GORDON C. ALLAN

A PLACE TO BE ME

A Novel

First published by Scholarcom Support Services Ltd. 2025

First edition

Cover art by Robert Jarocki

This book was professionally typeset on Reedsy. Find out more at reedsy.com

To my darling wife, Yully

Acknowledgments

In 2020, the year of COVID, I ended up spending the better part of my time in Taiwan, much of it by myself. During this period of solitude, the idea for A PLACE TO BE ME started to fully materialize, and eventually, pen was put to paper. It was also a time when my good friend back in Victoria, Marianna — a very social person — was looking for something to help her through what was clearly a very isolating time. So, when she heard about my novel-in-progress, she asked if she could be a silent editor. What a bonus! Her invaluable email and telephone counsel, constructive criticism, and ongoing encouragement kept me focused and motivated, and I'm not sure the book would have come to fruition had it not been for her ongoing support.

Chapter 1

Maybe it was because I was naive, or maybe I'd just been lucky, but I can honestly say that, prior to meeting her, I believed most people in this world to be quite reasonable. And for those few eccentric oddballs I did stumble across over the years, I could usually sympathize with them because they often had extenuating circumstances to justify their outrageous behavior. But not her.

Major Harriet T. Hunter, a.k.a. *The Major*, Head and CEO of Cothbert House School, introduced me to cynicism. It all began at an interview, of sorts, in Vancouver's *Bacchus Lounge* at the *Wedgewood Hotel*—a setting so totally at odds with who she was and what she represented. And yet, to be fair, that meeting would change my life and the lives of so many others forever.

"Ah, yes ... Mr. Gower," the manager acknowledged, looking down at his reservation book. "Welcome to our Afternoon Tea. Ms. Hunter asked me to seat you if you arrived before her."

He raised his eyebrows and signaled to a waiter, who led me to a table-for-two beside a tall, arched window overlooking the street. Seating myself, the waiter deftly flicked my white napkin, handing it to me while I stared in awe at the European-inspired lounge. High-back chairs, dark wooden walls framed by velvet curtains, and a vaulted ceiling exuded elegance and sophistication.

It was early June of 1995, and I had just turned thirty-four. Looking back, I now realize that what I had thought was just a series of unfortunate events was actually a premature mid-life crisis.

In January of the same year, I had resigned from a dead-end administrative position at a renowned private school in Eastern Canada after being passed over for more senior roles, sold everything I owned, and driven almost non-stop across several provinces of Canada, eventually arriving in Vancouver on Canada's West Coast. I told myself—and anyone else who bothered to ask—that I was going to *explore new opportunities*. And my mother, bless her heart, on hearing of my decision, exclaimed with passion, "It's fate. I can feel it in my bones. You must go, no matter what your father thinks."

Unfortunately, after six months of bravado and no new opportunities, reality settled in much quicker than anticipated, and my father's unmitigated displeasure was beginning to resonate as true. My bank account had dwindled to a few thousand dollars while I was getting distinct vibes from the family with whom I was staying in Vancouver (distant relatives, not one of whom my immediate family members had ever met) that I was starting to overstay my welcome.

There were certainly respectable private schools on the West Coast where I could have probably found employment, but none of them was hiring. It was therefore somewhat of a surprise when I discovered an ad in the paper for a principal at Cothbert House School. I say surprised because it was my understanding that Cothbert, a school well-known for accepting students who couldn't get accepted anywhere else, had gone belly-up in the 1980s. Apparently, an exchange student from California burned down much of the school's dormitory when his homemade chemistry set exploded. From what I'd been told, the school had attempted to carry on with makeshift accommodations and reassuring letters to parents, but it was never able to get fire insurance again and was therefore reduced to ruin.

"Are you Gower?" A gruff voice broke my reverie.

"Yes, that's me—Phil Gower," I said, scrambling to my feet, dropping my napkin.

A heavy-set woman with a buzz-cut and brown horn-rimmed glasses shook my hand.

"Major Harriet T. Hunter. You can call me Major," she said, scanning me as if deciding whether I was worth her time. "You look younger than I expected," she added, with noticeable surprise.

I smiled awkwardly. "Yes, I hear that a lot."

I had come to accept that my genes were set on preserving my eternal boyish appearance: a small frame, fine, light auburn hair that drooped no matter how I tried to style it, and impish blue eyes that still seemed to overlook the world's imperfections. Despite a few feeble attempts to grow facial hair and my investment in a carefully curated rotation of dark business jackets, I couldn't shake the look of an idealistic sophomore.

"Well, so be it," sighed the Major, dropping her stare. "Be seated, young man," she ordered, falling unceremoniously onto a chair opposite me and snapping her cell phone shut.

Her choice of clothing seemed unfitting for both the occasion and the setting. A houndstooth pant suit barely concealed her stained white shirt, on the top of which was affixed a carelessly-knotted plaid bow tie.

I sat down again, just as a young waiter rushed over to retrieve my fallen napkin.

"Hey, waiter," barked the Major, pulling a crumpled paper from her blazer pocket. "I've got a gift certificate for your Afternoon Tea."

She shoved the paper into the hovering waiter's hand and then dismissed him by twisting her body to look out the window.

"I've always thought there was money to be made in education, Gower," she began. "I know that's not very PC, but I don't give a damn. I haven't made my money by listening to whiners. And let me tell you, on the West Coast, there are a whole shitload of whiners: the tree huggers; the crappy craft people who live on the local islands; and your union workers, who sit around watching the clock half the time, complaining about job descriptions. That's why I'm interested in an Easterner like yourself. You people are different.

I'd never really classified myself as an Easterner nor considered it an advantage for a job interview.

"You know," she continued, "they say, that if you tipped Canada on its end, all the nuts would fall to the West Coast."

I laughed politely, not really knowing if she was joking.

"You ever heard of Cothbert House School?" she asked.

"Well, yes. If it's the one I think it is. I thought it went bankrupt in the eighties."

A waiter arrived carrying our tea along with a silver stand containing an assortment of baked goods and sandwiches.

"You're right. It went bankrupt in '85. Some American kid set the place on fire, and it never recovered." The Major turned around just as the waiter began to arrange our food. Before we had even been handed our plates, she was popping sandwiches in her mouth.

"Help yourself, Gower!" Then, turning to the waiter with a sandwich in her mouth, "Was that certificate okay there, son?"

"Yes, ma'am. You are entitled to two Afternoon Teas," he smiled awkwardly, pouring the tea into both our cups.

A couple of sandwiches later, the Major launched back into her story.

"Anyway, Gower, like I was saying, Cothbert went bankrupt in 1985 after some American prick bombed the place. It's been sitting vacant ever since. It was originally bought by a leftist charity organization that re-built the residence and tried renting out the campus to local church groups. But the charity found it was cheaper to just close it all down. It held onto the site for tax purposes, until finally it was busted by the local RCMP for running a marijuana grow-op. The site was then put up for auction."

The Major poured a second cup of tea for herself and then downed its contents.

"Help yourself, Gower," she said, dropping her cup loudly onto its saucer, all the time staring out the window in an obvious attempt to avoid eye contact.

I didn't need to be asked twice, so I quickly poured the remaining tea into my cup while I waited for the Major to continue her story. She had now shifted her focus to devouring the tower of sandwiches and cakes that threatened to overflow onto the pristine white tablecloth.

"So, did you buy Cothbert House School?" I finally asked, cautiously trying to move the conversation along.

"Of course I bought it," replied the Major, slithering back towards me. "That's why you're here. I want to start a new school, and I want to hire you as my principal."

"You want to hire me for a school that doesn't exist?"

"Look, here's the deal, Gower," said the Major, finally looking me in the eyes as she grabbed another handful of sandwiches. "There are a bunch of snotty-nosed private schools in Vancouver and over on Vancouver Island. Their noses are as high as kites, and most of them refuse to take international students who can't speak English. And let me tell you, there's been a bloody boom of them from Asia during the last couple of years. So, here's my idea. We offer a one-year program for international Asian students, give them all the bells and whistles of a regular boarding school, bring their English up to scratch, and then help them get accepted to them snotty-nosed schools a year later.

"So … basically you want to set up an ESL school," I responded, feeling a bit deflated.

"A what?"

"English as a Second Language School."

"Oh yeah, that's right. One of them," she said, wolfing down a scone heavily laden with Devonshire cream and raspberry jam. "Are you going to eat or what?"

"Oh, yes, thank you," I said, reaching for the last remaining sandwich.

I was skeptical about her proposal. I had been loosely involved in the world of ESL at my last school, where we ran a small program for children of newly-arrived immigrant families. I quickly discovered that ESL instruction is a

6

huge industry and that most of its major players are profit-making enterprises operating as pseudo schools granting bogus diplomas and certificates.

"Look, Major, I do appreciate your offer, but I have to be honest, ESL schools don't exactly have a great reputation. What makes you think the local private schools will even take notice of your school?"

"Good question, Gower. I like your thinking! My accountant asked me the same question. That's why I want to hire you. You've already worked at one of them private schools. You know what they want. And the schools will take notice because I'm going to hire qualified teachers."

That's reassuring, I thought. The Major caught my look.

"What I mean is that I'm not going to hire any of those certificate types. My teachers will have to have a teaching degree."

I took a sip of my tea, wishing it were something stronger.

"So? What do you think, Gower? Are you game?"

"Well … " I began, trying not to choke on my tea at her insolent bluntness. "I … I need more time to think about this. Also, I'm not entirely sure how you're going to structure the school. I mean, my experience with ESL is pretty limited."

"Look, here's the deal," she said, repeating her classic opening line. "I'll look after the minor issues, you know, like teachers and curriculum. I want you to focus on getting students."

I took another mouthful of tea as I tried to formulate a suitable response. I had never heard a Head of School refer to teachers and curriculum as 'minor issues'.

"Do you have any students enrolled yet?" I asked hesitantly.

"Not exactly. I've got about a dozen on the back burner.

But here's the beauty of all of this. I've crunched the numbers with my accountant. If we charge each student thirty thousand dollars a pop, I only need about twenty students to break even. The rest is gravy. Of course, we'll have to hire a few more teachers as the numbers rise, and buy a couple more books, but otherwise we're looking at big money."

By this time my head was spinning. The situation bordered on the absurd, yet the Major's passion for her misdirected vision was undeniable.

"Look, Gower, why don't you drive up to the school tomorrow and take a look around. I'll have a contract ready for you to sign and then we can get going."

The Major pulled a torn piece of paper out of her pocket, drew a map with directions to the school and, as an afterthought, jotted down her phone number.

"See you tomorrow, Gower. Let's say around 4:00 pm?"

Heaving herself out of her chair, the Major hustled off without even giving me a chance to respond. I curled both hands around my almost empty teacup, staring dully out the window as I tried to make sense of what had just happened.

Chapter 2

The Sea-to-Sky Highway, officially known as Highway 99, is a stretch of scenic roadway that runs north of Vancouver toward Whistler. Flanked by parts of the Pacific Ocean, distant glacial mountain peaks, and lush forests, the highway possessed an allure that was hard to resist. But as I made my way up this mountainous corridor toward Cothbert House School for my second interview with Major Harriet T. Hunter, Head and CEO, I could feel the weight of impostor syndrome pressing down on me. This wasn't the senior role I'd envisioned for myself, but the opportunity was real, and I knew I had to grab it. I was tired of being passed over. Maybe this was my chance to prove I could do it, even if it felt more like a last resort than a dream job.

According to the Major's map, Cothbert House School was a one-hour drive from Vancouver, just north of the town of Squamish and situated near the village of Timberline Lake, which the waiter at the Bacchus Lounge had described as a seedy resort town. The exit for Timberline Lake was clearly marked, and as soon as my Mazda left the highway, the pavement disappeared, and gravel rumbled under my tires. I continued along the road for about ten minutes until I finally caught sight of a dilapidated old sign. It was between a hedge of unkempt Ceanothus bushes and displayed a crest depicting a single rose around which were inscribed the words *Cothbert House School.*

The entrance to the school was overgrown, and twigs from previous windstorms littered the dusty driveway. My car crunched its way along the dirt track, at which point the road descended in a steep incline, weaving its way toward the lake. When at last the gravel gave way to pavement, a two-story, post-and-beam lodge came into view. Encased in stone and dark wooden siding, its entryway was framed by a stone portico etched with a faded sign that read: *School House.* What had once been a full-sized playing field on the opposite side of the road had, over years of neglect, been reseeded by nature and was now an overgrown wheat field of tall yellow grasses waving in the breeze. I eased the car further along the way, past the lodge and field, at which point the road made one more pitch toward the lake. The tree-lined driving path continued for about a hundred yards until at last I could see sparkling light reflecting off a body of water. Another largish building came into view: a newer wooden A-frame structure that had the name *Boarding House* painted above its two front doors. Beyond this facility, the road opened up onto a clearing, above which there was a tall wooden tower that resembled a park ranger's fire station, its glassed-in lookout deck providing a 360-degree view. In front of it was a parking lot, a few boat racks with an assortment of red and green cedar-canvas canoes, a beaten-up looking yellow mini-bus, and a section of land that jutted out from the hill with a set of wooden stairs that appeared to lead down to the lake.

I parked the car and got out to take a look at my surroundings and stretch. The crisp, cool air filled my lungs, and the serenity of the wilderness setting heightened my senses: the smell of pine and moss, the gentle breeze whispering its way through the leaves of the trees, the ranting birds overhead expressing their displeasure with my being on their turf, the pristine lake that stretched to a horizon of wooded hills—and then the sound of a gunshot.

"Goddamn raccoons. They got into the garbage last night and left a bloody mess everywhere."

The Major was wearing an old baseball hat, tweed shirt, overalls, and green rubber boots—and she was carrying a large shotgun.

"No trouble finding the place, Gower?" she asked, not really giving me much attention, bending forward and eyeing the woods suspiciously.

"Ah … no, Major … beautiful place you have here…"

"Yeah, it is! Now, let's see if it can make us some money," she said, storming up the hill. I took this as a cue to follow and ran to keep up with her. As we neared the Boarding House, the Major slowed down, cocked her gun, and fired a few shots into the woods.

"Missed the bastard," she said, reloading. "That's the slammer over there. You know, the Boarding House." She pointed her loaded gun at the front door of the A-framed structure while checking its sight. "Let's go and have a look, shall we?"

As we strolled toward the building, I noticed the tall lookout tower again.

"What's that used for?" I asked.

"Oh, that old thing? Nothing! It was built by one of Cothbert's previous goofy headmasters, who thought it would be a good idea to have a place to monitor the comings and goings of his kids. I guess Cothbert was a bit of a reform school in those days. Anyway, that thing's been boarded up for some time. I have no idea what's in there. Maybe the remains of old students," she cackled.

Her sense of humor was a bit off-putting as I thought about how hard it must have been for the students in those days. I continued to follow her into the front lobby of the Boarding House, which was paneled in light tongue-and-groove siding and furnished with four scruffy-looking leather chairs that sat in front of a gray mottled rug. A series of yellowed black-and-white photos decorated the walls.

"I found a whole lot of crap that belonged to the old Cothbert House School. Thought these photos would spruce the place up a little." The Major adjusted an old cricket team photo that barely clung to the wall.

"Hello, Major!" came a raucous voice. "To what do I owe the pleasure?"

A plump, older woman with disheveled graying hair emerged from an adjoining door. Wearing a blue smock and white apron, she carried an old-fashioned broom.

"Ah, Myrtle … this here's Gower," said the Major, waving her hand my way. "He's going to be the new principal in charge of admissions."

Already my job description was being embellished, and I hadn't even accepted the position.

"Oh, how wonderful," said Myrtle, beaming, while she bounced up and down on the balls of her feet. "Lovely to meet you, Gower. I'm Myrtle Green," she said, seizing my hand with both of hers. "Lovely indeed."

"It's Phil, actually—Phil Gower."

"Well, Gower, let me show you around the place. If you're going to sell the school to your potential families, you need to know what the place looks like, right?" she said, elbowing me and then breaking into a boisterous and exaggerated fit of laughter.

"Gower, you're in good hands with Myrtle here," said the Major. "When I bought the school, they threw in old Myrtle Green as a bonus."

Myrtle, by now, was laughing hysterically.

"She's been here since the early days of the school and stayed on during the years the charity ran the joint. She's going to be in charge of the slammer as my new Boarding House Director."

Myrtle paused for breath, wiping her eyes with a tissue.

"Oh, Major! You keep saying I'm going to be your new Boarding House Director, but I haven't even agreed to the job yet."

At least the Major's style of human resource management was consistent.

"Listen, Gower, I'll let Myrtle show you around. You two can share your ideas on the school. I'll see you up at the Big House in an hour." The Major then bolted out the front door before I could respond.

"The Big House?" I asked, turning to Myrtle.

"She means the School House—the main school lodge, dear. She loves using prison analogies to describe the school. Now let's go and have a look around, shall we?"

The Boarding House was divided into two floors, with all 28 of its bedrooms located upstairs and the lounge facilities and a duty master's office downstairs. The second floor, with its sloping white roof and dark cedar cross-beams, looked like the inside of a ski chalet. It was subdivided into a Boys' and a Girls' section separated by a sliding barn-style door in the hallway.

Myrtle decided to show me all the rooms, despite the fact each one was essentially the same, with a dormer-style window, built-in wooden furniture, and en-suite washroom. As we finally made it to the last room, she rattled off her sales pitch one last time: "You've got two beds with drawers underneath; two desks, two lockable wardrobes, and we provide all the linen plus a weekly laundry service. It's all quite lovely."

"Very nice," I said, checking my watch.

"And if we go back downstairs," she said, guiding me, "I'll show you the Common Room."

The bright Common Room, with a partial view of the lake, was a decently sized lounge featuring a low wooden ceiling. A few bean-bag chairs and a sagging couch sat in front of a gas fireplace, and a small kitchenette with bar stools was tucked nearby. Off to one side stood a pool table.

"You know," said Myrtle, starting to get the giggles again, "the senior boys used to refer to this room as the Make-Out Room."

She had wound herself up again, coughing and spluttering in between bouts of laughter.

"Do you think I should go up and see the Major now?" I asked hopefully.

"Oh, not yet, Gower," she said, regaining her composure. "Let's go and have some tea in my apartment. We'll have a lovely chat, and then you can walk up to the School House."

I wasn't sure if I could handle much more of 'old Myrtle,' but I agreed and followed her into her apartment.

Myrtle lived in a compact one-bedroom suite that had a gorgeous view of the lake. Her living room, with its beamed ceiling and bay window, had the appearance of an antique market, complete with assorted china figurines, hotel ashtrays, miniature dolls, and ornate lamps with shades from which there hung frayed baubles.

Myrtle stoked a fire that was smoldering in a small brick fireplace, surrounded by shelves full of hundreds of other knickknacks, including a collection of snow globes.

"Do you smoke?" she asked, turning around and handing me a cigarette and a crested ashtray that had the words *Best Western* printed on it.

"Ah, no … no, thank you."

"Alright then. Give me a few minutes and I'll brew us a lovely pot of tea," she said, exiting the room.

I examined the cluttered living room more closely, including an old picture of what looked like Cothbert House School students. I immediately recognized Myrtle in the middle of the group, looking a lot thinner and younger, while the students appeared somber as though they had just returned from the dentist. I wondered idly if the American bomber was among the group. There was also a photo of a soldier, but I couldn't tell if it was Myrtle's son or husband.

Myrtle returned a few minutes later with a tray of tea and a plate of biscuits.

"That's old Duncan, my husband," she said, placing down the tray as I adjusted the photo on the table, knocking over a prescription bottle. "He worked with the Major, you know … before he was killed."

"Oh, I'm so sorry. He was killed in action?"

"No. He fell in the shower. He wasn't even on duty. They

15

say he had been drinking. Idiot. Left me all alone at twenty-two—no children, no nothing. That's why I've always worked here. Those boarders have been like my children," she said, pointing to the school photo on the table.

There was an uncomfortable moment of silence, and I wondered if Myrtle was going to cry. At last, she poured the tea and then sat, peering over at me from behind her raised cup. It was as though she were about to disclose an important piece of information.

"I've always been good at judging people, you know. I think you are going to be very good for this school."

"Thank you, Myrtle," I said, stirring my tea. "Can … can I ask you something?"

"You want to know about the Major, right?"

I nodded.

"The Major and I go back a ways," she said, sipping her tea. "I've always admired her. Did you know she served in the Canadian Armed Forces?"

"Well, yes, I assumed so, given her title."

"You mean *Major*? She's not a Major. I think the highest rank she ever achieved was Second Lieutenant. Then she left the military. Some say she was kicked out. But no one knows for sure."

"I don't understand. She introduced herself to me as Major Harriet T. Hunter."

"She got the nickname Major because when she did serve in the military, she would always parade around town wearing her military uniform, even if she wasn't on duty. After a while, her drinking buddies started to tease her. They'd all stand at attention and salute her whenever she walked into our local pub. Eventually, everyone just started calling her

Major, and she sort of adopted the title."

"Oh, I see."

Myrtle stared out the window. "Anyway, she's always been good to me, particularly after Duncan died, you know. She helped me get settled and found me a job at the old Cothbert House School. But I have to admit, she is known in Timberline Lake for being a tough, no-nonsense person who has a knack for rubbing people the wrong way at times. She has very little business sense, flies by the seat of her pants, and loves it when everything is in various stages of crisis. Maybe she sees life as a big battlefield. But you know, despite everything, she always seems to protect herself with people who do know what they're doing. That's why you're here," she grinned.

There was another moment of silence, as I tried to digest what Myrtle was saying.

"Look," she said, laying out biscuits for me, "the reason the Major wants to hire you is she knows you can get this school on the map."

"But I can't do it alone," I implored. "I've already told the Major my experience with English as a Second Language is limited."

"Working with the Major won't be easy. But she'll get some good people to support you. Don't worry. Despite the Major's rough exterior, she does listen, and she will do what's necessary to make this school work. Deep down, she's a good person."

I was warming up to Myrtle and began to see the Major a little clearer.

"Are you going to sign on as the Boarding House Director?"

"Oh, of course. I just don't want the Major to think I'll

jump every time she waves her chequebook at me. Anyway, finish your tea, dear. You need to head up to the Big House to meet up with her."

"Thank you, Myrtle. I really appreciate your insight," I said, getting up from my chair.

"Listen … Phil, right?"

"Yes," I smiled.

"Phil, I have a good feeling about you. You're what the Major needs."

Chapter 3

There appeared to be no one around as I stamped my feet on the worn slate tiles inside the front door of the School House. To the right of the entryway, an abandoned reception counter and office sat tucked into a recessed alcove, while glass display cases, filled with tarnished trophies, faded athletic pennants and other assorted school paraphernalia, snaked their way down the dimly-lit wooden corridor.

The lingering smell of aged pine and old floor wax hung in the air as I moved further inside to examine a series of honey-colored wooden panels affixed to the wall. They profiled gilded lists of former school prefects and sports captains, hanging on opposite sides of a smoke-stained brick fireplace. Above the fireplace, the school crest displayed the same stylized rose I had noticed at the entrance. Beyond this area, a carved pine staircase guarded by two antique padded chairs, soared to the floor above.

The Major's decorating handiwork was also very much in evidence. A rather uneven trail of yellowed photos of the old Cothbert school wandered haphazardly along the paneled walls, abruptly ending at a stack of frames piled on the floor.

Curious, I decided to further investigate the lobby's nooks and crannies, the creaking floorboards coming to life underfoot. To the right of the fireplace was an over-sized door, a sign above it reading *Dining Hall.* Pulling on the door, I discovered it was locked, prompting me to try a set of doors on the opposite side labeled *Gymnasium* in faded letters. I managed to pry these doors open with a bit of difficulty, pleasantly surprised to find a small but functional gym, complete with scuffed hardwood floors and painted lines. At its far end stood a raised stage framed with heavy red curtains, a battered piano angled into one corner. A faint smell of rubber and sweat still clung to the air.

I closed the gym door and was considering whether to check the upper floor, when I heard laughter coming from somewhere at the end of the hall. Walking tentatively toward the sounds, I finally stopped in front of a large wooden door with a hand-written note affixed in duct tape. The note announced: Office of *Major Harriet T. Hunter, Head and CEO of Cothbert House School.*

Since the door was slightly ajar, I cautiously eased it open only to be enveloped by cigar smoke. Through a blue haze, I could barely make out the Major, who was seated on a stool opposite a man who bore a striking resemblance to the legendary British actor, Peter Ustinov. He looked vaguely familiar, but I couldn't place him. On a small table between them was a half-empty bottle of *Johnnie Walker* Scotch, its contents obviously contributing to the loud, unbridled mirth.

"Philly, my boy!" yelled the Major, pulling a cigar from her mouth when she noticed me. "Where the hell have you been? Pull up a stool!"

I think I preferred being called Gower. As I looked around for something to sit on, I was amazed by the lack of furniture in what was supposed to be a Head's Office. There were no chairs, no side tables, no bookcases or filing cabinets, nor indeed any kind of ornamentation. Most notably, there was no desk. The walls were covered with buckled, water-stained wallpaper, and the once decorative ceiling tiles now hung like stalactites warped from past leaks.

"Here you go, Philly," said the Major, handing me a chipped coffee cup full of Scotch.

Spying an old worn stool hidden in a corner I dragged it beside the gentleman.

"I'm Phil Gower," I said, placing my Scotch on the floor and extending my hand. The gesture felt almost like a statement—asserting my presence in a place where I wasn't sure I belonged. A part of me hoped it would make an impression.

"Harrison Tweedsmuir," he responded with a smile, grasping mine as he rose to his feet. "My friends call me Harris Tweed or just Harris is fine. Please have a seat and join us."

"Harris Tweed?" I repeated, a note of recognition creeping into my voice as I settled onto the stool and reached for my drink. "Did you speak at a conference once? I swear I've heard you talk before."

"Quite possibly," he said, letting his faint British accent slip just a little more dramatically. "I used to facilitate seminars on international education and cross-cultural studies." He positioned his small half-rim glasses as if to underline his academic credentials.

"Right! I remember now. You spoke at a conference I attended on Language and Culture. You're quite a guru in the field of International Education, aren't you?"

"Guru?" Harris chuckled, topping up his coffee mug with Scotch, "I wouldn't go that far. But I like to think I know a

21

little bit about cross cultural studies. My father's company used to manufacture boiled sweets in Bangkok, so I spent my childhood bouncing between Britain and Asia before moving to Canada. That gave me a unique perspective on various education systems and how foreign students have to adapt to them. Ended up doing my thesis on the whole topic."

He sucked on his smoldering cigar, releasing a particularly toxic plume of smoke.

"Philly," blurted the Major, cutting into the conversation, "meet your new Director of Academic Studies."

"Really," I said, looking over at Harris, who had disappeared into a cloud of gray. "That's great."

"Well, thank you, Phil," Harris said, reappearing through the smoke with a grin. "The Major talks highly of you as well. Looking forward to working together."

"I'll toast to that," yelled the Major, fumbling with her mug, and raising it triumphantly.

We followed the Major's lead, after which the Major refilled our mugs with more Scotch.

"We're not going to be like those other snotty-nosed private schools," she declared, starting to get quite animated.

She was referring to the handful of long-standing and very well-respected private schools on the West Coast.

"We're going to focus only on the basics — reading, writing and arithmetic. I'm not going to piss away money on useless things like calculators and computers the way they do. We're going to be a real school."

Harris threw me a mischievous wink, while the Major continued to expound on her various theories on education. As the amber contents of the whiskey bottle dropped lower and lower, the Major's face slowly turned crimson, while her pedagogical proclamations took on an evangelical tone.

"Take uniforms, for instance. Totally useless! Just a way to show off, like those fancy stick-in-the-mud private schools…"

"Oh, Christ Major! What the hell are you on about?" roared Harris suddenly, who himself had consumed his fair share of liquor. "Don't be so damn judgmental. Uniforms instill discipline; they create school spirit, and they prevent the students from being preoccupied with making fashion statements."

"Don't lecture me, Mr. High and Mighty." The Major reached for what was now an empty bottle. She peered into it quizzically, as though she couldn't understand what had happened to its contents and then turned to face me.

"Gower, Tweedle-dee here wants us to be like those stuck-up private schools. What do you think?"

I wasn't sure what to 'think' let alone say. I only knew I was damned if I did and damned if I didn't.

"Well," I stammered, anxiously looking over at Harris, who was sitting like a Cheshire Cat, enjoying the results of his provocation, "uniforms can be a good thing."

I sounded weak and unconvincing but I wasn't going to be drawn into a confrontation in what was still a job interview.

There was a tense moment of silence as the Major's face flushed deeper, her brain struggling to process the unanimous lack of support for her views on uniforms.

"*Yous* … two … university types think you're so special," she slurred. "I have the right mind to fire you both!"

"Fire us!" cried Harris. "You can't fire us because you haven't even hired us yet. And after tonight's performance, I'm not sure I want to work for you."

The Major glared at Harris and then looked imploringly over at me, obviously hoping I was going to bail her out.

"Maybe we've all had a bit too much to drink," I said, giving a weak laugh. "I think we should call it a night."

The Major responded by leaping up from her chair and bolting from the room. Her exit was followed by a particularly accentuated slam of the door after which the word 'ASSHOLES' echoed loudly down the hall.

I looked up at Harris, who seemed totally undaunted by the Major's frenzied exit and temper tantrum. He was moistening a newly unwrapped cigar.

"Well I guess I better start looking for another job," I announced, trying to solicit his reaction.

"What!" Harris exclaimed, reaching for a match. "Don't be so damned sensitive, Phil. If you want to work for the Major, you had better get used to scenes like this one. She's a bloody control freak, but she always backs down in the end. She knows that if she fired us, she'd be high and dry."

Harris lit his cigar in silence, shaking the match out with considerable force. I stared at him, unsure whether I was more worried about the school or the temperamental Major.

"So," I ventured, "how did you meet the Major?"

Harris waved his cigar toward the door, as if the Major herself had left a lingering mark on the room. "When our family moved to Timberline Lake in the late 60s, the Hunters were our next-door neighbors. We grew up together. After I started teaching in Toronto, I lost touch with her. It wasn't until a few years ago, after my mother passed away, that I came back here. I ran into her at a local pub called the *As You Like It* and we hit it off again. Became drinking buddies. It's been fun winding her up, especially about private schools.

24

She's got a personal vendetta against them—something to do with a cousin of hers who got accepted to one and used to rub her nose in it. That's why she's so determined to start this school. She wants to prove something to her cousin and other private school types, as she calls them, that she can be just like them.

I raised my eyebrow. "But why get involved if it's all about oneupmanship?"

Harris jerked his head towards me, his gaze hardening as he considered his answer.

"Well," he said finally, "I've been retired for three years. A failed marriage, which I'd like to forget. No hobbies to speak of. And no real social life up here. I guess I saw this as an opportunity to have one more challenge in my life — you know, to apply all the knowledge on international education I have amassed over the years. When the Major offered me the job, I thought, why not." He puffed on his cigar then waved it in the air again to make his point. "Besides, the school's a good idea. None of the big schools are accepting ESL students."

"But do you think the Major knows what she's getting herself into?" my skepticism growing.

Harris snorted. "Oh, she has no clue about the educational side of things. You saw it tonight. But we'll handle all that. As for the financial part, I'm not sure. To be honest, I don't really understand where she got all the money from to buy the school in the first place. She's well off but not that well off."

"Has she ever managed a business before?"

"Not on this scale. And that's my my biggest concern. If everything goes according to plan, she'll be responsible for a fairly large operating budget."

"Can't we share in that responsibility?'

"You have to understand the Major, Phil. When it comes to her money, she's as tight as a drum and she doesn't trust anyone. Maybe after we start enrolling students and prove our financial worth to her, she'll be more open with her finances. Until then, she's got a good accountant. He's actually a friend of mine. I think he'll watch over her."

"You mentioned enrolling students. I'm already worrying about that. The Major says there's been a boom of Asian international students recently and that she already has a dozen on the back burner, whatever that means. But, I have no idea how to get students from Asia in such a short time? I mean, I assume the school is supposed to open in September. That only gives us two and a half months to find twenty students."

"Rest assured … the Major has no students on the back burner. She probably talked to twelve people about her idea, and that's it. But there are ways you can get students in a fairly short time period. You know what, let's get out of here and go for dinner, and I'll fill you in on some tricks of the trade."

Twenty minutes later, Harris' Volvo pulled into the parking lot of the *As You Like It Pub and Grill,* a building framed by crooked wooden beams, all of which gave the impression you were standing in front of Anne Hathaway's cottage on steroids. I noticed across the street, above an industrial-looking red-brick structure, a large neon sign blinking the word *Kipling's*.

"What's that over there?" I asked, pointing to the sign.

"*Kipling's*? That's your general store in Timberline Lake.

Your only store. They sell everything from milk to microwaves. The place was originally owned by Bertie and Barbara Kipling, a couple of Brits who moved here in the 1930s."

"Do they still own the place?"

"No, Bertie went a bit batty in his old age and so Barbara put the store up for sale. It's exchanged hands a number of times, most recently to two Portuguese immigrants, Santiago and Matilde Almeda. Rumor has it the Almedas were taken advantage of and paid way too much for the place. They're a lovely couple—salt of the Earth, but I think they barely keep the place afloat these days. Anyway, listen, it's getting chilly out here. Let's go and have our dinner, shall we."

Harris ushered me through the front entrance to the *As You like It* where we were greeted by a cozy British pub-style atmosphere. A long wooden and brass bar with various gleaming beer taps was being manned by a cheerful woman who seemed to effortlessly charm the local patrons sitting in front of her.

We retreated to a booth. A crackling fire in an adjoining room provided just enough heat to take the chill out of the air, and the smell of spirits and hot food seemed to lull us into silence as we relaxed in the convivial ambiance, trying to forget the Major's antics.

"That Major," blurted Harris all at once. "I mean, honestly! Suggesting that the school won't have calculators and computers. What a nutcase. She really has no right to be within 500 feet of an educational establishment."

A waitress, who was chatting with customers at the next table, recognized Harris' obvious distress and moved quickly to our booth.

"Hello Tweedy! What'll it be today?"

"I just had a session with the Major, Sue. I am in desperate need of a double *Macallan* on ice. This is my new colleague, Phil Gower," he said, nodding toward me.

"Very nice to meet you, Phil," she answered smiling.

"Nice to meet you. I'll have your house wine. Red, please."

"Brave," she chuckled, scratching something on a small notepad, turning back towards Harris. "Now, Tweedy, haven't I warned you before about staying away from the Major? You know, every time you get near that woman, you become an alcoholic."

"After today, I'm actually contemplating harder substances, Sue."

Sue laughed her way towards the bar, while Harris grabbed a menu and pulled out his reading glasses. "The food's your basic pub fare here, all heavy, full of saturated fat, lots of salt and utterly delicious."

I opened my menu and surveyed its dessert-special for the day: *spotted dick.*

Harris reached for his glass. "You know, you haven't told me how *you* got roped into this whole Cothbert thing."

"Fate, I suppose. I had been in Montréal, working as an assistant school administrator in charge of timetables and general minutiae. After a while, the job became mind-numbing. I tried applying for more senior positions, even at other schools, but I was always passed over. One particularly boorish headhunter told me I needed to show my more cutthroat side—that I came across as too nice and, worse, too young-looking." I winced slightly, still feeling a stab of embarrassment at the memory.

"Charming. Don't ever listen to crap like that."

"I know. But after a while, you start to believe it. Anyway, I'd just had enough. After a couple of failed job interviews and a personal relationship that went sideways, I finally decided to head west in search of myself. Cliché, isn't it?"

"A bit," Harris said, toying with his Scotch glass. "But if there's one thing international schools need, it's empathetic leaders. My instincts tell me you're exactly that type. And maybe the Major sensed it too, though she'd never admit it."

"You're too kind. I'm all for empathy, but I also know I need to work on being more assertive."

"Well, you'll definitely get your chance working for the Major. If you're not assertive, she'll walk all over you."

"Understood," I laughed, but inwardly, I second-guessed myself.

"Now, I think you said you wanted to talk about admissions," said Harris glancing down at his menu.

"Yes, how exactly *are* we going to get ourselves students for this school anyway?"

Harris looked up again and contemplated my question. "Ah … yes, students. Rather important pieces of this educational jigsaw puzzle. If you thought the Major was a piece of work, you ain't seen nothin' yet. Your next foray into the world of international education will involve dealing with educational agents, euphemistically called educational consultants. While there are certainly some reputable professionals in the field, many, unfortunately, prey on vulnerable international students, charging exorbitant fees and directing them to schools that offer the highest commission."

"Are you saying we'll have to pay to get students?"

"Absolutely … at least initially, until the school develops its reputation. The key will be to sort through the riffraff and find those educational agents who actually give a damn about education."

"But how do we find the good ones?"

"Canadian Embassy can offer up a few names; but, not to worry, my friend. I already made a few phone calls to some of my contacts overseas and in Vancouver and I've been able to generate a short list. South Korea won't be easy, as there are more agents than there are Hyundai cars, but I believe I've got a few solid ones. Now, the key will be to focus on the countries that can deliver. In addition to Korea, I suggest Taiwan, Hong Kong, and Japan. We'll need to create a one-page profile of our program — description, curriculum, what's included, fees and, of course, a commission structure for the agents. And we had better do it soon, as schools in those countries will be out in a few weeks."

"What type of student would even consider a school like ours?"

"Good question! A lot of students in Asian countries are expected to write exams to move from middle to high school. Those who fail their exams are destined for trade schools or less than reputable private schools. A program like ours can keep them in an authentic academic stream and help them save face."

"So … what you are saying is that our best market is for dropouts?"

"Don't be so harsh. Many schools in Asia are brutal — 45 students per class, a curriculum devoted to the art of memorization and, in some countries, rampant corporal punishment. Most of those so-called drop-outs you refer to are often sensitive, creative students who simply don't fit the mold."

"And the rest?"

"A little needy," said Harris, with a wry smile.

Our drinks arrived and Sue took our food orders. Harris chose bangers and mash and I ordered fish and chips. As I attempted to savor what was clearly a musty glass of plonk, Harris, wasted no time downing his Scotch, which seemed to have the effect of making him rather morose. I contemplated this dumpy old man in front of me. His jowls hung like deflated balloons and his heavy breathing was clearly the product of carrying more than his share of weight. On the face of it, you couldn't imagine him having the stamina for the job. And yet, his interesting conversation earlier this evening reminded me of a lecture I once attended of his; where he wowed everyone with his warmth of personality, witty anecdotes and passionate knowledge of international education. Something about him just clicked—he felt like the right fit.

It was well after midnight when we made it back to the school. A dense, wet fog had descended on the campus, and, on more than one occasion, Harris had lost sight of the road.

We decided to bunk in the Boarding House for the night; first, because there was no way Harris could make it safely to his house on the other side of the lake on his own and secondly, because I still had no idea where the Major was expecting me to live on campus. I was now, for all intents and purposes, homeless.

Chapter 4

"Rise and Shine, dear!"

The bedroom door banged open, and an energetic Myrtle burst in, whipping back the curtains and flinging open the window wide. A cold draft of morning air accompanied this rude awakening. The fact I had slept in my underwear did not seem to faze her. She placed my shirt and dress-pants on a chair and neatly arranged my shoes beside it.

"The Major is waiting for you and Harris up at the Dining Hall. Breakfast is ready and I think she has papers for you to sign. You need to get going!"

Thankfully, dear old Myrtle had the foresight to put a toothbrush, razor, bar of soap, and a towel in the bathroom. After a quick shower, I was finally ready to face the day—and the Major. Racing down the Boarding House stairs, I found Harris standing in the lobby.

"Did Myrtle's idea of room service awaken you, Mr. Tweedsmuir?" I joked.

"Now listen, Phil," he admonished, without any pleasantries. "The Major will have contracts for us. Whatever you do, don't sign them!" He then barreled out of the door without warning.

"What … why?" I began, but Harris was already charging

up the hill to the School House.

"We need to play hard ball," he shouted over his shoulder. "If we give her the impression we want these jobs, she'll take control and we'll live to regret it."

"But I do want this job!" I almost stopped in my tracks. *Did I actually just say that?*

"That's beside the point," Harris tossed back at me. "The Major needs to learn who's running the ship here—and it ain't going to be her. Just follow my cues."

He slowed down and we walked the last few steps together.

The door to the Dining Hall stood open when we entered the School House. Peering inside, I noticed that, unlike the rest of the neglected facilities, this impressive church-like hall had recently been renovated. Its angular ceiling, supported by massive log posts, was dotted with wrought-iron candelabras. Tall mullioned windows provided commanding views of the lake, while solid oak tables with matching chairs sat atop heavy flagstone flooring near an imposing stone fireplace. Along one wood-paneled wall, a modern buffet counter, with stainless steel cavities, completed the room. This morning, however, the pièce de résistance was none other than the Major herself, standing behind the buffet in an outfit that only Julia Child could appreciate. Gone was her customary brown pant suit; she now sported a chef's hat and striped red, white and blue apron.

"Philly! Harris, my man! Good morning! Come on in and have some breakfast," she waved eagerly.

As we moved in front of the buffet counter, the Major's face telegraphed her satisfaction with the variety of breakfast items she had created, including a large platter of scrambled eggs, sausages, fried tomatoes, sautéed mushrooms, and a rack of toast.

"Coffee and juice are just over there," she said pointing to a filled carafe of coffee and a carton of orange juice.

"Thank you for all this," I replied, moving towards the coffee. "Everything looks great."

I poured some coffee and helped myself to the breakfast offerings. In contrast, Harris ignored both the Major and her breakfast extravaganza. He hastily splashed coffee into a mug and threw himself into a chair at the head of the table like a spoiled child. Placing my plate and coffee down, I joined him.

"Not eating?" I asked, cutting into a sausage.

Harris sipped his coffee while surveying the pastoral scene outside one of the windows. Without turning around, he muttered under his breath: "The trick with the Major is to look uninterested."

I couldn't help but notice the Major watching us uneasily, clearly suspecting Harris was going to be difficult. The second she disappeared through the swinging doors into the kitchen, Harris sprang up, loaded his plate, and rushed back to the table. I watched in silence as he tackled his food with gusto, still lost in his own thoughts and disinclined to small talk.

Looking out the same window, I contemplated the slow dawning of a June day. A soft mist hovered above the ground, punctuated by enormous red cedar trees. Flashes of forest green peaked through, revealing moss and lacy ferns growing over a rocky terrain. Far in the distance, Timberline Lake sparkled from the rays of early sunlight that were now dancing on its surface. Cradling my steaming cup of coffee, I surrendered to the magical allure of this west coast environment.

"It's really quite breathtaking, isn't it?" I observed in an attempt to initiate conversation.

"What?" said Harris looking up.

"The grounds," I said, pointing out the window. "They're all so beautiful."

"Hmm," he replied, his mind elsewhere.

My musings were interrupted by the familiar creak of the swinging door. The Major poked her head in, scanning for Harris. After a moment's hesitation, she pushed the door with confidence and marched towards us. Apron and hat removed, she had pulled on the same pants and jacket she'd worn at the *Bacchus Lounge*. Under her arm was a tattered brown briefcase.

Harris looked up and then snapped his head down again. "And here we go," he mumbled.

"Well *yous* two, I've got your contracts," the Major announced proudly, flicking the latches to her briefcase for effect and retrieving two sets of stapled sheets. She slid one set towards Harris and the other towards me. For a moment I thought Harris was going to ignore her but he reached into his shirt pocket for reading glasses and, looking somewhat professorial, flipped through the pages, wetting his finger with each turn for added effect.

I decided to read mine too, despite a distinct rise in tension Harris amplified with every grunt of disdain. The contract was straightforward: room and board, a one-bedroom apartment on the top floor of the School House, a generous salary, retirement contributions, and some mediocre health benefits. Not bad, I thought, particularly given the state of my finances twenty-four hours ago.

Harris finally peeled off his reading glasses and asked, "What about renovations?"

The Major frowned, wary. "I've already started to put up photos and I have a cleaning crew coming in next week, and..."

"That's not what I mean," Harris interrupted. "Parts of this building and the Boarding House look like a dump. If you think I'm going to promote an untested school that is in disrepair, think again. We need serious renovations. Oh ya, and uniforms, computers and calculators— I want them guaranteed in my contract too."

"Now just a second," the Major snapped. "If you think I'm going to piss away money when we don't even have any kids..."

Harris folded his reading glasses shut, stood, and stormed out of the room.

The Major turned to me, stunned. "Well, what's the matter with him? Got a bee in his bonnet— again?"

She stomped back into the kitchen, leaving me holding a contract I was still reading. I wondered if every meeting with them would result in such drama and sap so much energy. Looking at a portrait of a former Cothbert House Headmaster on the wall, I murmured, "So how would you have dealt with all of this ... sir?"

No response.

A few minutes later, Harris stuck his head through the door. "Looks like she's gone?"

"Yes, you blindsided her."

"Good!" He grinned, pouring more coffee. "She needs to know the ground rules. If this school is going to work, she has to take it seriously."

"But you basically told her off. I don't get it."

"Oh, don't be so thin-skinned. The Major will come around. Threats work."

I wondered if Harris was a bit bipolar. His antics reminded me of the advice from the headhunter back in Montréal about being more cutthroat. My stomach churned as I considered whether this was really the job for me.

For two hours, Harris and I pored over a spreadsheet of agents—local, overseas, and shady ones.

"Do you think any of them will actually visit?" I asked, overwhelmed by the sheer number of names and details.

"Yes," Harris replied confidently. "Violeta Kim from *Hyung Bo Consulting* in Seoul will be here in three weeks."

"Three weeks?" I gasped, "but the school is not nearly ready to show."

"Exactly. Now you see why I pushed the Major. Don't worry—she'll step up in time."

A tea trolley rattled in, pushed by Myrtle.

"What goodies do you have for us today?" Harris asked, his earlier bravado replaced with a sudden charm.

"Never you mind," Myrtle huffed. "You've got the Major in an awful state. What did you say to her this time?"

"Don't worry about the Major," Harris replied, waving her off. "She needs to understand what's at stake."

Myrtle sniffed but didn't argue. "Hmm. Maybe you're right, but a little honey goes a long way."

She poured tea for both of us.

"Anyway, I can see you've got your plates full," she added, trundling out of the room, chuckling at her own pun.

Harris and I spent the rest of the day tackling curriculum

plans, staffing needs, and marketing strategies. By dinner-time, we realized we'd worked through lunch.

After a quick meal at the *As You Like It*, this time without excessive alcohol, we agreed to meet again for breakfast the next morning.

As I climbed the stairs to my room, I thought about everything we had accomplished and everything still left undone. I paused at the top, glancing back out the window. The mist had returned, curling around the cedar trees like a protective shroud. Somewhere out there, Timberline Lake lay waiting, its surface now dark and still under the gathering twilight.

I sighed. This job was going to be an uphill battle. But for the first time in months, I felt something stirring—hope, maybe, or a sense of purpose. I wasn't sure yet.

I stepped into my room, closed the door, and leaned back against it. Myrtle had left a small note on the dresser:

Everything worth doing takes hard work. Sleep tight.

I smiled despite myself. Myrtle was right. Pulling back the covers, I slipped into bed.

Chapter 5

Unlike the previous morning, it wasn't Myrtle's abrupt entrance that woke me but the forceful banging of hammers and the high-pitched screech of saws. I leaned out of my window to see a group of men and women carrying ladders, paint cans and planks of lumber. In the midst of this chaotic circus stood the Major herself, barking out orders. Clipboard in hand, a pencil perched on her left ear, and dressed in her signature houndstooth pantsuit, she was clearly in her element.

Harris had been right after all.

Once dressed, I ran downstairs. The acrid smell of fresh paint filled the air, mingling with the shouts of the work crew. The Major's determination to have a new school rise phoenix-like from the ashes of the old was impossible to ignore.

Harris was already in the Dining Hall when I arrived. From the stacks of papers carefully spread across a large table by the window, it was clear he had been there for some time. He sat at a smaller table, his notebook open beside an empty breakfast tray, while Myrtle was hovering over his shoulder, refilling his coffee mug.

I began with a "Good Morning," but my voice was drowned

out by the harsh whine of an electric saw from down the hall.

"Oh, there you are," cried Myrtle over the noise, bouncing excitedly when she saw me. "I've got keys for you!" She dangled a massive key chain in front of me. Sliding through the keys, she announced: "Here's one for the buildings, one for your office, and, *ta-da!* one for your apartment!"

"Oh good, I had been wondering about my accommodations."

"Yes, well they're not quite ready yet because the Major is renovating everything. I've never seen her spend so much money. She said something about making sure the school is in good condition," she giggled, her other hand over her mouth.

"Ha!" snorted Harris, peering up over his reading glasses. "She's a piece of work! Making sure the school is in good condition. I mean really!"

"Trying to deflect Harris' comments, I asked, "So, what about my office?"

"Everything should be ready in a couple of weeks," Myrtle replied. The Major even arranged for new furniture. There's a hotel nearby that's closing and all its fixtures are practically being given away. The Major knows the owner and told him she's buying it all."

Great! Lamps with baubles and assorted hotel ashtrays. I can't wait.

Harris interrupted. "Phil, we'll need to hit the ground running once these renovations are complete. That means being accessible as soon as Asia opens for business each day. Late nights too, if we want meaningful connections. Oh, and that reminds me," he added, reaching under a pile of paper and pulling out a cell phone, "you can use this until we get the landlines working."

"Of course, I'm more than ready to do my bit," I replied., taking the phone.

"I know you are," Harris said warmly. "Take advantage of the chaos. Get your personal life sorted out — move out of your relative's place in Vancouver and settle in here. You won't have much free time once things start rolling. Meanwhile, I'll make some agent calls."

"Harris is right, dearie," Myrtle added. "While you get yourself sorted, I'll make sure your suite is *tickety-boo* for when you return."

I felt like asking her to define tickety-boo but I bit my tongue.

My unexpected return to the home of my relatives in Vancouver was met with a mix of trepidation and reluctant acceptance. While there was no grand homecoming, their faces softened when they learned I had secured a job and would soon be leaving—this time, for good. Their smiles, though somewhat forced, were genuine in their own way. They made a concerted effort to make my remaining time in Vancouver as pleasant as possible, even feigning emotional goodbyes when it came time to leave.

Though the weather had been beautiful during my two-week respite, my journey back to Cothbert was clouded by gray skies and relentless rain. The drive up the Sea-to-Sky Highway was shrouded in thick fog, with hairpin turns, slick roads, and the occasional hailstorm making it a harrowing experience.

Was this an omen?

By the time I turned onto the school grounds, my stomach felt queasy. *Would the Major and Harris still be going at each other? Would the school ever be ready for consultants, let alone students?* My eyes fell on a copy of the *Vancouver Tribune* newspaper on the passenger seat. I had a sudden urge to rip it open and scour the Help-Wanted ads.

But as I parked, I realized the rain had stopped. Stepping out of my car, a glimmer of sunlight edged the dense gray clouds with gold. I heard the rumbling of a car approaching and looked up just as Harris' bright yellow Volvo pulled in beside me.

"What timing, Phil. We both got back at the same time," he said, struggling to close his squeaky front door .

"You were away too?" I asked, with surprise.

"Yes. Myrtle convinced me to leave for two weeks so the Major could work without me 'poking my nose in.' Smart woman, that Myrtle." Smiling, "I've already made headway with some agents. Ready for a walkabout?"

We started up the hill toward the School House, the large portico coming into view first, followed by the familiar sight of the lodge-style building—weathered and unchanged. Stepping inside, it still felt as though we had entered a time capsule, as if nothing had been touched since the days of the old Cothbert.

"Not much different since the last time I was here," Harris muttered, his gaze sweeping over the entrance with a note of disapproval.

We made our way down the hallway to check the offices, starting with the Major's. Harris flung the door open, as though trying to catch her in a compromising position. Both of us gasped in surprise.

Gone were the sagging ceiling tiles and grotty wallpaper.

Freshly painted cream walls and a restored ceiling greeted us instead. The mismatched, decrepit furniture had been replaced with tall cabinets, comfortable chairs, and a sleek, modern desk. The haphazard photos that once cluttered the hallway were now arranged in neatly curated collages, showcasing the school's history and lending the space the aura of a distinguished old-world institution.

I glanced at Harris, who avoided meeting my eyes. He was conspicuously quiet. Without a word, we moved to inspect our own offices, where the smell of fresh paint lingered and new carpets had been laid. The furniture was clean, functional, and professional. Things were definitely looking up!

"Ah, there you are!" came a screech from out of nowhere that made us both jump. It was Myrtle. She was bounding toward us, unable to contain her excitement.

"You've got to give the Major credit," she said, laughing nervously. "The place is starting to look a lot better. And wait till you see what they're doing over at the Boarding House." Her eyes sparkled. "Oh, and Phil, come with me. I've just put some finishing touches on your apartment."

Myrtle grabbed my hand, and began pulling me along. I glanced back at Harris, who flashed his usual snide grin.

Myrtle gestured to us to follow her up a set of narrow back-stairs that led to a solitary wooden door marked *Private Residence*. I took a deep breath as she unlocked it. I entered cautiously and then exhaled a quiet sigh of relief. No baubles.

The apartment was clean, functional, and surprisingly charming. Hardwood floors in the small living room gleamed, complimented by two armchairs and an old brick fireplace. Recessed bookshelves lined one wall, creating the cozy feel of a private study.

The modest, open-concept kitchen featured newly painted cupboards, an under-the-counter fridge, and a hot plate.

"You won't need a stove, dearie," Myrtle announced. "You'll be eating with the students. Remember?"

"Not every night," I muttered under my breath.

The bedroom was small but comfortable with an en-suite washroom, that while dated, was spotless and functional.

I returned to the living room and pulled back the curtains on the large picture window, dismayed to see the strange watch tower partially obstructing the panoramic view of the lake.

Harris and I spent the next hour touring the rest of the School House. The classrooms upstairs, the gymnasium, the various washrooms, and the front office reception area were all in decent shape but in need of organizing and a through cleaning. By the time we returned to the main hallway, Harris had his second wind.

"Yes, well," he said, "it appears the Major has finally started listening to my advice. But she'll never manage the complete disrepair of the Boarding House. Let's see what she's been up to there."

I followed Harris outside, debating whether to say something. The Major had accomplished far more than he expected, yet he refused to give her credit.

Footsteps approached from behind. It was Myrtle, trying to catch her breath.

"So, what do you think of what the Major's done?" she asked eagerly.

"Myrtle," I said, choosing my words carefully, "how has the Major managed to accomplish so much in such a short time?"

"Well," she began, still puffing slightly, "as much as the Major can be a thorn in the side, she's always there when people need help. She's bailed out so many locals—lending them money, pitching in when things got tough. When she realized she needed to fix up this place, she called in all those favors. *Voilà!* Instant work crew: painters, drywallers, builders, even an interior designer. They owed her."

Harris remained silent, quickening his pace as we neared the Boarding House. As we stepped onto the porch, the door flew open. Holding it like a Ritz-Carlton doorman was the Major herself.

"Well, look what we have here!" she said, grinning. "If it ain't our two fancy educators. While *yous* two were busy planning the school's future, me and my team have been getting the Big House and the Slammer ship-shape. So, what do ya think, hmm?"

"I'm glad you finally listened to my advice," Harris shot back, brushing past her into the lobby.

The Major chased after him, indignant. "*Your* advice? Let me tell you, big guy, I was planning this long before you showed up!"

"Really?"

I stepped in quickly, pulling Harris aside. "Harris, please," I said under my breath. "Don't start! Let's look around, then stroke her ego a bit. We don't have time for more of this!"

Harris seemed startled by my directness but nodded. "You're right," he muttered, letting out a short breath.

The Boarding House renovations were still underway, but progress was evident. Fresh paint covered most walls, secondhand furniture was stacked neatly against the sides, and scattered plumbing fixtures suggested bathrooms were next on the list.

Harris set down his clipboard and turned to the Major. "I … I must congratulate you. You've done yeoman's work restoring this place. We're actually starting to look like a real boarding school."

The Major looked genuinely taken aback

"Does that mean *yous* two are finally going to sign them contracts I gave you?" she asked hopefully.

"Of course, Major," Harris said. "Right, Phil?"

"Absolutely."

For the moment, we were all one big happy family. Well, sort of.

Chapter 6

I was buried in a stack of resumes for potential teachers when I heard the distant sound of a car engine through my open office window. Pivoting in my chair, I was amazed to recognize a decrepit 1970s *Ford LTD* with comically soft suspension careening down the driveway. When it eventually stopped and the driver's door opened, a large white-brimmed hat with a matching veil gradually emerged. Next came a pair of white stilettos, followed by the body of a diminutive lady, her hands hidden by long white gloves. Reaching into the car, she slung a gleaming white purse on her arm before activating the car's alarm system. Once satisfied the car was secure from any woodland criminal element, she stood motionless, getting her bearings before carefully making her way to the front door of the School House.

"Violeta Kim is here," announced Harris, popping his head through the door.

I looked up.

"Remember? The rep from *Hyung Bo Consulting* in Seoul? Arriving at 10 a.m.?"

"Oh, yes, of course!"

Quickly grabbing my blazer, I trailed after him into the main hall; a welcoming committee of two.

A few moments later, the front door swung open, and Violeta made her entrance. The staccato clicking of her high-heeled shoes echoed in the hall as she trotted determinedly across the wooden floor towards Harris, one white-gloved hand extended as though expecting him to bow over it before kissing her upturned palm.

"Ah, Harris. How you doing?" she said, handing him a small gift bag.

"Wonderful. Thank you so much for coming to see us. You look stunning as always, Violeta. I don't know how you do it. You look exactly the same as you did five years ago."

"Harris, such a gentleman." She smiled innocently before adding, "Did you put on weight?"

Harris' grin faltered, and his face stiffened slightly as he glanced at me. I offered an innocent shrug.

"Yes … well … I'd like you to meet our principal. This is Phil Gower," he said, waving his hand in my direction.

"Nice to meet you, *Pil*," she replied, angling to size me up. "You look too young and handsome to be a principal," she said, one hand flowing gracefully toward mine as she gathered up the veil of her hat with her other hand. Fluttering her dark eyes, she paused for a moment, calculating her effect on me. Returning her smile, I awkwardly offered my hand, but she dismissed it with a nod, turning her attention back to Harris.

"So why don't we go on a tour first, and then we can chat afterwards," suggested Harris, placing the beautifully wrapped gift bag on the front desk counter and moving towards the door.

"Good. I need to take some photographs of the school for my clients."

Pulling a small camera from her bag, Violeta tapped her

way past Harris, who glanced back at me, rolling his eyes in mock exasperation.

I ran to hold the door open, then watched in amusement as Violeta stumbled down the road towards the Boarding House, her high-heeled shoes wobbling and sinking into the soft ground, her hat's veil fluttering like a tattered flag in the wind. She had one hand firmly clutching Harris's arm for support.

Unable to resist curiosity, I reached for the gift bag on the counter and took a quick peek inside. A small red box read: *'Ginseng Special Serum: Improves Your Virility.'*

Well, well, I thought to myself, chuckling. There must be a story here.

Forty-five minutes later, Harris and Violeta returned, Violeta looking a bit worse for wear. Her veil was entangled in the folds of her hat, while her shoes, better suited for chic city streets, were encrusted with soil.

"It looks like it was a bit windy out there," I began, trying to break the silence. Violeta gave me a strained look and, without replying, hastily tapped down the hall to the ladies' room.

"Not exactly the outdoorsy type," smiled Harris. "Oh, and she mentioned again how handsome you are, Phil—or should I say, *Pil.* I think she might have the hots for you."

"Yeah, right!" I replied, cringing at the prospect.

After what seemed like forever, Violeta reappeared from the ladies' room. She had magically transformed herself back to her original doll-like image; her hat and veil artistically arranged on her head, her high-heeled shoes gleaming again. As she had done earlier, she lifted her veil and fluttered her heavily mascaraed eyes at me.

"You know, *Pil*, there is a lot of potential here. I think I can get you about a dozen kids."

The casual way in which the word "dozen" rolled off her tongue made it sound like she was sending us a box of donuts rather than a group of eager students.

"That sounds wonderful," I responded, finally daring to hope that this school might actually succeed. "We look forward to working with you."

"And I look forward to working with you too, *Pil*," she whispered.

Fortunately, at that moment, Myrtle came to the rescue, pushing her trademark trolley with tea service.

"Ah, Myrtle, you are a savior," said Harris, introducing her to Violeta. "Violeta, why don't you and I go have a quick look at some classrooms and the gym, and then we can re-convene in the Dining Room for tea? Then we can talk about a contract."

Harris signaled to me that he wanted to handle this one alone, and although I was more than happy to oblige, Violeta would not hear of it.

"No, no! *Pil* needs to join us too, Harris. If I am to work with him, which I must, *Pil* has to understand my needs."

"Oh, heaven help me, please," I whispered under my breath.

A smiling but subdued Myrtle interrupted with, "Why don't I leave you on your own. I've brewed some coffee and a fresh pot of tea for Miss Kim. And there's a plate of sandwiches and shortbread cookies, so you can carry on your work undisturbed by me."

Myrtle shot me a cheeky grin before rattling off down the hall.

Following Harris' quick tour of the School House and Myrtle's refreshments, the three of us settled down to business. For almost an hour, we discussed students, agent contracts, and commissions. Despite Violeta's seemingly delicate demeanor, her business acumen was razor-sharp, convincing us to sign a contract that included additional commission incentives for reaching certain student targets. If even half of what she promised materialized, we could expect at least ten Korean students for the start of school, with more to follow.

"I have to go now," announced Violeta, signaling our meeting was over. "I need to return the *LTD* limousine to my friend later today. Tonight, I fly back to Seoul."

Her farewell included a rather prolonged kiss on my cheek. We stood at the door as she tapped her way out.

I was ready for some fresh air.

"How about a walk? We've been cooped up in here all day. I'd love to explore the grounds a bit."

"Wonderful idea," Harris boomed. "You see how easy all this is, Pil?" He exaggerated Violeta's mispronunciation of my name. "I think she really fancies you."

"By the way, interesting gift she left you," I retorted.

Harris looked inside the golden gift bag and fell silent.

"You sure it's me she fancies?"

"Ha!" Harris snorted.

We strolled leisurely past the playing field, the watchtower, and the Boarding House, following a small path that ended at the edge of a cliff overlooking Timberline Lake. Carefully navigating the rickety wooden stairs that hugged the rock face, we began our cautious descent to the beach below.

Harris stopped halfway down to catch his breath, pulling at a rotten handrail and throwing large, decayed shards of wood to the ground for dramatic effect.

"This is something else the Major will need to fix before the students arrive, or we'll never get insurance! This is bloody dangerous."

He was still harping on about the school's flaws, and it was beginning to wear thin.

At the base of the cliff, we paused, taking in the view before us: a long, warped dock stretching into the lake, its weathered boards sagging under the weight of two old blue Adirondack chairs at the end. Nearby, a small, sun-baked beach house crouched under the cliff's curve, half-hidden by overhanging tree branches. Beside it stood a boat rack holding a motley assortment of canoes, most in various stages of disrepair, their faded orange life jackets strewn about haphazardly.

We instinctively headed toward the dock, settling into the chairs. Harris pulled out a long cigar, wetting it with his lips before lighting it.

"This is what makes it all worthwhile, *Pil*," he said, satisfied his cigar was performing as it should.

I smiled in agreement, studying the waves slapping rhythmically against the dock, their foamy-white froth trapping bits of lake sediment. Far across the lake, a deep purple and gray sky warned of an impending storm, while overhead, an ever-shifting vee of geese honked in formation.

But then, I smelled something.

"Do you smell that?" I asked Harris. "It smells like wood smoke."

Harris pushed himself up from his chair, surveying the

shoreline.

"Over there," he said, pointing to the far end of the beach.

In the distance, Myrtle sat by a small campfire. Without a word, we made our way toward her. She looked up, startled to see us.

"Oh, what a nice surprise!" she exclaimed, bouncing to her feet. "Please, join me. I've brought sandwiches and hot coffee. There's enough to share."

Good old Myrtle. Always there when you needed her. The sandwiches and cookies were unmistakably leftovers from our meeting with Violeta, but I especially appreciated the hot coffee. One sip, however, revealed it wasn't quite the same brew—it was laced with liquor.

Harris caught my eye and gestured subtly: keep quiet.

We sat in companionable silence until Myrtle finally spoke.

"So, how are you two feeling about things? You must admit the Major has made huge progress with the campus."

I braced for Harris' cynicism, but he surprised me.

"Yes, the old bird has certainly shown us there's a school buried beneath the shambles."

"And how's it going with recruitment?" she asked cautiously.

"Slowly," said Harris, tapping his cigar. "We had an agent today—you know, that lady you prepared refreshments for."

"Oh, yes. Miss Kim. The one who likes Phil?"

"Yes, exactly," chortled Harris, shooting me a devilish sneer. "Anyway, she's promised to send us about ten students, but these agents always promise yet rarely deliver. We'll need to work the phones over the next little while if we hope to open with twenty students.

I turned to Myrtle and asked, "And what about you? How

are you feeling about all of this?"

Myrtle gave me a tentative look, nervously playing with a long stalk of grass she had pulled from the sand.

"I'm a bit anxious, to be honest. I haven't been responsible for a boarding house for years. I hope I can still do it, but I'm not sure." Her voice took on a tone of quiet desperation, and I could tell she was having second thoughts.

"Also," she continued, "I've never supervised Asian students before. But they're quiet, right?"

"They're not all quiet, Myrtle," said Harris, laughing. "That's pretty much a stereotype. They can be just as precocious as the next kid."

I could tell this wasn't what Myrtle wanted to hear. Her shoulders sagged as she cupped her chin in her hand, looking almost defeated.

"Oh, Myrtle, don't worry. You'll be great," I said, trying to buoy her spirits. But I could tell she wasn't convinced.

"Darn it! I guess that puts an end to enjoying time on the beach," I said, looking up at the dark sky. Drops of rain were now starting to fall.

Together we helped Myrtle douse the fire, gather up the remains of the picnic, and tuck everything into her knapsack before quickly climbing the wooden stairs.

Once we reached the top, Harris started discussing his plans for the evening. He and I would each take fifteen agents from Taiwan and Korea, he announced, and begin our sales pitch. I dreaded the prospect. It all sounded like tacky telephone solicitation. I would be making those annoying calls that I abhorred—those calls I would typically hang up on before the person on the other end of the line had a chance to give their well-versed speech. But I knew these calls were our lifeline to getting students, and I could sense from our discussion on the beach that Harris wasn't entirely convinced everything was going to fall into place without persistence.

When we reached the parking area, Myrtle waved goodbye and walked briskly through the icy raindrops to the boarding house. Harris collapsed on a large rock, puffing from the exertion.

"You okay, Harris?" came a voice from behind us.

We both whirled around to see Violeta. She was standing straight, holding a tall white umbrella.

"Violeta? I thought you'd already left. Didn't you have to return your car?" Harris asked, looking puzzled.

"I lost my car keys. I left them in your washroom after I took photographs of the campus with you."

"Oh, for goodness' sake! And I locked the School House, didn't I?" I admitted, kicking myself.

"I looked everywhere for you two. You didn't answer your phones. But your owner helped me."

Harris' eyes narrowed. "The Major?"

Violeta nodded, but I could tell from her face that something wasn't quite right.

"That lady wouldn't let me leave, you know," she continued, starting to sound upset. "She kept talking to me. She asked me what you and I had agreed to. Then she offered me a two-for-one special to get even more kids."

I glanced at Harris, whose eyes were blazing. But before he could explode, I stepped forward, my voice calm but firm.

"Violeta, I'm sorry for what you've been put through today," I said. "That's not how we operate, and it won't happen again. You're right—this is a school and Harris and I respect your professionalism. I promise you'll deal with us directly going forward."

Violeta studied me for a moment, her expression softening. "Good. That's what I needed to hear. I was so angry earlier, but I feel better now."

Harris nodded, still seething but holding himself in check. "Like Phil said, you have our word," he said tightly.

Violeta gave a faint smile, kissed us both on the cheek, and left. Her *LTD* wheezed its way up the driveway, clouds of dust trailing behind it. Then, as if summoned by the atmosphere, the silhouette of the Major appeared on the hill, waving her arms dramatically as Violeta's car drove by.

Before I could stop him, Harris bolted forward. "That bloody, interfering, good-for-nothing woman…"

To avoid inflaming the growing tempest, I decided to remain where I was. But it wasn't long before loud expletives started reverberating through the campus, interspersed with comments like, "How dare you interfere…" and "Who do you think you are?" and "If you expect us to do our job, let us do it!"

I stayed inconspicuous as I watched Harris flail his hands in front of the Major. Finally, the Major stormed off in one direction while Harris walked determinedly toward the School House. Like Harris, I sighed loudly, as if releasing an "om" in a yoga class. The students hadn't even arrived, and I was already dealing with playground conflict.

Chapter 7

For the next few weeks, the Major and Harris were able to strategically avoid each other. The Major continued her foray into construction management, running about, barking orders at weary-looking workers while wielding a clipboard like a weapon. But there were moments when I noticed her pausing in the middle of the chaos, her gaze lingering on the half-finished school building. The intensity in her eyes softened just briefly, and I wondered if she saw this place not as it was but as it could be.

Harris, on the other hand, stayed clear of the campus until late each evening, after ensuring the Major had gone home. He was consumed with his agent calls to Asia and had developed a nightly ritual of pacing the length of the School House, phone pressed to his ear, as he pitched the school.

In the midst of it all, I was juggling my own tasks. I had secured contracts from three young and energetic teachers Harris and I agreed would be good fits for the school. But finding a competent office manager was proving to be more difficult. Most of the candidates so far were local friends of the Major, with minimal experience and a general air of desperation that suggested they viewed the position as a lifeboat.

Late one afternoon, as I was about to call it quits for the day, there was a knock on my office door, that was partly ajar. A tall, immaculately dressed man bowed as I looked up.

"Sorry to bother you. My name is Koji. Koji Tanaka. I am applying for your office manager job. I don't have appointment. I thought I would just drop by to see you, if that's okay."

I stared at the naïve-looking man in front of me, who appeared to be barely in his twenties.

"Do you live nearby?" I asked, more to make conversation than out of any real interest.

"No. I am from Vancouver. But originally from Japan."

"You came all the way up from Vancouver?" I exclaimed.

"Sorry. I'm just interested in job."

Impressed by his effort, I felt compelled to invite him to come in and listen to what he had to say. "Please have a seat," I said, directing him to a chair in front of my desk.

Koji eagerly positioned himself, sitting up straight like an overzealous student ready to take notes. He was wearing a designer black suit with a white shirt, an orange Hermes tie, Ferragamo shoes, and a blue-tinged Rolex watch. I had to admit, there was something intriguing about him.

"Koji," I asked gently, "do you understand what this job entails?"

"I think so, sir. Organize office, greet people, manage student records, and speak English, Japanese, Chinese, and Korean on phone and at the counter."

"Please call me Phil. Wait ... you actually speak all those languages?"

"Yes, sir—I mean, Mr. Phil. Learning languages is easy for me but sometimes pronunciation and grammar is a problem."

"Where have you worked in the past?"

"Tokyo mainly, but I also worked for a Malaysian trading company in Vancouver because they do business with Japan. Here are my references," he said, eagerly handing me a sheet of paper.

As I reviewed the references, I noted they were quite complimentary, describing him as, "a can-do worker, an excellent troubleshooter, and someone with good common sense."

My concentration was broken by the squeak of my office door being carefully opened. Harris peeked in.

"Oh, sorry," he said, hesitating when he saw Koji. "I didn't realize you were with someone. I just wanted to see if you'd like to join me for dinner before our evening calls to Asia?"

I looked at Harris and then back at Koji. "Yes, but, before we go, I'd like you to meet someone."

"Sure!"

"Koji, I'm just going to have a quick chat with my colleague here and I'll be back in a minute."

"No problem," he beamed.

"Agent?" asked Harris, looking quizzical, as I walked into the hallway, closing my office door behind me.

"No. You know how challenging it's been for us to find a good office manager," I said in a hushed voice. "Well, the guy in there is interested in the job. I can't put my finger on it—but I think he might work hard for us if we gave him the chance. Would you mind chatting with him for a few minutes and let me know what you think?" I handed him Koji's references.

"Of course," replied Harris, smiling. "Let's see what we've got."

I waited in the hallway, looking at other résumés, while Harris spent time with Koji in my office. After about twenty minutes, he re-emerged.

"I think you nailed it. Your instincts are bang on," whispered Harris. "He also speaks a whole bunch of languages. I say we give him a try."

A week later, Koji arrived dressed to the nines for his first day at Cothbert House School. It was agreed that his remuneration package would include free lodging in the Boarding House in exchange for helping Myrtle with supervisory duties on the weekends.

"Where would you like me to start?" he asked, enthusiastically, laying an expensive leather briefcase on the reception counter.

I hadn't done much planning for Koji's arrival and was unprepared for his eagerness to get going. I stared at the tired office lying in total disarray behind the reception counter. There were a couple of old, abandoned computer terminals, a photocopier turned sideways, its parts scattered on the floor, and several dusty, outdated phones left ages ago on a steel chair.

"We want this office up and running, Koji," I explained, pointing to the equipment behind me. "See if any of those old computers are salvageable and whether that copier is functional. We'll also need to contact the phone company. Maybe you can get some quotes for a new phone system for the campus. And we need to look at getting connected to the Internet. Email is becoming more common for communication these days."

"No problem. I get on it ASAP."

As I turned to return to my office, the front door swung open and the Major swooped into the office like a storm front, her boots echoing ominously on the tile floor.

"Is something wrong?" I asked cautiously, already bracing myself.

"Yes, there is!" she barked, glaring at me. "Did you go and hire someone without consulting me? Who is this *Koojie* person anyway?"

Before I could respond, Koji stepped forward and bowed deeply. "I am Koji Tanaka. Very nice to meet you, Boss," he said, his smile bright and unshakable.

The Major's scowl faltered at the word *Boss*. She studied him, her arms crossed, as though deciding whether to chew him out or offer him a challenge.

"Hmm. Asian, eh? Any brothers and sisters?"

"Yes. Four brothers and three sisters."

"Are they looking for a good school? I can give them a package deal," she said, her tone shifting into a sales pitch, but her words carried less bite.

"Ah … well, thanks, but they are at university."

The Major nodded curtly. "Well, let's see how you do. I expect hard work from all my employees. And don't think I'll be going easy on you just because you're new."

As she left, I noticed her give Koji a sideways glance, as if assessing his merit. I turned around to see how Koji was coping with all this, but he seemed fine, still smiling and looking eager to begin.

"Don't mind her. She's a bit direct at times."

"Oh, it's okay. I am used to this. Had bosses like her before. You just need to show respect. She's a good person. I can tell. I will show her I am a hard worker."

"I'm sure you will," I grinned.

A couple of evenings later, I had just finished jotting down some notes on an agent who had appeared particularly enthusiastic about the school, when there was a soft knock on my office door. *Myrtle with coffee, perhaps? I thought.*

"Come in ... please," I called back.

The door slowly eased open to reveal Koji, who, on cue, bowed as soon as we made eye contact.

"Oh, Koji ... I've completely neglected you, haven't I? I'm so sorry. How are things going with the office? Do you need me to connect you with a phone provider?"

"No. It's okay. Thanks. Can you please come with me to the office so I can show you a few things?"

"Of course!" I replied, ready for a much-needed stretch break.

I followed him back out to the main hall reception area. When I reached the front office, the view that greeted me caused my jaw to drop. The previously dingy office space had morphed into a hub of activity. New overhead lighting shone down on the previously abandoned computers, each of which was humming along and actually displaying a workable desktop. The large photocopier, that had previously been laid to rest in pieces all over the floor, was now in full service, eagerly churning out copies of a school profile Harris had created. And there, sitting on the front counter, was a brand-new switchboard and fax machine.

"This is amazing, Koji. Amazing! How did you do all this in such a short time?"

Koji beamed with pride. "I know a lot about computers and office machines, and when I worked for Malaysian company in Vancouver, I helped them get the best deal for a phone system. By the way, there will be a phone in everyone's office by next week, as well as Internet. The company I chose also gave us a free payphone in the Boarding House as a thank you for signing the contract. I think it's a good idea. You know, the boarders may want to phone parents at nighttime."

"Yes, certainly makes sense … Wait a second! Did you say you signed a contract?"

"I know. The Major will be angry. To get the best deal, I had to sign right away."

"I see. But, Koji, next time you've got to check with me first. We're going to have some explaining to do with the Major over this."

"I'm not worried. You'll see," replied Koji confidently.

As expected, chaos erupted the next morning, with the Major at the center of it.

"You'd better come quick," bellowed Myrtle, bursting into my office. "The Major's tearing into Koji about the phone contract."

I rushed into the reception area to find the Major waving a paper in Koji's face. My stomach dropped. "How dare you sign a contract without my permission? Do you have any idea how much money you've wasted?" She slapped the paper against her palm. "I had the perfect deal lined up with a friend in town who actually knows this stuff—unlike you!"

Koji didn't flinch, standing with a steady posture. His calmness was enviable. "How much was your friend charging you?"

The Major paused, her tirade briefly stalled. She yanked a crumpled paper from her pocket, jamming her reading glasses on with an irritated huff. "Four hundred and fifty dollars a month for the whole system. What do you have to say to that?"

Koji nodded, his voice in control. "If you look at my contract, it's three hundred and eighty dollars a month. We also get Internet, a fax machine, and a payphone for the Boarding House. Your friend is overcharging you."

I held my breath, half expecting the Major to explode again. Instead, she studied the papers, her scowl softening into something resembling approval. "Fine," she muttered, her tone clipped as she regained control. "But don't you dare sign anything else without consulting me first.

"Yes, boss!"

"And you, Gower, what do you have to say about all this?"

"I trust Koji. That's why I hired him," I said, wondering where my unrestrained words were coming from.

"We'll see if this is the right place for him," snapped the Major, storming out the front door.

After she left, Koji turned to me, smiling. "She's tough, but I like her. She reminds me of my first boss in Tokyo."

I forced a laugh, still rattled. How did he stay so composed?

I recounted the incident to Harris later that evening at the *As You Like It.*

"You did what real leaders do, Phil—you stood by your people."

He took a swig of Scotch and added, "A principal I respect once told me something I'll never forget: If you want to be a strong leader, you need to keep your resignation letter in your back pocket at all times so you never lose your integrity."

His words hit harder than I expected. I wasn't quite there

yet—I wasn't sure I'd ever be—but for the first time, I felt like I was moving in the right direction. I wasn't just following orders anymore. I was standing my ground.

And it felt good.

Chapter 8

Harris and I were just returning from inspecting the progress being made in the Boarding House and feeling relieved that most of the renovations were nearly complete when a *FedEx* truck came rumbling down the driveway. It pulled up in front of the School House, and a courier leaped from the cab, darted inside the building, and was back in the van before we reached the front door.

Entering the reception area, we were greeted by a loud, "Look!" as Koji jumped out in front of us, handing me a white courier envelope. "It says *Pil* Gower, but I think it's for you. Right?"

I turned, blushing slightly, toward Harris, who was clearly relishing the moment.

"Right!" I replied, snatching the envelope from Koji's hand and ripping it open.

As I began flipping through the contents of the package and realized what I was staring at, my heart started to race.

"Holy shit!" I exclaimed, unable to contain my excitement.

"What is it?" asked Harris, clearly not used to hearing me swear.

Ignoring Harris, I started counting the documents in the envelope and shouted again, "Holy shit!" followed by, "I don't believe this! We just received ten applications. From Violeta!"

"What?" thundered Harris, yanking the envelope from my hand. Quickly scanning its contents, he handed the package back and gleefully yelled, "Yes!" while pulling down his clenched fist in a show of victory.

For a moment, we both stood there, stunned by the sudden breakthrough. The envelope felt heavier in my hands now—a lifeline we hadn't expected.

Harris turned to Koji, whacking him on the back. "Well, my friend, you've got your work cut out for you now. We're about to accept ten new students! Prepare their acceptance packages as soon as possible, exactly as I showed you the other day."

"Yes!" cheered Koji, imitating Harris. "I'll do it ASAP!"

"By the way, Koji, don't tell the Major about this yet," Harris added. "She'll get uppity, think it's a cinch to recruit students, and expect us to fill the school overnight. Do you understand?"

"Yes. *Mummies the word,*" he said, moving his forefinger in front of his lips and tittering like a child keeping a secret.

"That's 'Mum's the word,' Koji. Mum's the word."

As Koji nodded enthusiastically, a ripple of discomfort settled in my chest. I could see where Harris was coming from—managing the Major's expectations wasn't a bad idea in theory. But something about his dismissive tone didn't sit right with me.

"Phil?" Harris's voice cut through my thoughts. He was looking at me, his expression a mixture of amusement and impatience. "You okay there?"

I forced a smile. "Just thinking about the logistics," I replied vaguely.

"Well, don't overthink them," Harris said, brushing off my concern. "We've got momentum now, and that's all that matters."

But as Koji started organizing the paperwork, I couldn't shake the weight of the Major's expectations pressing down on me. I couldn't help but feel that she deserved to know what was happening. For better or worse, this was her school.

Behind the reception counter, Harris, Koji, and I carefully put the forms into ten separate piles. Six of the applications were from boys, while four were from girls. As I examined them more closely, I realized they spanned different grade and language levels.

"These students seem pretty good," I remarked. "Are they serious about coming here?"

"If you're basing your assessment on their report cards, don't!" said Harris bluntly. "They've probably been tampered with."

"You're not serious?"

"I'm damn serious. And the tampering wouldn't have been done for our benefit. Violeta knows too well that, at this stage of our existence, we'll take any warm body that comes along. No, it was probably done to convince *CIC*—also known as *Citizenship and Immigration Canada* —that these students are worthy of being admitted. If *CIC* thinks an applicant could become a burden on the Canadian Government, their *Study Permit* will be rejected outright, and they won't be able to enroll."

"So, you think some of these applicants have issues?" I asked.

"I can guarantee it. It could be anything. But believe me,

these applications are not as good as they look."

I took a deep breath and exhaled slowly as I stared at the dour, expressionless student photos stapled to the applications. So, who are you all, anyway?

"Listen, Phil," cut in Harris. "While this is a great present, we've only got four weeks until school starts, and we're still only halfway there. We can't stop now. We've got to keep working those phones every night. And Koji, whenever we accept a student, stay on top of their agent so everything unfolds quickly."

"Got it!" Koji replied, raising his thumb in the air, just as the sound of footsteps echoed down the hall.

"Hey, Joe!" Harris thundered as a small man in black-framed glasses, carrying a worn brown leather satchel, stepped up in front of us. "What are you doing here?"

The man, who had unusually pale skin, thinning greased-back hair, and wore a pin-striped navy suit, sneered at Harris. "You know exactly why I'm here," his deep voice laced with frustration.

"Ah yes, losing more sleep over you-know-who, are we?" quipped Harris with a belly laugh. "Phil, this is my good friend Joe Spitz. He and I go way back. These days, he has the unenviable task of managing the Major's finances."

"Oh, you're her accountant," I said, remembering how the Major referenced him during my interview. "I'm Phil Gower, Principal of Cothbert."

"Lucky you," replied Joe wryly, shaking my hand. Turning back to Harris, he added, "Joke all you want, Harris, but no one in accounting school prepared me for working with her."

"Relax, Joe!" Harris bantered, clapping him on the back. "Things are looking up. We just got ten firm applications today—$300K for the books."

Joe's expression remained serious as his eyes darted between us. Leaning closer, he lowered his voice. "Listen, you two need to get more involved with the school's finances—and fast. There are things happening under the surface that neither of you will want to deal with when they come to light."

"What do you mean?" I asked cautiously.

Joe paused. "The Major's bending the rules to keep this school afloat, but sooner or later, that's going to catch up with her. When it does, it won't just be her in hot water—it'll drag all of us down too. You need to keep a close eye on her."

Without elaborating further, Joe turned on his heel. "Take care of yourselves," he said before leaving.

Harris caught my concerned look. "Hey, I already suggested to the Major that she open her books, but she won't budge. She just gives me that spiel about how educators don't have any business sense."

"Maybe I can help," I offered. "I've got some budgeting experience. I'll dig into our fixed costs and put together a broad-based budget. At least we'll have a clearer sense of where we stand financially."

"Not a bad idea," Harris said, his tone turning more serious. "But obviously, something else is going on here. What? I have no bloody idea."

That night, in order to keep my mind off budgeting and the Major, I made significant progress through my agent list. By 11:00 p.m., just as I was wondering how many more calls I could reasonably manage, my phone rang unexpectedly. I jumped with surprise, fumbling for the receiver.

"Good evening, Cothbert House School. Phil Gower speaking," I answered.

There was dead silence on the other end of the phone.

"Hello? Hello?" I said again, more firmly.

Faint sounds of heavy breathing came through the receiver.

"Hello?" I repeated more loudly.

"Mr. Phil Gower?" a deep, low, breathy voice intoned, questioning the validity of my name despite my clear introduction.

"Yes?" I replied hesitantly.

There was more heavy breathing.

"Hello?" I repeated again, raising my tone slightly.

"This is Tarantino Tang," the deep voice announced with a strong accent. Considering the time of night, it felt ominous. I waited for him to continue, but again only silence.

"Yes, Mr. Tang. How can I help you?"

"I heard about your school."

"Oh, good... do you have questions about Cothbert?"

"I am coming there on July 25 at 2:00 p.m. to visit."

"Oh, I see. So, you want to make an appointment?"

"I will be there at 2:00 p.m. I will see you then."

There was a click, and the phone went dead.

What on earth was that? I asked myself, standing and then charging into the hall searching for Harris. I barged into his office where I found him on his landline. He signaled with his finger for me to have a seat and that he was almost finished. A few moments later, he put down the receiver.

"Just need to jot down a few notes before I forget what we talked about," he said, scribbling on his agent list. "I think we're winning over some of these agents with our generous commission. How are you making out?"

"I just got the strangest call from a man who called himself Tarantino Tang."

Harris sat upright in his chair, his pen dropping from his hand and his reading glasses sliding down his nose.

"You're kidding me, right?"

"No. Why?"

"I've been trying to connect with this guy for the past two weeks. What did he want?"

"Well, that's just it. I'm not quite sure. To be honest, I thought he was from the Mafia at first, the way he spoke. All he said was that he'd heard about our school and he would be visiting on July 25 at 2:00 p.m. Then he hung up."

"He's coming here? And he phoned you personally?"

"Yes. He knew my name. Who is this guy?"

"Strange," Harris said pensively before abruptly springing from his chair. He rubbed his hands together, reached into a cabinet beside him, and pulled out a bottle of *Laphroaig* Scotch and two stubby crystal glasses, filling each halfway. Handing me one, he took a swig from his own glass and then started pacing the room.

"Phil, this could be a game-changer for us," he said, taking another gulp.

"Why? Tell me who this guy is!"

"Tarantino Tang owns *Yingyucom*—one of the biggest chains of language schools in all of Asia. He's based out of Taiwan, where locals idolize him because so many of his graduates get accepted to Ivy Leagues in the U.S. I'd heard his company recently expanded into educational consulting, so I've been trying to connect with him. But I was never able to get past his bulldog of a receptionist. And no one ever returned my calls. I was ready to give up on him. But here he is phoning you personally out of the blue. I don't get it... but I like it!" he said, downing the remains of his glass.

"So, you've never even met this guy before?" I asked, still feeling a bit uneasy about the call.

"No. But, I've heard he can be a bit rough around the edges and that he has an ego the size of Vancouver. He was probably curt with you because you didn't gush when you heard his name. Anyway, when did you say he's coming to visit us?"

"July 25 at 2:00 p.m.... That's all he said!" I replied.

Harris looked over at his wall calendar. "Christ! That's this Friday—three days from now," he exclaimed. "We've got to make sure everything is perfect on that day," he continued, recharging his glass. "Koji must be ready to greet him as soon as he arrives, and Myrtle needs to prepare something in the way of food. But most importantly, I have to find a project for the Major to do off-campus or she'll torpedo the visit."

Harris continued to pace the room and was obviously wound up. "Wow, this is an interesting development." He paused and shook his head, "But I still don't get why he phoned you personally," he repeated.

We were all on high alert when, three days later, Tarantino Tang's visit was anticipated with apprehension. Harris had convinced the Major how important it was that she drive to Vancouver and negotiate a deal with a company that leased computers to schools. A deal that only she could broker, he told her, without blinking an eye. In the meantime, Myrtle transformed a table in the Dining Hall by setting up an appetizing buffet, while Koji was on a ladder in the lobby, changing burnt-out light bulbs.

It was just before 2:00 pm when I heard the sound of a

car engine outside my office window. Twisting my chair around to look, I could see a long black *Mercedes S-Class* that looked like it had been designed to carry a foreign dignitary, edge its way towards the School House, where it purred to a stop under the portico. Koji, already outside, was standing at attention. A few moments later, a uniformed driver got out, walked towards the back of the car, and opened a passenger door. I immediately took this as my cue to get to the reception area, where I found Harris, frantically trying to button his blazer.

"Now," we can't look too eager," he said, panting. "But we'll probably need to stroke Tarantino's ego a bit. A moderate amount of gushing and groveling may be necessary," he added, half-jokingly.

There was a gust of air, as the front door was opened by Koji to allow a short, pudgy man, followed by a tall, slim woman, to enter.

"Good afternoon. You must be Gower?" said the woman, swooping towards me. She wore a charcoal gray business suit, black pumps, and carried a white briefcase with a very obvious Chanel logo on it. Her sharply cut, bright silver dyed hair conveyed an air of confidence.

"Yes, I'm Phil Gower," I said, extending both of my hands with one of my business cards. "And this is my colleague, Harrison Tweedsmuir." Harris offered his card.

"Thank-you," she said, receiving our cards. "I am Bobo Chang, Mr. Tang's assistant." She handed us each two cards, one with her name on it and the other with Tarantino's. "Mr. Tang would like a tour of the campus and then a meeting with you afterward."

I looked over at Tarantino, who had chosen to remain at

74

the entrance, totally absorbed in a cell phone conversation. He was wearing a tailored, but tightly fitting black suit that failed to hide a rotund body that bulged in all the wrong places. A snow-white shirt, perfectly knotted blue silk tie, and black patent dress shoes were an advertisement to his self-proclaimed status. His tanned face, with sternly carved features, was exactly as I had envisioned during my late-night phone call with him. I couldn't help but think his black hair, slicked back over the top of his head and closely-shaved sides, were more characteristic of a Triad gang member than someone in whom you would entrust your child's education.

"Certainly, I'd be happy to show Mr. Tang around," I said, trying to get his eye contact.

"That won't be necessary. Mr. Tang will look around by himself—without the sales pitch."

"Oh, I see," I responded with a bit of chagrin.

Harris gestured with his hand to give them what they wanted.

"If you'd like, my assistant, Koji Tanaka, can go with you as a guide," I signaled to Koji. "You know, just to make sure you don't get lost."

Bobo moved back towards Tarantino, touching him on the shoulder. He covered his cell phone with his free hand, listening as she whispered in his ear. He nodded, expressionless, quickly whispering something in response, before continuing with his call.

"Yes, that's fine," said Bobo, flicking back her hair. "As long as there's no sales pitch."

"No problem," said Koji, stepping forward and bowing. *"Mummies the word*! Please, this way, Ma'am," he directed, then ushered Tarantino, who had still not acknowledged us, out the door.

I leaned against the wall, crossing my arms tightly. "Well, there's an engaging individual."

"Let's not judge him too quickly," said Harris. "He's obviously here for a reason, otherwise, he wouldn't have come all this way."

"If you say so."

All three returned to the School House about forty minutes later, toured the classrooms and gym, and then joined us in the Dining Hall, where Myrtle had performed her culinary magic.

"Thank you, Koji!" said Harris, indicating it was time for him to leave.

Koji bowed and exited. There was no acknowledgment from Tarantino or Bobo.

While I fully expected the two of them to ignore the refreshments Myrtle had laid out, I was pleasantly surprised when Tarantino, after surveying the food, picked up a plate and proceeded to fill it. Bobo followed behind, dutifully pouring Tarantino tea while at the same time serving herself. Once they both appeared ready to eat, Harris steered them towards a table, where we all sat down.

"So, how was the tour?" I asked, cautiously, as they got comfortable.

"Yes, I do hope Koji took good care of you," added Harris, trying to initiate conversation. Tarantino remained focused on his food and then reached for his tea, loudly slurping its contents. Bobo turned to Tarantino, appearing to translate.

"Mr. Tang says the tour was good."

Harris shot me a reassuring look.

At last, Mr. Tang sat up and swiveled in our direction. He didn't look so much at us but through us. His penetrating, yet powerful gaze remained focused on Harris and me, as though he were attempting to read our minds. I felt like we were being interrogated, even though nothing was spoken. Finally, after an extended and very awkward period of silence, he leaned toward Bobo and whispered again, prompting Bobo to open her Chanel case and remove a red file folder.

"Mr. Tang would like to speak now," said Bobo, opening the file.

I guess we should be honored, I thought cynically. *Where the hell is all this heading?* I felt more and more uncomfortable by the minute.

Tarantino stood up, leaned forward, carefully placing his hands on the table, and began to express what, to me, sounded like a rehearsed speech.

"Let me translate for you," said Bobo. "Mr. Tang believes he has been successful in his career because of his good intuition. Over the years, he has developed the ability to read people and determine quite quickly if a business has potential."

Tarantino continued speaking.

"Mr. Tang wants to apologize for being so aloof, but it was important for him to assess everything objectively, including both of you—without allowing false niceties and marketing to cloud his judgment."

I looked at Harris, who raised his eyebrows slightly. Tarantino paused for a moment before continuing.

Bobo listened intently and then turned to us with a smile.

"Mr. Tang likes you and thinks this school has great potential. He is now ready to sign an agent agreement. He thinks he already has about twelve students who would benefit from coming here this September."

"That *is* wonderful news," said Harris, sitting up as he tried to contain his excitement. "Bobo, please let Mr. Tang know that we are honored and humbled by his commitment to us and will do everything we can to prove his intuition correct."

Bobo translated Harris' comments, and, for the first time, Tarantino smiled. Then, after extending his hand to clasp each of ours in turn, he nodded to Bobo, who promptly removed two identical documents from the red file folder and slid one toward me. Harris moved in closer, adjusting his reading glasses as he looked over my shoulder. It was a standard agent agreement, but went one step further, promising a minimum of twelve students in year one and, as long as both parties were happy with each other, a minimum of fifteen students by year-two.

As I continued to read, I noticed a clause I hadn't seen before—the promise that we would participate in at least one *Yingyucom* education fair per year. I pointed to this section, but Harris waved me off, as though to say, 'no problem'.

"This looks very straightforward," declared Harris, snapping his reading glasses shut. "We'd be happy to sign it right now—as long as you're ready, of course."

Once again, Bobo translated, and Tarantino smiled for the second time.

"The contract has Phil's name on it," said Bobo, sliding the duplicate copy toward me. "He is the one who will have to sign both copies," handing me a large black *Mont Blanc* fountain pen.

I searched each document for my name, eagerly signing both on the dotted lines before swiveling them back to Bobo. She motioned to Tarantino, who pulled out his own gold

Mont Blanc and quickly drew Chinese characters on his signature lines, handing me back one of the signed contracts. He then leaned into Bobo, continuing to speak Mandarin.

"Mr. Tang will update you more specifically in the next twenty-four hours," said Bobo. "He just needs to consult with his head office in Taipei. He also understands that time is of the essence, but given his special relationship with the Canadian Consulate in Taiwan, he thinks he can get his applicants' study permits processed in no time at all."

"Excellent," I replied. "Please extend our sincere thanks again to Mr. Tang."

"Yes, we really do look forward to a long and fruitful relationship with *Yingyucom*," added Harris.

"Mr. Tang would also like to say thank you to Koji, who he thought was very professional," added Bobo.

"I will definitely let Koji know. I'm sure he will appreciate hearing that," I replied.

Bobo carefully inserted her signed contract into the red folder and slid the folder into her case.

Tarantino raised his eyebrows and nodded.

"So, I think we're done here!" announced Bobo, as the two of them simultaneously rose from their chairs.

I scrambled to my feet. "Please, this way," I said, shepherding them back out to the main hall. "I must say, Bobo, your English is impeccable. Where were you educated?"

"Stanford," she answered, nonchalantly.

"Impressive. By the way, may I ask where Mr. Tang got my name from?"

"His good friend in Seoul," replied Bobo. "Do you know an agent called Violeta Kim? Works for a company called *Hyung Bo Consulting*? She spoke very highly of you both—

particularly you, Mr. Gower."

I purposely avoided Harris' eye contact.

The minute Tarantino's Mercedes disappeared up the drive-way, Harris and I joyfully high-fived one another, our voices rising in a jubilant cheer so loud it must have echoed all the way to the far side of Timberline Lake. Our audible delirium prompted Koji to dash out the front door, his brow furrowed in confusion.

"What happened?" he asked, eyes darting between us.

"What happened, my friend," Harris said, pulling him into a huge bear hug, "is that we've just signed a big contract! It looks like we'll hit our minimum student quota in time for the school opening. And you, Koji, played a key role in closing the deal."

"Closing what deal?" came a voice from behind us. We whirled around in unison, startled to find the Major standing there in her gaudy tweed hunting outfit adjusting a rifle cradled carelessly in her arms.

"After those raccoons again, Major?" I asked, trying to diffuse the situation.

"What deal did you just close?" she demanded again, her tone sharpening with suspicion.

"I thought you were supposed to be in town," Harris shot back, stepping forward, a flash of frustration crossing his face. "Did you arrange for those computers?"

"Ha! You mean, did I deal with those crooks you recom-mended? No. I'm not throwing away $2,000 a month leasing from them." She waved her hand dismissively, still struggling to adjust the safety clip on her rifle. "Educators have no business sense," she muttered under her breath, echoing her usual mantra, the words laced with a mixture of contempt and irritation.

"Maybe you need second-hand computers?" Koji suggested, appearing oblivious to the Major's rising tension.

"What?" The Major looked up, narrowing her eyes as she tried to steady her rifle.

"I'll find you a much better deal on second-hand computers than $2,000 a month," Koji insisted.

The Major eyed him warily. "Alright, then, *Koojie*. Show me what you've got. But don't sign any damn contracts. Do you understand? Just get me the numbers and I'll decide if you're worth the money I'm paying you."

"Got it, Boss," Koji replied, almost bouncing on his heels before sprinting back inside the School House.

The Major shifted her gaze over to Harris and me. "Now, will one of *yous* tell me what deal you closed without my permission?"

Harris' expression hardened, as he looked like he was preparing to unleash a tirade. But I cut him off, stepping forward.

"We signed an important agent agreement," I said. "That's all, Major. An agent agreement."

"And we don't need your permission for those, do we?" Harris added, his voice edged with challenge. "Or have you forgotten that we're the ones who sign agent contracts around here?"

The Major stiffened, her eyes flashing with irritation. "I don't see them agent agreements bringing us any money yet. I've done my part—pissing away my own money making your damn campus look pretty. But there are still no damn kids. And we're supposed to be opening in a few weeks. So don't patronize me! Do your damn jobs and find us some bloody kids!"

Suddenly, a rustling noise from the woods caught her attention, and without another word, she abandoned the conversation. "Bloody educators," she muttered under her breath as she turned, clear-cutting her way through the brush.

I glanced at Harris who was seething, his arms crossed defiantly. None of this felt right.

"She's not wrong, you know," I said cautiously, my voice quieter now.

Harris' head snapped toward me, his eyes blazing. "Excuse me?"

"This tension, this mistrust—it's because we're keeping her in the dark," I said, meeting his gaze. "If you don't bring her up to speed, how can you expect her to back us? It's no wonder she hasn't opened her books to you. And frankly, I'm done with the negativity."

Harris blinked, caught off guard by the sudden bite in my tone. "Negativity?" he repeated.

"Yes," I said firmly, standing my ground. "You're seething all the time. And I get it, Harris, I do. It's hard to feel the joy when she's meddling, but—"

"She thinks we're lazy dreamers! She doesn't see the hours we're putting in, the calls to Asia, the agents who are finally coming on board. She doesn't understand what this place *means*! It's more than a business. You of all people should know that."

"Then show her!" I snapped, the frustration spilling out before I could stop it. "Show her everything—Violeta, Tarantino, the agents. Prove to her that her money is going to pay off. Once she sees that, maybe she'll stop treating us like employees she can bully and start working with us instead of against us."

Harris stared at me, his expression shifting as my words sunk in. For a moment, the tension between us hung in the air like a drawn breath. Then, slowly, he exhaled, rubbing his hand down his face.

"You're right," he admitted finally, his voice softer now, almost reluctant.

Suddenly, we were jolted by a loud gunshot that rang out from the woods, followed by an agonizing scream. I turned to Harris with wide eyes, my heart sank.

"Don't tell me…" I whispered in horror.

A few days later, with my phone on speaker, Harris and I listened as a doctor at Vancouver General Hospital updated us on the Major's condition. The bullet, which had firmly lodged itself in the Major's left foot, had been successfully extracted, although she would still require additional surgery. Apparently, her sister, Millicent Hunter, who lived in Vancouver, was now looking after everything and had agreed to take care of the Major until she was ready to use a wheelchair. As we ended the call, both shaking our heads, Koji stuck his head through the door.

"Mr. Phil. Mr. Harris. You must come quickly!"

Now what? Surely the Major can't have caused another crisis from her bed.

Harris and I followed Koji to the reception area just as he dashed behind the counter. Leaning on the front desk, we asked in unison: "What's wrong, Koji?"

"Nothing wrong. But look at this!" he exclaimed, holding

up reams of fax paper, like an unraveled toilet roll. "It just arrived from Mr. Tang. It's fourteen applications. Yes! I just said fourteen applications," he giggled, with unabashed delight.

Harris attacked the flowing mass of paper like a child ripping through wrapping paper on Christmas Day.

"Incredible, Koji. Can you believe this Phil?" he hollered, leaning toward me. Tarantino was true to his word."

"And then some," I added. "Fourteen applications. That puts us at twenty-four students for opening."

"Yeah!" cheered Koji, clapping.

I pulled aside a covering letter that was attached to the applications that reminded us of our need to participate in at least one of *Yingyucom's* annual education fairs.

"Harris," I said, pointing at the letter … "How's this actually going to work?"

Harris leaned over my shoulder. "Oh, that," he replied with recognition, waving his hand dismissively. "Simple. We just visit Taiwan and participate in their fair."

"Visit Taiwan? Really?"

"Absolutely," replied Harris. "And we'll need to go to Korea and probably Japan and Hong Kong as well. These agent relationships are built on mutual trust and commitment. They visit us and we visit them."

"Does the Major know she'll be flying us to Asia in the near future?"

"Ah, don't worry about her. We'll make a business case for the expense. Any international school worth its weight travels, both to maintain agent and parent relationships and to recruit new students. Now, Koji," he said, turning to the mass of paper that was falling over the reception counter, "let's get these applications processed ASAP."

"Yes, ASAP," he said, saluting in jest.

Chapter 9

The call connected with a faint crackle, and the Major's voice came through the speaker-phone, sharp and direct as ever. "Any kids yet?"

I watched Harris lean forward, his elbows on the desk, a grin tugging at his mouth. "We've done it, Major—we've hit our break-even."

For a moment, there was only silence on the line. The faint hum of static filled the lull until her voice returned, softened in a way that made the weight of her relief unmistakable. "Well, it's about time. Maybe *yous* two aren't a complete waste of my payroll after all."

"Our agent contracts paid off," added Harris, unable to let the Major have the last word.

After a beat, her tone snapped back to business. "Do we still have time to bring in more kids?"

Harris gave me a look, as if to say *I told you so.* But I couldn't help noticing the faint trace of satisfaction in her voice.

"We'll keep pushing our agents," I said, stepping in. "And we're already following up on some local students who might board with us."

"That's good, Philly," sounding as though we had completely disarmed her with our good news. "Do whatever it takes to lock them in," she added, slipping seamlessly into her hard-nosed, saleswoman persona.

"And how's the foot?" asked Harris, his tone hovering between sincere and teasing.

"Yeah, well, I really fumbled that damn gun, didn't I? Those raccoons will be the death of me." She let out an uncharacteristic belly laugh—a sharp, gravelly sound that felt entirely out of place and yet oddly satisfying. It took me by so completely by surprise that I couldn't help but chuckle, and even Harris joined in.

With our enrollment now well under control and a working budget in the draft stage, I decided to convene an evening staff meeting in the Dining Hall for all of our new hires. In preparation, Koji had designed an information folder for each participant that was embossed with the school's stylized rose-stem logo, while Myrtle had discovered an old dressmaker's mannequin on which she'd pinned a prototype of the new school uniform: a white dress shirt and navy-blue sweater bearing the Cothbert crest. Lying on a table beside it were a pair of gray slacks and a blue and gray kilt, as well as a mock-up of a sports uniform consisting of a blue gym shirt and matching sweatpants, both of which had the word *Cothbert* inscribed in bold white letters.

"Sorry I'm late," said Harris, rushing in, trying to catch his breath. "I'm afraid one of our teachers just bailed on us."

"Which one?" I asked, annoyed.

"The gym and art teacher."

"Cheryl Collins? She was one of our best."

"And that's why another school sweetened the pot and snapped her up."

"So now what?"

"Well… I went back through our shortlist of applications, and the only one I could secure at this late date was…"

"Don't tell me that Whipplehill girl?"

"Yup. She's already on her way. She lives just down the road."

An hour later, our three new staff members started arriving. Other than Harris' last-minute recruit, I was generally pleased with our hires, particularly given the relatively low salaries we were offering. The important question, though, was: Could they work together as a team? I needed to get a sense of the group chemistry, particularly since Harris and Koji were, so far, the only proven entities. Myrtle certainly had the background and experience, but I still wasn't sure about her emotional state. To get a better idea of who I'd be working with, I decided that, as an icebreaker, I would ask everyone to introduce themselves and talk about one of their passions in life.

Once we were all seated, Koji, to whom I'd given a heads-up earlier, launched into his presentation by explaining how much he loved anime and a little bit about the history of Japanese computer animation. Harris got the group laughing by convincing us that his passion in life was single-malt Scotch. Then Myrtle, who couldn't stop bouncing in her chair, made a bit of a scene as she giggled her way through her fondness for cooking and decoupage. By the time she'd finished, she was almost hyperventilating.

The first of the new teachers to introduce herself was the one I was most concerned about.

"So… my name is Chelsea Whipplehill," she said, her

intonation rising as though she were asking a question. "My friends call me Chill. So... ya."

Chelsea was a tall, angular woman with long hair that was pulled into a bun that sat on top of her head, resembling a bird's nest. There was an uncomfortable pause as we waited for her to continue.

"And your passion?" I said, trying to coax her along.

"Oh, ya. That would be yoga and the outdoors... that's why they call me Chill."

I could see Myrtle on the other side of the table trying valiantly to contain herself.

"And what will you be teaching?" asked Harris, whose tone suggested he wasn't overly impressed.

"I'm the art and phys-ed teacher here at the Cothbert School. Like, I'm so happy to be working with you, Horris, and you, Phil—and the rest of you around the table. I can tell you're all such nice people. Namaste!" she chanted, putting her hands together and bending forward.

"That's Harris, dear. Not Horris." Harris rolled his eyes at me.

But then Chill straightened up and added, "And I also believe in making education holistic—where body, mind, and spirit align. That's what drew me here. I've worked in places before where the focus was only on the academic side. But when you feel good in your body, you're open to learning better."

The other two hires nodded in agreement and Harris raised his eyes in surprise. Her thoughtful words and underlying conviction were not what I'd unexpected.

The next to speak was Pancho de Metz, a small man with a bronze complexion and big dark eyes that shone through black-framed glasses. Despite his studious look, there was a restless energy about him.

"So, hey guys, I'm Pancho. You can call me Pancho," he said grinning. "I'll be teaching math and drama. I've actually taught international students before in Japan and Mexico. Mexico is where I'm originally from."

"You speak Japanese?" asked Koji, sitting up excitedly.

"A little. Konnichiwa!"

"Oh, very good! Very good!" Koji cheered, clapping.

"Anyway, I really like traveling, and while it's certainly one of my passions, my real passion in life is acting. But in the meantime, as I told Phil and Harris, I need a real job, so here I am," he replied with a quick smile.

The last to introduce herself was Ida Plotnik, whose cropped gray hair signified she was older than either Chill or Pancho. Whatever challenges she had experienced in the past were immortalized in her deep furrowed brow, but there was an endearing warmth about her.

"Hi everyone. I'm Ida. I'm a local. I was a teacher in the public school system for many years, where I worked with special-needs kids. After the Government started cutting back funding for specialized programming, I decided I needed a new challenge. I'm really humbled by the experience around this table. What I truly love is music. I actually used to play in a jazz ensemble. I'll be a core science and social studies teacher."

"Wonderful," I said, reaching for my files. "Now, let's move on to other business…"

"Wait!" Chill interrupted. "You haven't told us about your passion."

"You're right," I said, hesitating slightly. "So, as you all know, I am the Principal, basically in charge of day-to-day operations as well as admissions. I work closely with Harris, who looks after all curricular matters. If you had asked me a few months ago what my passion is, I'm not sure I would have had an answer for you. But I have come to realize that it's actually running this place."

I paused for a moment before continuing.

"You know… I think we have a huge opportunity here to create a school from the ground up, but more importantly, for each of us to provide students who may have slipped through the cracks a chance to find themselves in meaningful and positive ways."

The group nodded and cheered enthusiastically.

"Thank you," I said, looking around the table. "Any other thoughts before we move to the agenda?"

No one responded.

"Right then. Harris, do you want to kick things off?"

"Sure. I've been really struggling with how we should structure our school's curriculum. We need to offer an adapted version of the Ministry Curriculum while we teach English as a Second Language, yet we have students who span a variety of grade and language levels."

"What about alphabetical order?" said Chill.

"Pardon?" Harris asked.

"Just arrange the students into different classes by their last name."

I avoided looking at Harris, and I could see Myrtle was really struggling to maintain her composure.

"Well, yes, that's one possibility," said Harris, showing incredible restraint. "But I think we should still divide them according to their age and grade level. Math, art, and phys-ed can easily be taught at grade level, regardless of a student's English ability, and even science can be adapted. The main challenge will be English and social studies. But we'll likely find that the older students already have a higher level of English proficiency because of the time they've spent learning it."

"I mostly agree with you," Ida cut in, leaning forward. "However, we may find that some of the younger students have been fast-tracked in ESL and could handle higher-level English instruction. I'd suggest building in some flexibility by creating closely aligned mixed classes. I'd build in a little flexibility by having closely aligned mixed classes. For example, we could offer a Grade 8 and 9 class, a Grade 9 and 10 class, and an 11 and 12 class. There will always be the odd student who might need to be moved up or down a level because of English, but given our small class sizes... only six to ten students, am I right?"

"Correct," said Harris.

"Yes, well, then, we should have the flexibility to custom-design our curriculum based on an individual's linguistic needs. It's actually a dream scenario when you think about it."

"I couldn't agree more," said Harris, slapping his hands down on the table.

"So, what are we going to call these mixed classes?" asked Chill, sitting up.

"Call them?" said Harris, raising his eyebrows.

"Ya. We should give them fun nicknames."

"Nicknames?"

"Look at this rose," said Chill, holding up one of the crested folders on the table. "What does this really mean to you all?"

she asked, looking at each of us in turn.

"It's a flower," replied Harris, exhaling deeply.

"Well, think about how this lovely flower came to be," she continued, a thoughtful expression crossing her face. "It started off as a seedling, then little stems emerged, which sprouted leaves and, eventually, over time, it grew to become this full-grown blossoming flower you see in this picture, with its strong foundation."

"I'm not sure where you're going with this…"

"Oh, I do," said Pancho, interjecting.

"You do?" said Harris, looking over at him in complete surprise.

"Chill is describing the flower as a metaphor. Chill, are you suggesting, for example, that we name our lower group the Seedlings, the middle group the Stems, and the older group…"

"Blossoms," Chill interrupted. "We'd call the older group Blossoms," she said proudly, looking dreamily at the school logo.

"I like it," said Ida. "It kind of makes the whole educational journey aspirational for the students. When they become blossoms, they will have fulfilled their journey."

"Exactly my idea," said Chill, beaming. "They will have fully blossomed."

"Well then," said Harris, looking totally blindsided. "Are we all in agreement?"

"Yes, I am," said Pancho. "I like it—Seedlings, Stems, and Blossoms. And as the school grows, we could even consider a group called the Buds…"

"Or Petals," added Chill."

"Done!" exclaimed Harris quickly, in an attempt to stifle

further flower analogies. "Back to you, Phil."

Chapter 10

The day before Cothbert House School was officially due to open, Harris and I enjoyed several pleasant hours at the *As You Like It*, congratulating ourselves on reaching this pivotal moment in the school's history. After what seemed like insurmountable odds, the campus was transformed, the staff hired and eager, and the minimum enrollment of twenty students exceeded. With the addition of some last-minute acceptances, our total population had now risen to twenty-seven, while tuition payments were sitting comfortably in the school's bank account. With my operating budget firmed up, I was convinced the entire venture was beginning to look financially feasible.

As our car limped its way out of the pub's parking lot, I reminded Harris I needed to pick up a few groceries.

"Okay," he replied. "Let's go to *Kipling's*," the tires of his Volvo squealing as he peeled dangerously across the road, hitting the curb before coming to a full stop.

"Have you met the owners yet?" he asked.

"No, I was always too much in a rush to stop and talk with anyone."

"Then let me formally introduce you to Santiago and Matilde," he offered, clambering out of the front seat, slamming his groaning door shut.

A hanging bell on the front door to the store announced our arrival while beneath our footsteps, the scuffed wooden flooring complained loudly. The familiar smells of cedar, roasted coffee, and lubricating oil greeted me as I marveled again at the organized chaos in front of me. Crooked, heaving shelves were stuffed with bags, cans, and boxes of food, while plastic milk crates filled to the brim with unrecognizable hardware parts sat next to inflatable fluorescent aquatic animals. High up in the rafters, a red cedar and canvas canoe appeared to hang precariously. To ensure every available space displayed salable merchandise—like dented kerosene lanterns, garish jigsaw puzzles, and mini jars of maple syrup—make-shift shelving had also been installed behind a cluttered wooden counter on which there stood an antique gold cash register.

"Harris!" came an excited voice from the depths of the store. A short man with wiry brown hair and baggy denim coveralls emerged from one of the aisles, pushing a tall hand-cart stacked with cardboard boxes.

"Hello, Santiago. Where's your better half today?" provoked Harris, cheerfully, thumping him on the back.

"Over here," came another voice. A woman with an angelic face partly hidden behind a mass of tangled salt-and-pepper hair came walking toward us. She was wearing a faded floral cotton dress and a pink plastic apron, her pockets bulging with pens, a calculator, and a small spiral notebook.

"I can't stay long," announced Harris, "but I wanted to introduce you to our principal, Phil Gower."

"Oh, yes," Santiago smiled, extending his hand. "You've been in here a few times. I wondered who you were. Thought you were a university student, to be honest. So young looking! Nice to meet you."

"Likewise," added Matilde. "How's it going over there, anyway? Have you got all the students you need?"

Harris grinned at me. "Basically, yes. But you know the Major. She'll always keep pushing for more."

Matilde and Santiago laughed, nodding their heads vigorously to show they knew exactly what the Major was like.

"Just so you know, Phil," said Santiago, turning to me, "I told Harris we'd give a ten percent discount to any of your students who shop here."

"And that includes you two as well," Matilde added cheerfully.

"Oh. I wish I'd known that earlier. Thank you," I said. "I'm actually here to stock up on a few things."

Without wasting any time, Matilde grabbed my hand and eagerly started maneuvering me through the store. Once done, and with the Volvo overflowing with shopping bags, Harris and I finally made our way back toward the school.

"Lovely couple," I uttered as Harris swerved his car to avoid a pothole.

"They are. But I hear they're really struggling financially."

"Oh, that's sad. They certainly seem to know all about the Major," I added.

"Everyone in the Community does. Don't get me wrong," he clarified, almost apologetically, knowing how I wanted to tone down the negativity, "I do feel sorry for the Major and appreciate all the work she's put into getting our campus up to speed, but I can't say I miss her being around. I mean, look at what we've been able to accomplish without having to waste our time keeping her happy."

"Oh, that reminds me. I spoke to her yesterday. She was a bit cranky. Apparently, her doctor wants to keep her off her feet for an extra two weeks."

"Excellent! The first two weeks of school without interference," beamed Harris, joyfully honking the horn of his car.

"You're so bad," I laughed, even though I had to admit I didn't miss the tension between the two of them. Harris was much easier to deal with without the Major's mercurial temperament getting under his skin.

As we bumped our way toward the school's front entrance, a flatbed truck just in front of us, transporting a large object wrapped in a dark tarp, signaled its intent to turn into the campus.

"What the hell is that?" asked Harris, squinting as he followed the truck closely behind. "Did you order something?"

"Maybe a few stationery items. But nothing that big. I hope Koji hasn't signed another contract for something without our permission."

The truck stopped in front of the School House, and we pulled up behind. The driver leaped out of his cab and walked toward us as Harris rolled down his window.

"Sorry to bother you," said the portly man, pushing his cap up. "Any idea where deliveries should be left?"

"I can deal with that," Harris declared as he got out of his car. "What've you got there, anyway?"

"A gas-powered golf-cart."

"A what? You must have the wrong place!"

"I don't think so," he replied, glancing down at a clipboard, flipping through some paperwork. "This is... Cothbert House School?"

98

"Yes, but…"

"Excuse me," I said, climbing out of the passenger side and joining them, "but who placed this order?"

"Let me see … oh, here we are. A Harriet T. Hunter."

"Christ! This is all we need," hollered Harris, holding out his hand for the paperwork, scribbling his signature so violently that the paper tore under his pen. "Maybe this is the sort of shit Joe was referring to."

In stunned silence, we stood watching the driver remove the tarp to reveal a used golf cart. It was silver with faded and chipped green trim and had over its top a weathered-looking green awning that was spotted with water stains and bird droppings. It was obvious this beauty hadn't been on a golf course for eons.

The driver lowered a ramp from the flatbed and then hopped onto the cart. As he turned the key to its ignition, the engine sputtered to life. He then flipped a lever, and the vehicle sprang backward down the ramp, where he parked it directly beside Harris and me.

"There you go," said the driver, returning the ramps with a clang. He then climbed back into his cab and drove down the hill to the parking lot in front of the Boarding House so he could turn back around.

"Enjoy!" he yelled out his window, tearing past us.

"Enjoy indeed! Bloody hell!" screamed Harris, whacking his hand on the side of the cart. "This can only mean trouble."

My cell phone started to vibrate. I flipped it open.

"Hello? Oh, hello, Major," I said, grinning at Harris. "Yes, it just arrived. We're standing beside it right now."

Harris slapped a hand to his forehead, letting out a long, frustrated groan.

"But you told me your doctor wants you to stay off your feet."

Harris nodded heartily in agreement.

"Oh, I see," I replied, as the Major kept chuntering on. "Uh-huh … yes. Right. Okay, I understand. Twelve-thirty tomorrow? Yes, of course I can pick you up."

Harris was mouthing "no damn way," his eyes flaring with renewed fury.

"Alright, see you then, Major."

"Phil, what the…?"

"The Major was given the cart by some friend of hers," I said, cutting him off. "She says she can stay off her feet by remaining in the cart while still being able to check out what's happening around campus. Because she only shot her left foot, she claims that using the accelerator and brake with her right foot shouldn't be a challenge."

Harris stared back at me, narrowing his eyes in complete disbelief. It was the first time I'd ever seen him speechless.

Chapter 11

The golden rays of the sun were quickly giving way to a palette of deep blue sky as my early-morning jog around the campus gave me a preview of the beauty Nature had bestowed on our official opening day at Cothbert House School. A temperate breeze rustled the leaves in the forest before dancing off to whisper to the lake that this was indeed an auspicious day.

The grounds looked magnificent—perhaps better than they had ever looked. Lawns around the buildings were clipped and lush, forming a verdant border for brightly colored flower beds. Chill, who had offered to help with the finishing touches, had done a magnificent job planting large pots of annuals, placing them strategically around the campus. The hedges now stood as neat walls of greenery, and the gravel road and walkways were free of debris, marking the end of years of neglect.

Any outdoor sport was now possible, as the tall weeds and scrub grass had been cleared, thanks to one of the Major's workers who had breathed new life into the field—spraying white perimeter lines and erecting goalposts. Peering over the steps down to the beach, I was pleasantly surprised to see that the rotting railings had been replaced. Koji, bless his heart, had mounted directional signs to all the buildings, though a couple had to be replaced at the last minute due to some creative spelling, including one that read "Boarded House."

In the parking lot, the once-neglected minibus now gleamed with a fresh coat of yellow paint, proudly displaying the name *Cothbert House School* in bold black letters. Chill had added to the festive mood by attaching large helium balloons over a *Welcome* sign that stood next to the vehicle.

Ecstatic at what I had seen, I doubled back to the Boarding House. Just as I walked through the front door, a familiar, excited voice called out, "Good morning, Phil!"

I spun around. Bouncing up and down furiously, clearly back to her ebullient self, was Myrtle—but something was different. She wore a light summery dress, a hint of lipstick, and had obviously been to the hair salon.

"Myrtle, you look beautiful. And ready to go," I said.

"Thank you, Phil. Come and have one last look around," she beamed, tugging on my arm.

She led me first to the bedrooms, which looked warm and cheerful with their new tartan duvet covers. Further down the hall, the common room had been re-carpeted, and two red couches with matching side tables and lamps anchored the décor, giving the room a relaxed and more contemporary feel.

"You've done a stellar job here, Myrtle."

"I couldn't have done it without the Major," she smiled, rocking on her feet. "Or without you and Harris badgering her." She poked me in the shoulder, bursting into a fit of laughter.

"Yes, well, thanks for all your hard work. I'm off to check

the rest of the campus. I think you can expect your first arrivals just before noon."

An anxious expression flitted across Myrtle's face for just a moment before she quickly masked it with a smile.

"I think I'm ready," she replied, her voice wavering slightly. Then, seeming to control her emotions, she brightened. "Oh, by the way, before you go, there's one last thing I have to show you. Stay right here. I'll be back in a moment."

She dashed into her suite and reappeared a moment later, cradling a small bundle in her arms. Gently, she placed it on the floor in front of me. I looked down, and two deep brown eyes gazed up at me.

"Oh, it's a puppy!" I exclaimed, squatting down to stroke its fluffy white back.

"I got him from the local pound. He's a bit of a Heinz 57, but he's very friendly. When young people are away from their families, having a pet can help ease the pain of separation, you know?" She crouched down beside me and gently patted the puppy's head. The puppy wagged its tail, licked her hand, and gave a high-pitched yap.

"This was so thoughtful of you, Myrtle. I'm sure the students will absolutely spoil him. What's his name?"

"Tofu," she said, smiling as she stroked his chin.

My next stop on the morning inspection was the School House, which was looking just as impressive. I strolled past reception, where Koji, wearing his trademark black suit and tie, was busy photocopying something. He looked up and waved at me.

"I'll see you in a minute," I called out.

I entered the Dining Hall, where more of Chill's creativity was on display: flowers on every table, and colorful streamers hanging from the ceiling. I introduced myself to Janice and Peg, two friendly retirees the Major had scrambled to hire at the last minute to run the kitchen. Wearing white aprons and cook's hats, they bantered like the best of friends. They told me breakfast would be ready in ten minutes.

Entering the gym, I encountered another of the Major's new hires—a man with frizzy brown hair and coveralls, pushing a cleaning cart.

"Hello, hello—the name's Frank. I'm the caretaker and bus driver around here," he grinned, extending a hand covered in a yellow rubber glove, now stained with cleaning chemicals.

"Just finished the toilets, I did!" he added proudly.

"Nice to meet you, Frank. My name's Phil," I said, politely avoiding the handshake.

"Phil, you say? You got that office down the hall, eh? Scrubbed it well for you, I did!"

Hopefully, before you cleaned the toilets.

"Glad to hear it, Frank, and thank you. The school has never looked cleaner."

Frank gave me a toothless grin and wheeled his squeaky cart out the door.

Before heading for breakfast, I quickly checked the classrooms. Each had been personalized by the teachers and arranged in a seminar-style layout. In addition to three homeroom classrooms, there was a makeshift science lab and a room set aside for art classes. As I walked back into the hallway, I bumped into Koji.

"Mr. Phil! Did you see the new computer room?" he asked, his eyes widening.

"No, not yet. I was on my way. Harris mentioned you were setting it up. Did you get a good deal for the Major?"

104

"Oh, yes. Computers from closed businesses. Only two hundred dollars each. Also got you and Mr. Harris laptops. Please, please, this way," he said, proudly leading me to a small room I hadn't noticed before.

Around the periphery of the room sat twenty computers, each displaying a colorful psychedelic screensaver. Office chairs were arranged in front of each terminal, and a giant printer stood on a separate stand.

"The printer is networked to the computers. It also has a scanner," Koji said, smiling. "And all the computers have Microsoft Office software."

"Koji, this is amazing. Well done! Are these hooked to the Internet?"

"Oh, yes. Also, the company that hooked up the computers wants to sign a service agreement. I said, 'wait, please,'" he said with a coy smile, handing me the contract for review.

"I'll get this approved and back to you as soon as possible. Thanks for looking after all this. Great job!"

Koji and I returned to the lobby, just as Harris and Myrtle arrived. The four of us wandered into the Dining Hall for breakfast, where Janice and Peg had arranged a small buffet of simple offerings.

"The place looks incredible, Harris," I said, filling my cup with coffee from a small urn.

"It certainly does. But it was a hell of a lot of work to get to this point."

"You know, Harris," Myrtle said, reaching for her tea, "I know how the Major gets under your skin, but you do need to give her some credit for all this."

"I know," Harris admitted begrudgingly, sitting at the head of the table. "But let's not forget this guy over here," he added, slapping Koji on the back, who was busily devouring his food. "He's done wonders with this place."

"Koji, you really have," I added. "That computer room is amazing."

"Thanks. I really enjoy working with you all," he beamed.

His comment resonated with me. Our ability to work as a team had been so instrumental in getting us to this point.

Chapter 12

Just before noon, our first family arrived in the school parking lot—the Lams from Hong Kong. Fourteen-year-old Stanley and fifteen-year-old Albert Lam had been last-minute acceptances. Initially enrolled in public schools in Vancouver, their mother realized she would need to return to Hong Kong to manage her business ventures and sought a boarding school for her boys.

I introduced myself to Mrs. Lam, who, with a dismissive glance and no acknowledgment, said, "Those are my sons," her voice dripping with disappointment as she waved a pointed finger at each of her boys disparagingly. "He is Albert, and he is Stanley."

Both lads stood dutifully at attention beside a dark SUV. Albert, in a white t-shirt, loose-fitting faded jeans, and a Lakers ball cap, hadn't stopped smiling, his dark eyes flitting behind heavy-framed glasses. Stanley, on the other hand, was a walking advertisement for the fashion industry. His baseball cap, embossed with a large Gucci logo, sat perched above his smiling face, while a fitted black sweatshirt, emblazoned with oversized reflective silver letters, read *Dolce & Gabbana*. On either side of his tailored sweatpants, the word *Versace* was prominent, while I immediately recognized that his matching running shoes were a highly sought-after *Nike* collectible recently profiled in *Sports Illustrated*.

I took a few minutes to welcome the boys, both of whom had reasonably good spoken English. Probably Blossoms, I said to myself, making a mental note of which class-level they should be assigned. Then, without warning, the door to the SUV slid open, and a wooden cane, tentatively seeking *terra firma*, planted itself. A brown-clad leg and shoe carefully exited next, followed by a dark bouffant pile of hair. At last, the complete body of an elderly woman emerged, pulling herself slowly upright. Black wraparound sunglasses turned towards me, and the woman launched into a high-pitched screaming tirade in Cantonese. Turning toward me, Mrs. Lam translated: "My mother-in-law wants you to know my boys are both very naughty," once more pointing to Stanley and Albert dismissively, "and that you must change their way of thinking."

I can only guess who's paying these boys' fees.

"Yes, well, please tell your mother-in-law we'll work very hard with her two grandsons."

Mrs. Lam translated, and her mother-in-law's piercing crescendo continued unabated.

"She wants the boys to go to Harvard. Worst-case scenario, Columbia."

"I see," I replied, not wanting to wade into that conversation.

"Why don't we get their bags and then the boys can settle into their rooms?" I suggested, frantically waving at Pancho, who dashed over to open the trunk.

With relief, Myrtle arrived on the scene, her hands outstretched. She proceeded to greet the Lam boys and then quickly turned her attention to their mother and grand-mother.

"Hello, I'm Myrtle Green. I will be looking after your sons in the Boarding House," she said, enthusiastically shaking each of their hands.

Myrtle kept chattering, laughing incessantly, no matter what the topic of the conversation, and it wasn't long before the two women were laughing with her. With both mother and grandmother distracted by Myrtle's overtures, Pancho signaled the boys to collect their luggage and make their escape. I then watched in amusement as they both dashed toward the Boarding House, dragging their cases behind them. I turned back towards Myrtle, who, with incredible finesse, had disarmed both mother and mother-in-law.

About thirty minutes later, another of our last-minute acceptances, fourteen-year-old Aki Ito from Japan, arrived with her parents. She had been slated to attend a public school in Vancouver when her homestay family suddenly bailed on her at the last minute. Mr. and Mrs. Ito readily took my hand, smiled, and bowed when I greeted them, but it was clear that neither of them could speak a word of English.

Aki was short for her age but carried herself with an air of quiet maturity. Her hair was styled in a natural, slightly tousled bob, and her pale skin highlighted her bright eyes. She wore a simple, comfortable outfit—a loose-fitting green sweater paired with tailored black pants and white sneakers. A denim jacket hung casually over her shoulder, giving her an effortless but well-put-together appearance. Though she stood beside her parents, she kept a reserved distance, her body language quietly betraying a shy disposition and a reticence to communicate with me.

Not quite sure what to do next, I was about to go in search of Koji, when he came dashing out of the School House. Recognizing the family as citizens of his own country, he welcomed them enthusiastically in Japanese. Not only were Aki and her parents relieved Koji could speak Japanese, I was as well. With the formalities over, the Itos and Koji appeared to relax, chatting unreservedly.

"They want me to take them on a tour of the school," said Koji, stepping away from the family.

"No problem. I'll ask Harris to look after the front desk."

"Got it!" he replied, directing the Ito's white Lexus towards the parking lot.

I looked at my watch and realized it was almost time to pick up the Major. The Major's sister, Millicent, was supposed to have dropped the Major at her house earlier this morning so she could get herself organized. It was now my job to shuttle her over to the school. I needed to be quick, though, because both Tarantino Tang's and Violeta Kim's groups would be arriving *en masse* shortly, having arranged to share a bus.

"I'm just on my way to get the Major," I said, looking in on Harris, who was at the School House preparing language testing for the first day of classes. "Would you mind covering the front office?"

"Sure, take all the time you need," he said, grimacing. "By the way, how are the new arrivals?"

"Let me see… one of them refuses to talk to me, and we need to ensure we get the other two into Harvard. Otherwise, they all seem very pleasant."

"Welcome to my world. You haven't seen anything yet."

The Major lived alone in a small lakeside cottage about five minutes from the school. She had informed me she would be waiting outside her front door, but when I arrived at the house, there was no one around. Just as I was contemplating leaving, a bright gold BMW 740 Series turned onto the driveway. The passenger window rolled down as the vehicle came to a stop.

"Morning, Philly," came the Major's voice from the shadows inside the car. "Help me get out of this bloody thing! We got stuck on the damn Sea-to-Sky, and my legs are killing me. My wheelchair is in the trunk."

"Yes, Major," I replied, gritting my teeth. I sidled over to the rear of the car just as the trunk popped open and took out her chair, setting it up. As I rolled it beside the passenger door, I heard footsteps approaching and looked up, momentarily stunned. Standing beside me was the Major, wearing a fitted dark dress suit and black high-heeled shoes. Her face had been smoothed over with tasteful make-up, and her hair professionally coiffed. She almost looked elegant. She dropped a suitcase on the ground.

"Major?" I asked, hesitating. "Why are you standing? I mean … you're not supposed to be on your feet."

This was followed by a loud screeching laugh. "I'm not the Major, my love. I'm her twin sister, Millicent."

"Twin … sister," I stammered.

"Yes, Philly, twin sister. Now get me the hell out of this car," yelled the Major, sticking her head out the passenger-door window.

I stared in shock and disbelief, looking from Millicent, then back to the Major.

"Well, come on, lovey," ordered Millicent, waving me over. "Let's get the old battleaxe out of my car. I need to get back to Vancouver."

I helped transfer the Major to her wheelchair, but obviously not fast enough for Millicent, who rushed around the car, waving and calling out over her shoulder, "Got to go. Harriet—remember, get back to me soon! I need a decision. Nice to meet you, Phil. Toodles," she added, climbing back into her car and roaring off.

I stood, paralyzed, still in shock from this new revelation, staring at the Major, who suddenly looked a bit sullen.

"Let's get my chair over to the passenger side of your car so I can pull myself in," she said at last. "Then you can chuck the chair in your trunk."

There will be no chucking, I said to myself, coming back to reality.

Without waiting for my assistance, the Major released the brake on her chair and barreled towards the opposite side of my car, twice dinging my paintwork. I was mentally calculating the cost of bodywork.

"Any kids arrive yet?" she hollered back, sounding like she was referring to an impending infestation of lotuses. As I walked over to help her into the car and retrieve the wheelchair, I updated her on the Lam boys and Aki.

"Well, don't forget to offer them a discount if they've got relatives. Two-for-one, if it'll close the deal."

"Yes, Major," I replied, collapsing her chair and carrying it to the trunk. *I clearly had no intention of initiating such conversations.*

A few minutes later, we pulled into the campus and parked beside the Major's sad-looking golf cart, which sat alongside the portico to the school. A Grinch-like smile started to creep across her face as she eyed the small vehicle.

"What a beauty!" she declared. "Philly, move your car closer so I can climb aboard!"

I eased beside the cart, but the Major didn't wait for me to get out and help her. She simply opened the passenger door, hitting it against the side of the golf cart, clambered out, and hauled herself onto the cart, using her right foot to kick my car door closed.

I adjusted my estimates for bodywork.

"You can throw my folded wheelchair on the back of the cart, Philly."

I did as I was told, while watching as the Major positioned herself upright in the cart's driver's seat, carefully placing her left leg on a small ledge below the dashboard. With a somewhat manic look on her face, she then turned the ignition key, and the engine choked before slowly coming to life. I heard footsteps above and looked up to see Harris on the portico's balcony. He was concealing himself from the Major, his arms crossed and looking down in disgust. The cart lunged back and, with a jump, shot forward, before racing off down the road towards the Boarding House.

Harris stepped down off the balcony and walked over to join me. "There's no telling what sort of mischief she'll be getting up to with that god-awful looking thing."

"I know," I responded, halfheartedly. "But, for the time being, I'm just going into denial."

"You're a stronger person than I am, Phil."

"By the way, you never told me the Major has a twin sister."

"You mean Millicent?" he replied curtly. "What about her?"

"Nothing," just surprised.

"Hmm," said Harris, appearing to avoid any further discussion about her.

Harris was usually all business, but something about the mention of Millicent made him uneasy.

Chapter 13

"The bus! The bus!" yelled Koji, tearing out the front door.

A long, dark coach, covered in billowing dust, appeared out of nowhere, roaring towards us, then slowly eased down the hill, pivoting into the parking lot. Harris, Koji, and I followed from behind, waiting to see what would happen next. It didn't take long. The passenger door swung open to the sound of escaping air, and a diminutive man, who looked like he was barely 18, jumped out, squinting as he tried to adjust his eyes to the brightness of the day. Dressed in a creased pale gray suit that draped over his thin body, he had carelessly added a gray tie that did little to complement his appearance.

"Hello, I'm Phil Gower," I said, walking towards him, my hand outstretched.

"Oh … oh, Mr. Gower. Yes … yes, I'm Hymie Chen. I'm here with the group from *Yingyucom*," he said nervously, offering a limp, damp handshake and his business card.

"Nice to meet you, Hymie. This is my colleague, Harris Tweedsmuir."

While Hymie scrambled to retrieve another business card and smiled at Harris, a young woman dressed in business attire exited the bus and joined us.

"Hello, I'm Hee-young Park," she announced, offering up her card. "I'm with the group from *Hyung-Bo*." She hesitated for a moment, "You're *Pil*, right?"

"Phil, actually."

"And I'm Harris Tweedsmuir," Harris cut in, accentuating his British accent, as he moved forward to shake her hand.

"Oh, yes. Violeta mentioned her lovely big friend."

I prodded Harris' arm. Harris gave a short grunt.

"Listen, I wonder if I could use you both to help translate?" I asked, turning to Hymie and Hee-young. "I need to explain a few things to the students while they are still on the bus—so they know what to do and where to go. I also want to make them aware of Ms. Myrtle Green, who will be their house mother and Head of Boarding."

"No problem," replied Hymie eagerly.

"Of course," nodded Hee-young.

I followed Hee-young and Hymie onto the bus and onto a step just above where the driver was sitting, wedging myself between the two of them. I could hear lively chatter coming from the back of the coach when, all at once, the bus went dead quiet as the students became aware of my presence. I stood, looking at the apprehensive faces that stared back.

Hee-young reached for the microphone hanging beside the driver and launched into a lively conversation in Korean, then handed the mic to Hymie for translation into Mandarin. At last, I heard the mention of my name, followed by clapping. Taking the proffered mic, I began. "Hello everybody. Welcome to Cothbert House School!" I sounded like I was kicking off a motivational retreat.

"H…e…l…l…o…M…r…G…o…w…e…r," came a simultaneous, monotone, and well-orchestrated response.

"So, I have a few things I'd like to discuss with you before you get off the bus," I continued. "Once you get your luggage, you'll be directed to the Boarding House, where you'll be assigned your room by your house mother, Ms. Myrtle Green, who is also Head of Boarding. Then, you'll have some time to tour the campus by yourselves. You must be back in the Boarding House no later than 5:00 pm for dinner. Tonight is a Welcome Barbecue."

I noticed both Hymie and Hee-young furiously writing on small pads of paper as I rattled off my prepared talk.

Whoops, I suddenly thought, checking myself. *Remember what Harris said—speak in short sound bites.*

Hymie and Hee-young relayed my comments, and towards the end of each of their translations, there was lively cheering, no doubt in response to the mention of the evening barbecue.

Looking like deer caught in headlights, the students stepped down from the bus to be welcomed individually by Myrtle and Harris, who positioned a lanyard with a name tag around each one's neck. While most of the Korean students had Korean names, the Taiwanese students all had English names. According to Harris, in Taiwan, a student's English name is typically assigned at a young age by a foreign teacher from one of the many *Buxibans* or cram schools the student has to attend.

"Myrtle," I said, tapping her on the shoulder. "I'll stay out of your way until you get everyone settled in the Boarding House. Are there any last-minute preparations I can help you with for tonight's barbecue?"

"Oh, no, thank you. Everything is under control. Ida has offered to help and we've been working with Janice and Peg in the kitchen. They'll have everything down on the beach by

117

5:00 pm, and Pancho promised me he would have a bonfire for us."

"Oh, before I forget, Myrtle, the two agents— Hymie and Hee-young, who I introduced you to earlier, will be here for one more night to make sure their students get settled. They'll be staying at the *Timberline Lake Arms Hotel* in town but will be on campus during the day if you need help with translation or any …"

The backfiring of a faulty motor interrupted our conversation as a golf cart came whipping around the corner, pulling up abruptly beside us.

"Hello, Major," exclaimed Myrtle, clearly happier to see her than I was. "What have you been up to?"

"Just had a great chat with the Lams — you know, Albert and Stanley from Hong Kong. I really like their grandmother. She handed me the boys' personal spending money. Ten thousand dollars! Can you believe it? Ten thousand dollars!" She waved the wad of cash in the air like lottery winnings. "Spoilt little shits."

"Major, did you count that money before you accepted it?" asked Myrtle.

"Not really…"

"Did you give them a receipt?" she continued, her face stern.

"Well, not exactly…"

"Major, in the future, if you have any parents who need to hand over money, passports, or anything else, for that matter, please direct them my way. That's my job. That's what you've paid me for. Is that clear?"

Pulling the bills from the Major's hand, Myrtle then stormed into the Boarding House.

The Major turned to me with a chagrined smile. Without a word, she reached for the lever to her golf cart and rattled backwards, then turned up the hill towards the School House.

Harris joined me a few moments later with some newly-arrived students with whom he was helping with luggage. After ushering them into the boarding house, I eagerly filled him in on Myrtle's *tête-à-tête* with the Major.

"Good for her! Good for her!" he proclaimed, rubbing his hands together. "Now's the time to draw our lines in the sand with the Major. She has to let us do our jobs."

So much for the peace accord, I thought.

By the time 5:00 pm rolled around, Harris and I had stationed ourselves outside the Boarding House, taking roll call in preparation for the barbecue. The squeaking rumble of a truck broke our concentration, and just as I looked up, a battered red pick-up pulled in beside us. Out hopped Frank, the caretaker, in a pair of tattered burgundy coveralls and Koji in his dark suit.

"We need to move the Major to the barbecue. Frank says there is a special service path to the beach we can use. But not big enough for vehicles," explained Koji, following Frank behind the truck. Harris and I watched in astonishment as they both reappeared, one in front of the other, carrying two long poles over their shoulders, the center of which dangled leather straps connected to a wheelchair with the Major sitting in it.

"Good evening Philly … Big Guy," the Major called out enthusiastically, "I'll see the two of *yous* on the beach." Then, like an empress from the Ming Dynasty, she waved on Frank and Koji.

119

"What were you saying about drawing lines in the sand?" I asked Harris, pursing my lips.

With the students all accounted for, and after a few additional announcements, Harris and I moseyed down to the beach, where the waterfront had been transformed into what could best be described as a pseudo Hawaiian luau. There were torches planted in the sand, colorful lanterns strewn over long portable tables with mismatched deck chairs, and a table overflowing with salads, rice, assorted Asian specialties, as well as fixings for hamburgers and hot dogs, all of which made for a veritable feast. Janice and Peg were busily grilling on two propane barbecues, while further up the beach, Chill was designing a make-your-own *s'more* station that held bowls of chocolate, marshmallows, and crackers. A huge bonfire was sending dancing sparks into the evening sky, and, around its perimeter, Pancho had positioned driftwood logs for a seating area.

"I haven't seen our illustrious Major yet," I remarked, more for effect.

Harris looked around. "At your three o'clock."

I turned to where he was indicating, and sure enough, there was the Major, holding court with Mrs. Lam and Mrs. Lam Senior. A makeshift platform had been installed for the Major's wheelchair, and I could see two short, stubby vessels with red, white, and gold labels that resembled bottles of kerosene sitting on the table in front of them. Grandmother Lam reached for one of the containers, poured a few ounces of clear liquid from it into plastic glasses, and, hollering in Cantonese, distributed one to her daughter-in-law and one to the Major. Mrs. Lam appeared to translate for the Major, just as glasses were raised and toasts called out. Then, like

120

university students at a frat party, they each threw their heads back and swallowed.

"This isn't going to end well," I said, staring in disbelief. "What is that stuff they're chugging back, anyway?"

Harris squinted to get a better look. "Yikes! It's *Maotai*," he replied. "It's from China. I'm guessing Grandmother Lam must have brought it over from Hong Kong. It's a distilled liquor made from fermented sorghum. As I recall, there are different variations that can range from your basic 80% proof to a paint-stripping 120% proof. So, yes, I would agree with you. This is not going to end well."

"Well, I need to put a stop to it before the students arrive," I announced, marching towards them with Harris trailing behind.

"This should be interesting," Harris mumbled, with anticipation in his voice.

"Excuse me, Mrs. Lam. But Mr. Tweedsmuir and I need to have a chat with the Major. Would you excuse us for a few moments?"

Mrs. Lam heaved a sigh at the inconvenience, reluctantly agreeing, as she helped her mother to a chair nearby.

"So, what's so important that you have to rudely interrupt us?" asked the Major, her scowl becoming particularly pronounced. "Can't you see I'm networking for *yous* two?"

"We're a school, Major," I implored, grabbing the bottles of *Moutai* from the table, "and like all schools, there needs to be a no-alcohol-allowed policy when we're in session."

"Assholes," she muttered under her breath.

Harris and I ignored her and walked over to the Lams, where we explained our no-alcohol policy and informed them that their bottles of *Moutai* would be waiting at the reception when they were ready to leave. But the second Mrs. Lam finished translating, Grandmother Lam exploded into a piercing tirade of hysteria, flailing her cane at me. Then, throwing it down, she snatched the bottles of *Moutai* from my hands.

"I guess we're leaving now," said Mrs. Lam coyly.

Grandmother Lam barked an order at Mrs. Lam, who immediately acquiesced and returned to the Major, placing a bottle of *Moutai* on the table, gently patting the Major on her back. Then, without further adieu, the Lams turned and painstakingly made their way along the shore, disappearing from view, while the grandmother's screeching protests grew more distant but no less expressive.

"Hey, *yous* two university types," hollered the Major, raising her plastic glass in the air. "Great way to treat your rich clients. Now you've gone and pissed them off."

"It's called ethics and morals," Harris yelled back. "You should try using them sometimes."

"Assholes!"

"Well, that went well," I said, smirking.

Chapter 14

There was a loud clatter behind us and then carefree cheering as Myrtle finally arrived on the beach with everyone from the Boarding House. Like dogs let off their leashes, the students impulsively flung off their shoes, racing around the sand in delight at being set free. Closer to the water, Pancho and Koji had erected a volleyball net, punting a ball back and forth; it wasn't long before others enthusiastically joined in, and a proper game commenced. With all the exhausting organization of the day, Harris and I were content to just stand and watch the action. Myrtle wandered over to join us, carrying Tofu, who, once let go on the sand, chased after two of the students as they laughed and tried to outrun him.

"Did you provoke the Major again?" she asked, turning to us with a look of alarm. "I just walked by her, and she launched into a rant, unleashing some interesting adjectives to describe the two of you."

"I'm not surprised," said Harris. "Let's just say she was up to her usual shenanigans."

"I figured as much when I smelled the alcohol on her breath."

Myrtle shook her head with dismay and turned to check on Tofu, giving us a rueful smile before strolling over to a few of the students who were congregating. It was obvious, even from a distance, that she had a special way with young people, enthusiastically bantering with the group like she was a close member of their families.

"She really is a natural at this, isn't she?" I said.

"Yup," replied Harris. "Unfortunately, she just doesn't know how good she really is."

The star attraction of the evening was the make-your-own *s'more* station, where students screamed with delight as their marshmallows burst into flaming blobs, leaving gooey smears across their faces.

At the start of the barbecue, the Koreans stayed close to their chaperone, Hee-young, and the Taiwanese to Hymie Chen, but as the evening wore on, more students began breaking away from their cultural groups and co-mingling. Aki Ito, whom I had been very worried about, looked much more relaxed, whispering and giggling with her Korean roommate. The Lam brothers, with huge smiles on their faces, were fraternizing with one student after another, plainly liberated by the departure of their mother and grandmother. As the evening light gave way to darkness and the glow of the fire cast shadows of happy students on the sand, I thought back to the early days of the school.

"Do you remember when all of this was just a half-baked idea of the Major's?" I said, turning to Harris.

"I do," he replied, smirking. "And see where we are tonight."

We continued to reminisce, completely oblivious to the set of twin girls cautiously edging our way. All at once, the two of them stood before Harris and me, looking at us through their matching steel-rimmed glasses with anxious expressions.

"Hello, girls!" I said eagerly. "And what are your names?"

"I am Pansy Huang," replied one of the girls.

"And I am Hibiscus Huang," said the other. "We are from Taiwan."

"You're both flowers," I said, jokingly.

Both girls looked at me with blank expressions.

"Is there something wrong?" I asked finally, when they didn't move. That's when I noticed the electronic gizmos in their hands, which resembled large calculators.

Pansy typed something into her device.

I have a problem announced the device in robotic English.

"Ah, an electronic translator," said Harris, leaning over with interest. "I've seen pictures of these before, but I've never seen one in action. So, what is your problem, Pansy?"

She typed again.

I stepped in defecation came the translator's response.

"Hmm," I said, biting my lip. "That's not very nice."

Myrtle, who was standing nearby, overheard the translator and exploded into laughter. The girls looked over at her, concerned that they had said something wrong.

"Tofu must have left his calling card," I said.

Pansy just shrugged and handed me her translator, pointing to its keyboard.

I typed: *Ms. Green's dog probably pooed on the beach, and you stepped in it.*

The translator spouted something in Mandarin, and at last, the girls started to laugh. I reached for the translator again: *Let's go down by the water, where we can help you clean off your shoes.*

The device translated my message out loud, and the girls appeared to relax, nodding eagerly.

By the time the four of us returned to the same spot, most

of the students were already making their way back up the steps toward the Boarding House. The Huang girls rushed to catch up.

"See you later, girls," I called out.

They responded with huge grins, waving back at us. Moments later, Ida and Chill sauntered over to bid us goodnight.

"I love how this evening got the students to mix and mingle," Ida remarked. "They all seemed to have such a great time, even with their language challenges."

"Yeah," began Chill, "like, who knew it could be so much fun eating *s'mores*!"

"I agree," said Harris. "We made a wonderful first impression tonight. Phil and I really appreciate all the help you two gave in making it such a success."

We could hear Janice and Peg cleaning up behind us.

"And you two ladies were miracle workers tonight," I began.

"Yes, you really were," added Harris. "And thanks for including all that traditional Asian food. I think it really helped to soften some of the culture shock."

"They seem like really nice kids," smiled Peg, scrubbing the grill. "Oh, before I forget, Pancho's looking for you two."

I started scouring the beach when Pancho came running over, panting.

"We have a small problem," he blurted.

"What's wrong?" I asked.

"Well, as you know, Frank and Koji carried the Major down to the beach."

"Yes, using poles. I remember. Don't tell me they've lost the poles?"

"No, the problem's not the poles. It's Koji."

"Koji?"

There was a rustling noise and the sound of someone tripping over something. Koji stumbled out of the darkness, swinging from side to side and singing a Japanese song wildly off-key. I looked over at the Major, who cheered us from a distance and then proceeded to yell something completely unintelligible.

"Koji, did the Major offer you a drink?"

"Yes," he squealed in a euphoric, high-pitched voice, clapping enthusiastically.

Frank came plodding over. "What are we gonna do now?" he asked.

I turned to Harris.

"Don't look at me. I have high blood pressure."

"I'll help," offered Pancho.

"Thanks, Pancho. But Harris, you're the one responsible for getting Koji to his room without being seen."

"Done!" he responded, putting Koji's arm over his shoulder as the two of them staggered off toward the wooden steps.

The next morning, when I arrived at the School House, I noticed Millicent's gold BMW sitting out front beside Frank, who was sawing a piece of plywood balanced on a couple of trestles.

"What are you up to, there, Frank?"

"The Major asked me to build her a ramp so she can get in and out of the Big House. That's what she calls the School House, you know."

"Yes, I do know," I replied, cringing.

I entered the building, but not without stopping by the reception area, where Koji was just getting off the phone. He looked up at me, gasped, and then, with a jolt, snapped his head back down, pretending to focus on the files on his desk.

"Good sleep last night?" I asked.

"Yes. Thank you," he replied stammering, nodding his head and refusing to look up.

I continued on to my office, snickering to myself. Harris was already waiting for me when I arrived, his reading glasses perched on his nose and the latest edition of the *Vancouver Tribune* in front of him. He peered over his paper as I walked in, reaching for a coffee beside him.

"Ah, there you are. I've got everything ready to go for our language assessment this morning. I'm going to administer it all in the Dining Hall ... as soon as Janice and Peg clean up," he added, just as there was a knock on the door.

"Come in!" he replied.

Koji peeked his head in, his face immediately starting to flush. "Can I talk to you both?" he asked.

Harris waved him in, giving me a devilish wink.

Koji slinked in front of us, struggling to make eye contact. "First, I want to apologize for my behavior last night," he said, bowing repeatedly.

"Koji, you were offered a drink by your boss. You didn't do anything wrong," assured Harris.

"I agree," I added.

"I am allergic to strong alcohol," Koji responded, talking quickly. "But Miss Major was very happy to offer me a drink, so I said, 'okay.' Then she kept giving me more and more. So I said 'okay.' Then I started to feel wonky, and my head went crazy. Then kaboom."

"Kaboom?" I queried.

"Kaboom, I lose my mind."

"Oh, I see. Well, don't let people ever force you to drink, Koji. You can always say 'no.' And while it's okay for us to drink in the privacy of our own homes, we shouldn't be drinking in front of the students."

"I understand. I agree. Sorry."

"Hey, forget about it," said Harris, patting him on the back. "Let's just pretend it never happened."

"Yes, but there is one other thing that did happen."

"Oh?" I said, looking back at Harris.

"When Miss Major got drunk, she gave me a promotion."

"Promotion?"

"Yes, she said, *'Koojie*— that's what she calls me —*'Koojie',* you are now my new Executive Assistant. Then she offered to increase my salary by five thousand dollars a year."

I could see Harris was about to explode.

"Where is the Major right now?" I asked.

"She's with Frank outside."

"That interfering bloody nuisance!" yelled Harris, storming from the room, his footsteps reverberating down the hall.

"Koji, don't worry," I said, watching his jaw drop. I gave him a friendly tap and then chased after Harris.

By the time I made it outside the building, the yelling was already in full swing.

"We hired Koji to run our office," thundered Harris. "He's already got a lot on his plate!"

"I pay the bills around here, big guy. If I want him to do something else, I have every right to ask him," roared back the Major, as she rolled her chair down the new ramp Frank had just completed for her, giving him the thumbs-up.

"Major, what exactly is it that you want him to do for you?"

I asked, moving in front of her.

"Help me with my letters…"

"Your letters?" scoffed Harris. "His first language is Japanese, for heaven's sake."

"He can type them, can't he?"

"What else?" asked Harris, accusingly.

"Well… take messages for me, send faxes and some of them emails, and sometimes drive me places."

I signaled to Harris to back down.

"Alright, Major, we can call him your Executive Assistant, but his first priority must always be to the front office. Can you live with that?" I asked, as Harris blurted a loud guffaw.

"Yes. But his title must be Executive Assistant to the CEO."

"Understood."

"For which, you do realize, you needlessly pissed away $5000," Harris reminded, emphasizing the word "pissed" for the Major's benefit.

"Yeah, I know. That part was a bit rash of me. I think I drank too much," she replied.

"You think?" muttered Harris under his breath.

I shot Harris a look indicating it was time for us to leave. The two of us moved back into the School House, where Koji was already waiting by the front door for us, looking totally stressed out.

"I'm sorry," he said again. "I made everybody so angry."

Harris turned to Koji with a grin. "Koji, like I said before, it wasn't your fault. Anyway, did you catch what the Major said out there?"

"Yes," Koji replied.

"Exactly. So, you're getting a new title and a salary increase for doing the same job you've always been doing. I'd say there's absolutely nothing for you to feel bad about."

Koji took a moment to process Harris's words. "You two are still my secret bosses, right?" he asked, a nervous smile spreading across his face.

"Right!" Harris and I answered in unison. "Secret bosses."

As soon as Koji left the room, I chuckled. "Looks like the Major has finally decided *Koojie* is worth the money she's paying him."

Harris laughed with me. "Yup! Took her long enough to figure out what we've known all along."

Chapter 15

While Harris and the rest of the staff were administering language testing in the Dining Hall, I had scheduled an early-morning meeting with Hymie Chen. Just before 9:00 a.m., Hymie's taxi pulled up in front of the School House, and I went out to greet him. For the second time, I noticed Millicent's car parked in the lot.

"Good morning, Mr. Gower," yelled Hymie, waving enthusiastically through the open taxi window.

"Good morning," I responded, opening the car door for him. "I hope the hotel was okay last night. I'm sure it was much smaller than you're accustomed to."

"Oh, no. It was great," he exclaimed, getting out. "So quiet!"

"You've already toured the Boarding House with your group, and I saw you enjoying the waterfront at last night's barbecue. Why don't I take you on a tour of our School House, and then we can go back to my office to chat."

"Oh, yes, thank you—that sounds very good," he replied, fumbling to straighten his disheveled gray suit as he followed me up the steps into the front lobby.

"So, are your students settling in alright?" I asked, directing him towards the staircase leading to the second floor.

"Of course. They really love it here. So do I. The air is so clean, and everything's so peaceful."

"I've never been to Taipei. What's it like?"

"It's not a very pretty city, but it's a fun city. It has close to three million people, and there's so much to do and so much to eat—almost entertainment twenty-four hours a day. I think that'll be the hardest part for my students to get used to: learning to make their own fun."

"That's a very interesting observation."

When we finally retreated to my office, Peg had put out a tray with a teapot and cookies.

"Please help yourself, Hymie. I just need to go and check on our language testing in the Dining Hall. I'll be right back, and then we can chat some more."

"No problem," he said, pouring himself a cup of tea. "Take your time."

Ida was administering the oral part of the language test when I arrived, while Chill and Pancho were circulating through the room, making sure the students were following along. The Dining Hall resembled a call center, with everyone wearing headsets Koji had managed to wangle off a struggling tech company. They were listening to a recording of a woman telling a story and filling out individual answer sheets in response to questions about its content.

"Any issues?" I whispered to Harris, who was leaning against a table, holding his coffee cup.

"So far so good. I hope to have the results by noon and finalize class levels by this afternoon. In the meantime, after lunch, the staff has organized writing and art activities for the students. Then it's off to first-term clubs."

"I'll be with Hymie for a bit, and then I'm meeting with Hee-young. Koji also informed me there's a family arriving from Macau later to look at the school for their son."

"Excellent. Can we meet to review the results of the language assessment just before clubs, then?"

"I think so," I replied, quietly moving to the door.

When I returned to my office, the cookies had evaporated and Hymie was on his cell phone, having a rather animated conversation in Mandarin. When he saw me, he immediately lowered his voice and cut the conversation short.

"You have a family from Macau visiting you this afternoon," he said abruptly.

"I do. Is it one of your clients?"

"Yes, and I'm afraid it's not an easy client. They're the Kangs. The boy's name is Thomas. He's fourteen years old. He's been bounced around from school to school because of bullying."

"Was he the bully, or was he bullied?" I asked.

"He was bullied."

"You said they are not easy clients?"

"No! That was the mother I was just arguing with on the phone. She said that because your tuition is so expensive, she wants me to guarantee that Thomas is not bullied and that he gets at least a B+ average by the end of the school year."

"Hymie, we're not in the business of offering guarantees like that. I can't make either of those promises."

"That's what I told her. But she said I'm her agent and need to negotiate for them."

"Does she speak English?"

"Yes, both the mother and the boy do, but not perfectly."

"Let me see what I can do when I meet them. I'm sorry she's putting you in this awkward position. If she makes things difficult for me, Thomas may be the first student whose application I end up rejecting."

"I understand. Sometimes, if you show them you don't need their business, they start to panic and back down."

"Are there any more of your students I need to be made aware of?"

"Just one. His name is Manfred Ma. He's a really nice boy, but ... well, he kind of gets hyper at times. I mean really hyper."

"What do you mean?"

"It's hard to explain. His mother recently started monitoring his diet to see if anything he was eating was triggering his behavior, but so far, she hasn't found anything."

"Could it be ADHD?"

"She doesn't know. But she says there haven't been any complaints from his teachers."

"I see. And there are no other students with any issues?" I asked, making notes about Manfred.

"No, I don't think so. Just regular kids with regular issues."

Though I suspected there was more to his "regular issues" comment, I didn't press him further.

"So, what are your plans for today?"

"I have a meeting with Miss Myrtle after I leave here, and then I'll be rejoining you when the Kangs arrive. Tonight, after Prep, I want to have one final get-together with my group."

"Well, you'll probably be able to meet early, as I don't anticipate too much homework will be assigned tonight. Also, if you have any spare time in-between your meetings, feel free to go to the beach. There's an area on the dock where you'll find a couple of comfortable chairs. That's where

Harris and I go when we want to run away from everything."

"Thank you. I will. You have a good life here at Cothbert."

"Well, it's not good every day, but I agree with you, it's a pretty nice place."

We were interrupted by the buzzing of my intercom.

"Yes, Koji?"

"Hee-young is sitting outside your door, waiting for you."

"Thanks!"

Hymie sprang to his feet, ready to leave.

"Thank you again, Hymie," I said, receiving his limp-fish handshake. "You fly back tomorrow?"

"Yes, tomorrow night."

"Well, I know you'll be joining my meeting with the Kangs this afternoon, but in case I forget, I wanted to let you know that I'll probably be in Taiwan later in the year to attend one of your fairs. Maybe, when I visit, you can show me around Taipei."

"I'd love to do that," he said, waving back as he exited. "We can go for some famous Taiwanese beef noodles."

As soon as Hymie was gone, I quickly made a few more notes, gathered my thoughts, and then stepped into the hall to greet Hee-young, who was waiting patiently. I ushered her into my office, just as Peg arrived to refresh the tea and cookies.

"Would you like a tour before we chat?" I asked.

"Oh, no thank you. I spent the last couple of hours looking around," Hee-young said, pulling a notepad and pen from her bag. "Lovely campus."

"And your accommodations were okay last night?"

"Oh yes, very nice."

"Can I offer you tea, then?" I asked, reaching for the teapot.

"Yes, please."

"So," I said, filling her a cup, "tell me what I need to know about your group."

"There's really only one student I need to talk to you about. But before I do that, I wanted to give you a bit of background information about Korean culture—so you better understand my students."

"Oh?" I said, curious.

Hee-young paused, glanced at her notes, and then looked directly at me.

"Phil, it's important you understand there's a strong sense of hierarchy in Korean society. The older you are, the greater respect you command."

"I don't think that's necessarily unique to Korea."

"Maybe not. But it's more important in Korea, and you'll even see it at the high school level."

"Really?"

"Yes. In Korea, younger children are often expected to show unconditional respect towards older children, particularly the oldest child in a peer group. While this is not always an issue, if the oldest student has a controlling personality, it can become a problem."

"You mean, a bullying problem."

"Exactly. While I don't want to tell you how to run your school, you do have a large group of Korean students staying with you. If I were you, I would get to know the oldest Korean boy and the oldest Korean girl and try to win them over. That way, they won't abuse their power out of respect for you. But if they don't respect you, you'll have some challenges to deal with."

"Meaning …?"

"The older students will become the Korean ring leaders. Think about a union. The oldest students will be wanting to negotiate with you on behalf of their peer group."

"I see. And who are the oldest Korean students?"

"Kyong-park is the oldest boy. I don't know too much about him, as he signed on quite late. And Hee-jin Lee is the oldest girl. She seems very down-to-earth, so I don't think she'll be an issue."

I quickly scribbled their names down and made additional notes.

"You mentioned you also wanted to discuss one student in particular. Is it one of those you just mentioned?"

"No, this one's a special case," she said, looking down at her notebook again. "His name is Byung-ju Lim. He is a very bright boy. In fact, he's been labeled gifted. The issue is, he has a mind of his own which, in Korean society, where it's all about deference to authority, doesn't really work very well."

"And that's why he's here?"

"One reason, yes. I think he's more suited for a Western environment. He's also consumed with old American movies."

She paused, taking a moment to collect her thoughts before continuing.

"Listen, I fully expect that he's going to be a challenge, but I really want to advocate for him."

"I see. Well, I appreciate the heads-up," I said, moving onto page five of my notes.

"One other thing you really need to know," added Hee-young, "Byung-ju's mother spoils him rotten—in fact, she's one of the main sources of his problems. He's her only son—only child, actually—so nothing Byung-ju does is ever wrong or ever his fault. It's Byung-ju's birthday in October, so she'll be visiting the school. You'll see what I mean then."

"Wow! You've given me a lot to think about today."

Hee-young smiled warmly. "It's only because I like what you're doing here and want you to succeed. We need more schools like this. I studied at Queen's University in Ontario, but it was ridiculous how hard I had to work to get there. The way they teach English in Korea is psychotic. You have to memorize everything. It's debilitating. If I'd had the opportunity to learn English at a place like this, it would have been so much easier."

"Well, that's very validating. By the way, Harris informs me we'll probably be visiting Violeta Kim in Seoul sometime during the year."

"Oh, I'm sure she'll be more than happy to host you," Hee-young said with a smirk. "She also likes what you're doing here. Although, she tells me she wasn't overly impressed with your owner."

"She made that abundantly clear," I laughed. "Abundantly."

Chapter 16

"The Kangs from Macau are late," I said to Koji, leaning over the reception counter. "Did they call to let us know when they'd be arriving?"

"No … because they are here already. They were just talking to Miss Major."

"What? Why didn't you tell me they arrived? They were supposed to be in my office over twenty-five minutes ago."

"Oh, I'm sorry. When they walked in, Miss Major tell me she will take them to your office. I thought you were already with them."

I marched down the hall to the Major's office. Peeking inside its open door, I could see the Major chatting away with an elegant woman, who was sitting across from her. Dressed immaculately in a tailored dark navy-blue dress with a brightly-patterned red and white silk scarf tied around her neck, the woman radiated affluence.

"Philly, said the Major, looking up at me from her wheel chair. "We were about to go to your office. But because Mrs. Kang just arrived from Macau, I thought I'd offer her a drink, and then we got chatting. Well, you know how it is," she said, laughing nervously.

I bit my tongue and gave Mrs. Kang a forced smile.

"Welcome, Mrs. Kang. Please, let's go to my office. We're running a bit late," I said, giving the Major a firm look.

"Thank you for your kindness, Miss Major," said Mrs. Kang, picking up her fuchsia *Birkin* purse."

The Major gave me a look as if to say, *See! I am useful.*

"Thank you, Major," I said begrudgingly.

Entering my office, I directed Mrs. Kang to a chair and pulled up a seat opposite her.

"Where's your son ... Thomas?" I asked.

"Oh, Mr. Hymie Chen take him to restroom."

"Well, while we wait, can you tell me a little bit about Thomas and why you want him to come to Cothbert."

Mrs. Kang straightened her dress and took a deep breath. "Thomas is very special boy; maybe a bit different," she qualified. "But he is also very sensitive. Other boys don't understand him. He is interested in things not popular with boys his age."

"For example?" I asked.

"Kangaroo."

"Kangaroo?"

"Yes, when he was young, other boys gave him nickname, Kangaroo. You know, because his last name is Kang ... and also, he likes to jump. Anyway, he started to read everything about the kangaroo. So later he become very serious about the kangaroo."

"What do you mean very serious?"

Just as Mrs. Kang was about to elaborate, the door to my office flung open and Hymie walked in, accompanied by a short, good-looking young boy. Moving up and down like he was doing squats in a gym, the boy then hopped towards

141

me, both hands extended in front of him, bent forward like paws.

"Hello Thomas," I said. "Welcome to Cothbert. I'm Mr. Gower— the Principal here."

"My name is not Thomas. It's Kanga — short for kangaroo."

"I hear you like kangaroos."

"Yes. Here are some facts about kangaroos you need to know," he blurted, avoiding any eye contact. "Kangaroos are marsupials. A male kangaroo is called a boomer and a female kangaroo is called a jill. A group of kangaroos is called a mob," he added, starting to titter.

"I see," I said. "So, you know a lot about kangaroos…"

"Babies are referred to as joeys," he continued, completely ignoring me. "Kangaroos are from Australia…"

Mrs. Kang suddenly yelled something in Cantonese, and Thomas immediately became quiet.

I stared at Thomas not knowing what to say next and then looked over at Mrs. Kang, who simply smiled back.

"So, Thomas … sorry, I mean, Kanga … I stuttered, how do you feel about coming to this school?"

"Good," he replied. "It is a nice school. Does it have bullies?"

Mrs. Kang's eyes welled up.

"Kanga, every school, every business, in fact, everywhere you go in life, has bullies. The trick is to learn how to manage bullies. Running away or being scared won't fix the problem. If you come here, I can't promise you that someone won't try to bully you. But, what I can promise you, is that we will help you learn how to deal with bullies, and I will punish anyone severely who tries to bully you."

"What happens to someone who is a bully at your school?"

"Well, they could get suspended or, if their behavior

continues, expelled. Bullying is not acceptable at our school, Kanga."

Thomas remained quiet and put his hand under his chin to show us that he was thinking about what I had just said.

"That sounds good," he replied at last.

"Do you want to get good marks at our school?" I continued.

"Yes. My mother really wants me to get good marks."

"Well, I can't promise you good marks either, unless of course you work hard and try your best. Does that make sense?"

"Yes. But you need to ask my mother."

I turned to Mrs. Kang, who was patting her eyes with a tissue. She nodded at me and placed her hand gently on Thomas' shoulder.

"Kanga, I would like to have a private chat with your mother and Mr. Chen. Would you mind waiting in the hall for five minutes?"

Thomas didn't say anything, as he rose from his chair and bounced out of my office. I turned to Mrs. Kang.

"Did you understand what I meant just now?" I asked, firmly.

She nodded, still dabbing her eyes.

"We are a school. We try our best to understand each child and help them to succeed. But we can't make any guarantees."

"I understand," replied Mrs. Kang.

"Mrs. Kang, I need to ask you a question and I hope you won't take offense to it, but has Thomas ever been assessed by anyone?"

"You mean psychologist, right?"

"Yes," I replied gently.

"No. It's not very common in Macau."

"Before you leave here today, I would like one of our staff to meet with Thomas. She used to work with children with special needs. It's important that we make sure Cothbert is the right place for Thomas. If we decide it's not, we'll help you to find a school that is."

"You are very kind and honest," replied Mrs. Kang. "You are not like his other principals. They just wanted my money. I want what's best for Thomas. I'd like to hear what your staff person has to say about him. If she says this school is not the right school, I accept. But, I really like your school."

I shot Hymie a wink just as Kanga bounced back in the room.

"Five minutes is up!" he announced.

"Let me see if I can free up my teacher now," I said, smiling at Mrs. Kang. "Her name is Ida Plotnik. Give me a second and I'll be right back."

I walked down the hall, and as I neared the Dining Hall, I heard squeaking noises behind me. I turned around, hitting my foot against the Major's wheelchair.

"So, did we sign up that Macau kid?"

"I don't know if he's the right fit for our school, Major. I'm going to have Ida assess him," I said, rubbing my foot.

"Not the right fit? What the hell does that mean? His mother looks like she can afford the fees."

"That's not what I'm talking about. The boy may have a developmental disability. I want to make sure we have the resources to support him."

"What more resources could you possibly need? This school is a bloody paradise already.

"I ignored the Major and entered the Dining Hall. Harris

was still leaning against the same table, now focused on grading the students' tests.

"Can I borrow Ida for an hour?" I asked him.

"Sure, what's up?"

"It's the boy from Macau. I think he may have a developmental disability. I want an objective assessment before deciding if we should accept him."

"Good call. Sure, I'm almost done here. The other staff can cover for her. Oh, and don't forget our meeting to review the results."

"Right," I said, feeling like I was being pulled in all directions.

I took Ida aside and explained what I needed from her while giving a brief synopsis of Thomas' situation; his history of being bullied, his unusual obsession with kangaroos and his overall social awkwardness."

"I can do some cursory psycho-educational testing, but I'm not trained to do a full-blown psychological assessment. The best I can offer is to benchmark him against other special needs students I've taught over the years and give you my gut feeling about what type of support he might need."

"That's perfect! That's all I need at this point," I replied, noticing through a gap in the open door to the hallway, the Major, still waiting outside and ready to pounce on me again. I quickly gave Ida a head-ups on what to expect so she wasn't caught off guard.

"You didn't answer my question," the Major snapped as soon as we stepped into the hallway. "What resources could you possibly need that you don't already have? You think I'm made of money? Why wouldn't you just accept this kid now?

We could lose him to another private school!"

Ida stepped in smoothly. "Phil," she said with deliberate emphasis, "psycho-educational testing will help us assess Thomas's emotional and intellectual development to ensure his cognitive abilities can compensate for any immaturity. It will also determine whether the Ministry would require extra funding for resource support."

The Major blinked, clearly thrown. "What does 'extra resource support' mean?"

"In simple terms," Ida replied, "it means hiring another teacher."

"No bloody way."

"Exactly why we need to evaluate him more thoroughly," I added, catching onto Ida's lead. "Accepting him prematurely could force us to incur unforeseen costs."

The Major glowered but didn't argue further. "Yes ... well, if he's not the right fit, then we shouldn't accept him. But we can accept him if we don't need to spend more money on him. Right?"

"Exactly what I was thinking Major," I replied. "Ida, shall we go and see Thomas now?"

"Yes," she said, determinedly. "We shouldn't keep him waiting."

As soon as we were out of earshot of the Major, we both broke down in laughter.

"Thank you so much for bailing me out!"

"No problem," Ida smiled back. "It's not the first time I've had to deal with money-crunchers like her. Did you enjoy the psycho-babble I fed her?"

"It was masterful. Particularly the comments about the Ministry of Education. They actually cover the cost of a teacher's aid."

"I know," Ida grinned back playfully.

We arrived at my office, where I introduced Ida to Mrs. Kang. Thomas, who was standing beside her, immediately began raising his body up and down, extending his hands as though they were paws.

"Are you going to accept me to your school? I like your school," he said, finally glancing at me then lowering his eyes again.

Ida looked over at me with a smile. "Thomas, is it okay if you and I go and have a chat. I don't know anything about kangaroos, and I'd love you to teach me about them."

"Sure! By the way, my name is Kanga. Let's go," he said, excitedly.

With Thomas escorted out by Ida, Hymie and I decided to kill time by touring Mrs. Kang through the campus.

"So, what do you do in Macau," I asked, as we walked down the hill towards the Boarding House.

"My husband and I own a few businesses."

"Oh, what type?"

"Just a casino, a few restaurants and a couple of shopping centers. You know."

I was glad the Major wasn't with us to hear all this.

"And Thomas went to school in Macau?"

"When he was young, he was in a boarding school in China."

"How old was he then?"

"Five years old."

"I see," I said, unable to fathom what it must have been like to be a boarder at such a young age.

"And after that?"

147

"He tried a couple of private schools in Hong Kong. But they weren't very good— and he was bullied a lot. Then he came back to Macau and he went to local public school until they inform us they could no longer teach him."

"What was their reason?"

"They said he was too disruptive; talked too much. I think it was because he was bullied, and they didn't know what to do."

"I see."

By the time we finished exploring the campus and returned to the School House, Ida was seated in my office with Thomas, sharing a book about kangaroos that he had brought with him.

"Mrs. Kang, please let me have a few moments with Mrs. Plotnik and then we'll share our thoughts."

Mrs. Kang nodded, but it was obvious she was becoming anxious. I signaled to Ida, who moved into the hall.

"So, what are we dealing with here?" I asked.

Ida looked down at her notes. "I did some cursory cognitive testing first. From what I can see, he is very bright. He has an almost photographic memory and an incredible eye for detail. His base in mathematics is above grade level. His English language is about two years behind, but of course he is ESL, so I'm not overly concerned about that."

"So, no learning disability?"

"No. I don't think so. But, as you saw in your office, he's does have social issues. Like I said, I'm not a psychologist, but his behavior reminds me of the children I used to manage who had *Asperger Syndrome*."

"Is this the right school for him, then?" I asked.

"*Asperger's* is a form of autism, and the autistic spectrum is huge. There are many students with *Asperger's* who function quite well in regular classes with moderate resource intervention. Others require a full-time teacher's-aid. While Thomas clearly has some quirky social issues and a lack of self-awareness, he also has attributes you wouldn't normally see in a student who was high on the autistic spectrum."

"Such as?"

"When I read him a story about a young girl who was born with a facial disfigurement, he was able to show empathy. While he is set in his ways, he did allow me to change things up a little bit without pushing back too much. And, I didn't see any delayed cognitive development. He was also willing to share his experience going to boarding school at five years of age. I think it was quite traumatic for him."

"Hmm. So, what do you think?"

"I don't think he needs a teacher's-aide. He requires a school with small classes. And he could benefit from being in social activities with children his own age. I think Cothbert could be perfect for him."

"What about the whole kangaroo thing. Won't the students eat him alive?"

"It's a coping mechanism. I'm more than happy to take him on as one of my special projects. I'm already going to be teaching the younger students anyway. My approach would be to be up front with his peer group about his challenges and then work collectively to wean him away from this kangaroo alter ego thing."

"So, it's a go?"

"Yes, but I think you should make his acceptance conditional on Mrs. Kang getting him tested by a psychologist before he starts — so we at least know for sure what we're dealing with. I can give her some names of people in Vancouver, if you'd like."

"That's a good idea. Listen, thanks for all this. I'll go and brief Mrs. Kang and get back to you if she asks for names of psychologists. I think she really wants Thomas to come here."

"I think he's worth the gamble," smiled Ida.

When I relayed the good news to Mrs. Kang, she was over the moon.

"Thank you! Thank you! This means so much to Thomas and me," she exclaimed, raising her voice with excitement and pointing to Thomas, who was now hopping around the room, a delighted smile spreading across his face.

"You do understand, Mrs. Kang, that we will need that psychological report before Thomas can start here?"

"Yes, Mr. Hymie Chen is going to arrange it for me. He knows a psychologist in Vancouver who can meet Thomas next week."

She grasped my hand and squeezed it with both of hers, her eyes shimmering with unshed tears. Then, with Thomas bouncing along behind her, she turned and walked out of my office.

Chapter 17

"Are you ready to review the language test results?" I asked, looking in on Harris, who was hidden behind piles of paperwork strewn across his desk.

"Sure, come on in," he said, gesturing me forward. "How'd everything turn out with that boy from Macau?"

I filled him in on our decision to accept Thomas, as well as Ida's observations.

"*Asperger's*, eh? Interesting. Thank goodness we have Ida on staff. I also think it's a good idea you requested an outside assessment."

"We did have a bit of push-back from the Major," I said, explaining the scene outside the Dining Hall.

"Well, no surprise there. Didn't someone tell me the Major would start focusing on the heart of the school once the money started rolling in?"

"I guess there's not enough rolling in yet," I quipped.

"There never will be," scoffed Harris.

"So, any surprises with the language tests?" I asked, glancing at his toppling stacks of paper.

"Actually, yes. Our Japanese girl, Aki Ito, tested almost off the charts. Very strong!"

"Really?"

"Yes! Who would have guessed? I'll keep her at her grade level for math and science, but I'm going to have to bump her up to the Blossoms for English and Social Studies. It took a bit of juggling, but I think I can make her timetable work."

"Wow. She's that good?"

"She is. Oh, and by the way, Albert and Stanley are not as strong as we originally thought. They're typical products of some of the schools in Hong Kong. Their understanding of grammar rules is strong, and their oral English and comprehension are decent, but they can't write. Their writing samples were incoherent. I'll still place them in Blossoms, but they'll need a lot of extra support."

"Anyone else we should be concerned about?"

"Actually, there is," Harris replied, pulling a sheet of paper out from one of his many work-piles. "This guy," he said, handing me a completed answer sheet.

"Manfred Ma?" I said, staring down at the name. "Hymie and I were just talking about him. Supposedly, he has a tendency to get himself excessively wound up about things."

"ADHD?"

"His mother doesn't know."

"Okay, well, his results were the lowest of the bunch, and I noticed letter reversals and unusual spelling in his writing sample. He'll definitely be a Seedling. Otherwise, everyone else kind of fell into their appropriate grade level."

"So, the teaching assignments remain the same?"

"Yes. I will look after math and science for the, ah, Blossoms," he said with a hint of disdain, "and you'll be picking up their English. Ida will look after the Seedlings, and Pancho will oversee the Stems. Chill will be in charge of physical education and art. I think she can also chip in with health science for the Seedlings and Stems."

"That means we're good to go with classes tomorrow, then?"

"Yup! I've generated basic timetables, and we can distribute textbooks right after breakfast. Myrtle is going to hand out uniforms for dinner tonight. Tomorrow, the fun begins."

There was good energy in the Dining Hall that evening when Harris and I seated ourselves for dinner. The sea of blue and gray uniforms sweeping through the room seemed to fill a void; it felt as though the school had been brought back to life again with the return of its long-lost friends. Sitting at a table, taking it all in, was the Major, looking happier than I had ever seen her.

"Don't they look smart?" she puffed, her chest swelling with pride.

Harris turned to me, shaking his head in disbelief. I bit my tongue, remembering the famous *asshole-escapade* when she had proclaimed that uniforms were completely useless.

"Yes, Major. Very smart," I replied, careful to keep my tone neutral.

Still, there was something in her expression—perhaps in the way she quietly scanned the room. It wasn't just pride; it carried a hint of introspection, perhaps even the realization that she was beginning to enjoy being a private school type.

I turned towards the buffet table, which was decorated with platters of roast beef, Yorkshire pudding, and Caesar salad, but also a choice of stir-fry and rice.

"Did you ask the kitchen to offer up those alternatives?" I whispered to Harris.

"I did. If there's one thing that can undermine a successful cross-cultural integration, it's not taking the time to understand a person's food needs. I've asked Janice and Peg to ensure there is white rice on the buffet table every night and congee for breakfast."

"Congee?"

"Asian oatmeal, except it's made from leftover rice."

I could see the students were making every effort to try the Western food choices but hadn't quite grasped the subtleties of the dishes or our table etiquette. Peg was beside herself that they had completely ignored using dinner plates in favor of ice cream bowls. They had filled these bowls with a multi-layered East-meets-West concoction that included Yorkshire pudding rolled around a pork stir-fry on top of roast beef and gravy, mixed with rice and a Caesar salad chaser.

After enjoying a bit of salad and stir-fry myself, I decided to work the room and check to see how everyone was doing. The students happily called out, "Hi, Mr. Gower," as I walked by, and even though I was still struggling to learn everyone's name, Myrtle had asked us all to wear our name tags for the first week. This allowed me to gain brownie points by responding on a first-name basis. I noticed Pansy Huang sitting by herself and decided to join her.

"Everything okay, Pansy?" I asked. She had her trusty translator with her and punched something on its keyboard.

I suffer from fatigue came the response.

I smiled as she handed me her device.

In English, we call it jet lag. It will only last a few days I typed.

She gave a look of recognition when she heard my response, then looked up, seeing her sister approach, balancing a bowl of East-Meets-West. Hibiscus carefully put her bowl and utensils down and sat opposite me.

"Hi, Hibiscus. How are you?"

She nodded politely but appeared preoccupied with re-directing Pansy's attention to a smart-looking boy sitting at the next table. With cryptic winks, the girls silently signaled back and forth to each other, glanced at me awkwardly, then rose in unison and nonchalantly wandered to the next table. Hoping they had fooled him into believing they had just happened to have arrived, the twins sat down on either side of the unsuspecting boy. I smiled inwardly, remembering my student days.

I was about to continue with my informal tour of the Dining Hall when a very disheveled boy, mumbling in Korean, slumped into a chair in front of me. I recognized the name pinned to his shirt: *Byung-ju Lim*. So, this was the lad Hee-young had mentioned. My curiosity piqued, I studied him a little more closely.

Short of stature and of medium build, he didn't appear to care too much about his appearance. His hair was long and concealed his eyes until he flicked it back, a gesture he repeated frequently. He had headphones on that were connected to a CD player. I moved towards him and tapped his shoulder. He jumped and looked up, removing his headset.

"Hi there. I'm Mr. Gower," I said. "I'm the Principal here at Cothbert."

He turned his head and gave me a sideways look, flicking back his hair. "Hello, I Byung-ju," he said, his face remaining expressionless. "I remember you from the bus."

"How are you liking it here?" I asked.

"Like prison camp," he said. "But okay."

Well, at least he's honest, I thought.

"I hear it's your birthday next month."

He gave me another sideways glance, and his sharp eyes started surveying me with a look that didn't miss a thing. "How do you know that?" he asked accusingly, his expression becoming suspicious.

"Ms. Hee-young told me … your chaperone. She also said your mother is coming to visit you next month."

"She bringing me videos for my birthday. I ask her for *Dead Poets Society*."

"Really? That's an old movie … but a great movie!"

"I like old movie. You see it before?" he asked, his face relaxing a bit.

"Many times. It's one of my all-time favorites."

"Me too."

"Why do you like it?"

"Students have secret place to go to without any annoying teachers."

"That's right. They read poems to each other. Do you like poetry?"

"No. Hate it! Make no sense. You have video player here?"

"Yes, I think there may be an old one sitting in the Boarding House Common Room. But you can only use it with Ms. Green's permission and only after you have finished your homework."

"Really sound like prison here." He shook his head at the concept.

"Anyway, Byung-ju, nice to meet you. I do hope you end up liking it at Cothbert," I said, getting up.

"Not sure," he replied, putting his earphones back on, not fully appreciating my attempt to be courteous.

The other person I wanted to look for was Manfred

Ma. What with Hymie's vague description of him being excessively hyper and his less-than-stellar test results, I really wanted to see what this boy was all about. I walked back to the table where Harris was demonstrating his skill with magic tricks to one of the girls.

"Harris, which one's Manfred Ma?" I asked.

"Over there," he pointed. "Where all that noise is coming from."

I'd heard the cheering coming from the far side of the Dining Hall but hadn't thought much of it. Now that the commotion had my attention, my eyes went directly to a table where a heavy-set lad seemed to be reenacting a story. Using exaggerated hand movements like in a game of charades, he began racing around the table, and as his story unfolded, occasionally jumping into the air while simultaneously shouting to simulate what sounded like an attack by wild animals. By this time, the others at his table were in hysterics. I moved closer, pulling up a chair to watch. Beads of sweat were rolling down Manfred's forehead as his narration reached a feverish pitch and he almost elevated himself off the ground until finally, his exuberance waned, and he appeared to bring his story to its conclusion. His audience clapped with fervor, and Manfred took his bows. He noticed me watching.

"Hi Mr. Gower," he said with an endearing smile. "Sorry, I was very noisy. Right?"

"You were a bit. This is a Dining Hall, remember."

"Yes, sorry. My mother always tells me I'm a bit too hyper."

"You're quite the actor."

"I like making people laugh. Laughter is best medicine. No?"

157

"Yes! Absolutely."

Out of the corner of my eye, I noticed the Major had positioned herself beside the buffet table and had a large box sitting on her lap.

"Attention! Attention, everyone!" she suddenly called out, wheeling herself to the front of the room. Her booming voice silenced the chatter as heads turned toward her.

"My name is Major Hunter. I am the owner of Cothbert House School."

The students started clapping politely, unsure of what to expect. Then, in one swift motion, she reached into a large box on her lap and began pitching chocolate bars, bags of chips, and assorted candy around the room like a coach at halftime.

Cheers erupted as students leapt from their seats, lunging for flying treats.

Harris walked up beside me, sighing.

"What exactly is going on here?" I asked, watching the chaos unfold.

"She just won them over with bribery," he deadpanned.

We both exited the Dining Hall like beaten soldiers.

Chapter 18

Morning classes seemed to go smoothly, and when I entered the Dining Hall for my recess break, Harris was already by the sink, dunking a tea bag in a cup of boiled water.

"So far, the staff feel we placed the students in their appropriate levels," he said, looking up at me over his reading glasses.

"That's good to hear. I was thinking I would sit in on the Seedlings this afternoon to get a feel for the class. Do you want to join me?"

"Not this afternoon. I'm still trying to track down some textbooks, and Pancho wants me to order a certain novel for the Stems that looks like it might be out of print. But I'll go on walkabout with you during afternoon clubs, if you'd like?"

"Sure. How'd it go with the Blossoms this morning? Didn't you have science and math with them?"

"It was fine, I guess. But you're definitely going to have your hands full in your English class. Some of their written skills are downright wacky."

"What does that mean?"

"Let's start with the Koreans. It seems that many of them have been drilled using a notorious cram-school book that boasts over 20,000 English words."

"Isn't that a good thing?" I asked, sitting opposite him. "I mean, their vocabulary must be pretty strong, no?"

"You'll see what the challenges are when you start marking their essays. Then there's Albert and Stanley. They love multiple-choice or fill-in-the-blank-style work. But, give them something to write or think about, and the best you'll get back from them is a stream of consciousness mumbo-jumbo. Oh, and some of the Taiwanese—they won't read anything without going in and out of their electronic translators. I say we ban those bloody contraptions, at least in class; otherwise, it'll take them hours to finish their work."

I was suddenly not looking forward to my afternoon class.

There were only seven students in Ida's Seedlings class when I arrived for my observation, although with the addition of Thomas, the number would climb to eight. I pulled myself up onto a table at the back of the classroom to get a better look. The students were playing a game in which they had to choose an idiom from a huge list on the wall and use it in a sentence with a partner. Most of the students were actively engaged in the activity, including a young Taiwanese girl called Celia Wu, who was enthusiastically typing every idiom she could into her electronic translator. However, one student who was not being overly serious was Manfred Ma. He was preoccupied with the idiom *caught with your pants down* and was gesturing with his swaying backside to whomever would watch as he released high-pitched shrieks.

"Manfred," hollered Ida. "I'm getting a little bit sick of your voice. Do you know what that expression means?"

Celia looked on with interest.

"It means we are tired of listening to you going on and on. I want to see you use six idioms by the end of this class, excluding *caught with your pants down*. Do you understand?"

Manfred laughed playfully, bobbing up and down in his chair. "Yes, ma'am," he replied, enjoying the attention.

By the time Ida called on Manfred to present his six idioms, he had decided to stand on his chair where, in dramatic fashion, he enthusiastically and quite amazingly performed *Pardon my French, It's all Greek to me, Kick the bucket, When pigs fly, Monkey business*, and *Wouldn't be caught dead in that*. The other students were in stitches watching him, and I had to admit I was trying very hard to contain myself. Luckily, the bell rang, signaling it was time to change class.

"That Manfred's pretty high energy," I exclaimed, getting ready to go to my English class.

"Didn't you say his agent said there were no behavioral issues?" asked Ida sarcastically.

"That's what he assured me," I smiled back.

The Blossoms class consisted of ten students, including the oldest Korean boy, Kyong-park, Aki Ito, and Albert and Stanley. I decided I would use this first class to get a sense of their reading and writing levels. I assigned an essay, the topic of which was, *Don't judge a book by its cover*. Then, I took each student individually out into the hallway and had them read to me.

By the time I had finished assessing the last student's reading level and returned to the classroom, completed essays were starting to gather on my desk. I glanced down at one of them, which was written by a Korean girl called Myung-hee. It began:

Are a person's gawks a symptom of what type of person they are? No. We should not judge someone by their gawks but who they are emphatically.

Another essay from a Korean boy called Jo-ho read:

Voluminous people adjudicate others by their looks instead of appreciating them very intimately.

So, this is what happens when your education system is based on fast-track memorization. Now I have to undo all this damage, I thought.

I noticed Stanley's submission. It began:

Looks don't judge. I mean, you must know the person, like if my friend only judge me by how I look, I don't feel good. Right?

Right! I said to myself, shaking my head. I was getting more and more depressed by the minute, wondering how I was going to tackle this mess.

I met up with Harris at the reception counter as soon as the bell for afternoon clubs sounded.

"So, how was your English class?" he asked smugly.

"If that's a rhetorical question, don't bother!"

Harris snorted with delight. "I did warn you."

"It's one big mess of mumbo-jumbo in there. I honestly don't know where to begin."

"What does mumbo-jumbo mean?" asked Koji, poking his head up from behind the counter.

"It's when what you say or write makes no sense."

"You mean, nonsense? I had that problem. When I first learned English, my teacher said I did not think properly about what I was writing, and that I was writing nonsense."

"How did she fix the problem?" I asked, halfheartedly.

"She told me I had to learn how to write all over again. She made me write sentences like I was in Grade 3."

"And there you have it!" proclaimed Harris. "His teacher was bang on. The solution to your mumbo-jumbo dilemma is to teach your students how to write all over over again. No translators. No 20,000-word vocabulary books. No grammar books. Just simple, controlled writing. I suggest daily journals that you correct and have them rewrite. Right now, the problem is they've lost control of the basics."

"They have mumbo-jumbo," repeated Koji, who seemed amused by the expression.

"I see," I replied, already structuring my next lesson plan in my head.

"Come on, cheer up," Harris said with a grin. "Let's go check out what our clubs are up to."

We caught up with Chill first, who had decided to organize a photography club. The Major had given her a few beaten-up cameras and, when we arrived, she was trying her best to demonstrate to her club how to use them. She had a diagram on the wall illustrating the key parts of a camera.

"And what is this called?" she asked, pointing to a re-tractable lens.

"*Loom lens*," came a loud, collective response.

"Yes, a zoom lens."

"And what are you going to use your camera for today?"

"To take interesting *potographs*," they all yelled.

"Yes, to take interesting photographs."

"Now, the goal of today's class is to take an interesting photograph of something outdoors that makes you feel good. Look at these prints, for example," she said, laying out a selection of shots she had taken of flowers, trees, and engaging wildlife. The class looked on with muted interest.

"Do you all understand?" she asked, enthusiastically.

Everyone nodded, eagerly grabbed a camera, and dashed off. However, I wasn't entirely convinced they really did understand, and this was shortly confirmed when they started noisily charging around campus, happily clicking at anything they encountered. I then noticed, out of the corner of my eye, the Huang twins, each of whom had positioned herself behind a clump of shrubs. They had pulled their baseball caps down to conceal their faces. I wasn't sure what they were up to until a boy walked by. All at once, there was a sudden flurry of shutter bursts. As the boy continued to walk on, unaware, the two girls hastily changed positions and angles, launching another rapid-fire series of clicking sounds with a fervor that bordered on the obsessive.

Harris and I strolled over, but the twins seemed oblivious to our presence, remaining fixated on another boy who was coming their way. At the very last moment, the boy veered off the path, and the girls groaned with disappointment.

"Girls, do you understand what the goal of today's class is?" I asked.

"Yes," replied Pansy. "To take a photo of something that makes you feel good."

"Well ... yes," I stammered, "but..."

"Do you really want to pursue this conversation any further?" asked Harris, raising his eyebrows irreverently.

"No, I suppose not. I guess you can't accuse them of not understanding the objective of the class."

Harris and I decided we still had time for one more visit, and walked over to the playing field, where Ida was hosting a soccer club. Only ten students had signed up, and only one of them was a girl. Of the nine boys, five were Koreans, including Kyong-park, and the other four, Taiwanese.

"Wow, look over there," I said to Harris, realizing that the only girl was Aki Ito. "I'm surprised. Other than her roommate, she's been keeping her distance from almost everyone since she arrived. You know, she still can't look me in the eye when I try to talk to her."

"Give her time," said Harris. "Remember, she's the only Japanese student at the school. It's really brave of her to come out today. That's why these clubs are so important; they build character and break down barriers. This could be good for her."

"Everyone, take a seat, please," ordered Ida with a commanding tone. The students positioned themselves on the grass, happily looking up at her.

"In order for me to get an idea of where I should focus your skill development, we're going to play a game of five-on-five. I'll pick the teams randomly and then each team can decide who it wants to have as its goalie."

"Why don't we play Korea against Taiwan?" asked Kyong-park, with an edge to his voice.

"I don't think so," replied Ida. "We're all Cothbert students here. It doesn't matter where we're from. Let's keep everything friendly."

I could see Kyong-park didn't like her response.

"I've put letters in a hat," she said, holding out a baseball cap. "You'll either be on Team A or Team B. Go ahead and pick a letter!"

Despite Ida's desire to avoid pitting one culture against the other, as luck would have it, one team ended up being exclusively comprised of Korean students and the other, Taiwanese students and Aki.

"Yes! Korea versus Taiwan," called out Kyong-park, as his teammates cheered from the sidelines.

"No, Korea versus Taiwan and Japan," said Mason Lee, one of the Taiwanese boys, jokingly.

As the teams huddled together, a whistle blew, and the players scattered, moving into position.

Team A had selected Tae Kim, one of the younger boys, as their goalie, while Team B had chosen Aki. Ida flipped a coin to see which team would have initial control of the ball, and Team A won the draw. Ida blew her whistle again, and the game was on.

Soccer is an obsession in Korea, and something young Korean students take very seriously. This was clearly evident as the Korean players demonstrated excellent footwork and passing skills. While players from Team B defended themselves admirably, it wasn't long before Kyong-park was able to fire off a blistering shot at their net. All at once, Aki hurled herself upwards, head-butting the ball away from the net. Players from B cheered, as players from Team A re-tooled, clearly peeved.

Team B was now in control of the ball, and Mason was able to release a shot on the Team A net, which hit the goal post and went bouncing out of bounds. A boy named Jung-sik took back control for Team A. He lobbed the ball back and forth to his teammates, keeping his opponents scrambling. Then, as soon as there was an opening, he kicked the ball forward to Kyong-park, who fired off his second powerful shot at the Team B net. Aki dove toward the net, grabbing the ball in midair before landing firmly back on the ground.

CHAPTER 18

She held the ball above her head for her teammates to see. They all shouted enthusiastically.

The school bell sounded, announcing that it was the end of clubs. Ida looked at her watch.

"Okay, last play."

A boy named Bernard maneuvered the ball back down the field towards Team A's net and was about to pass it forward when Kyong-park tried to intercept it from behind, kicking Bernard in the leg. Bernard fell to the ground, howling.

"That's a penalty shot," yelled Ida, rushing towards Bernard, who slowly got back on his feet and hobbled over to the sideline. After some brief massaging and stretching, he marched back onto the field again, ready to take the penalty kick. By this time, he was angry, and the force he was able to put behind his shot propelled the ball so rapidly, Tae never had a chance to stop it. The game was over. Team B: 1. Team A: 0.

Aki was lifted into the air by her teammates as a huge smile spread across her face.

"I guess we don't need to worry about Aki fitting in," I joked.

"Damn! She's good," proclaimed Harris.

There was a raucous noise behind me, as Kyong-park waved his teammates off the field and then stormed back towards the Boarding House. I remembered what Hee-young had said to me about the power of the oldest Korean boy and decided it was time Kyong-park and I had a little chat.

When I arrived at the Boarding House, Myrtle was in the lobby looking a bit flustered.

"What happened?" I asked.

"I don't know. Kyong-park and the other Korean boys

167

came storming into the house. I tried to talk to them, but they seemed angry about something and banged their way upstairs, slamming their doors. Why are they so upset?"

"Their egos have been hurt," I replied. "I'm going to take Kyong-park into the duty office for a chat. Can you ask him to come downstairs?"

A few moments later, Kyong-park walked into the office to stand in front of me, his face suffused with anger. He bent his head forward.

"Have a seat, Kyong-park."

He seated himself, avoiding my eye contact.

"Kyong-park, I want to share with you what I have learned over the years about great leaders."

He looked up, confused. "What do you mean?"

"Aren't you the oldest Korean boy?"

"Yes."

"And doesn't that mean your Korean friends expect you to be their leader?"

"Yes," he said, starting to look uncomfortable.

"Well, don't you want to know some tricks from the greatest leaders that ever lived?"

"So I can be a good leader with the Koreans?"

"Yes. But not just the Koreans. You want everyone to see you as a good leader, don't you?"

"Okay. Yes, I would be interested to learn," he said, relaxing a bit.

"Let's talk about respect first. What does respect mean to you?"

"Listening to those who are older than you are?"

"Good. But what happens if the person who is older than you is a bad person?"

"It's hard to show them respect."

"Exactly. Of all the books I have read about great leaders, the one thing that is repeated over and over is that good leaders work for the people they lead and earn their respect by being good role models themselves."

"I understand."

"Do you? Were you a good role model today?"

"I was angry."

"Kyong-park, what happens at the end of a professional soccer game in Korea?"

Kyong-park thought for a minute, and then I saw his face starting to blush. "They shake hands with each other."

"Yes. They don't go storming off the field or walking angrily past Ms. Green like you did, slamming doors behind them."

Kyong-park bowed his head again.

"Being a good leader is a tough job. I want to help you; give you some advice. Today, you were not a good leader. You need to show everyone that you can be humble and respectful, both when you win and when you lose. You have a huge responsibility being the oldest Korean boy. Don't screw it up!"

He looked up at me, surprised by my language.

"I will try much harder, Mr. Gower. Sorry."

"Sorry is an easy word to say. You need to show how sorry you are through your actions."

He nodded his head.

"Remember, I'm here to help. I know it's not easy."

"Thank you," he said, reaching for my hand.

"Now that's leadership," I said, smiling.

Chapter 19

The report arrived from Dr. R.J. Margulies in Vancouver. As Ida had suspected, Thomas 'Kanga' Kang was bright but mildly autistic, with Asperger Syndrome. As I waded through the detailed document, Koji buzzed me from reception. Mrs. Kang was already on the line, wanting to know when she could drop Thomas off. I confirmed that we would be willing to receive him the following day after classes but realized, as soon as I said that, I hadn't even thought through how best to prepare for his arrival—or whether the school community was even ready to receive him. The last thing I wanted was to be complicit in further bullying.

When the recess bell rang later that morning and the students started flocking to the Dining Hall for their snack, I decided to grab Dr. Margulies' report and head upstairs to find Ida. I wanted to share my concern about Thomas' arrival and look at strategies to avert any initial challenges. As I wandered past the reception area, I spotted Pansy and Hibiscus, both of whom were standing in front of a new student welcome sign Koji had posted that included a photo of Thomas. The girls were fawning over the image.

"Maybe they could help us with Thomas," I thought.

When I found Ida, she was sitting at her desk reviewing

writing samples with Harris.

"How are things going?" I asked.

"You mean, with the Seedlings?" Ida chuckled, shaking her head. "They're an interesting lot. I really enjoy them, but there's so much work ahead of us if we expect to get them accepted to mainstream English private schools."

"To add to your workload, this just arrived," I said, placing the report from Dr. Margulies in front of her. "I'll leave it with you, but basically, it reaffirms what you originally thought."

"Asperger's?"

"Yup. Mild. I have to say, though, I'm more concerned about all of the collateral damage caused by the years of bullying. It's so important that Thomas feels safe when he arrives tomorrow."

"As I mentioned to you before, my plan is to have a candid conversation with his classmates so they work with me and not against him."

"Oh, that reminds me. The Huang girls are in your class, right?"

"Yes, why?"

"Well, a few moments ago, I discovered our two lovebirds in the front lobby drooling over a photo of Thomas that was hanging on a welcome poster."

"Is that such a bad thing?" Ida quipped.

"No, that's my point. Maybe we can use it to our advantage. What if we approached the girls about becoming Thomas' big sisters?"

"As long as that's all they become," Harris chuntered to himself.

"I like your idea," said Ida. "Let me talk to them."

"The other person I need to meet with is Kyong-park," I added. "If I can get him behind us, I think it'll really help."

"I'll also check in with Myrtle to look at the best roommate fit for him," said Harris.

Kyong-park joined me in my office after lunch. He looked a lot more upbeat and relaxed compared to the last time we met.

"Any leadership challenges you want to discuss?" I asked, trying to break the ice.

"No. Not right now. But that thing you said about working for the people you lead—it really works."

"I'm glad to hear that. So, I have a leadership question for you."

"Me? Really? But you're the Principal."

"No leader has all the answers. If any leader tells you otherwise, they're an arrogant leader."

"Oh, yeah, right," he laughed stiffly.

"Kyong-park, do you know what a special-needs student is?"

"I think so. A student who has a learning problem?"

"Correct, but sometimes it can be a social problem too. Listen, there's a student arriving tomorrow. He's had a really rough time at his other schools, and—"

"He was bullied?" interrupted Kyong-park.

"Badly. I want to be honest with you because you'll meet him tomorrow. The boy, whose name is Thomas, has some personal challenges and still needs to understand how to get along with others. People will find his personality a little different—maybe even strange. That's why I need you to help me."

172

"Sure, how?"

"The most important thing right now is that we all remain patient with Thomas and accept him for who he is. Many of the other students will look at how you treat him. If you welcome him and ignore his personality differences, I think the other students will do the same. But if you laugh at him or make fun of him, everyone will start to pick on him. Any idea how you can show leadership and help me with this?"

Kyong-park thought for a moment, pondering the question seriously. "What if he was my roommate? Would that help?"

"Well, yes," I replied, surprised by the offer. "That's very generous of you. But don't you already have a roommate?"

"I do. But our room is really big. It has space for three beds."

"Kyong-park, are you sure you want to do this?"

"I need to become a strong leader. Strong leaders need to face challenges, right?"

"Absolutely. And this could be a big challenge. Thomas likes to pretend he is a kangaroo. In fact, he has changed his name to Kanga," I disclosed, watching for Kyong-park's reaction.

"My brother is like that too—always doing goofy things. I just ignore him."

The more Kyong-park talked, the more I realized that this plan might actually work.

Later that afternoon, I convened a staff meeting to review Thomas' arrival.

"So, we've got both the Huang twins and Kyong-park on board," I announced. "Myrtle, what about this three-person room idea? Is it going to work?"

"I think so. Frank's already moved in an extra bed and desk, and there's tons of cupboard space in that room. I'll keep a close watch on how everything goes."

"Good. We all have to keep our eyes open. If you sense any teasing or subtle bullying, we need to nip it in the bud right away."

"Ida, he's in the Seedlings with you," said Harris, looking at his files, "but from what I can see in his report from Dr. Margulies, he's pretty advanced in mathematics. Should I create a special timetable for him?"

"I don't think that's a good idea, Harris," she replied. "Frankly, right now, our priority is not his academics. It's helping him to fit in. He needs a simple routine with the same people. Let's keep him in the Seedlings for the time being. We can look at moving him later, if necessary."

"What about clubs?" asked Pancho. "Should we just assign him to a club?"

"I would like him in photography," piped in Chill. "He sounds like someone I could work with."

"Photography is probably the least risky club for him right now," agreed Ida.

"Settled, then," said Harris. "Tomorrow should be an interesting day."

"Aren't they all interesting?" I exclaimed.

With my English class finished for the day, I asked Kyung-park to accompany me to my office in preparation for Thomas' arrival. Passing through the reception area, I thought I felt a gentle tug on the hem of my jacket, and when I looked down, bouncing even more exuberantly than on his first visit, was Thomas, looking back up at me with an innocent gaze.

"Hi Mr. Gower! I'm back!" he announced, his eyes sparkling. "I'm really, really happy to be here!"

"Kanga … hi. Where's your mother?" I asked, looking around, totally caught off guard.

"She is outside with someone who said she is the owner of the school."

Of course she is.

"Kyung-park stepped forward. "Hi Kanga! I'm your roommate. My name is Kyung-park."

Thomas stuck out his hand in an exaggerated fashion.

"Thank you for being polite, Kanga," Kyung-park responded. "But, you know, next time, if you want someone's attention, you shouldn't pull on their jacket like you did with Mr. Gower. That's a little rude."

I turned quickly to see Thomas' reaction, but he just stood there with his hand under his chin in a reflective manner.

"Thank you. I didn't know that," he said. "What should I do next time, so I am not rude?"

"Just say, *excuse me.* That will get the person's attention."

"Okay."

"Can I show you your room now?"

"Excuse me … but do I get to sleep on a bunk bed? I like bunk beds. I slept on a bunk bed when I went to school in China."

"Kanga, bunk beds are for kids. You're not a kid anymore, are you?" asked Kyung-park.

Thomas shook his head.

"In this school, we all have our own beds like big people."

Thomas stroked his chin again. "That's good," he acknowledged.

175

"You know what, Thomas, let's go and see your mother," I suggested, gently shepherding him out the front door of the School House, signaling to Kyung-park to follow from behind.

Mrs. Kang and the Major were chatting away when we stepped into the warmth of the sunny fall day. As soon as Thomas presented himself, Mrs. Kang moved her focus from the Major towards her son, quickly acknowledging me with a deferential smile and a wave. I waved back, but my attention was being drawn to a curious-looking man who was hovering behind the two women, staring at me. He was a tall individual with arched shoulders, his hair pulled up into a ponytail. I couldn't put my finger on it, but there was something strangely exotic about his appearance, with his white Nero-style shirt, black baggy pants, and gold embroidered satchel slung over his shoulder.

"My name is Jake Zhou," announced the man as he stepped forward. "The Major was just telling us about all the work she put into starting this school."

I shook my head and muttered under my breath. Jake caught my fleeting reaction, turned slightly toward Mrs. Kang, and leaned closer to whisper in her ear. During this exchange, his eyes remained focused on me, almost like they were boring into my very soul. I started to feel a sense of unease. Mrs. Kang listened carefully, then jerked her head towards me, as if she had been told a secret of great importance. Jake walked over.

"You and I have a lot to talk about. But we'll wait until later."

I gave him a vacant look. I had no idea what he was referring to.

"Excuse me, everybody, but this is my friend," announced Thomas, breaking the brittle air and pointing to Kyung-park, who was now standing beside him. "He is going to show me to my room."

Mrs. Kang reached over to gently touch Kyung-park's shoulder. "Thank you for being Thomas' roommate. You are a good role model."

Kyung-park grinned and bowed bashfully, before looking back at me. I gave him a thumbs-up.

"Thank you. I will try my best," he said, just as we were descended on by a small group of students clicking on their cameras.

"That's the Photography Club," said Kyung-park, pointing at the group. "That's going to be your club too."

"I like taking photos," beamed Thomas. "Excuse me, but can we go to the Boarding House now?"

"Of course. Follow me," directed Kyung-park, as the two of them bounced down the hill.

As Mrs. Kang and Jake followed me up the steps into the reception area, I noticed Jake was still transfixed on me. I was starting to feel more and more uncomfortable.

"Don't worry. He is my friend," whispered Mrs. Kang, noticing my bewilderment. "You need to listen to what he has to say," she continued conspiratorially, leaning closer, as we stopped in front of the Reception Desk.

"Do you have tea?" Jake asked, following behind us. "I always like to talk over tea."

"Tea? Yes … yes, just a minute," I stammered, turning to Koji, who was eavesdropping from behind the reception counter. This was getting more mysterious by the minute.

"Koji, can you take Jake and Mrs. Kang to my office? I'll

177

go and see if Peg can get us some tea."

When I returned to my office a few minutes later, Mrs. Kang sprang from her seat in a rush of excitement and grabbed my hands. "Oh, Mr. Gower, Thomas couldn't sleep last night because he was so excited to come here."

"I am so gratified to hear that," motioning for her to sit back down. I carefully lowered myself to my usual chair, moving it slightly towards Mrs. Kang, but just opposite to where Jake had chosen to sit. His eyes continued to focus on mine, and the feeling of unease didn't let up.

"Well, I do hope Thomas enjoys it here," I added. "It sounds like he really needs a stable environment like Cothbert."

Mrs. Kang nodded, trying to hold back her emotions.

We were interrupted by a faint knock on the door, and Peg entered carrying a tea-service, placing it on the table in front of us.

"Thank you, Peg," I said, reaching for the teapot. "Don't worry, Mrs. Kang, we will work hard with Thomas. He's a lovely boy. You should be very proud of him."

"Thank you, Mr. Gower. I trust you."

I poured Mrs. Kang and Jake their tea and then settled into my chair. The word *trust* touched a raw nerve, reminding me of the incredible responsibility with which I had been entrusted.

With the exception of the occasional slurp of tea or clink of a teaspoon against a porcelain cup, the room became oppressively silent. Although Jake was actively drinking tea, his eyes never ceased their ongoing assessment of me, and the tension growing inside of me was becoming untenable. I wasn't sure where the conversation was heading when Mrs. Kang abruptly rose to her feet.

"I must go now. I wait in the car. You two have to talk. Thank you for looking after my son," she said, grasping my hand tightly with both of hers as she had done before. Mrs. Kang quietly left, and the overwhelming silence returned.

"So," I said, finally, feeling totally unnerved by the perpetual staring, "Jake, you mentioned you have something important to talk to me about?"

Jake rose from his chair and moved to my office window. "Please call me Zhou. You have a beautiful campus."

"Thank you. It didn't always look this good. We had to put a lot of work into it before we opened in September."

"Yes. The Major explained it all to us. She said that you and another guy have spent a lot of time working on this school."

I felt guilty about being so hard on the Major. She really did see what was going on, after all.

"A year ago, I was like you," continued Zhou. "Married to my stressful job, always on call, and without balance in my life."

"You were a school principal?" I asked.

"No, much worse than that," he laughed. "I was an investment advisor for one of the wealthiest families in Macau. But after years of dealing with their demanding personalities, I became burnt out. I knew that if I didn't take control of my life, the only direction I would be heading was straight downhill.

"What did you do?"

"I checked myself into a monastery in central Taiwan."

"A monastery?"

"Yes. I decided to become a monk."

"A monk? You're a monk?"

179

Zhou smiled at my reaction. "Were you expecting someone who looks like the Dalai Lama?"

"Actually, yes," I replied, sharing in his amusement.

"It only lasted a year, but it changed my outlook on life forever. But enough about me. Let's move onto you."

"Okay," I said, hesitating.

"When I became a monk, I had to go through a grueling spiritual and self-reflective process, much of which involved learning to trust my intuition. Before I left the monastery, I was taught that my spiritual transformation would not be complete until I shared my wisdom with three other people."

"Any three people?"

"No. We were told the three people would, in their own way, come to us; that we would feel an instant connection the moment we met them."

"Let me guess," I said. "You think I'm one of those people."

"When Mrs. Kang recounted her initial meeting with you and how you dealt with her son, and when I heard from the Major about the struggles you went through starting this school, I felt as though you might be one of my three people. But when I finally met you, this young, ambitious principal, it was as though I was hit with a surge of electricity. My intuition spoke to me. You, Phil Gower, are one of my chosen ones—one of the three people I must give back to."

Chapter 20

One morning, I was walking around the corner of the School House when I thought I heard bursts of foreign chatter coming from a radio somewhere. All at once, Byung-ju came barreling past me, yelling at something he had in his hand. He was wearing a tattered, wide-brimmed sable fedora.

"Byung-ju!" I yelled back.

Byung-ju slid to a stop, trying to conceal what was in his hand. "Yes, Teacher?"

"First of all, my name is not teacher—it's Mr. Gower. Second, the next time you run by a teacher, please stop and say hello. Remember to always be polite."

"Yes, Teacher."

"What have you got in your hand there, anyway?" I asked.

He gave me one of his sideways looks, his eyes taking on the pained expression of a student having to explain why he didn't do his homework.

"Byung-ju?" I said in a sterner voice.

"It's a *talkie-walkie*," he said, finally. "Mother gave it to me for my last birthday."

"You mean walkie-talkie."

"Yes, *talkie-walkie*."

"So, who's on the other end?"

"Number 2 *talkie-walkie*."

"Yes, I know that, but who are you talking to on your number 2 walkie-talkie?"

"My friend, Bo-sung. We play *Indiana Jones and the Cothbert of Doom*."

"You mean *Temple of Doom?*"

Byung-ju didn't respond.

"Okay, have fun. But remember your manners, Byung-ju."

"Yes, Teacher," he acknowledged with a half bow, tearing off.

A few days later, Chill came striding into my office looking less than pleased.

"I want you to know, I had a very unpleasant incident with Byung-ju today," she said, fidgeting with the bun on her head. "He was so rude in my class—swearing and slamming his fists against the wall. His behavior really disrupted the *qi* in my class."

"The *qi*?"

"The yin and the yang; the balance of our inner beings. He disturbed life's equilibrium."

"Byung-ju did all this by himself?"

"Yes... like I said, you need to have a talk with him."

"Did you try talking to him yourself?"

"I was too emotionally upset. My *qi* was grossly out of alignment after his inappropriate behavior."

"Okay, I'll talk to him, but you know, in the future, you need to take ownership of classroom management issues like these."

She looked back at me in puzzlement as though I had just spoken in a foreign language.

182

"Okay, tell him to meet me at my office before afternoon classes begin," I sighed.

Just after lunch, I found Byung-ju sitting outside my office, grumbling to himself in Korean.

"Please come in, Byung-ju."

I seated myself behind my desk and waved him forward, keeping him standing.

"What exactly happened in Ms. Whipplehill's class today?"

"I got angry," he scowled, flicking back his hair and crossing his arms.

"Did she do something to make you angry?"

"Not her. Someone else."

"Who?"

"The person who stole my number 2 *talkie-walkie*."

"And who was that?"

"I don't know. Major crime."

"I understand you are angry, Byung-ju, but Ms. Whipplehill found your behavior in class today very rude."

"I'm sorry," he said, craning his neck forward into a bow.

"It's not me you need to say sorry to. You must apologize to Ms. Whipplehill."

He looked up, nodded his head, and bent it back down again.

"I will ask our caretaker if he has seen your walkie-talkie."

"*Talkie-walkie* gone. Stolen," he said, his head still bent. "Criminal element."

"All right, off you go."

He bowed profusely and then zoomed out the door.

The weather continued to be seasonably warm during the first few weeks of school and, one afternoon, Harris convinced me that the two of us should take advantage of the Adirondack chairs on the dock. We had been cooped up in my office for most of the morning, discussing evaluation and reporting strategies, and I had to admit the prospect of continuing the conversation outside, beside the beauty of Timberline Lake, sounded far more enticing.

We gathered our paperwork and made our way down the hill to the wooden stairs that led to the beach. Just as we were about to descend the steps, Myrtle came bounding over, huffing and puffing.

"I need to talk with you both about Byung-ju," she said, trying to catch her breath.

"Not again. What's he done this time?" I asked.

"Chill told me she caught him spouting off inappropriate comments about Germans."

"Germans?"

"It's probably all part of the whole Indiana Jones persona," said Harris. "I seem to recall in those movies, there were some Nazi grave robbers who wanted to get their hands on the Holy Grail."

"I don't remember those movies," said Myrtle, indifferently. "And anyway, Harris, that's not the point. We can't have him parading around campus pretending we are under siege from the Germans. It's just not appropriate."

"I hear you," said Harris. "Where is he now?"

"I think he's in the Canoeing Club with Pancho, so he should be on the beach. I was just about to check in with Pancho to see if he needed my help. Do you want me to get Byung-ju and send him up to you?"

"No, don't bother," I replied. "Harris and I were on our way to the beach anyway. You know, as stubborn as he appears,

Byung-ju is a pretty smart boy. He responds to reason… with some persuasion. He just needs to work on his EQ."

"Thank you," said Myrtle. "Let me know how it goes. I promised Chill I would get back to her about how we were going to deal with him."

"How's everything else going in the Boarding House?" I asked cautiously.

"Phil, I can honestly say I've never been happier. The kids are wonderful. Tonight, I'm having some of the girls over to my suite," she said, sounding like an excited teenager. "It's the Huang twins' birthday tomorrow, you know, and we're going to bake them a cake."

"I was positive you'd be great at all this, Myrtle. You're such a natural."

"Thank you, Phil. Thank you both for believing in me."

Harris gave her an affectionate tap on the shoulder.

"Well, Phil and I must be off to see what our intrepid Indiana Byung-ju has been up to," he announced, turning towards the stairs to the beach.

As we navigated our way down the wooden steps, I thought about Myrtle's comment about having to report back to Chill.

"Harris, what's your take on Chill?"

"Well, from what I've observed, whenever she has a hiccup, she expects others to come to her rescue. I visited a few of her classes. She's not a bad teacher, but I think she struggles with troubleshooting. My suggestion with people like her is to give them some responsibility; put them in charge of something where they have no choice but to make some of their own decisions."

That's not a bad idea, I thought.

185

We arrived on the beach and were greeted by fairly strong gusts of wind. Closer to the Beach House, the Canoeing Club was in full swing, and Pancho was demonstrating how to do a roll-up with a canoe in preparation for portaging. Two orange pylons had been set up so each participant could practice portaging their canoe from point A to point B. As the exercise continued to unfold, a series of overturned red and green canoes with stubby legs started to emerge, each one wobbling and swaying its way between the two pylons.

"Everything okay?" I asked Pancho, who was lashing some paddles to the thwarts of a canoe. He was in bare feet and wearing reflective sunglasses, a blue cap, a yellow windbreaker, and salmon-colored shorts.

"Yes. Great! It's been a bit windy, so I've been teaching them some dry land procedures. The wind's supposed to ease off tonight, so Myrtle and I are hoping to get them out on the lake tomorrow."

"Have you seen Byung-ju around?"

"I just took attendance, and he hasn't arrived yet. He's always a bit of a straggler."

"Oh, look, there he is," said Harris, pointing to an area further up the beach.

"Why don't you let me deal with this," I suggested, handing over my paperwork to Harris. "I've built a bit of a relationship with him. I'll meet you back at the Adirondack chairs."

"Sounds good," he said, strolling off.

As I trudged through the sand towards Byung-ju, I could already see that he was intensely focused on his walkie-talkie again, holding it up against his ear. All at once, he moved the device in front of his face and leaned into it.

"Fuck you!" he screamed at it. "Fuck you!"

"Byung-ju," I hollered.

Byung-ju jumped and stood at attention. "Yes, Teacher?"

"Don't *Yes, Teacher me*," I yelled, getting closer to him. "What sort of language is that?"

"They stole my *talkie-walkie*!"

"Who stole your walkie-talkie?"

"The Germans."

"Now look, Byung-ju, you can't pretend that all the bad guys in your Indiana Jones game are Germans. It's not nice. In fact, it's racist."

"Not a game. No racist. True. Listen," he said, handing me his walkie-talkie.

I held the device up to my ear. At first, I could only hear static and then some chatter—chatter that was unmistakably being spoken in German.

Byung-ju bent over the walkie-talkie in my hand. "Shut up!" he screamed into it.

"Byung-ju!" I reprimanded, raising my voice again.

"Major criminal element found. Germans stole my *talkie-walkie*, Teacher."

"Listen, I will check on all of this, but I don't want to hear any more bad language. And no more comments about the Germans! Do you understand me?"

He nodded but was clearly not impressed with my reluctance to support his German conspiracy theory.

"Now, give me your walkie-talkie and go to canoeing. You're already late."

He gave me his usual suspicious sideways glance and then slapped the walkie-talkie into my hand, running towards the Beach House.

When I rejoined the group, I could see Byung-ju sitting on

the sand beside the Beach House, bent over with his head resting on his hands.

"Stop pouting!" I ordered. "Mr. de Metz is waiting for you."

"What is pouting, Teacher?"

ESL, Phil. ESL.

"Stop sitting there feeling sorry for yourself!"

Pancho heard us talking and came walking over.

"Hi, Byung-ju, where have you been? I've been looking for you everywhere. You're late, you know. Hey, by the way, last week when you returned your life jacket to the Boathouse, you left one of your walkie-talkie sets behind. It's still hanging on a hook in there."

Byung-ju looked up at Pancho, his eyes almost doubling in size. He jumped up, spraying Pancho and me with sand, and dove inside the Beach House, reappearing with his second walkie-talkie and a look as though he had found his long-lost pet.

"Byung-ju, come here," I ordered.

He shuffled towards me shamefacedly.

"Now, first, you can see that your missing walkie-talkie had nothing to do with the Germans. Am I correct?"

"Yes, Teacher," he said, bowing.

"Second, your behavior back there was very rude, and your language was very, very bad. I want to see you at recess tomorrow in my office for detention. Now hand me that walkie-talkie," I ordered. "You'll get your set back after you serve detention."

Byung-ju reluctantly handed over the unit, bowed, and slinked towards the rest of the students in the Canoe Club.

By the time I made it over to the Adirondack chairs, Harris

was fast asleep, a used cigar smoldering on his chair's armrest.

"Harris," I said, touching his arm.

Harris opened his eyes and looked up at me, dazed.

"You're back, oh chosen one," he chortled. He had been relentless in his teasing about my meeting with Zhou the monk. "How'd it go with Harrison Ford Junior?"

"Frustrating. Always calling me Teacher," I said, settling into my chair.

Harris sat up. "I'm not surprised. In many Asian schools, there is this type of impersonal distance that exists between student and teacher. A teacher is frequently referred to simply as Teacher. I wouldn't take it personally. He'll start using your name once he adapts to our approach. Anyway, what happened with his *talkie-walkie?*"

I recounted the whole episode while Harris roared loudly.

"I still don't understand where the German language was coming from, though," I said, joining in the amusement.

"Oh, I do," snorted Harris, who was now howling. "See that house next door to the school?" He pointed to a massive log house with a green metallic roof.

"Yes."

"It's owned by the Müllers—the Müllers from Germany. I've visited them on a few occasions, and, as I recall, their whole house is wired with a remote intercom system so they can keep track of their kids. If I was a betting man, I'd say their intercom system is programmed to the exact same frequency as Byung-ju's *talkie-walkies*. So, expect Indiana Byung-ju to hear back from the Germans."

Chapter 21

In order to provide Myrtle with some downtime and for all of us to get to know the students better, every week we would each take one evening duty in the Boarding House. This meant making sure the students remained quiet during their two-hour homework time, otherwise known as *Prep*, distributing evening snacks, then remaining on call after *Prep* while the students used the campus facilities. Finally, and most importantly, we ensured roll call and lights out were called just before ten, at which point we would hand the house and the responsibilities back to Myrtle.

It was following one such evening duty, when I was on my way out the door of the Boarding House, that the familiar stillness of the night was shattered by a piercing scream. As I turned in circles, frantically looking through the darkness for the source, a second, higher-pitched shriek sent a chill surging through my body. It appeared to be coming from the girls' section of the Boarding House, and in my haste to race back inside, I almost tripped over Tofu who, in his excitement, was running around, yapping frantically. Myrtle flung open her door, tearing out of her suite when she saw me.

"Phil, what's happened?" she screeched, her face contorted

with alarm.

Before I could answer, Koji came dashing down the stairs, hastily tossing on a navy-blue housecoat. "Hai! Who is screaming?" he panted.

"I have no idea," I called out impatiently, racing up the stairs two at a time. But before I could get very far, a parade of girls in assorted nightgowns came barreling past me, yelling at the top of their lungs, followed by a second wave of students, including many of the boys in pajamas, obviously curious to find out what was going on.

"Alright!" I yelled in frustration, flattening myself against the stairwell. "Enough! Everyone to the Common Room! Now!"

In the short time it took Myrtle, Koji, and me to follow the students into the Common Room, they had crammed themselves tightly onto both of the red couches, with several balancing on the armrests while others sat huddled on the floor by their feet. On the opposite side of the room, the rest of the students were bunched together, intensely engaged in whispered conversations.

"Okay, who would like to tell me what happened?"

In unison, all the girls swiveled their heads towards a small, fragile-looking girl named Portia Lu, who was sitting beside the fireplace, shaking and obviously distraught. Her roommate, Cho-he Park, was trying her best to console her.

"Portia? What happened?" I asked gently.

Portia appeared to be dazed and totally unable to stop her teeth from chattering. She looked at me mutely with eyes the size of saucers. Cho-he glanced up and spoke for her friend: "She saw a ghost."

The room reverberated with audible gasps.

"A ghost?"

"Yes! She was walking down the hall to go to the toilet. She saw a woman dressed in a pink robe coming for her."

"Are you sure it wasn't Ms. Green?"

"Oh, I don't own a pink robe," said Myrtle, shaking her head vehemently while patting the quilted blue dressing gown she was wearing.

Thank you, Myrtle. That really helps to diffuse the situation.

"Did anyone else see this ghost?"

Everyone shook their heads.

"First, let me reassure you, there are no such things as ghosts…"

"Yes, there are," piped up Albert Lam. "My grandmother saw one once. We had to take her to the village temple to get her cleaned."

"Mine too," confirmed another boy, Paxton Peng, nodding his head in agreement.

I looked on dumbfounded and wished Harris was here to advise me.

"Listen," I said calmly. "It could be that Portia saw a reflection that *looked* like a ghost. No one else has seen this ghost, and Ms. Green has been living in this Boarding House by herself for a very long time," then, turning to Myrtle, "You've never seen a ghost, have you, Ms. Green?"

"Never!" she replied, jiggling her head with such force that her dangling curlers clicked together like castanets. "I certainly wouldn't live here if there were a ghost —that's for sure."

Thank you again, Myrtle. Very supportive!

"So, I think we all need to go back to bed. There is no ghost," I reiterated firmly.

It was obvious to me that many of the students were very shaken by this incident and not entirely convinced that what I was saying was true, but slowly, in small groups, they began filtering out of the room, heads together in muffled conversation. Myrtle went over to Portia and put her arm around her.

"Do you want to sleep in my suite tonight, dearie?"

"No, thank you, Ms. Green. I'll go with Cho-he," she said, reaching for Cho-he's hand. Together, they rose from the chair and haltingly made their way up the stairs.

The normal chatter and laughter were missing in the Dining Hall the next morning, and I could sense that some of the students were still very much on edge. I sat down beside Myrtle, who was positioning a band-aid on the face of one of the older boys, who had attempted shaving for the first time.

"How were things after I left last night?" I asked, with trepidation, as soon as the boy walked away.

"It took them a while to settle down. They needed time to talk everything through, I guess. But a number of them did agree with what you said about there being no ghosts. They ended up accusing the worrywarts of being troublemakers."

"Well, that's not going to help things, either," I said, showing my frustration.

"Good morning!" announced Harris, dropping himself onto a chair beside us, his cup of coffee balanced on a plate loaded with scrambled eggs and bacon. "Why is it so quiet in here?"

I described the whole ghost episode, anticipating one of his flip responses. But his reaction was not what I expected.

"We really need to watch all this," he said, scooping up some eggs. "It's no use saying ghosts don't exist. These students come from families who are highly superstitious. Many of them celebrate special days, where the goal is to keep the ghosts of their ancestors at bay. I can tell you, if their parents get wind of the fact our school has a ghost we can't control, we'll have a mini-crisis on our hands."

"But our school doesn't have a ghost," I retorted, angrily.

"Relax! I'm just saying, we need to look at all of this through their eyes," said Harris, slurping back his coffee. "Listen, I'm on duty in the Boarding House tonight. Let me get a pulse of the situation."

While satisfied with Harris' explanations and support, I was still barely able to get through my daily routine of teaching English, responding to phone calls, and trying to be nice to the Major because my mind was squarely focused on the alleged haunting of Cothbert. By evening, the situation was slowly beginning to wear on me, and that night, I could barely sleep in anticipation of what new drama Harris would have to share at breakfast the following day.

"Before you ask," Harris began, laying down his breakfast plate, "it was quiet over there last night—but, as far as I'm concerned, it was too quiet. The atmosphere felt like a ticking time bomb — ready to explode at any moment."

"Wonderful analogy, Harris!" I said curtly. "If that's really the case, then we'd better have a staff meeting before the start of classes this morning so everyone's brought up to speed. I'm not in the mood for any bombs."

"I don't disagree. Like I said before, we need to handle this situation delicately."

194

The impromptu meeting was held in my office, where Harris decided to give a crash course on how certain Asian countries view the afterlife. Even Chill, who I thought wouldn't appreciate the importance of any of this, was feverishly taking notes and seemed intensely interested in what Harris had to say.

"The key," concluded Harris, "is to listen, be understanding, and not to judge. If you see or hear anything unusual, let Phil or me know, and we'll come and help you."

For the next few days, Harris and I were on tenterhooks, waiting for all hell to break loose in the Boarding House, but things remained quiet. Then, late one evening just as we thought the whole incident had finally blown over, the phone in my apartment rang.

"Phil, it's Ida. I'm really sorry to bother you so late, but I'm on Boarding Duty this evening, and there's been another ghost sighting — this time in the boys' section."

"Who saw the ghost?" I asked, tensing up.

"Albert Lam. He gave the same description as Portia Wu; a lady in a pink robe came running toward him."

"What's the mood like over there now?"

"Not great, but we were able to convince everyone to go back to bed. Unfortunately, not before some of them made phone calls home."

"And Albert?"

"He was quite unsettled, but Myrtle and his brother, Stanley calmed him down. He was one of the ones who phoned home ... to Hong Kong, I think."

"Oh brother! Okay then, I better convene another early-morning meeting tomorrow to get a handle on all of this,"

I said dejectedly. "Thanks for looking after everything, Ida. And I'm really sorry you had to stay up so late for this."

"Not to worry. Like Harris said, we can't judge them. We just need to convince them that everything's okay. See you tomorrow, Phil."

At our meeting the next morning, Harris proposed an idea he and I had been brainstorming. It involved having the evening person remain on duty for an extra hour each night after everyone was in bed, and physically sitting on a chair in the hallway to help reassure the students that everything was okay. We did, however, concede that it was a short-term solution.

Chill raised her hand.

"Yes, Chill," said Harris, not sounding like he was in the mood for any of her zany input.

"Like … I'm okay with the extra duty time, but have you guys considered an exorcism? I think I know somebody who could do one for us."

"An exorcism?" I exclaimed, incredulously.

"Yeah, you know," said Pancho, humming the theme song to the movie *The Exorcist.* "One of those spiritual cleansing things."

Myrtle started to jiggle on the other side of the table.

"Go on, Chill," said Harris, giving her the benefit of the doubt.

"Well … I was telling one of my friends in Vancouver about our ghost dilemma, and she said there is this elder guy in the Chinese community who performs exorcisms. A lot of Chinese businesses have used his services over the years."

"He's a ghost buster?" asked Pancho, smirking.

"I guess so … yeah, you could call him that," said Chill earnestly, completely oblivious to Pancho's sarcasm.

"Well, I think we should consider approaching him," said Ida. "It doesn't really matter what any of us believes. It's the students we need to convince. Otherwise, the situation could get worse. The optics of a full-blown exorcism, as ridiculous as they may look to us, might actually do the trick."

"I agree with Ida," said Myrtle, who I could tell had become more unsettled since the second ghost sighting.

"Chill, can you make some calls and see whether I can have a chat with this exorcist guy?" I asked, not really believing I was even considering such a wacky idea. "I'll cover your first-period class for you."

"Sure."

"In the meantime, the rest of us need to keep this under wraps," added Harris. "I know it's a bit of a stretch for some of you, but, as Ida pointed out, the status quo is not really an option."

Everyone nodded in agreement.

"Mum's the word," added a tired-looking Koji.

As the bell for period 2 chimed, I was just walking out of the class I'd been covering when Chill came running in, panting.

"I got hold of him … the exorcist guy," she said, catching her breath.

"And?" I asked quickly. "Will he talk to us?"

I was almost sounding eager.

"Yes! He said he'd give you a call later this afternoon. Got to get to class. See you," she chirped, charging off.

The exorcist guy. Sounds like one of those self-help gurus.

Shortly before clubs, Koji buzzed through to my office.

197

"There is a Master Shen Wang on the line who wants to speak with you."

"Thanks, Koji," I said, inhaling deeply and then pressing the flashing button on my phone.

"Master Wang, thank you for phoning back. This is Phil Gower," I said, exhaling.

"Uh-huh," came a soft voice. "What happened, Mr. Gower?" he asked, forgoing any pleasantries.

I explained the two ghost sightings in the Boarding House.

"Uh-huh. I see. So, has anyone ever died at your school before?"

"Died? Ah, no … not that I'm aware of. There was a fire at the school, if that helps."

"Uh-huh. I see … no, doesn't help. What about grave-yards?"

"Graveyards?"

"Are there any near your school?"

"Oh, I see. Um, no!" I responded, wondering where he was going with his line of questioning.

"And your students, you say, are all from Asia?"

"Yes."

"International students?"

"That's right."

"When did they arrive, exactly?"

"About a month ago."

"Uh-huh. I see. Interesting."

There was a brief moment of silence, and then Master Wang cleared his throat.

"Based on your situation, I believe your ghost followed your students from Asia because it is not happy they aban-doned their ancestors. It is trying to scare them into returning home."

A plausible explanation, I thought.

"Okay, Master Wang, thanks for that. But, can you help us get rid of our ghost?"

"Uh-huh. I'll be there tomorrow morning to perform an exorcism. That should fix your issue," he replied, sounding like a plumber, scheduling an appointment to unclog a blocked drain.

"How much do you charge for this type of service?"

"A donation of $300 should be enough. Cash only. No tax receipt."

Donation. Interesting choice of words.

"After you finish your exorcism, will we be able to convince the students the ghost has really gone and won't return?"

"If you need me to put a full-blown anti-ghost curse on your entire campus to make sure there will be no more ghosts in the future, that will be another $100. Cash only."

More donating.

"I see," I replied, not sounding like I really did. "Okay, let's go for the full monty."

"Pardon?"

"The full service — the $400 service you just mentioned. Let's go with that. I'll meet you at our Boarding House tomorrow," I said, giving him our address. "Does 10:30 am work for you?"

"Uh-huh."

"Is there anything you need from us for this exorcism?"

"Yes, I will need all the doors to the Boarding House left open. Also, I will require one of your student's suitcases. I will be setting fire to it."

Of course, you will!

After dinner, I had a quick follow-up staff meeting.

"So, the exorcism is a go," I announced, realizing how stupid that sounded. "The plan is to have all the students in front of the Boarding House no later than 10:00 am for a fire drill. Following the drill, Master Wang will arrive, at which point I will explain to everyone that, as a precaution, I have invited him to perform a special exorcism that will prevent ghosts from ever being able to come on our campus."

"Will they be able to witness the exorcism?" asked Ida.

"Yes, but only if they want to."

"That's good. I think some of them may need to experience the event as a type of catharsis."

"Yes, but, if any of them feel upset about some of this, we'll need to take them back to the School House," added Harris. "This may not be everyone's cup of tea."

"Just out of interest, what are you going to tell the parents?" asked Pancho.

"The truth. That we respect the fact some of our students are superstitious; that we felt it necessary to perform this ceremony because two of the students believed they saw a ghost."

The staff went quiet and stared at me. I had the feeling they were starting to question my sanity.

"That's perfect," said Ida finally.

"Yes," said Pancho. "Excellent strategy."

"Well, if we pull this whole thing off, we'll have Chill to thank for it all," said Harris.

"Thank you, Chill," said Myrtle, with a bit of desperation in her voice.

Chill put her arm over Myrtle's shoulder. "It'll all work out, Myrtle. You'll see."

"Oh, and Koji, I'll need $400 from petty cash," I added.

"Hai! I'll get onto it ASAP."

That evening, still feeling anxious about everything, I decided to visit the Boarding House to check in on things. I noticed, as I exited the School House, Millicent's BMW sitting in the parking lot again. When I arrived, it was already Prep, and Pancho was manning the fort in the Duty Office on the main floor.

"So far, so good," he said, raising his thumb when he saw me. I grabbed some water from a nearby cooler and sat facing him.

"Pancho, I know you think this whole exorcism idea is a bit of a crock, but I do hope you understand our reasoning behind it all."

"I do," he responded, seriously. "I was just trying to provide a bit of levity during our meetings. I meant no disrespect. I know this ghost thing is very real for some of these kids."

"It's interesting, isn't it?" I said out loud.

"What is?"

"You know, how, depending on your cultural upbringing, you can have such a different world view."

Pancho smiled. "Or, maybe you're overthinking everything and that ghosts just prefer to live in Asia."

"That's possible too," I said, laughing.

Our conversation was interrupted by the backfiring of an engine and the squealing of brakes outside the office window. This was followed by some clattering noises and swearing, and then the sound of the front door to the Boarding House being flung open. Pancho and I walked out of the Duty Office.

"Gower, I want a word with you," demanded the Major, looking up at us from her chair. Then, noticing Pancho, "In private!"

Pancho flashed me an anxious look. "I'll go make the rounds," he said, quickly walking to the stairs.

The Major wheeled into the Duty Office, and as soon as I moved behind the desk, she slammed the door.

"*Koojie* brought me this receipt to sign for $400—for a frickin exorcism!" she yelled, slamming the offending paper down on the table. "What sort of crap is this?" she challenged, her face slowly beginning to flush with anger. "Do you understand how tight things are around here right now?"

"Major, we have a serious situation in the Boarding House. Some of the students have been seeing ghosts…"

"I really think you and the big guy have lost it this time. Kids see ghosts all the time. It doesn't mean we need to piss away money on hiring some Voodoo doctor."

I knew this conversation wasn't going to go anywhere, but I didn't really care what the Major thought at this point.

"Major, this is a cultural issue," I said calmly. "If we don't handle it sensitively, your students will end up going home and we won't have a school to run. As for pissing away your money, if you don't trust our judgment, then I'll pay the $400 myself. Now, do you need me to help put your chair back on your golf cart?"

Ignoring me, the Major clumsily maneuvered her way out of the office, spouting her mantra about how educators have no business sense. A few moments later, the clattering and swearing returned until finally, the sound of her golf cart could be heard sputtering off into the darkness.

By 9:30 a.m. the next morning, the students were rapidly pushing each other out the front door of the School House, clearly motivated by the fact they were missing class. I grabbed my coat and followed behind, as Harris and Koji came walking up from the rear. When I recounted the previous night's confrontation with Harris, he just shook his head in disgust.

"It's getting worse," I added. "She seemed particularly angry this time. And, I don't really understand her comment about things being tight. My budgeting shows we are well within the black."

"Joe warned us something else was going on," Harris admonished. "We really need to get our hands on her books!"

"Here's your money," interrupted Koji, handing me four one-hundred-dollar bills.

"What?" I said, looking up, surprised. "The Major gave you permission to release this?"

"Yes. She changed her mind when she got an angry fax from Grandmother Lam this morning. Grandmother threatened the Major to take the boys home if she doesn't scare away the ghost."

"Ah, her good old drinking buddy," said Harris, sniggering. "It's just amazing who she puts her trust in."

"It's not about trust," I added. "It's her bank account she's worried about."

"Touché! Look who's finally seen the light."

The fire drill was uneventful, and as Harris gave some final reminders to the students about what to do in the event of a real fire, I was starting to get a little concerned that Master Wang was not coming when a few of the students pointed towards a rather odd-shaped yellow vehicle hopping its way down the road towards us. It had a frame like a van, but was stubby with an extra-high roof. As it pulled up in front of us, a large man wearing yellow ceremonial robes with an unusually tall, crown-like hat on his head stepped out. His shiny, layered attire, with its red and blue embroidered images of snakes and dragons, ballooned in the breeze, capturing the undivided attention of the assembled students and staff.

"That looks like the man who cleaned my grandmother," said Albert Lam.

"Welcome, Master Wang," I said, stepping forward. "I'm Phil Gower."

"Uh huh. Let's begin," he replied, looking bored.

He opened the hatch to his van and removed two over-sized bags.

"Do you have my money?" he asked, like I was about to purchase contraband.

"Yes. You want it now?"

"Uh huh."

"Master Wang, I would like to introduce you to the students before you begin, if that's alright," I said, counting out his four hundred dollars and handing them to him.

"Uh huh," he responded, re-counting the money. "That's fine."

As I gathered the students around me, it was obvious they were more than intrigued by our flamboyant visitor.

"This is Master Wang," I announced. "I have invited him here today because two of you think you saw a ghost."

The eyes of many of the students started to widen as they took this statement in.

"As I said to you before, I don't think there was ever a ghost. But it is important we treat what people believe with respect. Master Wang is an elder from the Chinese community, and he will perform what is called an *exorcism* — a ceremony that has been proven to scare away ghosts."

Nervous chatter erupted.

"Quiet, please," I demanded. "Now, before we get going, I have an unusual request. As part of this ceremony, Master Wang will need to burn an empty suitcase belonging to one of you."

Everyone started to laugh.

"Of course, if we end up burning your case, the school will pay you for a new one of equal value. Does anyone want to volunteer their case?"

"I will," said Stanley Lam, raising his hand. "I want to support my brother. I believe what he said about a ghost is true."

"Thank you, Stanley. That's very kind of you."

"Mr. Gower?" called Harris from the back. "I wanted to mention that if anyone is not comfortable watching this ceremony, I will personally walk you back to the School House now."

No one took him up on his offer.

I turned back to Master Wang. "In that case, I guess we can begin."

Master Wang shuffled over to the front of the Boarding House. "So, just to confirm," he said, pointing at the building, "the ghosts were seen in there, right?"

"Yes," I replied.

"Then I will begin the ceremony outside this building." He turned to Stanley. "Please go and get your suitcase and bring it to me."

Myrtle accompanied Stanley into the Boarding House, and the two of them reappeared a couple of minutes later with a dark brown suitcase embellished with beige monograms.

Master Wang opened one of his own bags and removed a large, tightly-wound bundle of wooden tinder, which he placed on the ground. He then took out a box of incense sticks and placed it on a large rock beside him. From a second bag, he pulled out a long rattle that clattered in the wind and two small, free-standing ceremonial drums.

"Who saw the ghosts?" he asked, scanning the onlooking students.

Albert eagerly raised his hand, and then Portia slowly raised hers.

Master Wang waved them both forward. "Please sit in front of a drum and wait for my instructions."

Albert and Portia did as they were told just as a now-familiar sputtering engine could be heard behind us. I turned to see the Major's golf cart coming our way and couldn't hold back a very audible groan as the cart pulled up beside me.

"Everything under control, Philly?"

"Yes, Major."

"Did my Executive Assistant give you the $400?"

"Yes, thank you."

"It's a good idea we're doing this exorcist thing, you know. It'll help keep the kids happy," she said.

Not to mention your bank account, I thought, realizing this was the closest I was going to get to an apology.

"Agreed, Major."

"Has the voodoo guy started yet?"

"He's just about to."

"Good. We can watch him together."

We were now best-buddies.

Master Wang began by untying the tinder, which was made up of various sizes of dried wooden sticks and fashioned them carefully into a pyramid shape. Then, taking a lighter from inside his robe, he lit the pile of sticks, which, once ignited, soon became a small fire. Next, he pulled out a miniature gold box from his robe and emptied a small amount of pink-colored powder into one of his hands.

"Start beating your drums!" he commanded, looking at Albert and Portia.

The two of them pounded in a rather discordant fashion. A few moments later, Master Wang began prancing around the fire with accentuated leg movements, waving a rattle over his head, swinging it from side to side as it jingled and clanged. Chanting loud incantations in Chinese, his eyes rolled back as he fell into a type of trance. All at once, he dusted a liberal amount of the pinkish powder from his hand, cascading it over the fire. There was a loud bang, followed by crackling noises and then a surge of pink and blue flames. The students reacted by oohing and aahing, like they were watching a fireworks demonstration.

"Quite the showman, eh, Philly?" said the Major, looking up at me.

"Yes, Major."

Master Wang's performance went on for about twenty minutes, with the students getting more and more excited with every release of the pink powder. At last, Master Wang signaled to Stanley to drop his luggage into the fire, which, by this time, had grown considerably in size. Another liberal toss of the pink powder caused the luggage to ignite and almost evaporate before everyone's eyes. The students reacted to this performance with enthusiastic cheering.

"That's grandmother Lam's kid," said the Major, sitting up. "Does she know we just set fire to her grandson's luggage?"

"Not yet, Major. He just volunteered it as part of the ceremony. I told him the school would reimburse him for a new case."

The Major's face started to twitch, but she remained quiet.

"Your campus is clean," proclaimed Master Wang, signaling to Albert and Portia to stop drumming. "But, just in case there is a ghost still hiding out in the Boarding House, I will now get rid of it," he assured the onlookers, reaching for the bundle of incense sticks he had left on the rock and lighting them. Holding the wad in his right hand, he waved it about as a woody fragrance started to waft through the air. With his left hand, he shook his rattle and recommenced the loud incantations in Chinese.

As he had requested, all the Boarding House doors had been left open, and Master Wang entered the building, where we could hear his incantations reverberating from within. As he wove his way through the building, we caught glimpses of yellow flashes from some of the bedroom windows. At last, he walked back out the front door, and as he did, I could have sworn I felt a rush of cold air.

"If there was a ghost in here, it is gone. Your Boarding House and campus are now completely safe," he announced. "It is impossible for a ghost to exist here any longer."

The cheering began once again as the students reacted to this reassuring proclamation.

"Thank you, Master Wang. Thank you very much. You have been a big help," I said, feeling a palpable release of tension among some of the students.

"Yes, thanks Mr. Wing," said the Major, who had wheeled herself up beside him. "I'm Major Harriet Hunter. I own this place."

"Uh huh," replied Master Wang, starting to repack his bags.

"I guess we won't be seeing you again," said the Major, half-jokingly.

"My guarantee is only good for five years," he replied with a straight face, closing the hatch of his van.

I decided not to pursue any additional insurance policy. *No more donations.*

Chapter 22

An evening stroll through the campus was a rare and luxurious event. The bustle of Cothbert life meant there was always something to deal with: a Harris-Major skirmish, student-roommate conflicts, curricular challenges, behavioral issues, or complaints about the food. But tonight, with the full moon overhead, the crisp air carrying the scent of autumn, and campus lights accentuating the red and orange hues of fall, the simplicity of life felt within reach again.

Tofu had joined me for his nightly walk. He was on high alert for squirrels and the Major's ultimate nemeses, the pesky raccoons, lurking in the woods and ready to descend on any discarded dinner leftovers that made it to the trash.

Tofu gave a few yaps as something in the woods moved, but then lost interest when he realized his more immediate priority was to leave a territorial mark on his favorite tree. As we continued our stroll, his intermittent yapping reminded the world not to mess with him. Then, all at once, something triggered a deep, low growl. He crouched down, staring at the watch tower—a building so out of place on campus that it was easy to forget it even existed.

I stared at the strange edifice, unable to imagine what had possessed someone to build something so inappropriate for a school. For a moment, I thought I saw a flicker of motion in one of the top windows. I squinted, but there was nothing.

Probably my imagination, I thought.

Tofu growled more intensely, as if urging me to take a second look. Then I saw it—something flitting from one window to the next.

Could the ghost have returned? Surely not. I had a five-year guarantee from Master Wang. We were still under warranty.

I froze as faint voices drifted from inside the tower. Tofu heard them too, his agitation growing with each passing second.

I obviously had to find out who was inside the building, but I wasn't taking my furry friend along—he'd blow my cover. I dashed back to the Boarding House and left Tofu with Myrtle. As I prepared to head out again, Koji came down the stairs.

"Hi, Mr. Phil. Are you here to visit boarders?"

"No, Koji. I'm checking on something else," I said, explaining what I'd seen and heard.

"Oh, I come with you," he said, getting excited. "We be like Hardy Boys solving mystery."

"How do you know about the Hardy Boys?"

"My ESL teacher used old Hardy Boys books to teach me English."

Not a bad idea, I thought. Maybe we should look into that for our students.

"Okay, my friend, do you want to be Frank or Joe Hardy?"

"I be Joe," he laughed.

The two of us set off on our Hardy Boys mystery-quest, arriving at the base of the watch tower a few moments later. Koji immediately spotted the same flicker of motion I had seen and gasped.

"I think I see a body?" he said.

"A body?" I asked, glancing anxiously at him. "Where?"

"Up there," he replied, pointing to the top of the tower.

"Oh, I see. You mean you saw somebody."

"Look, more bodies!" he exclaimed in a strained whisper.

I glanced up again and saw the silhouettes of two heads in the window.

"Alright! Let's do this," I blurted. "Are you ready to go in?"

"Yes," squealed Koji, like a child sneaking up on his best friend.

The front door to the tower was unlocked. I opened it slowly to avoid too much creaking, and the two of us eased ourselves inside. The moment the door closed, we were plunged into total darkness. The air was damp and musty, carrying the scent of a summer cottage sealed up for the winter.

"Damn, I should have brought a flashlight," I grumbled.

"No problem. Joe Hardy has one with keys," said Koji.

I could hear a jingle as he scrambled to pull out a keychain from his pocket. There was a soft click, and then a beam of light cut through the room. As we got our bearings, I could see shelves filled with dust-encrusted old textbooks, assorted school clothing, and some comic books that had no doubt been confiscated from delinquent students. A black, metallic spiral staircase stood in the center of the room. I signaled for Koji to follow me as we quietly began our ascent to the top floor. Fresh footprints stood out on the grimy steps, and the faint voices I'd heard before became more distinct. Then, one voice became instantly recognizable.

"Byung-ju!" we both whispered simultaneously.

We reached a small alcove at the top of the staircase. The area was dimly lit by a thin shaft of light spilling from a door left ajar. We slid ourselves over to the door, which I gently pried further open to peek inside. I could see a group of six students—four boys and two girls—sitting in front of a portable TV set with a built-in VHS cassette player. I immediately recognized a scene from the movie *Forrest Gump* being displayed on the screen. Abruptly, Byung-ju stopped the film and pointed to one of the boys seated on the floor.

"Your turn!" he announced.

The boy rose and moved in front of the group, turning to face them'.

"That's Manfred Ma," whispered Koji.

Manfred sat down on a crate, his back upright and his knees clasped tightly together. His facial expression became earnest.

"*My mama always said, 'Life was like a box of chocolates.'*"

His delivery was an uncanny imitation of Forrest Gump's Alabama-style accent.

"*Stupid is as stupid does,*" he continued.

Everyone in the room clapped.

"Who next?" asked Byung-ju, looking down at the others.

"I am," said a girl getting up off the floor.

I was stunned to see Aki Ito take the stage.

"Play the video," she ordered.

Byung-ju replaced *Forrest Gump* with another cassette. As soon as it started playing, I recognized Han Solo and Princess Leia, bantering with each other in the movie *Star Wars*. Aki stopped the video and turned back to the others. With a self-assured look, she moved directly in front of Byung-ju, transforming herself into Princess Leia.

"Why, Han Solo, you stuck-up, half-witted, scruffy-looking Nerf-herder!" she hollered.

Everyone burst into laughter.

Byung-ju handled the verbal abuse quite well, but I could tell he wanted a piece of the action.

"Okay," he said with a restrained smirk. "My turn."

He popped out the video and replaced it with another cassette, fast-forwarding it to the section he wanted. When it finally started to play, there was Jack Nicholson in full military garb as Colonel Nathan Jessup in the movie *A Few Good Men*. Byung-ju stopped the video, called Aki back to the front, and turned to her.

With an American-style twang, he leaned into her, his face intense.

"Aki, you can't handle the truth!" he taunted.

Everyone erupted in laughter.

A school bell started chiming, indicating that lights-out in the Boarding House was fifteen minutes away.

"That's it for *The Old Movie Society*," announced Byung-ju. "We meet again Thursday."

I pulled Koji into the shadows of the alcove so as not to be seen while the students exited the room and moved back downstairs.

"Why you not stop them? You not angry?" he whispered.

I waited until I could hear the door closing downstairs and turned towards Koji.

"Why should I be angry? We never told them this building was out of bounds. They're at our school to learn English. Look at what they're doing here. They're watching English movies, learning intonation, and having fun. They're not off smoking weed. No, I'm not angry. I'm impressed."

"Oh, I see," said Koji. "You make good sense."

The following morning, I asked Harris and Pancho to join me in my office. I reviewed what happened the previous evening and asked them what they thought we should do.

"Capitalize on it, of course," bellowed Harris. "I assume that's why Pancho is sitting here."

"Yes," I said, turning towards him. "Pancho, I know you're already going to teach these students drama, but this group is obviously ready for something more. With your passion for acting, any suggestions on what we could do to support them?"

Pancho stared at me for a few moments and then snapped his raised finger in the air, like he had just had an epiphany.

"What about a movie?"

"Make a movie?"

"Yes, yes," he implored. "I have the equipment at home. Why not ask them to make a movie about the day-in-the-life of Cothbert? When you go recruiting for new students, you can use it as a marketing tool."

"That's brilliant!" I blurted. "Don't you think so, Harris?"

"I do. I like it! A lot."

"Okay," I said, standing. "I'll work on our friend Byung-ju without letting on what I saw last night. If we can funnel his energy and enthusiasm for movies into managing this project, it might just get him fired up about other areas of school."

"I'm happy to be his mentor," offered Pancho.

"That's kind of you," replied Harris. "He'll need your checks and balances, or knowing him, he'll create an X-rated film."

Later that day, I saw Byung-ju walking down the hall and asked him to join me in my office.

"I in trouble again?" he asked flippantly.

"Have you done anything wrong?"

"No. I don't think so."

"Good then. Because I need your advice."

His head arched to the side, and suspicion started to creep across his face.

"Remember when you and I talked about *Dead Poets Society*?"

"Oh, ya. I remember."

"You like good movies, don't you?"

"Yes. I really like."

"Okay, then. I wanted to ask you if you'd be willing to help me make a movie."

"Make movie?" he asked, sitting up a bit.

"Yes. In the next few months, I am going to Asia. I will be meeting with families who might want to send their kids to our school. But I have nothing to show them except boring photographs. I want to make a movie about a day at Cothbert House School."

"Why you not pay movie company to make it?"

"Two reasons, Byung-ju. First, the people who work for a movie company don't live and study here like you do. They won't be able to show what life is really like. It will be a fake movie. Second, we are a small school without a lot of money. We can't afford to pay a big production company."

I could see from Byung-ju's face that the wheels were turning.

"How long you want movie?"

"About five, maybe seven minutes. No longer, or people

will get bored."

"You have camera?"

"Yes. Mr. de Metz does. He is interested in becoming an actor, so movie-making is one of his hobbies."

Byung-ju arched his face a second time.

"What you want me to do?"

"I need a director. Someone who can work with Mr. de Metz. He has experience editing movies. You love good movies. Why not try directing one?"

Byung-ju was clearly thinking about the idea, although I could tell he was trying really hard to conceal his excitement.

"Okay, I do it."

"Wonderful."

"But you need to speak to Kyong-park first."

"Why? What does this have to do with him?"

"He oldest Korean boy. He not like that you give me so much power."

I hadn't thought about that. But he was probably right.

"What if I made him the producer? Can you work with him?"

"Yes. You just need to give him more power. Producer is bigger than director. Right?"

"Not necessarily. But I can make him senior producer. Leave that to me, Byung-ju. Do we have a deal?"

"Yes," he said, trying his best to be casual about everything. "And can I also work with Aki?"

"You can work with whomever you want, Byung-ju. You're the director."

As a precaution, I caught up with Kyong-park after breakfast and invited him to my office, explaining the idea of the movie.

"I asked Byung-ju to be the director, but I need a senior producer … you know, someone to oversee the project. Are you interested?"

"Yes," he declared happily.

"Well, you'll need to recruit people to help you. If you're a good leader, you'll find positive ways to work with as many students as possible so no one feels left out."

"I understand."

"Do you remember what I said to you in our first chat?"

"Yes. Good leaders work for the people they lead."

"Exactly. If you run into any problems, drop by my office and we can share ideas on how to deal with them."

"Really?"

"Really."

"I would like you and Byung-ju to announce the project at Assembly tomorrow so you can start getting others in the school involved. Can you guys do that?"

"Yes. I will talk to Byung-ju."

"Good. Make your presentation together. Show that you are a team."

"I understand, Mr. Gower."

"Hey, before you leave, how's it going with Thomas?"

"Okay, I guess, but it's hard to tell what he's thinking at times."

"Ah. There's another skill good leaders need. The ability to read minds."

"You crack me up, Mr. Gower," he laughed.

The smell of cigar smoke wafted over our Adirondack chairs as Harris and I enjoyed an hour of peace by the lake before dinner.

"So, is Francis Ford Byung-ju on board?" asked Harris, drawing on his cigar.

"He is. And I think Kyong-park is too."

"Well, let's see what our movie moguls come up with. The idea of immortalizing our gong show on film is a bit disconcerting."

"True. I can't imagine anyone would believe half of what goes on here."

Chapter 23

October ushered in British Columbia's rainy season: relentless downpours that drenched the lake and dampened campus morale. Even though a Thanksgiving weekend-break was just around the corner, and I'd successfully negotiated with the Major to open up her cheque book and splurge for a special feast in celebration, I felt like we were still in need of something else to lift everyone's spirits and kick-off the holiday. Remembering Harris' advice, I decided to give the responsibility to Chill along with Koji, who I thought might complement her well. In the meantime, I had to broach our trip to Asia with the Major. I had just received a formal invitation from Hymie Chan at *Yingyucom* to attend his company's annual Taipei school fair in late November. I knew, if I did end up going, it would make sense for me to visit Seoul at the same time. Harris could then look after Japan and Hong Kong. I decided to book a meeting with the Major, albeit through Koji, so Harris and I wouldn't have to explain ahead of time what we wanted to talk to her about.

On the day of our scheduled meeting, Koji alerted me that the Major was in a particularly foul mood. Millicent had visited her earlier in the day, during which they had exchanged heated words about something. To make matters worse, despite having recently transitioned to crutches, her doctor in Vancouver had just reviewed her most recent X-rays and determined she would need to remain on them for a few more weeks. I would have to be diplomatic in my approach if I had any hope of convincing her to "piss away" more of her money flying us to Asi

I looked down at my watch, realizing our meeting should have started ten minutes ago, when there was a loud bang, followed by my office door being flung open. Using her crutches, the Major catapulted herself into my office. A few moments later, Harris arrived, panting and trying to catch his breath.

"Sorry, I'm late. Pancho is away today, and I had to cover his classes. Phil, have you already started the discussion?"

"No, not yet..."

"Then I'll get right to the point," Harris said, taking the lead. "Major, Phil and I want to let you know that we'll be going to Asia in November to attend an educational fair hosted by our biggest agent. We'll also be touching base with some of our other agents and families while we're there."

I looked over at the Major to see her reaction. Her face was now twitching uncontrollably, as though she were experiencing an extreme allergic reaction.

"Are you two nuts—"

"No, Major. Stop right there and listen to me," Harris cut in.

The Major's scowl became even more intense.

"I've been in this business much longer than you have, and this is how it's done."

"Now, you just wait one minute, big guy—"

"Major, do you realize," Harris continued, ignoring her,

"that if we pick up just one new student, a trip like this will more than pay for itself? And if we pick up two students, the additional revenue would be huge. And, just so we're clear, we cannot continue to grow this school over the phone. We need to be out there meeting people and giving this place some international exposure. Oh, and one more thing—just so you know—a bunch of the other BC private schools will be supporting the fair too!" He handed the Major a list of those schools that had already confirmed their registration.

The Major fumbled with her reading glasses and stared suspiciously at the list.

"Okay," she responded at last, "let's say we did pick up a couple of kids from this fair. Does that mean we'd still have to pay those crooked agents their usual commissions?"

"Yes, it does. These fairs are a win-win for everyone."

"And exactly how much is this junket of yours going to cost me?"

"If Phil takes Taipei and Korea, and I take Hong Kong and Japan, the cost of flights, accommodations, and registration at the fair will be around $8,000."

"You're joking," she choked, looking first at Harris then at me as if we had both lost our minds.

Harris held up his hand. "Before you say anything more, Major, I can guarantee you we'll pick up at least one new student. So, you'll still be well ahead financially. There's really nothing to lose and a hell of a lot to gain."

The Major's scowl started to wane as she digested what Harris was saying.

"Give me twenty-four hours to think about it. Oh, and by the way, do you realize one of your parents hasn't paid her fees yet?"

222

"What? Which one?" I asked, taken aback.

"That fancy mother from Macau."

"Thomas' mother? There must be a mistake. She certainly has the means—"

"Don't worry. My accountant already phoned her."

"I hope Joe was diplomatic."

"You see, that's your problem. You're too nice. No business sense!" she added, abruptly adjusting her crutches before propelling herself out the door.

You're too nice. There it was again—my defining flaw.

Harris and I walked together down the hall toward the dining hall, the sound of our footsteps echoing in the quiet corridor.

"I'd better get on top of this fee issue," I said. "Maybe I should give Hymie a call."

"Probably a good idea if we want to defuse the Major's grouchiness."

"Speaking of which, what's the story with Millicent?"

Harris stopped mid-stride and shot me a look, his jaw tightening. "What do you mean? Why do you need to know?"

"Her car is always here, and Koji mentioned something about her and the Major having a heated exchange earlier," I said, trying to sound casual.

"Phil, take my advice," Harris said, resuming his pace. "Stay as far away from that woman as possible."

"Why? What's the issue?"

"Let's just say she has a tendency to drag people down with her, and once she's done, she moves on to the next sucker."

"And what about her heated relationship with the Major?"

"Oh, they've been fighting like cats and dogs ever since they were kids. It's who they are—always clawing at each other, then pretending like nothing happened."

There seemed to be more to the story, but Harris's clipped tone told me he wasn't about to share. That was fine by me—for now. But something told me I wouldn't be able to avoid it for long.

"Let's go and get some coffee and cake first," said Harris, quickly changing the topic and rubbing his hands together in anticipation.

All at once, Byung-ju and Aki stepped out in front of us. They were both wearing black berets and had video cameras Velcroed to their arms. Standing behind them were two other students, one holding a silver bounce board and the other a tall, raised spotlight.

"We want to film you like it's a typical day … pretending to work," Byung-ju announced.

I stared back at him, stunned by his impertinence.

"Byung-ju," I said, slowly sucking in air, "Mr. Tweedsmuir and I do not pretend to work. Furthermore, if you'd like to film us, will you please ask us politely and then we might consider your request."

Byung-ju arched his head, flicking back his hair. "Sorry," he blurted. "Can we *please* film you two pretending to work?"

Harris and I never made it to the Dining Hall for coffee. Instead, Byung-ju requested that we perform multiple outtakes, during which we would walk down the hall and then stop to interact with some students he had commandeered. After his eighth call of 'CUT!', he whispered in Aki's ear who, in turn, yelled an order to one of the helpers, who nodded before racing off. Byung-ju turned to us with a look of profound disappointment.

"You guys too stiff."

I couldn't help but grin.

"Well, Byung-ju, you're the director, what do you suggest we do to solve our stiffness?"

But before he could answer, his breathless helper came running back, accompanied by Manfred Ma.

"Manfred going to make you loose," he announced. "You walk down hall and try one more time. *Please!*" he emphasized, as an insincere afterthought.

We did as Byung-ju directed, and as soon as we were in front of his entourage of students, Manfred stepped forward and immediately launched into a rap, gesticulating to its beat for effect:

Manfred Ma is the name
Learning idioms play the game
I'm sick of your voice Plotnik screamed
Caught with my pants down so it seemed.

Harris and I couldn't keep a straight face.

"That's a take!" yelled Byung-ju, all at once.

"I guess we got loose," I said, eyeing Harris.

"Brilliant!" he snorted back. "Sheer brilliance!"

I looked over at Manfred. "Did you write that yourself?"

"Not myself. I had help from Kyong-park. I gave him the ideas and he helped me put it together."

"It was very funny."

"Thank you. It was really fun to make."

A clopping sound echoed through the hall as the Major hopped towards us on her crutches.

"What's going on over here, Bing-ju?"

"Oh, hi, Miss Major. We make movie about your school

for Mr. Gower so he can buy new students."

"Really?" I could see the Major was intrigued. "Have you filmed anything outside yet?"

"No. But on my schedule to do."

"Maybe I can help you with that part. Come on, follow me," she commanded, pivoting and moving towards the front door. Byung-ju, Aki and their film crew eagerly trailed behind."

This can't be good, I thought.

Later that afternoon, as I was making my way over to the playing field, I heard the misfiring engine of the Major's golf cart approaching from behind me. As it peeled past me, I did a double-take. Byung-ju was draped over the top of the cart's canopy roof, his camera panning the campus, while Aki was hanging precariously off the back struggling to hold up a large bounce board. All the time, the Major was leaning into the steering wheel, relishing the moment.

I'm going to pretend I didn't just see that.

Two days later, Chill and Koji invited Harris and me to a working lunch in the art room. They wanted to share with us what they had planned as a fun activity to kick off Thanksgiving weekend. As Peg finished unwrapping a plate of sandwiches and cookies, Chill and Koji stood proudly at the front of the classroom. Chill reached for a blue felt marker and wrote the words *Backwards Day* on the whiteboard.

"We will have a day where everything is turned upside down," tittered Koji.

"Sounds like a regular day at Cothbert to me," I joked.

"Oh, and Mr. Phil, before I forget, Byung-ju's mother sent

a fax. She will be visiting the same day because it is also Byung-ju's birthday."

How fitting.

Chapter 24

"What a day in Vancouver. I'm bloody exhausted!" Harris bemoaned, collapsing into a dining hall chair and dramatically dropping his dinner tray for effect.

"Oh, yes, of course. This was your Saturday to play escort. Did the students give poor Mr. Tweedsmuir a hard time?" I asked jokingly.

Harris gave an exaggerated huff. "The first issue occurred just after the bus dropped everyone off at the parking lot near Chinatown. The Koreans let it be known that they felt snubbed. They've decided to rename the area in front of a Korean grocery store 'Koreatown' and have requested that we drop them off there in the future."

"Yeah, right. Like that's going to happen!"

"That's what I told them. Then," he continued, "we were almost thirty minutes late leaving because of a few stragglers. But the biggest pain-in-the-butt was that we hit a traffic jam going over that damn bridge you have to take from Vancouver to get to the Sea-to-Sky..."

"The Lions Gate?"

"That's the one. Anyway, we were stuck for so long that Manfred nearly blew out his bladder. I had to get him a Coke bottle and conceal him at the back of the bus so he could relieve himself."

"Sounds to me like Mr. Tweedsmuir needs a trip to the *As You Like It*," I teased.

"Now you're talking!"

"Good. Because there have been some developments."

"That sounds ominous! Okay, let me take a shower and change first."

"You know what, I've got some shopping to do at *Kipling's*. Why don't I meet you at the pub?"

An hour later, drinks in hand, Harris and I were lounging in a booth beside the pub's fireplace.

"So, what are these developments?" Harris asked, downing some of his Scotch.

"I spoke with Joe this afternoon. He confirmed that nothing has been paid towards Thomas' fees and that, when he phoned Mrs. Kang, she just listened, grunted, and then hung up on him."

"That's strange. What about Hymie? Did you get in touch with him?"

"He already emailed me. He's had an earful from Mrs. Kang, who says we're a bunch of crooks. Anyway, I'm going to phone her personally and see what's going on. But something doesn't smell right."

"I'd concur."

"But that's not the half of it. It also appears the Major's haphazard budgeting assumptions were not entirely on the mark. According to Joe, we've already blown through our budget and need to rein in expenses—which doesn't make any sense to me when I look at my own budgeting."

"You mean twenty students wasn't our break-even?"

"Apparently not. But I'm not sure why, because my calculations still show twenty as the correct number. I also let Joe know we haven't been frivolous in our spending—delivery costs for a golf cart and an unnecessary salary increase aside, of course."

"Let's not forget it cost us almost $4,000 to replace Stanley Lam's *Louis Vuitton* suitcase we set on fire during the exorcism."

"True! The Major practically had a meltdown when Koji shared that news with her. Honestly, though, who sends a teenager off to boarding school with a four-thousand-dollar suitcase?"

"Not sure," Harris sighed, staring at his glass as though the answer lay hidden in the amber depths. "So, what exactly is our damn break-even? And why the sudden change?"

"I actually asked Joe those exact questions. And his reply was as vague and noncommittal as last time: 'Just stay closely involved in the school's finances,' is all he said."

Harris shook his head. "Well, if we really are in debt, that would explain this message I got today." He reached into his jacket pocket and pulled out a *Post-it* note.

I glanced down at the crinkled yellow paper in his hand. It read: *okay, yous two can go to Asia but I will book the flights!!!*

"The Major?"

"Of course, she couldn't tell me to my face. Anyway, the good news is that Violeta and Hymie will probably look after your hotels, and I'm going to make some overtures to the Itos and Lams and see if they'll help me with mine. So, we won't have to worry about the Major booking us into some seedy hiker's hostel."

"Okay. Good. But what about timing? *Yingyucom* has its

Taipei fair on the 23rd of November."

"Yes, it's a two-day event. I suggest you fly to Korea a couple of days ahead of time."

"So, two nights in Seoul and three nights in Taipei?"

"Yes, that should do it. And as soon as you return, I'll fly to Tokyo and Hong Kong. Next year, one of us can do the whole circuit, but I don't think either of us should be away for more than a week this year."

"Agreed! Which reminds me, we're long overdue for a staff meeting. We need updates on how the students are doing," I said, downing my glass of Merlot.

"Alright, why don't we have lunch in my office tomorrow. But that's enough shop talk for today," he said, signaling to Sue for more drinks.

With our refilled glasses, the warmth of the fire, and the camaraderie we'd developed over the past months, we finally started to relax.

"So, my chosen one," Harris said cheekily, "any updates on your monk-friend?"

"I don't know, really. He said he'd check in from time to time and counsel me if needed. He also gave me his phone number in case of urgent help."

"1-800-MONK?" Harris lobbed, downing his *Balvenie*.

"Something like that."

At the staff meeting the next day, everyone seemed upbeat about the first few weeks of school and the progress of the students, particularly Aki, who had become a lot more self-confident and was excelling in almost all of her classes. A few concerns were raised about Byung-ju sticking his camera in everyone's face and Manfred, who continued to be on

231

overdrive.

"I do have one other student I'd like to discuss," Chill declared, sitting up. "Thomas—you know, that Kanga guy."

Ida leaned forward, a frown creasing her forehead. "Chill, I'm overseeing Thomas's progress," she said gently but with an anxious edge to her tone. "We did expect some challenges. What's your concern? Maybe I can help you."

"Well, it's this whole kangaroo thing," she said in a whiny voice. "In my art class, no matter what I assign the students to do, Thomas just sketches or makes models of kangaroos. In my photography club, he'll draw the shape of a kangaroo in the sand and then take a photo of it."

"I know what she means!" added Pancho. "The other day, I was in the Boarding House and I got angry with Thomas for not tidying his room. He then grabbed his sketch pad, sat on the floor, and started drawing an angry-looking kangaroo wearing a pair of glasses just like mine."

The room burst into laughter.

"You know, Pancho, it's strange about his room being messy," said Myrtle, jumping into the conversation. "He keeps his own cupboard military-tidy. But when it comes to the rest of his room, he just doesn't seem to care. It's like he doesn't realize it's his. Kyong-park is working hard to fix the problem. He and the other roommate in there—Bernard Lu—have made a daily duty roster for everyone to follow. We'll see if that helps."

"That's a good strategy," said Ida, quickly jotting in her notebook. "Keep me updated on how it goes. And listen, everyone," she said, her face becoming solemn. "It's just going to take time. We all need to be patient."

"Ida's right," added Harris. "At least there haven't been any

232

bullying issues. And the Huang twins have definitely taken him under their wings."

"Yes, he adores them," I remarked.

"Oh, before everyone leaves," interrupted Pancho, "I wanted to remind you that we're going to the Salmon Hatchery tomorrow to watch the annual salmon run."

"Hey Pancho, while we're there, would it be okay if I did some open-air art work with the students?" Chill asked. "I love painting nature."

"For sure, for sure," replied Pancho. "After we tour them through the facility, you can have as much time as you want to do your artwork. I'll then distribute the box lunches the kitchen's preparing. It'll be nice to get everyone off campus, and the weather's supposed to be good tomorrow. We should be back in time for clubs."

"Looking forward to it, Pancho," I smiled. "Thanks for arranging all this."

The Hatchery was an hour's drive from the school, renowned for its annual salmon run, where onlookers can view the many Chum, Coho, and Chinook that make the ultimate circle-of-life journey upstream to return to the place from which they were hatched. During this process, the exterior of their bodies changes color from steel blue to brilliant red, while their heads turn bright green. This transformation helps them attract mates so they can spawn the next generation before dying.

Frank pulled our bus into the Hatchery's parking lot, where we hastily herded everyone to the Visitor's Center. A park guide was waiting for us when we arrived. Harris, Myrtle, Tofu, and I took up the rear of the group, while the rest of the staff helped the instructor quiet down the students as she explained the story of the salmon's trek. Everyone seemed engaged in the interactive tour and discussion, although many of the students were now holding their noses as the smell of rotting fish became more overpowering.

"Why do the salmon have to die?" blurted Thomas suddenly.

Ida and I exchanged looks.

"Good question," replied the instructor. "While we're not entirely sure, we think their dead bodies fertilize the stream, giving young fish a better chance to survive and grow strong."

Thomas started to stroke his chin and look contemplative.

"Thank you for your interesting answer," he replied at last.

"Well, thank you for your great question," smiled the instructor.

By the end of the presentation, Chill had the students settle at several designated picnic tables, while Byung-ju set up his tripod and camera to film everything. She then passed out large sheets of paper and watercolor paints so the students could express themselves artistically and reflect on what they had just seen. I sauntered from table to table, bantering with the students while they busily painted. All at once, Ida touched me on the shoulder, pulling me aside.

"I told you we just needed to be patient. See, over there!" She pointed at a picnic table where Kyong-park was bent over the shoulder of Thomas, who was already on his third painting of brightly colored, stylized salmon swimming upstream. A senior park official, wearing a name tag that read *Sarah*, looked on with interest.

"Wow, that's incredible," she said, staring down at Thomas's painting. "May I see your other pieces?" she asked gently.

Thomas nodded his head but didn't look up.

Sarah leafed through his pieces. "Amazing. These are beautiful," she said.

Thomas slowly turned his head toward her, unsure how to respond.

"What's your name?" Sarah asked.

"My name is Kanga." Thomas then hesitated, remaining focused on his painting. After a moment, he slowly raised his head again. "My name is really Thomas," he said, correcting himself.

"Thomas, would you be willing to lend us these paintings to hang on the walls of our Visitor's Center for a couple of weeks? They're truly magical."

"What does magical mean?" he asked, still appearing very awkward.

"It means something that has a special power to make people feel good," replied Sarah.

Thomas placed his hand under his chin pensively. "Yes, you can borrow these paintings," he said after a few seconds. He was now smiling. "Will you return them to me?"

"I will personally drive them back to your school in two weeks, if that's okay with you."

"That's okay," he said matter-of-factly, lowering his gaze to the paper as he picked up his brush, dipping it into green paint. It was a signal to the park official that he was once again immersed in his own creative world, oblivious to others but at ease under the immense trees that reached for the blue sky.

I could see Ida's eyes brimming with tears, and I, too, was struggling to hold back my emotion. We had just witnessed a monumental event.

Following lunch, we all stood by the stream, mesmerized by the rainbow of lunging fish struggling to make their way upstream for their final calling. After a while, some of the students started to become restless. Manfred asked Myrtle if he could take Tofu, who was leashed to a nearby tree, for a walk. But Manfred was not one for walking. As soon as she gave him permission, he and an exuberant Tofu began a fast-paced game of tag along the park's trails.

As we neared the end of our stay, I felt a certain bond, almost a school spirit, starting to captivate us all. I mentioned this to Harris, who shared the same sentiments.

"It's the simple things in life, oh chosen one—those less complicated things that bring out the best in all of us. It was a good day.

We strolled back toward the parking lot, where I noticed some of our group had discovered students from a well-known girls' school also visiting the park. A few moments later, Aki and our oldest Korean girl, Hee-jin Lee, walked over.

"Mr. Gower," said Hee-jin, "that school over there has a band. Can we have a band?"

Ida, who was standing beside me, looked over at the girls from the other school.

"Well, Hee-jin, I was actually planning on launching a jazz band after Christmas. But if you're keen, we can get started right away."

"Yes, please. A lot of us already play instruments. Some of us even brought our own with us!"

"Okay with me," said Ida, turning toward me.

"As long as you have the time, Ms. Plotnik."

"Their school has band uniforms," said Aki, pointing back

at the girls. "Can we have uniforms too?"

"You know what, Aki," said Harris, "I think you should ask Miss Major about your uniform idea. See what she has to say."

"Okay. But Ms. Plotnik, you'll still help us get going, right?"

"I will," she replied, tapping Aki gently on the back. "I will!"

We finally returned to line up outside the bus. After Pancho took roll call, everyone began climbing aboard. But just as Harris and I started up the steps, a river of bodies came rushing back out again, hands clamped firmly over their noses and mouths.

"What's wrong?" I asked.

"It's Tofu," uttered Aki under her breath as she held her nose. "He's brought a dead salmon onto the bus and is rolling in it."

"How did Tofu get off his leash?" I asked.

"I tied him up after the game of tag," said Manfred. "He must have escaped."

"Harris, what were you saying about the simple things in life? Do you want to deal with this one?"

Harris sneered at me as he climbed onto the bus. I could hear him trying to negotiate with poor Tofu.

"All right, there's a good Tofu. There we go. Give me the fishy."

This was followed by ominous growling and then a sharp, pained cry.

"Bloody hell! You damn dog. I'm bleeding!"

Harris bolted from the bus, grasping his arm. The students found this immensely amusing. At last, Myrtle reappeared carrying a lunch cooler.

"Has anyone seen Tofu?" she asked.

The students started to giggle as Myrtle noticed Harris grimacing and clutching his arm.

"What's going on?" she asked impatiently. "What happened?"

Manfred stepped forward. "Miss, Tofu took a dead salmon onto the bus. When Mr. Tweedsmuir tried to take it away, Tofu bit him. I'm really sorry. I think I didn't tie up Tofu tight enough."

Myrtle looked over at Harris and shook her head.

"Oh, for goodness' sake. Do I have to do everything around here?" she said, trudging onto the bus. A moment later, she reappeared holding the smelly, limp salmon in one hand and a sheepish-looking Tofu in the other.

While the removal of the dead salmon had cleared the air a bit, the bus was still nothing short of a stink bomb on wheels as it made its way back up the Sea-to-Sky. All the windows on the bus were pried open, with students sticking their heads out, gasping for air.

"Mr. Gower, I have perfume mist I can spray on bus," offered Pansy Huang.

"Please, please spray the dog too," came a gagging voice from the back of the bus.

"Sure, go ahead, Pansy," I replied. "Thanks for trying to help out. It is getting pretty toxic in here."

"Toxic?" queried Pansy.

"Super stinky," I clarified.

By the time the bus was ready to take the exit to the school, Pansy had sprayed the entire inside of the vehicle with her mist, including saturating poor Tofu to the point that even he was gasping for air.

"Mr. Gower, I've finished the bottle of spray!" cried Pansy from the back of the bus.

"Pansy, thank you for all your efforts. It does smell much better in here. The school will buy you a new bottle. What's that spray called?" I yelled back.

"*Chanel Number 5*," came the response.

Harris, seated behind me, leaned over my shoulder. "Please let me be there when you give that receipt to the Major," he snickered. "Pretty please!"

"Whatever," I retorted, slinking down in my seat.

Chapter 25

Of course, I knew she was coming. Koji had reminded us all at our staff meeting two weeks earlier. But how could I have not foreseen the total gong show that Byung-ju's mother would get to witness on our carefully planned Backwards Day—not to mention her perfectly justifiable accusation that Cothbert was a total looney bin? Of all the potential cross-cultural misfires for which Harris had prepped me, not one of them even remotely included trying to explain to an irate mother, who barely understood a word of English, why the students and staff at her son's expensive private school were, at 7:30 in the morning, sitting in the dining hall with their uniforms on backward, eating pizza, drinking soda, and wolfing back sugar-glazed jelly doughnuts; or why, for that matter, I, as the principal of the school, was seen presenting my morning announcements with my back turned to the students. To add insult to injury, she even observed her son filming the whole fiasco. It simply confirmed to Mrs. Lim the need to have Cothbert House School condemned immediately. Luckily, however, it wasn't Mrs. Lim I had to clarify all of this mayhem to but rather Hee-young, the calm and understanding chaperone from *Hyung-Bo Consulting* in Seoul.

Her emergency phone call to me was patched through by Koji at 8:05 a.m., the result of a spirited call she had received from Mrs. Lim on her cellphone, threatening to withdraw Byung-ju from Cothbert and launch a full-blown investigation with the Ministry of Education. By the time I was able to explain everything, Hee-young couldn't stop laughing.

"I'll deal with Mrs. Lim," she replied. "You guys are hilarious!"

But as soon as I felt a bit more at ease, there was a simultaneous ding from my computer. I stared down at an email from Hymie that read: *Urgent. Phone me back right away.*

I reached for my phone just as Koji stuck his head around my office door.

"Sorry, I just want to remind you we are having the Backwards Painting Competition," he said proudly.

"I'll be there shortly. I've got to call Hymie first. I've got a small crisis to deal with. It appears Mrs. Kang never paid her fees and that she's upset at us."

"But she did pay her fees," blurted Koji adamantly.

"She did?"

"Yes. I remember exactly—she handed a thick envelope of money to that man who came with her just before I took them to your office for tea."

"Zhou?"

"Yes! Yes! That guy. He promised to look after the fees for her during his meeting with you."

"Oh, did he? Interesting. My beloved mentor might be a thief."

"Wow! What are you going to do now?"

241

"Phone Hymie and tell him the truth. I'll be at your competition as soon as I can. But this can't wait."

"Okay, got it."

Hymie answered on the first ring.

"Oh, Mr. Gower. It's you. Thank God. You need to do something. Mrs. Kang is so angry," blurted Hymie. "She screamed at me for ten minutes and—"

"Hymie, calm down and listen," I said, interrupting. "Do you remember that guy who was with the Kangs?"

There was a short pause and then, "You mean the guy dressed in the funny clothes?" he said hesitantly.

"Yes. Him," I said, explaining exactly what Koji had told me.

"Oh, this is terrible," exclaimed Hymie. "So, you're not the criminal."

"No, of course I'm not the criminal. And I'm counting on you to convince Mrs. Kang and get her to understand her monk buddy has stolen $30K from her."

"Okay. I'll speak to her."

"Let me know if you want me to phone her too. I just thought it would be better coming from you so I don't embarrass her."

"Yes. I will. I'll let you know how it goes."

In case anyone missed getting their sugar fix at the breakfast junk-food fest, that same afternoon, the kitchen had arranged for an outdoor lunch, which included a hot dog station, bowls of potato chips, more soda, and chocolate-dipped ice cream bars. While Janice and Peg barbecued, Pancho, who was seated behind a long decorative table wearing reflective shades and a tie-dye shirt, assumed the role of DJ, blasting a selection of dance music that caused the energy level to climb. By the time we had all stuffed ourselves for a second time that day, I could tell we were more than ready for some sort of activity—particularly Manfred, who, I feared, was going to self-implode. Luckily, Koji and Chill had arranged for a game of Backwards Soccer.

As I stood beside Koji and Chill, watching the students charge around the field, frequently backing into each other and exploding into high-pitched fits of laughter, Harris walked up from behind, tapping me on the shoulder.

"Just a heads-up, Phil! Over there—where Byung-ju is," he pointed, directing Chill and Koji to follow him to another part of the field. I looked over at Byung-ju, who was panning with his tripod. Standing beside him was a short woman wearing a long cream *Burberry*-style trench coat and a tall man dressed in a black suit. The woman caught my eye, nodded to her companion, and together they sidled over, stepping up beside me.

"Hello, Mr. Gower. This is Mrs. Lim, and I am her assistant, Johnston. I will be translating for her today."

Almost on cue, Mrs. Lim moved directly in front of me, speaking rapidly in Korean, her face mirroring her remorse for what had occurred.

"Mrs. Lim is truly, truly sorry for all the harm she has caused," said Johnston, translating.

"Oh, please tell Mrs. Lim there's been no harm—just a funny miscommunication," I smiled, trying to inject some levity into the situation.

Mrs. Lim looked somewhat ill at ease as Johnston conveyed my sentiments and then, visibly relaxing, carried on with her rapid-fire Korean monologue. Johnston listened attentively, then turned back to me.

"Mrs. Lim now realizes how much progress Byung-ju has made at Cothbert. She says he truly loves it here and that he couldn't stop talking about his filming project. She is deeply indebted to you and your staff."

"Well, please tell Mrs. Lim she has a very special and very creative son. He keeps us all on our toes!"

Mrs. Lim leaned towards Johnston, listening while he explained, and then, beaming, broke into a genuine laugh.

"Johnston, tell Mrs. Lim to look over there," I interrupted, seeing a trolley being wheeled out by Janice. On the cart was a large cake with the words *Happy Birthday Byung-ju* written over top.

Johnston translated for Mrs. Lim, who immediately cheered, "*Gamsahabnida! Gamsahabnida!*"

"That means thank you in Korean," smiled Johnston by way of explanation. Mrs. Lim ruefully caught my eye, then, looking at her watch, tugged on Johnston's arm, launching into what sounded like an urgent plea. After a few moments, Johnston interpreted:

"I'm really sorry, but Mrs. Lim just informed me we have to leave now to catch a plane. She promises she will be in touch and looks forward to seeing you when you come to Seoul. Also, she wanted you to know that she left seven boxes of birthday presents for Byung-ju with Miss Myrtle."

Only seven. Poor guy, I thought.

Looking back over her shoulder and waving effusively, Mrs. Lim then hurried over to say goodbye to Byung-ju.

When the students finally settled back into their nighttime

boarding house routine, I joined Harris at our Adirondack chairs on the dock. He was already puffing on a cigar, gazing up at the panoply of stars when I arrived. As I sat beside him, a cool breeze nipped at my neck, reminding me that winter was close at hand.

"That was some day," Harris said, putting his stretched arms behind his head.

"You don't even know the half of it," I said, recounting what Koji had said about Zhou the monk.

"You mean your famous guru is a wayward felon?" Harris replied, sitting up in surprise. "You're not really the chosen one?"

"So it would appear."

Re-lighting his new cigar, Harris jesting, "Can you now see how this whole Backwards Day was a metaphor for this gong show of a school?"

"Yup."

True to Harris' description, the following day, in an absolute tizzy, Koji buzzed me in my office. "Mr. Phil! Mr. Phil! Urgent call for you from Hymie. I will patch him through."

"So, how'd it go, Hymie?" I asked, with trepidation on hearing his nervous "hello" on the other end of the receiver.

"Not well, Mr. Gower! Mrs. Kang doesn't believe you. She spoke with Mr. Zhou. Mr. Zhou swears he gave you the money and that you're the one who is lying. He also said he's canceling his spiritual support for you, whatever that means."

"What? This is crazy, Hymie! I mean, honestly … I hope you're not buying any of this."

"I do trust you. And when I explained what was going on

to my boss, he said he believes you too. He told me he's seen similar games like this played before. But he also said this is your problem, not ours, and everything better not escalate or it will damage your school's reputation, and we won't be able to represent you anymore."

"Escalate?"

"Yes, Mrs. Kang is threatening legal action and more."

"And more? What does that even mean?"

"I don't know. She says you're just like all the other schools in Hong Kong and Macau Thomas attended, and it's time someone stood up to schools like yours."

"I see. And what does she propose to do about Thomas?"

"I'm to have him picked up today."

"Oh no! Do you realize how much progress he's been making?"

"I know. But she just doesn't trust you or your school anymore."

"Alright then, I'll try to reach out to her. Keep me posted if you get any further updates from your end."

As soon as I hung up, I dialed Mrs. Kang's number, which immediately went to voicemail:

Mrs. Kang. This is Phil Gower phoning from Cothbert House School. We obviously need to talk as soon as possible. Please phone me back.

I then remembered Zhou had given me his personal number. I decided to give it a shot. But, as anticipated, a message confirmed there was no service to the number I had dialed. As I sat fuming, there was another buzz from Koji.

"Now what?" I replied, realizing how on edge I sounded.

"You need to come to the front office ASAP," he said in his clipped tones. "Big boxes arrive. With your name."

Probably explosives from Mrs. Kang, I thought.

When I arrived at the reception counter, sure enough, there—stacked on the floor—were two very large boxes and a small package, each addressed to me. I could see that one of the boxes was stamped with a colorful image of a Macintosh computer, while another one had a drawing of a mixing board. I opened the package, which was unmarked. It contained discs labeled 'Video-Editing Software' and a white envelope with my name handwritten on the outside. Ripping open the envelope, I read the enclosed note.

Dear Mr. Gower,

This video editing equipment is a gift to Cothbert House School. It is my way of expressing my thanks to you and your staff for motivating and taking care of my Byung-ju.

Respectfully, Mrs. Lim

I tucked the letter into my jacket pocket and stared back at the boxes, trying to process what we had been gifted, when Pancho walked through the door. Showing him the delivery, he did a double take.

"Whoa! Do you realize how much all this stuff costs?" Not waiting for an answer, he began to rummage through the boxes like a child opening birthday presents. He pointed at the computer.

"That Macintosh alone, with its huge processor and memory, has got to be close to seven grand," he cried out. "And the sound-editing switchboard, probably another three grand. And I know for a fact that this software is at least two grand," he added, holding up the disks. "I've wanted to get my hands on this for some time but have never been able to afford it. It's like we now have our own production studio. I mean, this is totally awesome. We're now a miniature *DreamWorks*."

"Really?" I said, suddenly appreciating what was sitting in front of me. "I guess we need to decide where to set all of it up. Unfortunately, we don't have any spare rooms at the moment."

"What about the watchtower? Seems fitting, given that's where all this excitement began," Pancho joked.

"Actually, that's not a bad idea. I'll need to get the Major's approval first, but I don't think it should be an issue. Leave it with me!"

The Major, who had recently forgone her crutches for a cane, hobbled into the dining hall to join me for dinner that evening, and I took the opportunity to discuss with her Mrs. Lim's gift and my plan for using the watchtower.

"Do we really need to keep all that crap?" she asked, picking up a large slice of roast chicken from her plate with her fingers. "I mean, that's a lot of money. We could sell it all and use the money for something else."

By 'something else,' I knew she meant her own pocket. I felt totally deflated by her complete lack of appreciation for what made our school tick.

"Major, this was a gift from Mrs. Lim. She will be checking in with Byung-ju to make sure he's using the equipment," I said emphatically, trying to contain the frustration in my voice. "Our school has next to no facilities. I can guarantee that none of the other big boarding schools in the area has anything like this. According to Pancho, this is industry-standard equipment. We'll be able to advertise movie production as one of our signature programs."

I realized as soon as I said this, the comment would probably go over her head.

"You say none of the other boarding schools have got this stuff?"

"No … no way … like I said, this is really unique equipment. We'll have the best video production of any school in BC, maybe even all of Canada."

Everything was a competition with the Major, and I knew I had hit the right nerve. After pretending to mull the idea over, she finally looked up.

"Yeah, I think the top of the watchtower probably makes the most sense. You know what, I'll get Frank to build a counter up there to put everything on and get you a few swivel chairs, like the ones in the computer room."

"That's a fabulous idea, Major. Thank you for your generosity."

"Well, I just want to keep the kids happy, you know," she explained, tearing apart another piece of roast chicken she had picked up.

"Yes, of course you do. I can see that now," I said, knowing Harris would be so proud of me at this moment.

Chapter 26

With only a day left before I flew to Asia and still no further word from Mrs. Kang, despite leaving four separate voicemails, Byung-ju finally informed me his video was ready for showing. When I'd asked him a few days earlier if I could get a preview, he flatly refused, requesting instead an official opening night for its release to the entire school community. I was livid with our little *prima donna*.

"Oh, come on, what's the worst that could happen?" said Harris sarcastically, trying to console me as we deliberated whether this was a good idea.

"Oh, I don't know," I replied, "How about a mockumentary about our German family next door or a completely tasteless satire of us? Anything could happen with Byung-ju in charge."

"Pancho hasn't said there's a problem, and he's supposed to be monitoring everything."

"Yes, except he mentioned Byung-ju has been doing most of the final editing for the film without him because he wants the finished version to be a surprise. That's what worries me—Byung-ju's definition of surprise."

"Hmm, I see," Harris smirked. "But didn't you say his mother told you he loves the school?"

"Yes, but—"

"Then let him have his Hollywood premiere. If he screws up, we'll deal with it then."

"Fine," I replied dejectedly.

That night at the opening, the school community waited in single-file outside the gym on a red paper carpet Chill and her art classes had taped to the floor. On either side of the homemade runner, strands of white Christmas lights sparkled. Sitting on an easel, just to the right of the entrance to the gym, a very professional sign read:

A DAY IN THE LIFE OF COTHBERT
   A Kyong-Park Production, Directed by Byung-ju Lim | Assistant Director, Aki Ito | Staff Supporter, Mr. P. De Metz

At last, loud orchestral music started blasting from a boom box as Kyong-park, Byung-ju, and Aki came strolling around the corner. Pansy and Hibiscus pogoed alongside them, angling their flashing cameras while everyone started screaming and cheering. Both Kyong-park and Byung-ju were decked out in dress clothes and had their hair gelled back, while Aki wore a long, glittering white dress that Myrtle had pieced together. The stars paraded along the mock red carpet, waving to their adoring fans. The doors to the gym then opened, and we all dutifully followed the celebrities inside, seating ourselves behind a VIP section specifically reserved for them. On the wall in front of the room hung a large projection screen. Just when I felt like commenting on the whole ego trip, Byung-ju waved Harris and me over.

"What an honor," I said snippily under my breath, getting

to my feet.

"Behave yourself," said Harris, as we both moved to the front, seating ourselves on two assigned chairs on either side of Byung-ju and Pancho.

Within minutes, the lights started to dim, and a moving musical score, sounding like a piece from film composer Hans Zimmer, started playing. The image of Byung-ju in uniform, standing beside the entrance to the school property, emerged from a mist as he welcomed the viewer to Cothbert House School. From here, he narrated a series of interviews with students who gushed about their experiences at Cothbert. These interviews transitioned to action shots profiling the campus and different school activities, from food services, clubs, and boarding house life to our trip to the Hatchery and Backwards Day. There were heartfelt close-ups of staff and students interacting with each other, including Chill working alongside Thomas on an art project, Ida sitting patiently beside Manfred, helping him with journal writing, Myrtle laughing in her kitchen with a group of students who were preparing a birthday cake while Tofu yapped, and a shot of Pancho and Byung-ju working on video editing. There was even a segment showing the Major handing out free junk food in the Dining Hall. The infamous shot of Harris and me, which took multiple takes, came across as lively and genuine. The video slowly concluded with more moving music, as bold text moved slowly across the screen that read:

Cothbert House School. Where you can find yourself.

This was followed by reams of credits listing all the various students who had contributed in some way or another. At that moment, I couldn't contain the emotion building up inside of me as tears rolled down my cheeks.

Byung-ju, Kyong-park, and Aki stood up and took their bows as we all rose to our feet, while the gymnasium erupted in applause. Byung-ju looked back over at me and saw my face.

"You don't like it?" he said with a worried look.

I stepped towards him and gave him a hug. "I loved it. It was so amazing," I replied effusively. I then extended hugs to Kyong-park and Aki, both of whom looked back at me awkwardly.

"Kyong-park, I was really impressed that you got so many people involved in making this."

"Good, leader, right?" he joked with a confident look.

"Great leader," I fired back, shaking his hand.

"I agree," Pancho gushed. "You guys nailed it. I was blown away!"

"Does blown away mean *good*?" asked Aki.

"Aki, blown away means very, very surprised … in a good way," explained Harris. "I mean, come on, you all made poor Mr. Gower here cry," he bantered, patting me on the back like a dejected child. "I can't even do that."

The three of them exploded in laughter.

The Major tottered up beside us. I could tell she was over the moon.

"So, Major, what do you think of our professional film crew?" asked Harris.

"That thing was great. Really great. I really liked the shots of me and you guys driving around the campus."

Byung-ju bowed in response.

"Thank you, Miss Major, and thank you for all your help," replied Kyong-park, as both he and Aki followed with further bows.

As the gym started to empty, Harris turned towards me. "Did you enjoy a bit of humble pie tonight? I think it's fair to say Byung-ju knows the definition of a surprise. Wouldn't you say?"

"I can't wait to show this in Asia."

A tap on my shoulder startled me. Koji moved in beside me.

"Sorry, Mr. Phil, but a courier delivered this for you before dinner. I just realized who it was from, so I thought I'd better give it to you before you went home," he said, handing me a large manila envelope.

My stomach felt queasy as I stared down at the sender's name: *Leung and Associates, Barristers and Solicitors, Macau.*

Harris peered over to look. "Oh, shit!"

I ripped open the envelope and retrieved the solitary letter inside.

"So?" snipped Harris impatiently as I scanned its contents.

"So ... it says we have 20 days to transfer $50,000 for tuition and expenses to them or else they will proceed with legal action."

I looked to the front of the gym where the Major was hobnobbing with some of the students.

"Major!" I called out, waving her over. "I need a word."

I quickly summarized the contents of the letter and waited for her reaction.

"But I don't have $50,000. We're already in debt."

"I know, Major. And we shouldn't have to pay this. I'm off to Asia tomorrow. Can you and Harris discuss this letter with the school's lawyer? The way I see it, it's their word against ours. They don't have a case."

"Okay," said the Major. Fear flickered across her face as she looked down, silent."

"Harris, can you stay on top of this? I'll continue to try and connect with Mrs. Kang once I'm in Asia."

"Of course. This is bloody absurd! I'll deal with our lawyer."

Chapter 27

Allowing the Major to oversee any significant purchase was always a risk. It invariably resulted in the cheapest option available, regardless of whether it made any sense. This point was driven home once again as I made my way to a center-aisle seat at the very back of the charter plane the Major had booked for me to Seoul. I shook my head, staring both at my assigned seat, which looked like it could barely fit a preschooler, and my ticket. Despite the fact that three major airline carriers offered direct flights to Seoul from Vancouver in just under 11 hours, the Major's itinerary included a 9-hour layover in Tokyo.

Twenty hours later, unable to feel my legs from being twisted in front of me, my back in agony from what felt like a pinched nerve, and the ongoing stress over the Kang situation weighing heavily on me, I hobbled off the no-name carrier into Seoul's *Gimpo International Airport*, feeling physically and emotionally drained. Leaning on my baggage cart for support, I exited immigration into a swarm of locals waving welcome signs. Towering above all this chaos was an enormous hand-made sign that simply read, *PIL*. I waved to catch the attention of the person holding it up, and a man signaled for me to exit to the right. I staggered towards him, cringing in pain.

"My name is Tony," said the man, reaching for my luggage. "You okay? You look a bit sick."

Tony was a solid-looking man with a bulbous face, a crew cut, and the physique of a small sumo wrestler. The top button below his starched white shirt collar was ready to spring at any moment, and his ultra-thin black necktie hung like a reluctant afterthought.

"I think I pulled my back," I replied, jerking my body as I felt another spasm surge down my spine.

Tony's phone started ringing.

"Please wait a minute," he said, touching his headset. I could hear him chatting in Korean. All at once, he handed me his phone.

"Hello?"

"*Pil.* You in pain?"

It was Violeta.

"Yes. I think I pulled my back. Maybe after a good night's sleep it will get better."

"I doubt it," came the blunt response. "Tony going to take you to *Kim's Golden Body Clinic.* Only ten minutes away. They check you over."

"Are you sure it's no trouble?"

"A little trouble."

Kim's Golden Body Clinic was a bit of a hole-in-the-wall, located in a shopping mall sandwiched between a gaudy lingerie boutique and a rather dubious-looking spa with its blinds pulled down. A receptionist jumped to attention as soon as I walked in, clearly not used to having Western visitors. There was a strange smell in the air—a mixture of antiseptic wipes and garlic.

"You wait here. They look after you," instructed Tony. "I go meet Violeta. She's coming soon."

As soon as Tony left, I started to feel more and more uncomfortable. I looked up at the wall in front of me and noticed a crooked frame displaying an English speech, allegedly delivered by a doctor named Hak at a medical symposium in Boston. I struggled to stand up and read what it said. It was worse than one of Stanley Lam's essays: mumbo jumbo at its finest. I felt sorry for whoever was in the audience that day.

I continued to wait patiently until two young men dressed in surgical garb emerged from a steel door beside me. They proceeded to throw themselves onto one of the benches opposite me, grunting and puffing, as they tore off their masks in a way that accentuated their apparent exhaustion—no doubt from lancing a boil or performing a particularly complex ingrown toenail removal.

The steel door opened again, and a short, balding man, also wearing overly elaborate operating attire, walked towards me carrying a clipboard.

"Mr. Phil Gower?"

"Yes?"

"I am Dr. Kim. Please come in," he motioned.

Despite the showy waiting room theatrics, Dr. Kim's office was more restrained, comprised of a solitary examination table, an unusually bright overhead lamp, a saline stand, and a respirator.

"You have back problem?" Dr. Kim asked, looking down at his clipboard.

"Yes. I think it was caused by my long flight from

Vancouver."

"Please lie down on the table and turn on your side," he said.

I climbed onto the table, struggling in agony to position myself. Without warning, Dr. Kim started manipulating my legs and pushing on my back. I cringed, unable to hold back cries of pain.

"Too tense," he announced. "Pinched nerve. Let me give you muscle relaxant."

I knew this meant a needle. I couldn't stand needles. I turned my head to avoid looking.

"This needle is a bit longer than usual," Dr. Kim announced, shoving something resembling a knitting needle in front of my face. He started to insert it into my arm, and I immediately became light-headed.

"You okay?" he asked, noticing my distress.

"I think I'm going to faint. I'm not good with needles."

A buzzer sounded, and I could barely make out the blur of the two young medical assistants from the waiting room, rushing around me as Dr. Kim barked out orders. A respirator was placed over my mouth, and a blood-pressure cuff started inflating around my arm. I could feel the needle being withdrawn, just as another one was inserted into my arm. I looked up to see the saline bag swinging above.

I had experienced similar reactions to needles in the past, all of which were resolved with a low-key approach that usually included a glass of orange juice and a short lie-down. Nonetheless, this ER-level dramatization had the same result: about ten minutes later, I started feeling better.

"*Pil! Pil!*" came a familiar voice from somewhere. I turned and squinted. Violeta's diminutive figure was hovering over me. She was wearing a pink woolen jacket and an unusual pink hat with a gigantic white bow protruding from its side.

"You okay? Doctor says you sissy with needles?"

I didn't have the energy to defend myself.

"Yes, I am."

"Here," she said, handing me a clear envelope full of horse-sized pills. "Super painkillers. Don't take too much or you go unconscious. Tony now drive you to your hotel. When you arrive, you pop one pill and relax. Tomorrow, I arrange physio for you. We have breakfast at seven in lobby, okay? See you later, *Pil*," she said, not waiting for my response.

Tony informed me that the drive to Seoul would take between forty-five minutes to an hour, depending on traffic. I tried to stay awake as our car wended its way along a congested highway, punctuated by depressing, Soviet-style apartment buildings with large numbers painted on their exteriors. It wasn't until the sound of a car horn jolted me that I realized I had dozed off. The highway had given way to shiny office towers, luxury designer boutiques, and five-star hotels. We had arrived in the *Gangnam-Gu District*. A few moments later, Tony pulled his SUV under a brightly lit awning where two doormen stood at attention, wearing long tuxedo jackets and exceptionally tall hats.

"Welcome to *Hotel InterContinental*," they announced in unison as I exited the car, almost toppling over as another spasm hit me.

By the time I had checked in and navigated the marbled lobby up to my suite, all I wanted to do was collapse on the inviting king-sized bed. I quickly opened my suitcase, booted up my laptop, and surveyed my new temporary home. The room was spacious and tastefully decorated, with a modern, Asian-inspired teak desk and matching chest of drawers. Decorative shutters framed a large picture window through which the flickering lights of bustling Seoul shone back. Affixed to the building across the road was a massive TV screen displaying various ads, casting hues of red, blue, and purple over my bed.

After a quick shower and clean-up, I checked my voicemail for the umpteenth time to see if Mrs. Kang had phoned back. When I saw no messages, I phoned her again, leaving my fifth voicemail. Then, popping one of Dr. Kim's horse pills, I closed the shutters, fell onto the bed, and was fast asleep within minutes, immersed in a series of lucid dreams.

The last of these dreams involved my return to Cothbert, where I discovered the Major had fired all my staff and was now running the school by herself. The students, pale and thin, stood in a line, waiting to be fed. As they approached the serving area, they extended their bowls toward Janice and Peg, who nervously ladled gray-looking gruel into them. The Major stood behind them, screaming, "Not too much! Not too much! I don't want to piss away any more money on food!" It was like a scene from *Oliver Twist*. Suddenly, a strange light appeared, and a bell started sounding. At first, I thought it was the school's fire alarm. The light grew brighter. *Where am I? What is this?* I wondered, staring through the darkness at streams of light cutting through some shutters. Then I remembered: Seoul. *Hotel InterContinental.*

I turned toward the ringing bell. My travel clock was bouncing around the bedside table, blaring its alarm. It read six o'clock. I fumbled to turn it off, sitting up slowly, relieved that my return to Cothbert had only been a dream. However, the sharp pain in my back reminded me I wasn't off the hook entirely. Swearing at the Major the whole time, I struggled to pull myself out of bed and into the shower. Dressing was another ordeal; every movement was a fresh trigger for my back spasms.

A quick check of my phone and computer revealed no calls or emails from Mrs. Kang. Violeta was waiting for me in the lobby when I exited the elevator. She was dressed in a pale blue and white outfit and wore a matching hat perched jauntily on the side of her head, making her look uncannily like a *Pan Am* flight attendant.

"Your back still has problem?" she asked, grabbing my arm as we trotted toward the restaurant where breakfast was served.

"Yes. You were right, Violeta. It's still pretty bad," I replied as another wave of spasms shook me.

We settled into a booth, and I reeled when I saw it was a buffet.

"Don't worry, Pil," she said, noticing my grimace. "I get you food. Bacon, egg, toast okay?"

"Yes. And coffee, please. Lots of coffee!"

Violeta cackled and sauntered off, returning shortly with my food and a waiter, who deposited a steel carafe of coffee on our table.

"So, here's the plan for today," she announced, positioning herself opposite me. "I take you sightseeing in Seoul. Don't worry about back. I have a solution."

You're joking, I thought. What about the physio?

"Then, tonight we have a special dinner with families who are interested in Cothbert."

"Really?" I replied, perking up. "Are these parents looking for next September?"

"No. They want to start January. As soon as they can get study permit. Korean people very impulsive, you know. They like to get going on something right away. By the way, I also invited a few of your current parents to join us."

"Oh, good. So, how many potential new students are we talking about?"

"Could be six. Maybe more. So, you need to give a nice presentation."

The pain in my back eased a bit as I started calculating the tuition numbers in my head.

Following breakfast, we agreed that we would meet again in fifteen minutes outside the front doors of the hotel in preparation for my sightseeing tour. I went back up to my room. With still nothing showing on my computer, I gathered my personal belongings, popped another one of Dr. Kim's horse pills, and waddled out the door of my suite, taking the elevator back down to the lobby.

Tony was already waiting outside the hotel when I arrived. It was a cool morning, and although the weather forecast called for a mainly sunny day, Seoul's dense pollution had ensured the skies were gray and dreary. I could also smell an unsavory odor in the air: a combination of car exhaust and open sewers.

"Your back is better, Mr. Gower?" Tony asked.

"Not exactly, Tony," I said, forcing a smile.

"No problem! Violeta arranged special physio for you today?"

Now that sounded good.

"So, no sightseeing?" I asked, hopefully, as I walked towards his car.

"You go in that car," he said, stopping me and pointing

towards a large minibus.

I climbed into the long vehicle and was surprised to be met by a burly, middle-aged woman wearing a short, white lab coat. When I searched for a place to sit, I realized the bus had no passenger seats. In their place was a solitary massage table. Violeta stuck her head through the vehicle's open door.

"*Pil*, during your drive to places, Jang-mi here will give you a massage," she said, pointing to the dour-looking woman in the white jacket. I looked more closely at Jang-mi, who I now realized had the physique of an Olympic bodybuilder.

"Our first stop will be the *Royal Palace*. See you there," she said, at which point Violeta slammed shut the sliding door. Jang-mi ushered me to the massage table.

"Thank you," I replied, lying face down.

"No speak English," she snapped.

The driver of the bus indicated we were ready to depart and pulled out onto the main road. As soon as this happened, Jang-mi sprang into action, pounding on my back while I screamed incessantly. I wondered how the driver was able to stay focused on the road with all the racket. When we did finally arrive at the *Royal Palace* for our tour, I couldn't wait to bail, no matter how painful it was going to be. Anything was better than more pummeling from Jang-mi.

"This way," ordered Violeta, helping me from the bus and leading me towards the palace entrance. "You get good physio?"

"Yes, thank you, Violeta. Jang-mi is very tough … I mean, very good at what she does." I wasn't going to be called a sissy again.

"You feel better later on. Trust me."

In truth, my horse pill, combined with Jang-mi's various

forms of manipulation treatment, was easing the pain some-what and, for the most part, the stroll through the historic palace grounds was bearable.

Following the tour, we had a quick lunch and then, af-ter popping another horse pill, toured the *National Palace Museum*, which was also located on the same grounds. The museum houses over 40,000 artifacts and royal treasures from the palaces of the Joseon Dynasty and the Korean Empire. It was a peaceful and fascinating place to spend a couple of hours.

By 3:00 pm, I was back on the bus with Jang-mi, the bodybuilder, who was eager to pounce again.

"The next stop is shopping in *Itaewon*," announced the driver. Pulling back into traffic, he added, "We should be there in about 15 minutes."

Only fifteen minutes of suffering, I thought. But little did I know that this next round of bodywork would be even worse than the previous one. Jang-mi decided to administer a Chinese technique known as *Gua sha*, which I later learned was designed to improve the body's circulation. The barbaric treatment entailed scraping—or in my case gouging—my skin with a strange-shaped jade tool. As our bus pulled up to an intersection, I was convinced nearby pedestrians, on hearing my agonizing screams of "Stop!" would have no choice but to alert local officials and, at any moment, the Seoul Vice squad would be descending on our bus prepared to rescue me. But, alas, this was not to be.

"We're here," announced the driver at last. I slowly opened the sliding door and limped towards Violeta, who was already there waiting.

"Feeling better?" she asked wryly.

"Oh, yes. That was … very invigorating." I was still adamant she wasn't going to hurl another sissy accusation at me.

"We don't have much time before dinner. I take you to fake shopping," she declared, grabbing my hand.

"Fake shopping?" Normally, I don't mind shopping, but with my back now on fire, I just wanted to go back to the hotel.

Violeta ushered me to a series of makeshift covered tables beside which vendors were sitting on cracked plastic stools flogging *Burberry* and *Polo* look-alike shirts, imitation *Mont Blanc* pens, and copycat *Coach* leatherwear. I now realized what she had meant by fake shopping. *Itaewon*, a favorite hangout for expats and foreigners, was also notorious for its inexpensive, high-quality counterfeit goods.

We walked briskly from stall to stall, and whenever I indicated an interest in something, Violeta would gently push me aside, ask for the price of the item, and then launch into an aggressive verbal attack on the vendor. The vendor would invariably bow his head in shame, look apologetically in my direction, and then reduce his price by almost half.

"You are a white foreigner," declared Violeta, reaching for my hand. "If I was not here with you, they would clean you out. They all are robbers!"

By the time we were ready to leave again, I had completed my Christmas shopping.

"Before I forget," said Violeta, just as I was about to climb back onto the bus, "at tonight's dinner, you must let me do most of the talking, okay? You be quiet until you give your presentation. Just make small-talk, like about the weather. You understand?"

"Yes. You're in charge, Violeta!"

I was more than happy to let her close the deals. If she was anywhere near as good at selling Cothbert as she was at negotiating the price of a fake *Coach* briefcase, we would have no trouble landing six students by the end of the night.

"Don't worry, *Pil*. I know how to control people," she added.

I'm sure you do.

The bus proceeded back towards the hotel, and the last round of Jang-mi's physical abuse seemed a bit more manageable and did not involve additional instruments of torture. Instead, she emptied a small vial of warm lavender oil over my skin and proceeded to softly massage what was left of my back. When we pulled up in front of the entrance to the *InterContinental*, I sat up, thanked Jang-mi, and handed her a generous tip. She smiled for the very first time.

Thankfully, Violeta informed me that our dinner with prospective families was being held at a restaurant near the hotel. I still had time for a bath and to change into my suit before everyone arrived. When I returned to my suite, I checked in vain for any messages. Before climbing into my steaming bath, I turned around to get a glimpse of my burning back in the bathroom mirror and gasped at the appearance of the random black-and-blue stripes from Jang-mi's onslaught. And yet, I had to admit, despite how painful it all looked and the lingering burning sensation, my back did feel better—much better. By the time I was making final adjustments to the knot on my necktie, I felt like a new man.

Chapter 28

The restaurant that Violeta had booked for our event was within easy walking distance of the hotel. She had requested a private room, which a waiter directed me to as soon as I arrived. It was a medium-sized function room with warm, subdued lighting. An enormous painting, depicting a monastery perched on distant blue and gray mountains encased in a dream-like mist, was recessed into an ornate, orange silk-padded wall. Eight round tables had been artfully set for a Korean dinner, complete with red and black chopsticks and starched white napkins fashioned to look like Birds of Paradise. At the front of the room, a podium with two microphones had been set up in front of a projection screen.

"Hello, Phil," came a familiar voice. I turned around to find Hee-young standing behind me, looking professional as always, in her charcoal gray business attire.

"I thought you might need some help with translation," she said with a smile.

"You mean to avoid another Backwards Day fiasco?"

"Hey, be careful, Byung-ju's mother is coming tonight."

"I think we're on good terms now," I joked.

"I think you are too. That's why she's coming. She's going

to help Violeta with the sales pitch."

"Really?"

"Really. She's so happy with Byung-ju's progress. She's never seen him so focused on school. That filming project you gave him was a brilliant idea."

"Did you know Mrs. Lim helped us outfit a room at our school with expensive video-editing equipment?"

"I heard. Like I said, she's a happy camper."

"Hey, stop gossiping, you two!" interrupted Violeta. "The parents will be here any moment. Remember, *Pil*, just talk about the weather and small stuff like that."

"Understood," I replied, giving Hee-young a playful wink.

In addition to six of our existing families, there were five prospective families with a total of six children who had come to learn more about Cothbert. As soon as everyone was seated, Violeta moved behind the podium to extend her welcome in both Korean and English. After introducing Hee-young and me, she invited Byung-ju's mother to the front to say a few words. Mrs. Lim, dressed in a green cocktail dress that glittered under the spotlights, looked like she had stepped out of a fashion magazine. Her meticulously made-up face and auburn-streaked hair, styled into a flawless, seemingly immovable shape, complemented her commanding presence. Smiling warmly, she launched into an animated speech as Hee-young leaned in to whisper translations.

"She's telling everyone that Cothbert changed her son's life," said Hee-young. "She's saying that the Korean education system had beaten him down, and he now has a purpose in life because the school found his passion for filmmaking."

I noticed tears welling in Mrs. Lim's eyes as she continued

her passionate pitch.

"She's calling Cothbert a special place," added Hee-young. "Not just for learning English, but for discovering who your child is as a person. She's emphasizing the life skills in your program."

I couldn't have said it better myself, the lump in my throat tightening.

When Mrs. Lim finished, the room burst into applause. As she bowed and slid back to her seat, Violeta formally thanked her and announced that dinner would be served momentarily and that I would be presenting during dessert.

I was seated at a table with Mr. and Mrs. Lee and their daughter, Minji, who sat directly across from me. With her long hair and glasses that constantly slid down her nose, she was a gangly but spirited 15-year-old. The rest of the diners appeared to be extended family, who seemed like they might have come mainly for the free food.

"My name means 'smart intellect,'" Minji announced proudly, turning to me. "I already read about Cothbert. I want to play on the soccer team and in the band. And I want my roommate to be from another country."

Her confidence made me laugh. As I jotted notes in my *Moleskine* notebook, I remembered Violeta's warning to avoid detailed discussions. Steering the conversation back to the food, I asked about the colorful spread on the table.

Minji's father, fluent in English, explained each dish: a rich stew of pork and fermented soybean paste, zucchini pancakes with thinly sliced onions and green chili peppers, crispy fried chicken glazed in a sweet and spicy sauce, stir-fried noodles with seafood, and sweet dumplings filled with red bean paste, honey, chestnut, and sesame.

A waiter arrived with red wine, but given that I was presenting shortly, I reluctantly declined.

When we finally made it to dessert, Violeta beckoned me to start making my way up to the front. Hee-young followed me from behind. We both situated ourselves beside Violeta, who immediately took charge, launching into a lengthy talk in Korean peppered with the words "Cothbert" and "Mr. Gower." At last, she pointed to me and yelled, "Mr. *Pil* Gower!" The room broke out in applause. Hee-young nodded for me to begin.

I stood behind the podium and took a deep breath. "Good evening, everyone. It is such an honor to be talking with you in such a marvelous city surrounded by such great company and food," I began, as Hee-young translated. More applause filled the room.

"Before I give my formal presentation, I want to share with you a short introductory video of Cothbert House School—a video created by Mrs. Lim's son, Byung-ju."

Mrs. Lim looked around the room, smiling and nodding her head proudly. Violeta dimmed the lights, and everyone turned their focus toward the screen. When the video finished playing, there was an ominous silence; however, as soon as the lights started coming up again, everyone rose to their feet. I could see a teary-eyed Mrs. Lim being cheered on by boisterous parents.

With such a captive audience, I quickly transitioned to my PowerPoint presentation, concluding with a slide that read *Questions and Answers.* Before I could reach for the microphone and field the first question, I remembered who was in charge. Violeta gave me the eye and stepped in front of me.

Violeta fielded most of the questions with ease, although she did allow me to respond to a few that dealt with the curriculum, clubs, and discipline. When the formal part of the night was over, there was finally time for me to meet with all of our existing Korean families. During each of these meetings, Violeta helped me with translation, although I could tell she was putting her own spin on my responses to questions.

The last to leave was Mrs. Lim, who simply hugged me and said "thank you" in broken English before bursting into tears. I then collapsed on a chair.

"Would you like that wine now?" asked Hee-young, with an exaggerated smile, holding a decanter in her hand. "I noticed how disappointed you appeared when you had to decline the offer earlier."

"You read my mind," I replied, beaming.

As we sipped, Violeta joined us, pouring herself tea. "They're all super interested. Tomorrow, Hee-young, set up interviews for *Pil*."

"Interviews?" I asked.

Violeta smiled. "It's all about perception, *Pil*. They believe there are limited spaces. Make them eager. Then, in a few days, fax me their acceptance letters."

"I understand. I'll inform my office right away."

"So, Hee-young can fill your morning with interviews?"

"Yes. I have one meeting with another Korean agent later in the afternoon before I fly to Taiwan, but otherwise, my day is open."

"Hmm," Violeta responded, turning to Hee-young. "I need to talk with *Pil* a bit. I'll see you tomorrow, okay?"

As Hee-young bid me goodnight with a faint smirk, Violeta

turned back to me. "Can I have some of that wine?" she asked, gesturing toward the bottle on the table.

I found an empty wine glass and poured her some. She took a slow sip, fixing me with an intense gaze, as though carefully considering her next words.

"*Pil*, do you trust me?"

"Do I trust you? Of course, I trust you," I replied, feeling my stomach tighten a bit.

"How many Korean students do you have now?"

"Excuse me?"

"At Cothbert. How many Korean students do you have?"

"Just the ten you sent me."

"And if we accept the six from tonight, you'll have sixteen, right?"

"That sounds about right."

"So, I will have sent you sixteen students. That means more than half your school is Korean students. Why do you need to go and visit more Korean agents?"

I thought about her question. The simple answer was, I wanted to cover my bases in case she didn't send us students in future years; to not put all my eggs in one basket.

"Look, *Pil*, I want you to think about something. You can discuss it with Harris. Your school needs students from all over the world. You already have too many Koreans. That's okay for now, but in the future, if people think you are just a Korean school, they won't send you students."

"What are you proposing?"

"Sign an exclusive agreement with me to manage your Korean market. Together, we can set targets, and you can focus your time and money on other markets. You won't even have to visit us if you don't want to. I'll look after everything

273

here."

The obvious question, though, was: *What happens if you don't meet those targets?* Harris already told me agents love to request exclusive agreements, but I remember he wasn't a big fan of them because most agents were notorious for not delivering on their promises.

"I was going to phone Harris tonight anyway. Let me pitch your idea and see what he says," I replied, reassuringly.

"Good, please do! Now, enough business talk. So, how's your love life?" she blurted, reaching for her wine again.

I nearly choked. "Pardon me?"

"Do you have a girlfriend?"

Oh God, here we go.

"No … I've been too busy with Cothbert to have time for girlfriends," I stammered. "Also, Timberline Lake is not exactly a hot spot for eligible women."

Violeta coddled her wine glass and stared into my eyes. "When I was your age, I was like you. Very ambitious. Only focused on work. By the time I wanted to get married, it was very hard to find the right person."

"Did you get married?"

"Nearly. I got engaged but I got cold feet. Now I am alone. But it's okay, I guess."

I slid my fingers down the stem of my glass, wondering what to say next.

"What about Hee-young? She is quite cute. And she's eligible," Violeta smiled.

I had to admit, I did like Hee-young, and she was quite attractive, but I hadn't really thought about her in those terms. I was starting to feel more and more uncomfortable with the conversation.

274

"She is very nice," I replied, trying not to open up a can of worms. "Anyway, Violeta, listen, I obviously have a busy day tomorrow and I still need to phone Harris." I downed the remaining wine in my glass to signal that I was ready to leave.

"Okay. Sorry, I embarrassed you, right?"

"Well..."

"No pressure. Just remember what I said, *Pil*. You are a good man, and I don't want you to grow up lonely."

I suddenly felt sorry for Violeta and realized that under that tough veneer was a caring and vulnerable person.

Chapter 29

"Well, if it isn't our intrepid jet-setter," boomed Harris, retrieving my call. "How are things?"

I happily recounted my disastrous flight, trip to *Kim's Golden Body Clinic*, and my mobile physio nightmare with Jang-mi. Harris could barely contain himself, snorting and howling at my misadventures.

"Listen, not to be a party pooper," he said finally, "but I was just about to phone you. I'm afraid things are getting worse with Mrs. Kang."

"Why? What happened?" I asked, cringing.

"Her driver just picked up Thomas."

"I expected that…"

"And dropped off another letter from her legal cronies, telling you to cease and desist with your harassing voice-mails."

"Harassing? I just want to talk to her."

"I know. Anyway, our lawyer has drafted a response to everything, basically accusing them of defaming the school's and your reputation with unfounded accusations and confirming the fees were never paid and that, as a result, we have no intention of reimbursing her anything. We will, however, be filing our own suit for non-payment. I'll get

Koji to forward you a copy."

"And the Major?"

"Sullen and non-communicative. Strange, actually."

"Wow, this is all so surreal."

"Yes, well, just to further complicate matters, I finally got Joe to open up the books."

"What? How the heck did you arrange that?"

"Oh, the usual. Told the Major I would quit unless she authorized it; that we couldn't continue to run the school without full transparency."

"Nice! So, let me guess. We're broke?"

"We're not good. The Major has been adding all sorts of personal items to our budget. That's why you couldn't reconcile the numbers."

"What sorts of items?"

"You name it … a mortgage, some personal utility bills, oh ya, and some inflated charges for the work her so-called volunteer friends did to renovate the campus."

"You mean she was invoiced for that work?"

"Yes. And for some reason, she paid each invoice in cash."

"Cash? That doesn't sound right."

"No, it doesn't!"

"No wonder Joe was so concerned. It almost hints of money laundering."

"My sentiments exactly. Anyway, the bottom line is, we have another $60,000 on our books we haven't budgeted for."

"Yikes! Well, some help might be on the way… I've got six students who want to start in January."

"You're kidding?"

"No. Violeta's been a miracle worker," I said, describing the success of this evening's presentation.

"Wow! Okay, just a minute. Let me do the math."

I could hear Harris tapping on his calculator.

"If we add your additional six students," he said finally, "even with their fees being prorated to the start of January, I think it should still cover the shortfall and give us a small cushion."

"You mean, as long as the Major doesn't add any more unexpected expenses."

"Don't worry about that. I'm taking over budgeting from now on, so it won't happen."

"That's comforting to know. And in the midst of all this chaos, how are the students holding up?"

"Oh, they're fine. Ida tracked down some used instruments and has already started practicing with her Jazz Band, and the Major found them new uniforms."

"Great! Listen, I do need to talk to you about one other thing before I fly to Taiwan," I added, outlining what Violeta had proposed this evening.

"Hmm," Harris muttered, pondering the proposal. "You know what, if it was anyone else, I'd say *no*. But I've known Violeta for some time. I trust her. And based on what you described happened tonight, I say, let's do it. One less market for us to worry about."

"That'll make her happy."

"Speaking of which, did she try to make you happy?"

"Yes, but not in the way you are implying. She thinks I need to get hitched, and not with her. She proposed Hee-young as a possibility."

"Not a bad choice."

"I know, but the last thing I need right now is for someone to be my matchmaker. That's not my style."

"Well, luckily you're heading to Taipei. She'll soon be out of your hair. Oh, speaking of which, Manfred's father sent me an email asking whether you wanted to clear Taiwanese customs quickly. I responded on your behalf to thank him and said, sure."

"Fine with me … whatever that means. Anyway, please let Koji know I'll be sending him some information tomorrow on the six students we'll be accepting. He'll need to have their acceptance letters ready to fax back to Violeta in a few days."

"Will do."

"Are you ready for your trip to Hong Kong and Japan?"

"Yup! Aki's parents have arranged my hotel in Tokyo, and Evil Grandmother Lam is meeting me at the airport in Hong Kong and has also agreed to look after my accommodations."

"I'd also follow up on your flight arrangements, if I were you."

"Don't worry, after hearing you describe what you went through, as soon as I hang up, the Major and I will be having a little heart-to-heart about my own travel plans."

"Well, good luck with that one. How's her foot doing?"

"Much better. Still using a cane but far too mobile for my liking."

"You're so bad. Now, I've got to get some sleep. Apparently, I've got a full morning of interviews tomorrow."

After slipping into my PJs, I checked my emails one last time and noticed that Koji had forwarded our lawyer's letter. Quickly scanning it, I gave a dejected sigh, and threw myself on my bed where, within minutes, I succumbed to a deep slumber.

Violeta's company was located in a nondescript office building, a seven-minute walk from the hotel. A receptionist,
sitting at a rounded chrome-and-glass desk, welcomed me
as soon as I walked in and told me to have a seat. I looked up
at the red wall behind her. Large golden letters spelled out
the words, *Hyung-bo Consulting Ltd.*

"There you are," rejoiced Hee-young, swooping into the
reception area. "We're all set for your interviews. Your first
family has already arrived. They're sitting in my office."

I followed Hee-young through an adjoining doorway into
an open-area workspace where a number of employees in
cubicles were typing industriously at their computers. A few
of them stopped to look up, then quickly resumed their work,
no doubt used to seeing school reps in their office.

I was assigned a small interview room that had a view
of the city and was furnished with a round table and a few
comfortable chairs. A counter was set up with coffee, bottled
water, and local Korean snacks.

"If you need anything else, just give me a shout," advised
Hee-young. "My office is two doors down. I'll go and get
your first family now."

The morning went by quickly, and by 11:00 am, I had finished
five half-hour interviews. I could recite my questions by
heart: *What do you like to read? ... What's your favorite
subject? ... Why do you want to attend Cothbert?"* After a
while, it all became rather repetitive, and I could also tell
the applicants knew what I was going to ask even before I
posed my questions, often responding with robotic, well-
rehearsed answers. Their English levels were reasonably
good, and I fully expected, once enrolled at Cothbert, they

would be either Stems or Blossoms.

The last student to walk in was Minji Lee, who had sat at my table the previous night at the reception. She was the perfect applicant for my final interview as she dominated the conversation, responding to each question with such depth that all I had to do was smile and nod my head. Unlike the other applicants, Minji's responses were heartfelt and spontaneous, with the exception of her last response to my question about why she wanted to attend Cothbert:

"I need to embellish my language," she began. "I cannot rely on perfunctory learning from cram schools. I must accentuate my experience with a residential pedagogical experience like Cothbert's."

Another overdose of that infamous 20,000 word vocabulary book, I thought.

With the interviews complete, I enjoyed a bento box-style lunch with Hee-young before spending the rest of the afternoon by the hotel pool, having canceled my late-afternoon agent appointment. Despite the tranquil setting, I struggled to relax, my thoughts still preoccupied with the Kang situation. By 4:00 p.m., after an overly prolonged send-off from Violeta, I found myself back among the familiar Soviet-style buildings, heading to *Gimpo Airport*.

The three-hour flight to Taipei was far more comfortable than the one I had experienced from Vancouver — this time, it actually included legroom. With a time difference of one hour, it was 7:00 pm when the plane began its descent into *Chiang Kai-Shek International Airport*. Forty minutes later, I was exiting into the terminal where I was hit by a surge of hot, humid air.

Scanning a series of English directional signs, I walked into the Immigration Hall, where in the distance there were huge lineups behind counters staffed by uniformed officials. A monitor up above was flashing arrival information showing that, in addition to our flight, there were arrivals from JFK, Bangkok, Manila, and Singapore. I took a deep breath as I joined the back of one of the lines. However, as I did, a tall, elderly man dressed in full military regalia stepped out in front of me. In an exuberant voice that everyone in the hall could hear, he asked:

"Are you Dr. Gower?"

"Well…yes…I mean, I'm Phil Gower," I stuttered.

"Oh, Dr. Gower," the man saluted, "our country is so honored to host you. Please…please, do follow me," he beckoned with a sense of deference.

Waiting passengers stared at me, some with suspicion and others in awe. As I was paraded in ceremonial fashion to a counter reserved exclusively for diplomats and VIPs, my passport was promptly stamped. By the time we descended to the luggage area, a younger man wearing a neatly tailored black suit and white gloves was already there waiting for us with my luggage stacked carefully on a cart.

"I am Tyler, Mr. Ma's driver," the man introduced, in perfect English. "I will be driving you to the *Grand Hyatt Hotel.*"

Thanking my military attaché, who continued to reiterate, for anyone still interested, his immense honor in welcoming me to Taiwan, we made our way outside into a surge of heat. A black *Range Rover* was waiting for us in a cordoned-off area beside yet another man in uniform.

The drive into Taipei felt worlds apart from Seoul's sterility: lush greenery and towering mountains lined the high-way. As we neared the outskirts of the city's core, a massive red and gold building, not unlike one of the pavilions I had seen at the *Royal Palace* in Seoul, came into view.

"What's that?" I asked Tyler.

"Oh, that's the *Grand Hotel*," he replied. "It was built by Chiang Kai-shek to host dignitaries. But it had a bad fire two years ago and has been under reconstruction."

"Oh, I'm sorry to hear that."

"Do you know about the hotel you're staying at?" Tyler asked somewhat hesitantly.

"*The Grand Hyatt?* Not really, other than it's a pretty fancy place and very popular."

"Yes, but some people say it's haunted," he revealed.

Oh no. Here we go again, I thought, reliving the ghost episode at school.

"The hotel was built on a former prisoner of war camp," he continued in a cautionary voice, "where a number of executions took place. Some people believe the ghosts of those prisoners still haunt the hotel."

"They've seen these ghosts?" I asked, more to humor him than anything.

"Not exactly. But there are two Taoist talismans at the front door of the hotel to ward off spirits, although the hotel denies that's what they're there for."

"And what do you think, Tyler?"

"Oh, I'm not sure I could stay there," he intoned solemnly.

Once Tyler dropped me off, I entered through the massive doors of *The Grand Hyatt Hotel*, taking careful note of the talismans on either side. The lobby was immense, almost the size of a football field, decadently embellished in creamy marble with tall white Romanesque-style pillars. After an efficient check-in, I rode the elevator up to my suite, which was an enormous space with tasteful earth-tone decorations and marble accents. A welcome package from *Yingyucom* was waiting for me on a desk. I briefly flicked through its contents, which included a map of the fair's ballroom, my table number, and a name tag. The fair was scheduled to open at 9:00 a.m. the following day.

After setting up my laptop, I started to unpack, when there was a ding from my computer. Normally, I would not have rushed to see what it was, but with the Kang situation, I was constantly on edge. The message was from Harris with the caption: *Sit down before reading.*

Oh no. Now what? I thought, perching on the edge of the chair in front of the computer. I read further:

Koji just confided in me that the Major flew to Taipei and will be joining you at the Yingyucom Education Fair tomorrow.

Sorry, Harris.

"Holy shit! No! Please, no!" I yelled out loud. "No! No! No!"

Given the time difference, it was too early to phone Harris back, so I decided to drown my sorrows at a restaurant on the first floor called *Cheers*. Plopping down at its bar, I realized I desperately needed some Western food and ordered a hamburger, fries, and a glass of Shiraz. I was still in shock over Harris' message, but by the time I was reaching for my second glass of wine, I had resigned myself to the fact I really didn't care.

As I savored my burger and thought at length about tomorrow's fair, my train of thought was suddenly jolted by a familiar voice.

"Philly!"

The Major was standing beside me, resting on her cane, grinning from ear to ear. "I thought you might be here," she added excitedly.

"Major. What a surprise," I feigned astonishment.

"Wait a sec," she interrupted, raising her hand. "Hey, bartender. A Scotch! Whatever is the cheapest."

Some of the other patrons sitting at the bar gave us disapproving looks.

The Major sat on a stool next to me. "So … a bit of a shock, eh Philly?" she gloated, patting me on the back.

"Yes, Major, I just learned from Harris you were coming … totally caught off guard."

"How'd big guy know?" she scowled, looking disappointed that I hadn't experienced the full impact of her bombshell.

"Not sure," I lied.

"Well, anyway, I just thought it would be even better if the two of us were working the fair together, particularly given some of my previous experience in sales. That way we might get double the number of kids. Don't you think?"

"Um, yes, that's a possibility, but…"

"Now listen, Philly, I'll stay completely out of your way," her shark-like grin saying otherwise. "You won't even know I'm here. I'll work the room over the next two days … you know, convincing kids to come to our table, and then you and me can close the deals together. How does that sound?"

I wanted to say 'hellish'.

I rubbed my tired eyes, feeling totally defeated. "Yes, that sounds like a plan, Major," I finally responded halfheartedly. "Anyway, listen, I'm a bit tired after Seoul. I hope you don't mind, but I think I'll just finish up my burger and head up to my room so I'm well refreshed for tomorrow's fair."

The Major's Scotch arrived, and she took a swig before her eyes shot back at me. "So, how was that junket in Seoul?" she asked accusingly.

"Not bad."

"What does not bad mean?" she demanded, forcefully putting her glass down on the bar.

"Oh, I think I signed about six students for January," I said casually.

The Major cleared her throat, her eyes enlarging.

"So, Major," I added gleefully, "I do hope you'll be able to deliver at tomorrow's fair with at least that number of kids."

Her face visibly paled as she reached for her Scotch again. "Yes … I will do what I can," she stammered. "But we'll be working together on that. Right?"

"Oh, I'm sure you'll deliver on your own," I smiled, climbing off the bar stool, "particularly with that sales background you mentioned. Anyway, I'll see you in the Grand Ballroom tomorrow — say around 8:15 a.m. for set-up?"

The Major nodded, but I could tell I had successfully thrown down the gauntlet.

"We're at table number 27, by the way. Have a good night, Major," I called out, exiting with a self-satisfied smile but quietly bracing for tomorrow's showdown.

"It was 11:00 p.m. when I made it back to my room — 8:00 a.m. in Vancouver. I figured Harris was already in his office.

"Now, don't shoot the messenger," Harris called out defensively, realizing it was me on the other end of the phone. But his tone suggested he was relishing every moment of this situation.

"We've already met," I blurted. "I went for a drink after I read your message and the Major just appeared, seemingly out of nowhere — like she always does."

"Well, if it's any consolation, I never got to see her about my flight arrangements, and they don't look any better than yours."

"Harris, I just don't know if I have the stamina to manage her over the next couple of days of the fair. I'm already feeling exhausted after Seoul."

"Just do your own thing. She'll realize soon enough that it's not as easy as it all looks."

"I've already planted that seed. She asked me about Seoul, and when I informed her about how many students I landed, I told her I expect her to get at least that many in Taipei."

"Ha, that'll shut her down. You're really learning how to manage her, aren't you? I'm impressed!"

"I did mentor under a master," I laughed. "Oh, listen. Before you hang up, any further news on Mrs. Kang?"

"No. Nothing more. No calls to you either?"

"Nope. I've also stopped my harassing calls," I added sarcastically.

Harris chuckled. "Alright, I'll let you know if I hear anything more. Good luck with your sidekick."

"Thanks! I'm so looking forward to it."

Chapter 30

The next morning, I ordered room service and, over a croissant and coffee, I reviewed my welcome package, practiced my sales pitch, and spread out all of my marketing props on the bed. A handmade tablecloth with the school's logo, neatly stitched by Myrtle, anchored the setup. Photocopied informational packets and laminated activity photos added a personal but modest touch, and, of course, there was Byungju's video. I had already made arrangements with the fair organizers to rent a small TV-VHS unit, which they promised would be waiting for me when I arrived. The plan was to position it on a corner of my table and run a continuous loop of the video throughout the fair. With a smile, I packed my presentation materials into my carry-on. I felt confident and ready to introduce Cothbert House School to the Taiwanese.

It wasn't until after I checked in at the Welcome Desk and entered the main exhibition hall that my feelings of self-confidence slowly started to wane. A number of school reps had already set up their tables—or state-of-the-art booths, to be more precise, with their self-contained lighting and professionally branded backdrops, enhanced by stunning photography. Below these flashy displays were tables with matching crested tablecloths showcasing glossy brochures and inviting swag bags. Suddenly, Myrtle's handmade tablecloth and Koji's photocopied informational packets made our table look more like a stall at a local church bazaar.

Feeling a bit deflated, I finished setting up and then went in search of my second cup of coffee. All at once, I became aware of a very familiar, grating voice. Wincing, I struggled to compose myself as the voice rose in volume, becoming more unsettled. Quickly scanning the hall, I noticed the Major gesturing wildly in front of the Help Desk. She was waving her finger accusingly at Hymie Chen and berating him so loudly that the entire hall could hear her tirade. Hymie was sitting at his desk, stupefied with embarrassment, and from the looks of things, it was he who was the one in need of help.

"What's going on?" I asked, quickly striding to the Help Desk.

Hymie stood up as soon as he recognized me. "Oh … Hello, Mr. Gower. We … we have a small problem," he said, walking out from behind the desk.

"Crooks!" exclaimed the Major. "That's the problem. Crooks!"

"Hymie, what's the matter?" I puffed, feeling in no mood for the Major's theatrics.

Like a cowering dog, Hymie moved uncomfortably close to me, eyeing the Major defensively.

"Well, Mr. Gower, as you know, you paid for one representative to be at the fair. We did not know Miss Hunter would also be coming. So … so, she will need to pay an additional three hundred dollars as a second rep. See, it says so right here," he added, frantically flipping to a page in the fair procedural guide he had in his hand. "The additional cost does include lunch," he added, as though this information would somehow defuse the situation.

"Give us a moment," I said, pulling the Major aside to a less prominent area of the hall. Hymie moved back behind the Help Desk where he pretended to arrange pamphlets, nervously raising his head every so often to glance at us.

"Rip-off. Total rip-off," the Major scowled, avoiding eye contact.

"Major," I said with determination. "This is how these fairs work. Hymie's only doing his job. And he's correct. I remember seeing the price list for the fair. He has every right to charge us for a second person. You know," I said, shrugging my shoulders, "if you're not comfortable with the added expense…"

"Fine!" the Major snapped, glaring at me. She then whirled around and hobbled over to Hymie, who quickly jumped to his feet. I watched in horrified fascination as she reached inside a pocket of her slacks, pulled out an assortment of crumpled bills, and proceeded to slam them down in an unorganized heap onto Hymie's table.

"Canadian money okay for you, son?" she barked. "Or maybe you'd prefer gold bullion?"

"Canadian is okay," Hymie stammered, looking uneasily in my direction.

The Major carefully counted out three hundred dollars before hastily grabbing the remaining money from the table and stuffing it back into her pocket.

"All settled now, Major?" I asked, moving in beside her, knowing full well she was fuming inside.

"Never mind. Let's just get us some bloody kids to pay for all this racket!"

"Yes, Major," I replied, not having the energy to fight her on this one. As I ushered her towards our booth, I turned slightly and gave Hymie a signal not to worry. I caught his grin.

At 9:00 a.m. sharp, a gong sounded, signaling for hordes of people to spill into the Hall. Unfortunately, most of the visitors who chose to swing by our table were not familiar with the concept of an ESL boarding school. Using Chill's photos and Byung-ju's video, I did my best to explain it to them, but as soon as they caught wind of our fee schedule, they quickly tuned out, eventually bolting for another booth. It didn't help that our table was sandwiched between two questionable-looking language academies. These schools charged a third of our fees and haggled with families, frequently offering them what they called "scholarships" to secure deals. In truth, these were nothing more than feel-good fee discounts that had no correlation to an applicant's scholastic ability. To make matters worse, the Major was starting to take an acute interest in the way the reps at these language academies were pushing their services, and I could tell her own wheels were turning.

"I'm going on a walkabout," she announced abruptly, reaching for her cane, just as a father picked up one of our fee schedules, released a loud grunt, and promptly steered his daughter to the next table.

"See you later, Major," I replied, trying to contain my sense of relief.

A few seconds later, Hymie slipped over, his eyes shifting from side to side to make sure the Major was nowhere in sight.

"Any news from Mrs. Kang?" he whispered.

"She's now accusing me of harassment, but our lawyer is on top of it all and calling her bluff."

"Okay, well, I guess that's good," he said tentatively. "Is everything alright with the fair?" he asked proudly.

"To be honest, Hymie, no, not great. Next year, our table needs to be beside the other boarding schools in the room. People think we're your basic language academy," I said, pointing at the tables beside me. "They don't get the whole boarding thing. And they certainly don't get our fees."

"I think you're right. Our mistake. Sorry about that. Let me see if I can steer some of the right types of families your way. Oh, and Mr. Gower, our office just got a call from Mr. Ma—you know, Manfred's father. He wants to host you and Miss Hunter for dinner tonight at his private club, if that's okay."

"That's very kind of him," I replied, still feeling tired and preferring an evening to myself. "Sure, I'd love to," I conceded, putting on a brave face. "And I know Miss Hunter will certainly be honored."

"Oh, good. I'll let Mr. Ma know. We'll send the details to your hotel room later today."

Attendance at the fair remained steady, and Hymie finally delivered on his promise of sending over some mission-appropriate families. By the time lunch arrived, I had three strong prospects for the following September.

I hadn't seen the Major for some time and was hoping she would come and relieve me when I noticed her leading a set of parents with two school-aged boys hurriedly towards our table. The parents were smiling awkwardly as the Major corralled them with her cane in front of me.

292

"Philly," she called out loudly. "Got some hot ones for you. Offered them fifty percent off or two-for-one, whichever they prefer."

"You offered them what?" I asked incredulously.

"You know, scholarships."

I gritted my teeth as the family seated themselves in front of me, looking totally bewildered.

"Got to go," said the Major. "I'm on a roll. You close the deal."

While the two children took an interest in Byung-ju's video, their parents sat politely, waiting for me to begin.

"So, would you like me to tell you a little bit about Cothbert?" I ventured hesitantly.

No response.

I tried a different tack.

"So, what do your boys do for fun?"

More silent stares.

After further prodding, I finally realized they didn't understand a single word of English. Luckily, there were translators roaming the fair, identifiable by their bright pink shirts, and I waved one over.

"Hello, my name is Nancy," said the translator, pulling up beside me. "How can I help you today?"

"Hi, Nancy. My colleague brought this family to see me. Can you ask them what they know about our school and whether they have any questions for me?"

Nancy started talking to the parents in Mandarin, and I could see them getting a bit agitated as the conversation unfolded.

Nancy swiveled back towards me with a strained look on her face. "They don't know anything about your school. They were about to sit down with another school their friends had recommended when your colleague started yelling, 'Big scholarships! Big scholarships! Come with me!' She wouldn't stop yelling at them, so they agreed to follow her out of courtesy."

Oh, great! They're abductees.

"Look … Nancy, let me explain what our school is all about, and then they can decide if we're the right fit. Tell them no pressure, okay?"

The parents seemed to relax a bit as I gave them my pitch while Nancy provided simultaneous translation, but when they eventually realized we were a boarding school, they started vehemently shaking their heads from side to side and motioning with their hands that they were no longer interested.

"I don't think this is what they're looking for," said Nancy diplomatically. "They plan to accompany their children to Canada. They don't need boarding."

I forced a smile, shook their hands, and, with the help of Nancy, wished them good luck in their search.

As I watched them depart, I just wanted the day to end. A few moments later, the Major returned, this time without any hostages.

"So, did you close the deal?"

"I've got to go to the Men's Room, Major. I'll talk to you when I get back," I said brusquely, charging towards the other side of the room. Unfortunately, I hadn't made it very far when Hymie stepped out in front of me.

"We have another problem to deal with," he said, anxiously. "Mr. Tang's assistant, Bobo, just phoned me. Some of the other school reps have launched complaints against

Cothbert."

"Complaints? About what?"

"Bobo emailed them to me. Would you like me to read them to you?"

"Sure, why not," I replied, feeling totally crestfallen.

Hymie looked down at his clipboard. "One rep wrote: *Like a shady used car-saleswoman, a lady from Cothbert House School has been purposely intercepting our potential clients. This is totally unethical behavior and needs to be addressed immediately.* Another rep wrote: *An unscrupulous representative from Cothbert House School has been bribing families in an attempt to stop them from visiting our table. We cannot continue to support Yingyucom fairs if these are the types of people you are going to represent.*"

"Damn her!" I blurted. "Hymie, you know this is not what we're all about. Do you think this is going to jeopardize your ability to represent our school in the future?"

"No, I don't think so … your school is very popular with our parents. But this situation is serious. It could hurt both of our reputations. I did explain to Bobo that the problem is not you, but your boss."

"And?"

"And, she told me she'd deal with it."

After finally making it to the Men's Room, I took my time walking back to our booth, not knowing how best to manage the mess the Major had made, when Hymie zipped past me, stopping in front of our table, where I could see him saying something to the Major before handing her his cell phone. I watched from a distance as the Major's expression went from an obstinate scowl to child-like humiliation. Moving in closer, I could hear her starting to grovel.

"Yes, Bobo, I understand. It won't happen again … Of course, Cothbert truly appreciates all the money … I mean, students you have been sending us … No, I don't like lawsuits either … Yes, I will certainly talk to them right away … I agree, they have every right to be … appalled. Thank you for calling, Bobo."

As soon as the Major handed Hymie back his phone, I strolled up to our table.

"Everything alright, Major?" I asked, casually.

"Yes … why?" she replied, her face flushing as she turned to avoid me.

"Oh, nothing. Just asking."

"Um … I need to go and check on something," she announced, fidgeting nervously. "I'll be right back."

"Okay," I said, content to let the situation play itself out.

A family stepped in front of our table, so I turned my focus back to my sales pitch. Thirty minutes later, with another strong prospect in the bag, the Major returned looking a bit beaten up.

"Tomorrow … if it's okay … I'm going to sit with you at our table … you know, so I can watch how you market the school."

"Yes, Major. That's good with me. Very good. Oh, before I forget, we've been invited to dinner tonight by Manfred's father. I told Hymie you would be attending. I do hope that's okay."

"Oh, yes. That would be very nice. It's been such a long day."

"Yes, hasn't it, though," I replied, rolling my eyes.

Later that evening, Mr. Ma's driver, Tyler, pulled up his black

Range Rover in front of an imposing glass tower. A young woman in business attire stood by the entrance, her posture crisp and professional as she waited to greet us.

"Mr. Gower?" she called over politely as I exited the car.

"Yes," I said, moving toward her.

"Oh… good, good, good. Welcome. Mr. Ma is expecting you and Miss Hunter upstairs…"

A rattling noise broke our attention, and we both turned back toward the car, where the Major was clambering awkwardly out of the front passenger side. Before I could offer my help, the young woman rushed forward to assist her.

"And you must be the owner of Cothbert House School," she said, reaching for the Major's arm. "I'm Poppy Ping."

"Hi there, Poopy! Harriet Hunter," the Major huffed as she steadied herself with her cane, gawking at the building. "Yeah, I'm the owner, but our school ain't as fancy as this place."

Poppy smiled, her professionalism never faltering, as she directed us through a revolving glass door into a vast lobby. Steering us into a glass elevator, she turned a key on its control pad. As the elevator began its ascent, the spectacular evening lights of Taipei sparkled back at us. The enormity of the city spread out below, glowing against the night sky. In the distance, the *Grand Hotel* stood like a beacon, its golden silhouette unmistakable.

"Mr. Ma's private dining room is on the 50th floor," Poppy explained, just as the elevator car slowed to a stop. The doors then slid open, and a tall man stepped out in front of us. He had a contrived business look about him, with his round, horn-rimmed glasses, perfectly gelled black hair, and tightly

297

fitting double-breasted light gray plaid suit.

"I'm Lafayette Lu, Mr. Ma's personal assistant," he said, with an air of pretension. "Please follow me."

Lafayette led us down a softly lit hallway with amber-colored walls adorned with a series of abstract oil paintings.

"Wow, Philly, this place must have cost a chunk of change, don't you think?" the Major said, her head swiveling from side to side.

"Hmm, Major," I replied, wincing inwardly.

When we finally stopped, it was in front of two enormous teak doors. Lafayette pulled one open. "Go ahead, please." He nodded slightly, ushering us through.

We walked into a tastefully furnished room with antique furniture complemented by huge decorative blue vases. At the room's center, under bright lighting and atop a deep Oriental blue carpet, stood a round table elegantly set with blue-and-white china, neatly folded napkins, and gold chopsticks

The majority of the invitees were already seated. It seemed, at first glance, that there were about a dozen well-dressed people engaged in lively discussions. But the moment they noticed us, they stopped talking, stood up, and, as one, turned in our direction.

"Ah, my friends from Cothbert House School! Welcome to Taipei!" called an enthusiastic voice from the far side of the table. A few seconds later, a man hurried towards us.

"Digby Ma," he greeted, eagerly reaching out his hand towards me. "I'm so glad you had time for me. I know how busy you must be. But I had to meet the young principal Manfred has talked so much about."

Digby was tall, thin and exuded sophistication, with his

black silk suit, starched white shirt, and tightly knotted gold tie. His mischievous smile looked exactly like his son's.

"Very nice to meet you too, Mr. Ma. This is our school's owner, Major Harriet Hunter," I said, directing him to the Major.

"Oh, yes. Very nice to meet you too. I've never met a real major before. How long did you serve in the military?"

I turned to the Major, curious to hear her response.

"Oh … a few years," she stammered. "I was going to be re-posted, but I didn't want to leave Canada … so … so, I quit."

"Oh, I didn't know that," I said, enjoying the way she wove the tale."Where exactly did they want to send you?" I asked innocently.

"Oh … somewhere in Northern Europe. Yes, Spain, I believe."

Digby gave her a curious look and then waved his hand. "This way, please," he said, walking us briskly towards the opposite side of the table, where a woman with white porcelain skin and hair swept back into a sleek chignon at the nape of her neck stood waiting for us. She was wearing a scarlet-colored *qipao* that radiated timeless elegance.

"This is my wife, Doris," he introduced.

"Welcome, Mr. Gower… Major Hunter. It is our honor to host you," Doris said, extending her hand. She had a natural elegance and a twinkle of playfulness in her eyes.

Like a soldier taking his post, Digby moved behind his chair while Doris, seated on his right-hand side, invited the Major to sit next to her. Digby then pulled out a chair on his left for me. Finally, clapping his hands, he asked everyone in the room to be seated.

"These are my dear friends from Canada," he announced proudly, first introducing us individually and then adding, "and they have the near-impossible task of educating my son."

The room responded with spirited laughter.

"And, Major Hunter and Mr. Gower," he continued with a smile, while extending his arms towards the guests sitting around the table, "the motley crew you see before you are my business colleagues."

More laughter.

Several waiters appeared and placed small menu cards by each guest's plate as the room buzzed with conversation once more.

I reached for the card in front of me. It read:

Mr. Digby Ma and Mrs. Doris Ko have the honor of welcoming Major Harriet Hunter and Mr. Phil Gower to Taiwan.

Following that was a description of the courses to follow: assorted small appetizers and drunken chicken as starters, double-boiled seafood soup, braised beef shank, lobster, abalone, steamed vegetables, and noodles as main courses, and sweet red bean soup and fresh fruit for dessert.

"Do you drink wine, Mr. Gower?" asked Digby, as a waiter hovered behind us holding a bottle wrapped in a white napkin.

"Only in excess," I joked.

"Good ... good! Me too," he cheered, flicking his hand rapidly. The waiter poured a small amount of wine into each of our glasses.

"May I make a toast first, Mr. Ma?" I asked, raising my glass. "To your son ... Manfred?"

"Oh, yes, thank you. You are too kind. Doris!" he called out, leaning towards her. "Mr. Gower is making a toast to

Manfred."

I could see Doris smiling as she lifted her glass. But before I could even take a sip, Digby gently tapped me on the shoulder. He had downed his wine and was showing me his empty glass as a gesture of respect. I was about to follow his lead when he signaled with a friendly wave that it wasn't necessary.

"This is a wonderful wine, Mr. Ma," I said finally, realizing how much better it was than any of the cheap plonk I drank at the *As You Like It.*

"Please, call me Digby."

"And me Phil," I added.

"Phil, you have a very good palate." He waved for the waiter to hand him the bottle. "This is a *1985 Pichon Longueville Comtesse de Lalande*—from the Pauillac region of France," he said authoritatively, pointing at the bottle's gold-and-white label. "It's a Grand Cru—from my private collection. One of my favorites."

I took another sip and could only imagine how much the rich, robust nectar cost.

The waiters arrived, balancing trays laden with food, and the noise level subsided as conversation was replaced by people enjoying their host's cuisine.

"So, Digby, what do you do in Taiwan?" I asked, pulling apart a succulent piece of chicken.

"Well, what I used to do and what I do now are two different things," he said, reaching with his chopsticks for a plate of wood ear mushroom salad rotating on a lazy Susan in the center of the table. "I started out working in the construction industry when I was only twenty, just after returning from studying business at a small university in Australia that had given me a full-ride scholarship."

301

"Oh, that's why your English is so strong," I interjected.

"If you say so. Anyway, my experience studying overseas paid off, and by the time Taiwan's economy started to grow, I had risen to become president of the company. But after twenty-five years of slogging away, I'd had enough and chose to retire."

"You don't look old enough to be retired."

"Thank you. I'm not. But I'd had it with office politics, and given that I'm financially well-off, I didn't see the need for the hassles anymore. Doris and I now put all our energies into managing a foundation to support start-up companies."

"Wow, that's interesting!"

"Yes, but tied to some sad memories, I'm afraid." Digby bowed his head solemnly, as though choosing his next set of words carefully. "I came from a large family," he said finally. "Eleven children. My mother and three of my siblings died of starvation."

"Oh, Digby, I am so sorry—how awful for you."

"It was tough going for my father, who tried to keep everything afloat during very difficult times. Taiwan wasn't always the Tiger it's known for today, you know. Anyway, my father had an entrepreneurial spirit. He recognized early on that Taiwan was becoming a global manufacturing hub and planned to invest in the packaging industry. He thought it would become big business. And, of course, he was right. But, in the end, the banks wouldn't give him the time of day, even after he offered up our family's farm as collateral. When my youngest brother died, my father's spirit was broken, and he just gave up, passing a year later. I swore I would never allow what happened to him to happen to anyone else. And so, now, Doris and I—and the crew you see sitting in front of you—roll the dice on passionate people who have great ideas but not enough start-up funds to bring them to life."

"That's a very noble and worthwhile cause."

"Well, thank you. I'm hoping one day Manfred will be able to take over the reins of the foundation, but he's not quite there yet. Am I right?"

"Well…"

"It's okay. I know my son. He's got the same energy my father had. It just needs to be channeled. It'll take time. But with people like you guiding him, he'll end up being well-grounded."

"To your father," I said, raising my glass again, my voice breaking with emotion.

Digby gave me another soft pat on the back and tossed back the contents of his glass.

As the courses kept coming, Digby and I continued to enjoy each other's company, and I started to develop an immense sense of admiration for his empathetic view of humanity. It wasn't until dessert was served that I finally looked up to see what else was going on in the room. The noise level had climbed again, particularly where Doris and the Major were sitting. I leaned forward to get a better look just as the two of them yelled out something, enthusiastically clinking their glasses together so forcefully that they shattered. Sparkling shards of glass scattered across the table, while wine began pooling on the white tablecloth. I felt a sense of déjà vu, recalling when the Major and Grandmother Lam had drunk too much *Moutai* on opening day.

"Oh, oh," I said out loud.

Luckily, energetic waiters sprang into action immediately,

armed with white napkins to contain the mess.

Digby shook his head. "You know, it's usually me who gets in trouble for drinking too much. I'll enjoy recounting this moment with my wife at breakfast tomorrow."

We both clinked our wine glasses together.

"If you don't mind, Digby," I said, looking over at the Major again, "I think it's probably time I got my owner back to the hotel. We have another full day at the fair tomorrow."

"The trials and tribulations of running a business, my friend. Never a dull moment."

For some reason, his comment resonated with me and made me think about the Kang situation. While I knew it was probably not very ethical to air my dirty laundry in front of a parent, there was something about Digby's personality that made me feel I could trust him—not to mention Zhou had alleged he had stayed at a monastery in Taiwan.

"Digby, can I ask you for some advice on a rather delicate matter I'm dealing with?"

"Of course, you can. How can I help?"

I carefully summarized the entire Kang affair, avoiding the family's name but sharing details about my meeting with Jake Zhou, whose name I had no qualms disclosing.

"Hmm," said Digby, contemplating what I had just described. "You know, in the future, I would only accept wire transfers or certified cheques for your fees. That way everyone has receipts. The moment I hear of someone trying to pay you $30,000 in cash, I immediately become suspicious. But listen, let me do some digging for you. I'm used to coordinating complex background checks on anyone who wants to benefit from our foundation. I'll use my contacts, including police contacts, to see if anything surfaces on your friend Jake Zhou and whether he joined any of our monasteries in Taiwan. I'll get my team on it right away."

"Digby, I really appreciate this."

"Phil, I'm the one who should be thanking you. We have tremendous respect for those who teach in Taiwan, and what you've accomplished in one term with Manfred is worthy of my total respect. I hate to hear that your efforts are being undermined by some fraudster."

"Thank you," I replied, somewhat self-consciously.

"Are you flying home tomorrow?"

"Yes, tomorrow night. *Air Canada*. I'm hoping it will be a step up from the Mickey Mouse charter flight I took from Vancouver to Seoul." I had already shared my mobile-massage experience with him.

"Well, I'll have Lafayette check on the flight for you, and we'll look after your transportation to the airport. Just let him know your departure details."

After going around the room to shake hands with some of the other guests, then saying my goodbyes and thank-yous, Lafayette arranged for Tyler to drive us back to the hotel. Thirty minutes later, we were pulling up the long driveway to The *Grand Hyatt*. As I maneuvered a swaggering Major through the hotel's front entrance, I glanced up at the two Taoist talismans, hoping for their support.

The following day, with the Major slumped in a chair at our table, clearly suffering from a hangover, the fair proved to be a bit of a bust, generating far fewer visitors.

"Hey, Philly," snorted the Major, emerging from her co-matose state, "my leg is aching. I'm not used to all this walking, you know."

I looked down at her farcical bundle of sorriness and wondered exactly what sort of walking she was referring to.

"I think I'm gonna have to lie down for a few hours," she continued, trying earnestly to sound sorry for herself. "I'm sure you'll be able to manage without me."

I'll try, I thought.

With that, the Major picked up her cane and walked unsteadily towards the elevators. I quietly hoped she would remain in her room until the fair closed.

Thankfully, Hymie had organized my schedule to include a few appointments with our existing parents, and I knew, without the Major's interruptions and her attempts to upstage me by constantly reminding everyone she was the owner of the school, those meetings would run smoothly.

Overall, I was pleased with the interest shown in Cothbert—a promising first step toward proving the school could thrive. But as the day came to a close, the lingering concern over the Kang situation and Harris's disclosure about the Major's strange budgeting weighed on my mind. Despite the progress made, I couldn't help but shake the feeling that something unresolved lingered, quietly threatening to disrupt the calm.

Chapter 31

Due to the miracle of time zones, the Major and I arrived at *Vancouver International Airport* just after lunchtime on the same day we left Taipei. After eleven hours in flight, I was relieved to have been spared the back pain and spasms that plagued me on my outward-bound flight from Vancouver to Seoul. The fact that Digby Ma had upgraded us to Business Class helped, and I was also thankful for not sitting next to the Major, our seats being on opposite sides of the plane. This also meant I didn't have to listen to her complain about how much of her own money she had poured into the school.

Once landed, the Major and I cleared immigration and, forty-five minutes later, were wheeling our luggage out into the waiting area, where I noticed a waving sign that read, *Welcome Home, Pil*.

"Thought I'd say hello before I fly to Tokyo," Harris beamed, moving in beside me. He was towing a large black suitcase with Frank following behind, looking more presentable than usual. I stared at Harris' natty attire.

"Not to your liking?" he asked, raising his eyebrows and modeling his outfit for effect.

"Well, the plaid sports jacket certainly makes a statement— and it's definitely one of a kind." Then I realized the significance of the black suitcase.

"You're leaving? Now? I was hoping we'd have at least a couple of days to reconnect."

"I need to be efficient with my time."

"And my money," chimed in the Major, who had edged closer. "Make sure you bring us back some students to pay for your junket."

"And exactly how many students did you bring back, Major?" Harris asked.

"Well, Philly got six in Seoul, and I think he and I landed another six in Taipei for September."

"That remains to be seen, Major," I cautioned. "But overall, it was a productive trip."

"So, we're expecting the same thing from you too, big guy."

I could tell the Major had succeeded in getting under Harris' skin in record time.

"Major, I just need to have a word with Harris ... you know, to get caught up on what needs to be done in his absence."

"Fine," the Major huffed. "Frank and I will go and get a coffee while you two gossip. Phone me when you're ready." Steering Frank towards the Food Court, I could hear her asking him, "Got any money?"

After double-checking that they were out of earshot, I turned to Harris. "Listen, before you say anything, she was just awful in Taipei—borderline unhinged. We were almost blacklisted by *Yingyucom* because of her antics," I said, recounting her seedy marketing tactics.

"I don't know how you're still in one piece."

"Any further news from the Kangs?" I asked anxiously.

"Nope. I guess they're just counting the days until they get their money which, if my calculations are correct, is supposed to be tomorrow."

"Great!"

"I know. Scares me too. Who knows what their plan B will be?"

"Okay, enough about that. How's everything else?"

"Not bad. Ida's new jazz band is unbelievable—in a good way. Chill is still expecting us to step in whenever she has the slightest hiccup, and Byung-ju has kept his nose clean ever since we set up the editing room for him in the watchtower. Oh, and the Huang twins are in love with a new Japanese boy who just arrived."

"Oh? I didn't know we were getting a new student."

"Yes. It was a bit out of the blue. His name is Saburo. He was originally accepted to an American prep school in California but ran into some visa issues and was told he couldn't remain in the U.S."

"I see. What's he like?"

"Strange. A sixteen-year-old who behaves like a forty-year-old man. Even Koji struggles to relate to him."

"Another needy one?"

"I'm afraid so," Harris grinned. "Listen, I'm sorry, but I have to run," he said, reaching for his suitcase. "Oh, and remember. You need to cover my classes."

"I remember. Thanks for covering mine, by the way. And good luck. You do realize the next time we see each other, it'll almost be Christmas?"

"I know. The term has certainly flown by."

That night, with my internal clock still fixed on Taiwan time, I tossed and turned, unable to rest as I imagined any number of forms of retaliation from Mrs. Kang. By 6:30 a.m., I finally gave up on sleep. Filling my thermos with hot coffee, I grabbed a warm jacket and went for a stroll around the campus. The temperature outside seemed markedly cooler than what I remembered before leaving for Asia. The trees had shed the last of their brilliant foliage, and there was a pronounced damp mustiness to everything. Purple and black clouds loitered ominously on the horizon, and a frigid breeze was blowing from the east—a harbinger that cooler weather was on its way.

Wandering down to the beach, I made my way to one of the Adirondack chairs and sat down. Staring out at the restless water, I savored my hot coffee as I took in the stillness of the morning. With memories of my wacky Asian trip still lingering, these peaceful yet starkly beautiful surroundings reminded me, again, of just how lucky I was to live on Canada's West Coast.

By 7:45 a.m., feeling greatly refreshed and more energized, I walked into Morning Assembly to cheers and high-fives. It felt like being welcomed home by my own family—and in a way, I was. Like any family member returning from a trip, I recounted the highlights of my travels, making sure to laud both Korea and Taiwan equally. From their rapt faces, it was obvious the students were pleased I had shared in their diverse cultures. In their eyes, I was now more authentic because I had a better understanding of who they were and the far-off places they called home.

Shortly after returning to my office, Harris phoned from Japan.

"*Konnichiwa,*" I chimed excitedly. "And how's Tokyo?"

"A shit show," came Harris's blunt reply.

"Why? What's happened?"

"What's happened is the Itos didn't clue into the fact that the *Tokyo Motor Show* is in town, and every decent hotel room is booked solid. I was unceremoniously dropped off at something called the Tokyo Center Place. It's a glorified youth hostel. The room is so damn small I have to step into the hallway to get dressed, and my bathroom—if you can even call it that—is the size of an airplane toilet. There's not even a defined shower area. When you turn on the spray, the whole room fills with water. And if I want to watch the only English channel in town, I have to feed coins into this minuscule TV perched at the foot of my single bed. I mean, honestly. It's totally pathetic!"

"Oh dear, that does sound hellish," I replied, realizing a sarcastic quip wouldn't go over well right now.

"The Itos have promised to try and find me something better. Even a YMCA would be a step up from this hole."

"I hear you. So, what's on your agenda tomorrow?"

Harris gave a prolonged grunt. "Just a sec." I heard him rifling through papers. "Let me see," he responded with disinterest, "Canadian Embassy at ten, an agent at noon, another agent at 2:00 p.m., and then a dinner with the Itos at a restaurant—apparently with some interested families in tow. Then back to this hellhole."

"I'm sorry, Harris. I do hope things get better. At least you're only there for three nights."

"True. Anything more from the Kangs?"

"No. Nothing."

"Well, I'll touch base tomorrow for a follow-up. Right now, I need to go out into the hallway and change into my pajamas. Bye for now."

The phone went dead.

Poor Harris, I mused. And I thought he was going to have it easy compared to my circus in Seoul. But as soon as I put down the phone, it wasn't long before I longed to get on a plane and join him.

Another call came through. "Manfred's father from Taiwan," Koji buzzed enthusiastically.

"Digby! How are you?" I called back over the receiver. "Thank you so much for the seat upgrade. It made a world of difference."

"My pleasure. Now listen, my team is getting closer to finding out more about your Jake Zhou friend, but I really need a headshot of him. By any chance, did you happen to take any parting photos of him when the family visited your school?"

I was about to say no when I remembered Chill's photography class swarming us before my meeting with Zhou.

"Let me check, Digby. I might have something, but I'm really not sure."

"Okay, I'll wait to hear from you."

I quickly buzzed back Koji. "Koji, remember the day the Kangs visited to drop off Thomas?"

"You mean when I heard Mr. Zhou say he would give you Mrs. Kang's fees?"

"Yes, that day. I think Chill's photography class took photos of us while we were outside, and I need copies of them as quickly as possible. Can you get to Chill? Tell her I need her SD card with all the photos from that day. It's urgent."

"On it," replied Koji eagerly.

The phone buzzed again. "That was quick, Koji," I replied.

"No. It's some man," Koji said. "He won't give his name."

I pressed the flashing button and said, 'Hello, Phil Gower

speaking.'"

"Mr. Gower, my name is Joseph Stone. I'm a reporter for the *Vancouver Tribune.* I wanted to let you know we'll be running a story tomorrow about your school."

"Oh? About what?" I asked, swallowing hard.

"We have sources who claim you've been withholding tuition fees from international families and forcing special-needs students to leave your school. I thought I'd give you the opportunity to respond before we run the story."

I realized I had to be careful not to say anything that could come back to haunt me.

"Mr. Stone, we are aware of the allegations and are conducting our own investigation. All I can say is that we have never knowingly withheld anyone's fees, and the idea that we would force out special-needs children is ludicrous and slanderous. Our school is committed to meeting the needs of all students, including those with special needs."

"I see. So, that's all you're going to say?"

"Yes."

As the line went dead, I could feel a cold sweat breaking out. I started to envision a less-than-flattering headshot of myself on the front page of the *Vancouver Tribune* beside a caption that read: *School Principal Accused of Theft and Discrimination.*

Eventually getting hold of myself, I reached for a business card Harris had left on my desk: *Christine Hendry, Attorney at Law — Johnson, Hendry, and Roy, Vancouver BC.* I dialed her number. Her assistant informed me she was in court but promised she'd call back as soon as possible. I emphasized it was urgent.

"I've got them!" called out Koji, running into my office.

"The photos?"

313

"Yes. Here," he said, plugging a card reader into my computer.

"Okay, let's see if we can find a shot of the infamous Zhou."

One by one, the photos appeared on my screen. It was clear that Chill's photography club had yet to grasp the subtleties of photography. Most of the photos were either blurry or poorly framed — full of thumbs and the backs of heads — but just as I was about to give up, Koji blurted, "That one!" He directed my attention to a close-up of the Kangs. In the middle, as clear as day, was Zhou.

"That's it, Koji! I need to email this to Manfred's father right away!"

After attaching the photo, I quickly wrote:

Hi Digby, Attached is a photo of Jake Zhou—third person from the left. I've also just learned that one of our parents contacted a local reporter, who says he'll be running a story tomorrow accusing our school of withholding fees and expelling special-needs students. Time is of the essence.

Thanks, Phil.

Trying to take my mind off everything, I decided to wade through the pile of mail that had accumulated in my absence until Koji reminded me Chill was waiting for our scheduled meeting. At that moment, the meeting seemed like an incredible annoyance. Flouncing into my office, she immediately demanded I intervene in a number of her trivial classroom management issues.

"Chill, remember what I said about taking ownership of things like this?" I asked, listening to her babble about:

1. A student who uses 'bad' words,

314

2. Another student who was delinquent in completing his assigned homework,
3. And Byung-ju's unwillingness to smile at her.

"Like, ya, I do remember, but my *qi* is struggling to cope with these ones," she replied nonchalantly.

"Listen," I said, trying to contain my frustration. "I am not going to solve these for you, but I will let you sit in on my afternoon classes. I have English and Harris' Science. Maybe some of my classroom management techniques will give you a little inspiration on how you might deal with your own students' issues."

Chill grimaced, pulling hard on the bun on top of her head. It was clear this wasn't the answer she was hoping for.

"I thought my job was to teach, and your job was to discipline," she said finally.

"It's not as simple as that. If you send me your students every time there's a discipline issue, they'll have no respect for you. I'm here to support you with the big issues. What you've described aren't really big ones."

After rolling her eyes and nodding reluctantly, she agreed to join my back-to-back afternoon classes. I could tell she wasn't convinced.

"By the way, how were my photos? Helpful?" she asked, snapping me back to the larger crisis at hand.

"Very. Thank you."

The school bell rang just as my phone buzzed. I was relieved to hear Digby's voice on the other end.

"Got him!" he called out excitedly. "Jake Zhou, a.k.a. Joseph Zhou, a.k.a. William Zhou, a.k.a. Dragon Zhou. His face lit up the police database like Christmas lights. He's a wanted man—a professional scammer operating under multiple aliases. He was actually truthful when he said he worked for a heavy-weight family in Macau but left out the part where he skimmed large sums from their investments for his own Ponzi scheme. He fled before they could arrest him. Then, yes, he hid out as a monk in central Taiwan, where he bilked officials out of thousands in donations he collected on their behalf."

"Oh my God. Really?"

"I'm afraid so. Here's what I suggest you do: It's too late to connect with your parent or her lawyer now—it's almost 1:30 a.m. in Macau…"

"Oh, Digby, I'm sorry. I forgot the time difference. I'm keeping you up so late."

"Don't be silly. I didn't mind working late—it felt good to prove my suspicions right. Anyway, I've just emailed you my full investigative report on Jake, including details of his criminal record and photos under all his aliases. Pass it to your lawyer and have them email it to the lawyers in Macau, so it's in their inbox by the time their office opens—probably around 6:00 p.m. your time. Also, your lawyer should contact the reporter to inform him that one of his sources is a wanted criminal and that you'll sue for defamation if the story runs. Lastly, request that the parent retracts her claims immediately or face a lawsuit herself."

"I can't thank you enough, Digby."

"No time for thank-yous. Get on the phone with your lawyer—quickly."

I called our lawyer, and this time her assistant put me straight through.

"Christine Hendry," came the reply.

Carefully, I updated Christine on this new turn of events and emailed her the report as we spoke. She was very understanding and was quick to agree with everything Digby had proposed, informing me that, as soon as she got off the phone, she would set all the legal wheels in motion. Though I felt a bit relieved, I knew until I saw a copy of the following day's *Vancouver Tribune*, I would not be totally at ease. But I also realized it was time I got back to running the school.

I filled Koji in on the latest developments during recess.

"Wow. He really was a criminal?"

"I'm afraid so. Oh, before I forget, what can you tell me about the new Japanese student? I'm meeting him for the first time in a couple of Blossoms classes this afternoon."

Koji frowned. "He is not like normal Japanese, you know. Very strange."

"In what way?"

"He is not friendly. He also has big nose in air."

"You mean he's snobby?"

"Yes. He told other students he is not really Asian because he is Japanese. Now they think he is racist. You will see what I mean."

Can't wait, I thought, realizing I hadn't prepared my handouts for that class.

"Anything else, Mr. Phil?"

"Yes. Can you drive into *Kipling's* early tomorrow and pick me up a copy of the *Vancouver Tribune*?"

"Of course. No problem."

"Oh, and have you seen the Major? I need to update her on the Kang situation."

"I saw her before, when her sister was here, but she left to go into town. She said she had a meeting with her bank."

"I see. Her sister is here a lot."

"Yes, and always fighting with Miss Major!"

I was greeted with more enthusiasm when I walked into my afternoon classes. A few moments later, Chill sauntered in and sat in the back. After fielding all manner of questions about my trip, I soon realized I was being carefully manipulated away from the day's lessons.

"I understand we have a new student in the class," I said finally, regaining control of the classroom.

Instantly, a slim, very tall boy with coiffed black hair and tortoise-shell glasses shot out of his seat and stood at attention.

"My name is Saburo Endo, and I will tell you about me."

Saburo had altered his Cothbert uniform to include brown leather suspenders and his own gray-flannel pants, tapered and finished off with turned-up cuffs. Paisley socks rose above a pair of highly polished penny loafers.

"Okay, Saburo, please go ahead."

"I am from the Kagoshima. Do you know it?"

"No, I don't…"

"Well, you should. It is seaside city on Japan's Kyushu Island where there is also an active volcano called Sakurajima. Do you know about Sakurajima?"

"No. Sorry, I…"

"Well, you should…"

I swallowed hard.

"Okay, thank you for that…"

"I am not finished…"

"What did you just say?" I demanded, my jaw dropping.

"You interrupt me. I am not finished…"

"Oh, yes, Saburo, you *are* finished!" I responded loudly, my voice rising a few decibels as I felt my blood pressure spiking.

A hush descended over the class, and you could hear a pin drop. I noticed Aki and Stanley sliding further down into their seats, hoping to become invisible. I stole a glance in Chill's direction, wondering if I'd picked the wrong day for her to sit in on my classes, but she simply tilted her head and offered a halfhearted smile.

"Sit down, Saburo! Right now!" I responded with authority. "And see me after class!"

Saburo fell back into his chair, subdued.

"Can I stay and observe your talk with Saburo?" asked Chill quietly once both classes had ended. "I'll sit to the side."

I hesitated but nodded and then closed the classroom door. I asked Saburo to move his seat in front of mine.

"Saburo, do you know why I raised my voice?" I asked softly, pulling up my chair. I could tell he was tense.

"Not really," he replied curtly.

I looked over at Chill. "Miss Whipplehill, do you know why I raised my voice?"

"Of course. Saburo was very rude to you."

"Really?" Saburo questioned. "I thought you were rude because you interrupted me."

He was beginning to sound defensive.

"Let's start with your tone, Saburo," I replied, ignoring his slight. "You asked me if I knew where you live. Do you remember that?"

"Yes. And you say you don't know my town Kagoshima."

319

"Then you asked me if I knew about the volcano."

"Yes. Sakurajima."

"Miss Whipplehill, do you remember what Saburo said after I didn't know the answers to his questions?"

"Oh, yes! He said 'that you should know.' I was very shocked that he would be disrespectful to a teacher that way."

"Why?" asked Saburo. "Everyone knows Kagoshima and Sakurajima."

I took a deep breath. "Saburo, do you know Montréal?" I asked.

"No."

"Why not? You should. Everyone knows Montréal."

"Do you know what year Canada became a country?"

"No."

"Why not? Everybody does."

Saburo's cheeks slowly reddened.

"How do you feel when I talk to you like that?"

Saburo wrinkled his forehead, his eyes dropping to the floor. "Not very good," he finally responded, reluctantly.

"Saburo, I want to give you a special homework assignment—it's just for you. I want you to look up the meaning of the word 'empathy.' I'm not sure if there's a Japanese word that means the same thing. When we meet tomorrow, I want you to explain why you think I gave you this assignment."

"Okay," he said solemnly. "How do you spell the word?"

After writing down the correct spelling, I watched him leave the room looking forlorn. I wondered if I'd made any headway or just exacerbated the situation. I quietly closed the door.

"That was great!" cheered Chill, loudly, causing me to jump.

I spun around to face her.

"In what way?" I asked, curious about her take on the meeting.

"You didn't scream at him. You didn't get angry. You just got him to think about what he did…what he said. I like this approach. I never thought about doing that before."

"It doesn't always work, Chill, and sometimes I do have to scream. But the goal should always be for the students to learn how to change themselves—not for us to force them to change," I explained. "But I'm glad you thought your visit was fruitful."

Just after dinner, still feeling the weight of the world on my shoulders, I dropped in on Ida, who was on call in the duty office at the Boarding House, wading through a stack of student files.

"I hope I'm not interrupting, but have you had a chance to meet our new student?" I asked, dropping down on a chair in front of her.

Ida removed her glasses. "You mean our pretentious Saburo?" she quipped.

"Yes. I'm afraid I almost lost it with him today in my English class. Any suggestions on how I might temper his attitude? Harris told me the Huang twins like him. Do you think a romantic tryst might soften him up a bit?"

"It might, but it's too late for that now. The Huangs are no longer interested. Like everyone else who comes in contact with Saburo, he rubs them the wrong way. The only one who'd talk to him was Thomas, but he's gone."

"You heard what happened, right?"

"Yes, Harris told me. That mother is out of her mind. She

has no idea how good Thomas had it here."

"I know," I said, feeling another knot in my stomach as I recalled the events of the morning. "Anyway, getting back to Saburo, I asked him to do a little research on the word *empathy.*"

"Not a bad idea. But we'll still need to immerse him in some real-life situations if we truly want to help him understand how his attitude and behavior affect others."

"What do you know about him?"

"Funny you should ask. I was just looking at his file. He has an uber-wealthy father, his mother passed away when he was a baby, and he was raised by his grandmother and her hired help. I'm guessing he grew up getting whatever he wanted. We call it 'Little Emperor Syndrome.' But that's not exactly a clinical term," she smiled.

"That explains a lot. I know you'll keep an eye on him, but I'd like to spend some time getting to know him as well. What room is he in?"

Ida glanced down at a clipboard. "Room 204. Unfortunately, right now it looks like he doesn't have a roommate, which is not ideal for someone who has EQ challenges."

Thanking Ida for her insight, I climbed upstairs and wandered along the long corridor that connected the boys' and girls' sections. The lights had been dimmed and Prep was in session, as soft yellow glows from desk lamps cast shadows on the hall carpet. I stopped at Room 204 and saw Saburo bent over his desk, diligently writing. I tapped on his door before asking, "How are things?"

Saburo looked up, then stiffened when he realized it was me. "Fine...thank you, Mr. Gower. Just reading about empathy."

"Good. We'll talk more about that tomorrow."

My eyes were drawn to a haphazard pile of glossy magazines balancing on the corner of his desk. The shiny covers were splashed with photographs of luxury cars.

"You like cars?"

"Yes. I really love cars," he replied, perking up. "My father says I am allowed to get my driver's license if I want. Do you know how I can do that?"

"Let me look into that for you," I said, realizing a potential opening to connect.

While tiredness had badgered me all day, by the time I retired to my suite that evening, I was no longer sleepy and firmly back on Taiwan time. Sitting down on my couch with a bottle of red wine as company, I was still anxious about whether the story would get printed. As the night lingered and the contents of the bottle dwindled, my jet lag eventually returned with a vengeance. It wasn't until I was awakened by the ringing of my cell phone that I realized I had slept through until the following morning.

"Hello," I responded groggily.

"Phil, it's Christine Hendry. Sorry for the early-morning call, but I've got an important update for you."

"Okay," I said tentatively.

"Relax, it's all good. I just heard back from Mrs. Kang's lawyer in Macau. He has been instructed by Mrs. Kang to withdraw all claims as well as the request for a refund. Also, he was able to contact the reporter just before the story went to print, and it is my understanding the story won't be running."

I heaved a sigh of relief. "Anything from Mrs. Kang?"

323

"No, but I'm sure the revelation of who Jake Zhou really is will come as a total shock to her. I'd give her some space."

"Fair enough. Christine, thank you for your prompt attention to all this."

"I think it's your friend, Mr. Ma, you should be thanking. He prevented a mini-disaster from occurring."

I couldn't have agreed more with Christine's sentiments, and as soon as I made it over to my office, I phoned Digby.

"I'm so relieved for you, Phil. You didn't deserve all that rubbish," said Digby on hearing the news. "Let's stay in touch. I'm more than happy to help you and your school any way I can."

"Digby, you've been a godsend."

"Let's see how you feel after a few more months with Manfred."

As I laughed back and hung up, Koji walked through the doorway carrying a newspaper. My adrenaline started to surge. I flipped quickly through the paper, scanning each page and every story. There was nothing about Cothbert. I could literally feel the stress exiting my body.

Chapter 32

For the first time since we'd returned to school, I finally caught sight of the Major, who was leaving her office, followed by her sister, Millicent. As I tried to stop her in the hall to update her on the Kang situation, she brushed me aside and stormed out of the School House, clearly in a huff about something.

"Is something wrong with the Major?" I asked, as Millicent walked by.

"There's always something wrong with her. She just can't accept reality," said Millicent offhandedly, disappearing down the front stairwell.

With the Major out of sight and Millicent unwilling to explain, I pushed the matter aside for now. The day wasn't slowing down. As I entered the reception area, Koji was just hanging up the phone.

"Koji, I need you to look into getting Saburo his driver's license."

"Why?" he asked, looking perplexed.

"We have to guide this boy. He loves cars, and his dad's given him permission to get his license. I thought it might be a good way for me to connect with him in a more meaningful way and help him with his personality issues."

I could see Koji processing what I was saying.

"Okay. Makes sense, I guess. I'll check for you," he said.

Later at lunch, Koji slipped up beside me, placing his food tray on the table.

"I already looked into the driver's license for you. Pretty easy to do. But Saburo should go to driver's school before taking the test."

"That's what I thought. Are there any driving schools in the area?"

"There is one in Squamish. But they aren't taking new students until January—after Christmas break. But the good news is the driver will come to our school to pick up Saburo."

"Okay. Good. Can you book him in for one of their January classes? I'll let him know the good news."

I'd asked Saburo to meet me in the Dining Hall after English class to review his homework assignment. I thought a less intimidating environment might help him relax and speak more freely.

"I understand what you mean," he said before I could even begin.

It took me a second to realize what he was referring to.

"In Japanese, we call empathy *kyōkan*."

I smiled, then said, "Saburo, there is a proverb ... or a famous saying ... that our First Nations people have."

"First Nations?"

"Native North Americans..."

"You mean Indians?"

"We don't call them that anymore. We call them First Nations People. Anyway, their proverb says *you should never*

326

judge another man until you have walked a mile in his moccasins."

"What is moccasins?"

"Shoes. Soft shoes sewn out of animal skin."

He paused for a moment and then said, "Oh, I understand. Walking in their moccasins means understanding them. Right?"

"Yes. I think you say things to hurt people without realizing how they might feel and without getting to know them properly."

"Saburo's eyes watered slightly. 'I have no friends. No one likes me here,' he said, wiping his tears with his sleeve.

I hesitated, thinking back to my own struggles with being misunderstood. "I've been there," I said quietly. "I know what it's like when people don't understand you. Sometimes it's very frustrating. But the thing is, it's not about being liked by everyone—it's about understanding how your words and actions affect others."

Saburo looked at me, unsure, but there was something in his eyes that made me feel like he was listening.

"Given the way you spoke to me yesterday, I didn't like you much either. But I can see you are a good person deep down. You just need to stop and think before saying something. You can't expect everyone to be like you or to know what you know. Listen, I'm here to help you, and I think I might have some good news for you."

"What?" he asked, sniffling.

"I've booked you in for a driving course in January."

"Really? You did that for me?"

"Yes. As long as you remember what we talked about today. If you want people to like you, you have to start treating them more sensitively. I saw you liked cars and found out you'd like to learn how to drive. So, I'm helping you because you're feeling down. That's called empathy."

"Okay. I understand," he said finally, his voice cracking as he tried to hold back his emotions.

The following day, just before finishing my Boarding House duty, the phone rang. It was Harris.

"Hello, Phil," he gushed over the receiver, sounding much more upbeat.

"Where the hell are you?" I blurted out. "I thought maybe you'd eloped with a nice Japanese lady."

"Let's not talk about Japan, shall we. Now, before I tell you about my excellent trip, where are we with the Kang situation?"

"We're in a very good place, finally," I said, relaying in detail the roller-coaster ride of events that had transpired during the past twenty-four hours.

"Wow. It's actually over," cheered Harris. "Well done, Phil! So much for that headhunter back east who accused you of not being tough enough."

His comment jolted me, but then I realized he was actually right.

"Thanks. But, you know, I still don't get why Zhou wasted my time with his whole monk spiel."

"These psychotic types like to befriend their victims to make them believe they are trustworthy. He was certainly able to win over Mrs. Kang."

"True. But I think he actually believes he has healing powers."

"Which he can share with his fellow inmates when he ends up going to jail. Anyway, I don't care about the reason. I'm just happy it all worked out. Too bad about Thomas, though."

"Yes, he was the biggest casualty in all this."

"So, what I'm hearing from you is there is no pressing need for me to return."

"If you're thinking about extending your tour, don't! We've got end-of-term exams coming up and then Christmas departure."

"But I kinda like it here. I am presently lounging beside a pool at the Shangrila Hotel in Central Hong Kong, talking to you on Grandmother Lam's cell phone."

"I take it the hotel is a step-up from that other place you were staying in—the Tokyo something or other?"

"Ha! The bathroom here is bigger than that whole place combined. Anyway, seriously, though, I'm not sure Japan is a huge market. I did meet some interested families, but they're looking for a few years down the road. From what I gather, if you're a decent student in Japan, you don't usually study overseas. Those who do go away are typically shipped off to avoid disgracing their families."

"Meaning?"

"They can't cope with the regular school system… for whatever reason."

"Hmm. And what about Hong Kong?"

"A completely different story. Grandmother Lam held a reception at the hotel for me, and ten really interested families showed up—all ready to enroll in September."

"Wow, that is great…"

"Oh, and you can tell the Major her partner-in-crime will be loading me up with two canisters of *Moutai* to bring back for her."

"Yes, well, she could use them. She seems particularly grouchy these days for some reason." I purposely avoided mentioning Millicent's name, given how upbeat Harris seemed. "So, when exactly are you returning home?" I added.

"Don't worry, I'll be there in a couple of days. I've already arranged for Frank to pick me up."

"Well, happy travels then. And enjoy the pool while I slave away here," I said, hoping to guilt him into feeling sorry for me.

After checking in at the Boarding House, I was about to go home when Pancho came bounding into the lobby, setting off Tofu's high-pitched yapping.

"Hey, Phil, we're having an impromptu late-night coffee house. The jazz band's playing. You should come and watch. They're really good, you know."

Myrtle stepped out of her suite, clearly interested in what all the noise was about. "What's going on?" she asked, bending down to quiet Tofu.

"I was just telling Phil about the Coffee House," said Pancho. "That he should come and see the band play."

"Oh, yes, Phil. Pancho's right," Myrtle agreed, bouncing back up. "You must go. They are quite remarkable. I'm letting everyone stay up late so they can watch."

"Of course, I'll go," I smiled. "I wouldn't miss it for the world."

The tables in the Dining Hall had been pushed back when Pancho and I arrived, and a selection of musical instruments was carefully arranged in front of the fireplace. Byung-ju's tripod was already in place to film the event, while a number of students were sprawled across the floor, enjoying each other's company. I could see that, in lieu of coffee, Peg and Janice had prepared hot chocolate and Nanaimo Bars.

"Hi, Mr. Gower," the students called, realizing I was standing over them.

I looked down, joking with them, before pulling a chair from under a table and sliding it to one side. A few minutes later, with the hall now almost full, Ida and the jazz players walked in, proudly modeling their new burgundy uniforms. After taking a couple of bows to raucous cheering, the recital began.

The focus of the concert was mostly well-known pop songs, and with each set, I became more and more spellbound by the sheer talent of this little group of musicians. There was Aki and Stanley, joyfully swinging their saxophones in unison; Manfred, bursting forth with a rapid-fire trill on his drums; and a confident Portia Lu blowing her bright, brassy trumpet, a dramatic contrast to that totally devastated student I had to comfort the night of the ghost incident.

I joined Ida after the concert, watching as she was encircled by enthusiastic members of staff.

"I almost cried, Ida," rejoiced Myrtle, giving her a hug. "So moving! So moving!"

"Yes, really awesome," added Koji. "I move too."

"A truly remarkable show," I finally piped in. "You've accomplished miracles. Do we know if Saburo plays an instrument?" I asked coyly.

Ida winced and then stopped herself. "Good question. Let me look into that. You might be onto something there, Phil."

The Major, who I noticed had been sitting in the back, cautiously strolled over to join us. "Nice tunes, eh, Philly?" she said, leaning on her cane, looking a bit more upbeat than when I'd seen her in the School House but still not totally herself.

"Lots of talent, Major. Lots of talent. As you can see, education is not all about books."

"How's the new kid, Subaru?" she replied, her tone sharp, quickly shifting focus.

"You mean, Saburo."

"That's what I said."

"There are some issues, but I think he'll settle in eventually."

She didn't respond immediately, glancing around the room with a tight expression. "Let's hope so. We can't afford to lose anyone else."

She turned back to me, her voice suddenly brisk, almost forced. "We need the revenue."

"I understand. By the way, Mrs. Kang has withdrawn her claim for a refund."

The Major's posture stiffened, and she gave a quick nod, but there was a slight edge to her voice as she repeated, "Good. We need the revenue."

Chapter 33

The day before the students left for the Christmas holidays, Timberlane Lake was blanketed by one of the biggest snowfalls in its history, and Cothbert House School was miraculously transformed into something resembling the whimsy of a Grandma Moses painting. Minions of all sizes and ages, each wearing white-trimmed, pointy-red caps generously gifted to the school by Violeta, frolicked in the snow, pitching snowballs, rolling snow men, and sliding down the hill from the School House on large plastic bucket-lids commandeered from the kitchen.

"We made it," I exhaled, just as Stanley whizzed by on a makeshift sleigh followed by the Huang girls in heavy pursuit.

"And you're still sure you want to hang around here all by yourself over the holidays?" Harris asked, rubbing his hands together to stay warm just as a snowball soared precariously overhead. "Frankly, I don't get it."

"Well, it's just…"

"Wait a sec," he signaled, then cupping his hands around his mouth, "Manfred!" he hollered. "Didn't I say no throwing snowballs?"

Manfred waved back with an appeasing smile, gave a halfhearted bow, and then tore off towards another boy, tackling him to the ground before executing a double-flip in the air.

"That boy is clearly on something," said Harris, punching his hands into his coat pockets. "Anyway, sorry, Phil, you were going to tell me why you can't seem to part with this place?"

"Oh, right ... I have to stay here, Harris. Violeta asked me to make sure we have someone on site in case any of the January arrivals experience visa issues or need additional documents. Don't worry, I'll be fine. I've already explained it all to my family. They completely understand. Anyway, after my Asia trip, I don't really have it in me to board another plane."

"I hear you. I'm not going too far either; just to Vancouver to visit friends. No more planes for me as well."

"What about Myrtle?"

"Oh, she's going on a cruise with an old friend."

"Wow, now that sounds nice. She deserves it, though. She's worked so hard keeping our boarding house humming along. Any chance we could convince her to take the Major along with her? She seems to be in a foul mood these days."

"Huh! Don't worry about her. According to Koji, she's off to Las Vegas with somebody to hit the slot machines."

"And does Koji have somewhere to go?"

"Well, here's the thing about Koji," Harris smirked, leaning towards me. "I have it on good authority from a friend in town he has befriended a certain Japanese girl who happens to be residing with a local homestay family over the holidays."

"Koji's got a girlfriend?"

"Yup. She's participating in some sort of business exchange program with a student at the University of British Columbia.

But, listen, don't say anything to him. You know how easily he gets embarrassed. He'll have a complete meltdown if he finds out we know about his secret courtship."

"I hope it works out for him."

"So do I," said Harris. "He could do with a bit more balance in his life."

The school bell chimed through the wintry campus, signaling it was time for the final dinner of the term. Chill's art classes had decorated the Dining Hall with homemade streamers, cut-out paper snowflakes, and student artwork from the past term. Looking at the artwork, I felt emotionally torn, given the highlight of the display were Thomas' magnificent paintings of salmon.

I just hope he is still in one piece, I thought.

Beside the warmth of the fireplace, where the crackling of burning logs added to the wintry atmosphere, a long table framed with holly, cedar branches, and large pulsating candles displayed the full-blown Christmas buffet Janice and Peg had masterfully created. Creamy pumpkin soup, roast turkey with cranberry-pork stuffing and gravy, scalloped and mashed potatoes, fried rice, stir-fried cabbage, an array of salads, homemade hot apple pie, ice cream, Christmas cookies, and a punch bowl brimming with chilled eggnog were all on display. I was intrigued as I watched the students neatly loading up their plates, realizing how far they'd come since the early days of East-meets-West concoctions in ice-cream bowl.

After dinner, Ida's Jazz Band filled the hall with a repertoire of Christmas songs, and a few of the students started singing along, even if their renditions were a bit imaginative at times.

Finally, in keeping with the reputation she had gained for handing out freebies, and to great fanfare, the Major, decked out in a Santa Claus outfit, paraded into the room yelling, "Merry Christmas" at the top of her lungs while she liberally threw candy canes about. The effect on the students was to be expected, as they broke into cheers, drowning out the Jazz Band. I chuckled to myself, catching a chagrined Harris.

Once the night's festivities were over, I returned to the Boarding House to see packed luggage ready for the following day's departure spilling out into the hallway. Carefully making my way around the backpacks and suitcases, I also realized we had reached an important milestone in our school's brief history; we'd made it to the end of the first term of Cothbert House School.

Early the following morning, Frank shuttled the students to *Vancouver International Airport* after a tearful Myrtle sent them off with hugs and well-wishes. In truth, I too felt a lump in my throat as I bid farewell. By mid-afternoon, the school resembled a forgotten ghost town, its buildings empty and devoid of activity or the strident voices of students going to and from class. The staff, including Harris, Koji, Myrtle, and the Major, had all but disappeared to be with their families and friends over the holidays. So, there was just me.

The silence in the halls was heavier than I expected. The absence of the students, so full of energy just hours before, left a strange void behind. The quiet felt...different. I'd wanted the time alone—needed it, even. But the emptiness wasn't as peaceful as I'd imagined. There was a kind of restlessness, like I had slipped out of sync with the rhythm of the school, and now I was trying to remember what it felt like to belong.

Myrtle had left me in charge of Tofu, or maybe it was the other way around, but in any case, the two of us enjoyed a saunter along the beach, where I unfastened Tofu's collar from his leash so he was free to explore on his own. Eventually, we found our way to the Adirondack chairs, which were blanketed with a thick layer of snow. Even though the air was frigid, something beckoned me to take a seat and relish the moment. I brushed off what snow I could from one of the chairs and cautiously sat down. The old wood of the chair was cold, and I could feel my pants becoming damp from the skiff of snow, but just when I thought about getting up and leaving, Tofu jumped onto my lap and turned his body to sit upright, almost proudly as though he recognized it was an honor to be allowed to sit on one of our famous blue thrones. The two of us remained in silence, listening to the lapping of the water and gazing out at the lingering snowflakes leisurely falling from the sky. There was something spiritual about it all; a calm during which I could look back on everything this past term and finally feel an extraordinary sense of accomplishment. By the time we climbed back up the steps, the empty school bus was just pulling into the parking lot.

"Everything went smoothly, Mr. Gower," Frank yelled, leaning out the driver's window.

"Great. Thanks, Frank. What are you up to for the holidays?"

"Oh, me and the missus will be having our grandchildren over. But don't worry, if anything goes wrong over here, you just give me a call and I'll come right away."

"I'm sure everything will be fine. You enjoy your Christmas."

"Oh, ya, and don't forget to turn the furnace down to four degrees. Major's orders. And turn off all the lights — you know, and anything else that costs money."

"Got it. Have a good one, Frank."

Frank hopped off the bus and jumped into the cab of his truck, waving back at me as he sped up the driveway.

"It's just you and me now," I said, looking down at Tofu's deep brown eyes.

Tofu barked and began running in circles as if he knew he had more freedom than usual. Once back in my suite, he quickly curled himself up in front of my fireplace like he was a permanent fixture.

Before retiring that night, I ventured over to the Boarding House to ensure the furnace was, indeed, turned to 4 degrees and then returned to my office to have one final check of my email. I noticed my phone's message-light flashing when I arrived. It was a message from Hymie to call him back.

"Merry Christmas, Mr. Gower," came Hymie's upbeat response when he realized it was me on the line.

"Same to you too, Hymie. So, what's up?" I asked, almost defensively, realizing I really did need a break.

There was a pause, and then Hymie spoke softly. "Mrs. Kang phoned."

"Oh, yes," I said stiffening up.

"She is very embarrassed and so sorry about everything that happened and wants to know if you'd ever consider having Thomas come back. He really misses the school. She says she is willing to pay you double."

"Hymie, of course, I'll take him back. Beginning in January. But on two conditions."

"You want triple?"

"No … No! Condition number one is she agrees to pay the regular prorated fees like everybody else. I need her to understand we are not like those other money-grabbing schools Thomas attended. Secondly, she has to trust us unconditionally. I understand she was misled by Mr. Zhou, but she really left us high and dry. We are her friends, and we are here to work with her, not against her. Can you get her to understand that?"

"I think so. By the way, my boss also wanted to say thank you for getting to the bottom of your situation. He knew you didn't steal the money."

"No, I didn't, did I?" I responded, almost flippantly. "Please say thank you for me," I added, catching myself. "It has been a difficult time. Which reminds me, from now on, your families have to pay their fees using either wire transfer or certified cheque. No more cash transactions."

"I'll make sure of that, Mr. Gower. Got to go to a meeting. I hope you have a very nice holiday."

"You too, Hymie."

"Oh, we don't celebrate Christmas here — but we will celebrate New Year."

"Okay. Well, have a wonderful New Year. I'll speak to you again in January. And by the way, I'm still waiting for those Taiwanese beef noodles you promised."

"Next time you are in Taipei, I promise," he laughed back.

On Christmas Eve, I decided to venture into town and stop at the *As You Like It* for a drink. A local band was playing seasonal favorites when I walked in, and I noticed Santiago and Matilde laughing away at the bar. They saw me, waving me over.

"All alone for the holidays?" Santiago teased.

"Yes. My choice. A little less wackiness and a little more peace," I joked.

"Totally understand. Hey, why don't you join us?" he offered, calling over Sue to take my drink order.

"Yes, we're all alone as well," added Matilde, sipping on a glass of sherry. "Our children are too busy with their own lives to visit us right now.

After multiple refills of drinks, the three of us were all relaxed enough to truly enjoy each other's company. We talked about our families, Christmases gone by, the school, and the Major, frequently bursting into uncontrolled laughter. It wasn't until Santiago shifted the topic of discussion to *Kipling's* that the mood suddenly chilled.

"Everyone knows we were bilked when we bought that store," he ranted, slouching on his stool, his eyes looking forlorn and contemplative. "We were a couple of naïve immigrants, ready for the picking. What an embarrassment. If my father were alive today, he'd throttle me for being so stupid," smashing his hand down on the bar for effect.

"Let's not talk about this again?" lectured Matilde, sounding frustrated at what was clearly a frequent bone of contention. "It's over. We bought the place and we have to make the best of it. How many times do we need to beat this to death?"

"Is it a challenge managing the store?" I asked gently.

"It makes some profit," sighed Matilde, "but the building is so run-down. The heat escapes through cracks in its walls, and the poorly-fitted windows don't keep out the dampness. And our flickering lights are always blowing fuses. We're just waiting for something big to go wrong — like the furnace or refrigeration units. If that happens, we'll be in big trouble."

"Because we paid too much for the damn place," hissed Santiago in a slow, breathy voice. He had now drunk himself into his own self-indulgent stupor.

"Enough!" said Matilde in a stern but whispered voice so no one in the bar would hear.

Santiago stumbled off his stool. "I'm going to the Men's Room," he announced dejectedly.

Recognizing it was time to leave, I slowly rose to my feet. "This was a wonderful evening," I added. "Thank you so much for including me, Matilde."

"I think we ruined your evening."

"Not at all…"

"You have to understand, he's a proud man," she continued, "and the state of the store wears him down at times, but it'll all be fine. We believe in Fate … and God. We can't change our destiny."

I wanted to disagree with her, but thought better of it, picking up my coat and hugging her as I walked into the night.

Santiago phoned me the next day to apologize for his behavior and to invite me to join them again for New Year's Eve, but I explained that as much as I would like to, I had made previous plans. New Year's Eve, I decided, would be a perfect time to phone my family and extend holiday wishes and then enjoy a quiet evening by the fire with Tofu at my feet. Unlike the rest of my world, he never seemed to complain about anything.

Chapter 34

Like everything at Cothbert, the holidays zoomed by, and before I knew it, Janice and Peg were laying out coffee and cookies on a Dining Hall table for our first staff meeting of the new year. After reviewing the second term's timetables and club schedule, I asked Koji to update us on student-travel, all of which he had carefully arranged ahead of time and distributed as a handout.

Scanning Koji's spreadsheet, Harris said, "I don't see Thomas Kang's name anywhere on here. Isn't he supposed to be coming back?"

"Oh, yes. Sorry. You won't believe this," said Koji, sitting up. "I just heard he is arriving at our school by helicopter tomorrow—before noon. Can you believe it? Helicopter!"

Harris rolled his eyes. "Nothing surprises me anymore!"

"Don't worry. I'll greet him when he arrives," I offered, feeling somewhat responsible for his current predicament.

"Fine! So if there are no further arrivals... say by air balloon or submarine, for example, are we good to go?"

"I think so," Koji responded innocently, re-checking his spreadsheet.

The group dissolved into laughter.

"Good!" Harris raised his coffee mug in the air and

announced, "Then let the games begin!"

"You sound like the Head of the IOC kicking off the Olympics," I joked, standing up and pouring myself some more coffee.

"Oh, but the Olympic Games will be happening soon, Mr. Phil," Koji piped in excitedly. "In my home country … in the City of Nagano … in two years' time."

"That's right, Koji. They will," said Harris, taking an interest. "You know what, I think we might be able to dovetail an Olympic-based theme into our curriculum. We could separate the school into teams and motivate the students by awarding points for competitive games and hard work. It'll help us get through dreary January."

"I like it!" I responded.

The rest of the staff nodded enthusiastically in agreement.

The roaring cobalt-blue helicopter hovered over the school's playing field while I tried to hang onto my hat. Eventually finding a place to land a few feet from where I was standing, the chopper's blades gradually came to a stop, and as the engine noise subsided, a door popped open. A tall, smartly dressed man, accompanied by Thomas, exited. I could see Thomas pointing at me. I waved back as they slowly made their way over, each carrying a suitcase.

"Mr. Gower?" queried the expressionless man, putting down his case.

"Yes," I replied, as Thomas dropped his case and moved in beside me, proceeding to lean into my body.

"I'm Peter Kang. Thomas' father," he said, handing me an envelope. "This is a money order for his fees."

"Oh, thank you," I said, taking it sheepishly. "By the way,

we've never met before. Welcome to Cothbert. Can you join us for lunch?"

"No, sorry. I need to fly back to Vancouver right away—so I can make my flight to Macau later tonight," he replied, glancing at his watch.

"But my wife wanted me to tell you how grateful she is that you've agreed to keep looking after our son," he said, almost as an afterthought.

"We are happy to have Thomas back. You should be very proud of your son."

Mr. Kang turned to me with a look of surprise and then over at Thomas. "Yes, well... I'll see you back in Macau in the summer, okay, son?"

"Yes, father," said Thomas, leaning further into my body.

Without looking back, Mr. Kang reentered the helicopter.

"Can we go to the Boarding House now?" asked Thomas eagerly.

I smiled and nodded at him, just as the blades of the chopper started to spin and the deafening roar of its engine came alive again. As we strolled away from the field, I could feel the blowback from the helicopter as it started to rise. With his luggage in tow, Thomas never looked back.

With the Cothbert Winter Olympics a week away, Koji had transformed himself and the entire school into a walking advertisement for the upcoming Nagano games. His family in Japan had couriered him a box full of Olympic paraphernalia. Almost overnight, the school was deluged with everything Nagano, as Koji successfully convinced everyone to rally around the global spectacle.

At a special ceremony hosted two days before the official

opening of the Cothbert Olympic Games, Koji, wearing a rather garish Nagano Olympic tie, announced the participating countries as well as who would be on each team. The random draw included Belgium, Uganda, Turkey, and Belarus. I further explained to everyone that the goal was to learn about and write about the countries they were representing while enjoying some friendly competition.

On the night of the Opening Ceremonies, the Major was allowed to launch the games, which she did by firing a shotgun into the sky, although Harris and I had made sure it was not the same one that had almost blown off her foot. At 9:00 pm, Ida paraded the athletes down to the beach where a makeshift torch was lit. The students had painted their faces the colors of the countries they were each representing and brought oversized flags Chill had helped them to design in art class. I noticed Thomas, who was smiling for once, as he proudly waved his Ugandan flag, exhibiting a newfound confidence I hadn't seen before.

As he had done at our opening staff meeting, Harris then announced: Let the games begin!. This was followed enthusiastically by Pancho and Chill setting off a volley of fireworks and firecrackers — all of which were totally illegal and subject to massive municipal fines, but we decided the risk was worth it.

Over the next two weeks, there were canoe races, basketball games, obstacle courses, and tug-of-war competitions. Everything from room cleanliness in the Boarding House to performance and effort on tests and assignments was used to generate scores for each team, and everyone took it all very seriously.

It was during week two of the games that Harris also

345

received some good news: he had been invited to be a keynote speaker at a Ministry of Education conference being held at the *Vancouver Convention Center*, where he would profile his unique experience in running an ESL boarding school.

"It's nice to know I'm still appreciated," said Harris, joining me for coffee in the Dining Hall at recess.

"Oh, come on, Big Guy, we all appreciate you. Anyway, it'll be great exposure for the school."

"Speaking of which, under no circumstances tell the Major about my talk or she'll pull the same stunt she did in Taiwan and drop in on me unexpectedly to wreak havoc."

"As long as you're nice to me and cover some of my duty, I'll think about it."

"That's blackmail."

"What's your point?"

Harris slurped his coffee. "Flaky Easterner!"

"So, when exactly are you blessing these educators with your presence?"

"Friday."

"Friday? Why such short notice?"

"I … I forgot to mention, I'm a last-minute replacement for someone who got the mumps."

"An afterthought, eh. Well, we still think you're special."

"Like I said. Flaky Easterner."

Chapter 35

I heard it as soon as I entered the Boarding House lobby for my evening duty: gut-wrenching sobs interspersed with ragged, truncated gasps. Instinctively, I raced towards the stairs of the second floor, believing the crying was coming from a student's bedroom, but I abruptly stopped when I realized it was originating from inside Myrtle's suite on the main floor.

Was Myrtle trying to console a student? I wondered.

I hesitated to investigate further, fearing I would be unwelcome if, indeed, a troubled student was using Myrtle's shoulder to cry on; however, something prompted me to open the door to her apartment. Moving down a tiny hall, I arrived at her living room, where the sound of the weeping intensified. As my eyes adjusted to the dim light, I spotted Myrtle, sitting on the floor in a heap, despondently rocking back and forth, sobbing uncontrollably, clutching a framed photo close to her chest.

"Myrtle?" I whispered softly.

Myrtle looked up, her face red and blotchy, covered with tears, eyes bloodshot and swollen. Seeing me, she snapped her head away, buried it in her hands, and then jumped up, charging towards the kitchen.

"I'm sorry, Phil," she cried, running past me.

"Myrtle!" I called out. "What's happened? What's wrong?"

Pacing anxiously, I waited, considering whether to follow her, but a few moments later, she reappeared, her tear-streaked face wiped clean.

"Phil, I'm sorry. It's not normally as bad as this," she said, dropping into an armchair, her head falling forward into her hands.

"What is?" I asked, timidly.

Myrtle wavered, took a deep breath, and finally looked directly up at me. "Today is the anniversary of when my husband, Duncan, died," she said, her shoulders shaking as tears began anew.

I walked up behind her chair and put my hands on her shoulders, choosing to remain quiet, allowing her space to grieve. After a while, she reached for one of my hands, squeezing it tightly.

"Phil, thank you. Please sit down. Please. I'm okay now. Really."

I remained silent as I pulled up a chair and sat facing her.

"I think it's because I realized this is the thirtieth year since his death," she said, breaking the tension in the air. "It seems like such a long time ago … and here I am … still alone," she said, stressing the word 'alone.'

I thought for a moment she was going to break down again, but as she began to get control of her emotions, the breathless sobs slowly subsided. She reached for a prescription bottle on a nearby table, opened it, and popped a pill.

"You're not alone, Myrtle," I said softly. "Your students love you. We love you. You have a different type of family now. But it's still your family."

Myrtle nodded slightly, but as the tension in the room became palpable once more, an idea popped into my head.

"You know," I began, choosing my words carefully, "maybe there's a way we can honor him. Something that keeps his memory alive. What if ... we planted a tree in Duncan's honor? You choose somewhere on campus. I'll get Frank to build a bench to put under it, and then every year at this time we can remember Duncan's anniversary together on that bench. Just you and me."

There was more silence, and then: "You'd do that for me?" she said, wiping her eyes with her sleeve.

"Like I said, we're family."

While the weather was not conducive to planting, as the earth was still frozen, Myrtle decided later in the spring she would get a spruce tree. Rather than ask Frank to get involved—which invariably meant involving the Major—I bought a garden bench through *Kipling's*, arranging to have it delivered the same day and carried down to a secluded spot Myrtle selected overlooking the beach. That night, with the waves lapping against the shore and a crisp, clear sky sheltering us with a canopy of flickering stars, we christened the bench with a bottle of *Dom Perignon*.

"Thank you, Phil. This means so much to me," said Myrtle, sipping from a plastic champagne flute. "But do you mind if we keep this to ourselves ... you know, private?"

"Of course. But next year, you and I are going to plan for this day together. It will be a celebration of Duncan's life. A great event. Okay?"

"Okay," Myrtle smiled. "Family," she uttered quietly, leaning forward to clink my glass with hers.

349

"Speaking of which, I think some of our family members are involved in an Olympic basketball game in the gym in ten minutes."

"Maybe family is not all it's cracked up to be," she sniffled, getting to her feet with a faint smile.

After Myrtle left, I stayed on the bench for a few moments longer, staring at the space she had just occupied. Her parting joke—"Maybe family isn't all it's cracked up to be"—stuck with me. Even with all she'd lost, Myrtle didn't seem untethered. There was a quiet assurance about her, as if family could mean more than what was missing, as if the concept of family could shift and grow over time. For now, I felt secure in knowing that Cothbert was my family. And I could see that the students felt the same way

On the Friday morning, just before Harris was to leave for Vancouver to deliver his speech, I was in the front lobby updating our Olympic scoreboard when the Major came strolling through the front door.

"Can I see you and Harris in your office?" she said in a rather subdued tone.

"Sure, I replied. I knew Harris was putting the final touches on his speech. I buzzed him from the front desk.

"The Major needs to see us in my office about something," I said.

"Tell him it's very important," the Major yelled out, hearing me on the phone.

"She says…"

"I heard her," Harris called back. "I'll be right there."

Entering my office, I offered the Major a seat but she shook her head choosing instead to remain standing, avoiding eye contact. As we both pulled up our chairs, the Major began: "*Yous* two have done a lot for my school."

I shot Harris a surprised look.

"Well, thank you, Major," I stuttered. "We appreciate that…"

"But the school is closing," she continued sharply, cutting me off.

For a moment I wasn't sure I'd heard her properly.

"Closing? What do you mean?" I asked flitting my head back and forth between her and Harris. Harris looked like he was now in a confused stupor.

"We are broke. We don't have enough money to pay the bills. We don't have enough money to buy any more food. We have to close. It's over."

As she spoke, I noticed she was very tense and beginning to wobble on her feet. I quickly rose from my chair.

"Major, have a seat," I said, reaching for a bottle of water from my bar-fridge, handing it to her.

The Major dropped into the proffered chair and took a swallow from the bottle as some color returned to her face.

"Major, none of what you are saying makes any sense," said Harris getting his second wind, leaning forward in his chair. "I've been monitoring the budget. In fact, even before Christmas, Joe confirmed with me Phil's new intakes and Saburo's tuition had put our finances well in the black and we'd probably end the year with a small profit."

"The money from Asia has been spent. So too has Subaru's," blurted the Major, who was now picking at the label on her water bottle, still avoiding looking at us.

I could see Harris was starting to get that look he often got just before he launched one of his verbal attacks. I signaled to him to back down.

"Major, did you spend all that money," I asked calmly.

"Not me. My sister."

"Millicent?" growled Harris, bolting upright.

"Yes."

"Okay, now I'm totally confused," I added. "Can you explain exactly what happened."

The Major shot us a worried glance and then appeared to gather her thoughts. Taking a swig from her bottle of water, she began: "When this here school property came up for sale two years ago, it was basically a fire sale. The bank wanted to unload it because it had been sitting empty for so long. So, they offered it up for just over a million bucks, which I thought was a steal. I had to have it. But I didn't have that sort of cash lying around and could only come up with about half that amount. So, I spoke with my sister and asked if she wanted to invest. She had recently come into a lot of money so I knew she had the coin. Anyway, she agreed to become a fifty-percent shareholder of the school."

"But?" said Harris, who also seemed to be losing color to his face.

"Harris, you know Millicent's problem," said the Major, with sadness in her eyes.

"What problem, Harris?" I glared back.

"Let her finish, Phil. I'll explain everything in a minute."

The Major continued, "She came to see me just after the school opened saying she was in debt and wanted all her investment back. I tried to put her off by using some of the school's finances."

"What do you mean?" asked Harris soberly.

The Major cleared her throat. "Well, during renovations,

I arranged for my volunteer workers to bill me. I then had the school pay them in cash which they returned to me so I could hand it all over to Millicent. I also had the school take over her mortgage and some of her utility bills."

"But it didn't work?"

"It did for a while. But towards the end of last term, she became desperate and was visiting me almost daily. Then, one day, just before the Christmas break, my banker tipped me off she had withdrawn all the money from the school's account. When I confronted her, she told me not to worry; that she was going to double it so I wouldn't need to repay her."

"By doubling it, she meant gamble it. Right?" sputtered Harris.

"Right," said the Major, somberly. "So, when she told me she was going to Las Vegas for Christmas, I asked to tag along. I wanted to try and stop her from going crazy. But you know her, Harris."

I pivoted towards Harris again. "What the hell is she talking about, Harris?" I fired back. "Why does she keep saying, *you know, Harris*? Know what?"

"Phil, bear with me on this one. You'll understand everything in a sec," he replied impatiently. "So, Major," he continued, "are you telling me Millicent burned through every last penny in our account?"

"Yes, I told you that already. It's all gone. And she just phoned to say she's declaring personal bankruptcy. We have to close the school. Once her creditors find out they'll be coming after the school. And like I said, we also have no money left to continue running this place."

"But, we do have a credit line. Joe showed it to me," Harris said indignantly.

"That credit line is under Millicent's name. Also, nothing left after Vegas."

"Christ, Major," Harris blurted, dropping his head into his hands.

My mind was all over the place as I tried to digest what the Major was saying and why Harris seemed to know more about it all than I did.

"Major, do you have any idea what will happen if we shut our doors now and force a school full of international students out on the street?" I cut in angrily, raising my voice. "If you think the Thomas Kang situation was a risk to our reputation, it paled in comparison to this debacle. Our sordid story will be all over the national news, maybe even international news, and I doubt any school in their right mind will ever want to hire me again. I'll become a pariah overnight."

"I know," said the Major dejectedly. "I know."

The room became unbearably quiet as we each waited for the other to say something. Finally, Harris spoke.

"Major, I want to talk to Phil alone about all this. I know we just took delivery of food for the next couple of weeks, so I think we'll be okay for the short-term. In the meantime, you need to promise me to keep all of this completely under wraps and wait until we've looked at all the options."

"Okay. If you want. I promise. I'll hold off for a couple of days," the Major replied, getting slowly up from her chair. "But, like I said, there's no more money so I'm not sure what you think you can do."

With the door closed, I turned abruptly towards Harris. "Harris, what the hell is going on here? This doesn't make any sense."

Harris reached for his own bottle of water from the fridge and took a sip. Exhaling through his nose, he composed himself.

"Do you remember when we first met? When you and I were sitting in the Major's office having Scotch and you asked me how I got involved in the school."

"Yes."

"And do you remember I mentioned a failed marriage I'd rather not talk about?"

"I do. Wait …. oh, my God… Millicent?"

"Yup!" Harris took another sip of water.

"I was married to her for less than six months, during which time I almost went bankrupt. When we first started dating, she gave me the impression she was well off, which I guess at the time she was because she'd made a huge killing at some high-stakes poker game. But shortly after we got married, things spiraled out of control. She started asking me for money—big sums. She told me she'd give it back the following month, that she needed to cash out some of her bonds. By the time I discovered her gambling addiction, she owed me over 200k, and God knows how much more to other people. I tried to get her into therapy, but she refused, and then one day a collection agency arrived at our house and cleaned out all our appliances and took away my car. That was the final straw."

I was stunned into silence. The pieces suddenly fell into place—Harris's guarded demeanor, his discomfort whenever Millicent's name came up—now it all made sense.

"Oh, Harris. How awful," I whispered.

"It was. I filed for divorce and had to get legal protection against more of my personal belongings being taken away. It was a horror show. So, as you can see, Phil, what the Major is describing now is one big fucking déjà vu."

I jumped as Harris slammed his water bottle down in anger and frustration.

"So, what can we do?" I pleaded, as I tried to come to terms with this horrible turn of events.

"Well, there is no bloody way we're going to close the school in the middle of the year, I can tell you that much."

"I think we may still have the $15,000 for Thomas' tuition. Koji only deposited it last week."

"Good. Hopefully Millicent hasn't clued into that yet. We'll need it for food. Luckily payroll is a month away. Anyway, I've got my speech this afternoon in Vancouver. I'm going to see if I can swing by my own financial advisor after it's over."

"Really, Harris? You want to go there?"

"I do. I really do. And in the meantime, you, need to put on a good face and keep our cherubs happy with their Olympics. We can't let anyone know how bad things are right now or we will be finished for sure."

"I'll try," I said, forcing a smile. "I'll try."

For the rest of the afternoon, I wandered aimlessly around campus, feigning a smile at anyone who passed by, while the rest of the staff handled the last few Olympic competitions before the Closing Ceremonies. Finally, unable to bear the stress any longer, I made my way down to the beach and collapsed into one of the blue Adirondack chairs. Peering out at the ominous sky, I became attuned to the raging waves sloshing violently beneath the dock. For the first time, the beauty of the West Coast felt oppressive—almost dangerous—and I wondered if I'd made a huge mistake in moving out here.

I thought about Harris visiting his financial advisor in Vancouver. Of course, I knew what he was up to, but I also knew this wasn't just about him—it was about me deciding whether I still wanted to be part of Cothbert. The place felt precarious, as if it could fall into chaos at any moment. *But then again, I thought, reflecting on my conversation with Myrtle, that's what families are: fragile, messy, imperfect.*

After deliberating for over an hour and weighing all the options, I finally arrived at my decision.

Chapter 36

After immersing myself in a very successful Closing Ceremonies on the beach, my focus abruptly returned to the impending closure of the school. Exhausted and demoralized, I trudged back through blustery conditions to the School House for the night. But as I finally made it to the stairs to my suite, my heart skipped a beat. Hovering in front of my door was the silhouette of a man.

"Harris?" I said, finally realizing who it was.

"I have libations," he smiled back cheekily, raising two bottles in the air.

"You scared the hell out of me," I exclaimed, reaching for my keys in my coat. "Come on in," I added, shaking my head.

Harris followed me inside, proceeding directly to my kitchen counter.

"One bottle of *Macallan* and one bottle of *Penfolds Shiraz*," he proclaimed proudly, placing each one down.

"You mean one bottle for each of us?" I said, reaching for glasses from a cabinet above.

"Why not!"

"That bad, eh?"

"No. It's not," he replied reassuringly, removing the casing from the top of the wine bottle. "Have you got a corkscrew?"

I retrieved one from a drawer, handed it to him, and then sat down on my couch, just as I heard the familiar pop of a cork. Handing me a drink, Harris sat opposite me on a chair.

"I've made a decision," he announced, getting himself comfortable. "I'm going to buy out Millicent."

"That's a lot of money, Harris," I said, taking a sip of wine, watching him over the rim of my glass.

"It is, but I think it's worth the risk. Like the Major said earlier, she bought the property well under its market value. So, at the very least, I'm looking at this as a good property investment."

I took another sip and then leaned forward. "Harris, I've also been thinking a lot about all this. I kind of figured you'd come back with some sort of buy-out strategy."

"You don't think it's a good idea?"

"No. I do. But when I sat there in this morning's meeting, listening to you and the Major talk about Millicent, I suddenly felt... out of place. Like the two of you had this whole thing worked out, and I was just there for the ride. It made me wonder if I really belonged here. And I realized—I can't keep doing this unless I'm part of it, really part of it."

"I'm sorry about that. Like I said before, I wanted to forget that marriage."

"I'm not blaming you. What I'm saying is I can't continue to work here unless I'm part of your shareholder arrangements."

"Okay. What are you proposing?"

"My grandfather left me some retirement income. At last check, it was valued at about $300,000. While he wanted me to grow the money until I retired, I've decided if you're going to take a risk then so am I. I want in on this."

For a brief moment, the thought of risking my grandfather's hard-earned money sent a pang of anxiety through me, but the logic held.

"Hmm," said Harris, twirling his glass of Scotch. "I mean, that's great and will certainly lessen the financial burden on me. But that's your retirement income you're gambling with, Phil."

"Please don't use the word 'gambling,'" I said as the wind outside rattled my living room window.

"Sorry, poor choice of words."

"I understand the risk. I've thought it through. I also came to the same conclusion you did about this being an investment in property. So, I'm comfortable with the gamble, as you call it, because I believe my retirement income can still grow under this plan."

Harris nodded, then leaned back in his chair. "Speaking of risks, there's something else I've been considering."

"Oh?"

"How would you feel if we became a regular school?"

"You mean, not a boarding school?"

"No, I mean not the model we have now, where our students have to exit after a year, but a proper, fully accredited high school that can accept any type of student—including local day-students, students we'd see through to graduation."

"Interesting," I said, walking over to the fireplace. It was already set for a fire, so I struck a match. The warmth from the first flames was comforting as I turned his idea over in my mind.

"I have to be honest," I said after a moment, placing the matches back on the mantelpiece, looking toward the end of this year, the idea that all our students will leave for good does feel a little off."

"It's actually been on my mind for a while," Harris said, settling deeper into his chair as I returned to the couch. "A proper high school could transform everything here. It would stabilize us. Secure us." His voice carried a mix of excitement and conviction that made me sit up straighter.

"So how do we get the ball rolling?"

"Well, when I was at the conference today—where, I should add, I was quite amazing…"

"Naturally."

"I met this Ministry official in charge of private school inspections—Tina Wade's her name. Lovely lady. Bright, engaged, and curious about our setup. She doesn't understand our model either. She asked if we wanted to be accredited."

"To which you said?"

"We'd seriously consider it. And the more I thought about it, the more compelling the idea became. Think about it: more kids, more revenue, more appeal for international boarders—they always want to be surrounded by native English-speakers—not to mention North American kids. It's a no-brainer."

"What's the downside?"

"Not sure there is one. I think the Major will go for it too."

"Because of the money?"

"And the stability. A hundred percent attrition every year is asking for trouble. I'm sure Joe has pointed this out to her more than once. And as new investors, it should be a concern for us as well."

"So, how do we get the ball rolling?"

"Let's you and I chat with the Major once we get this ownership matter sorted out. If she's on board, we'll need to submit an application and a bunch of paperwork as quickly as possible. Normally you're supposed to do this a year in advance of opening but because we're already up and running and Tina seems to like what we've been doing here, she's going to fast-track everything. She says by March we should get interim certification and by May receive our formal inspection and official designation."

"So, if we get the interim certificate in March, can we notify our agents and convince some of our kids to come back next year?"

"Absolutely."

"Let's do it then," I said, raising my glass.

"Full steam ahead," clinked back Harris. "You see how valuable I am to you."

"Not really."

"Flaky Easterner."

The next morning, Harris presented me with a draft of a shareholders' agreement, which included, among other things, strict checks and balances to prohibit any one shareholder from withdrawing money from the school's account without the consent of the others. After agreeing to this initial draft, we asked the Major if we could meet in her office.

The Major was seated behind her desk when we walked in, and as Harris and I pulled up our chairs, I noticed she seemed surprisingly jovial compared to the last time we met. I wondered if she had gotten wind of our plans.

"Before *yous* two tell me what you have to talk about, I have just received some great news," she announced. "Joe has found one of them vulture capitalists to invest in Cothbert."

Harris shook his head. "You mean, venture capitalist, don't

you?"

"Ya. One of them. He is willing to buy out most of Millicent's debt, and Joe says we should then be able to get a credit line for the rest."

The Major's gaze shifted between Harris and me, her face scrunching in confusion as she waited for our reaction. "Isn't this what you wanted?"

"Well, Major, before you jump at that offer," said Harris, selecting his words carefully, "the reason Phil and I have scheduled this meeting is to inform you that we are prepared to buy out all of Millicent's stake."

Her eyes widened in surprise. "*Yous* two have that sort of money?" Her head darted back and forth between us, as if trying to make sense of it.

"We do," I assured her. "We have the means to finance becoming your 50% partner."

The Major leaned back on her squeaky executive chair, her hands clasped together in front of her as she mulled over the news. I could see she wasn't exactly sure what to do next.

"Do you need to talk to Joe?" I asked at last.

"Ah … ya, ya. Good idea!"

"That's fine," Harris interjected, leaning forward slightly. "But just so you know, our offer is only good for twenty-four hours. Right, Phil?" he said, touching my arm.

"Yes … yes," I stammered, realizing Harris was now in full-court press mode.

"Okay," said the Major, her brow furrowing as she processed the information. "I'll get back to you tonight. I think I can see Joe later this afternoon."

"Good!" I said, signaling to Harris that it was time to leave. "We'll see you tonight, then."

As soon as we retreated to my office, Harris screamed, "Fuck!" at the top of his lungs before flopping onto my couch, his body crashing into the cushions like a man exhausted by a long day.

"Harris! Shh! The students will hear you," I whispered urgently, glancing nervously at the door.

Harris threw up his hands in exasperation before turning back to me. "Joe's going to push her straight into that venture capitalist's den. Guaranteed."

"Why would he do that?" I asked, frowning.

"Because it's actually safer," Harris said with a bitter laugh. "Secure backing, extra cash for expansion, a safety net for hard times—you name it. They'll sell her the dream, Phil. The problem is, she won't see the nightmare waiting behind it."

"What kind of nightmare?" I pressed, leaning forward, suddenly wary.

Harris shook his head. "Profit-driven owners don't care about the vision, only the numbers. Worst-case scenario? Imagine staff turnover through the roof, teachers leaving because they're overworked, constant cost-cutting that destroys the heart of the place, parents pulling their kids out because it's no longer a school but a factory. Do you want me to continue?"

"No. I hear you," I sighed, trying to process the magnitude of it all.

"If you think the focus was on making money with the Major in charge, just wait until a venture capitalist takes control. It'll be all about the bottom line, nothing more."

"Do you really think it could come to that?"

"I've seen it happen before," Harris said, his voice quieter now, almost resigned. "And if this pans out, I'm out of here, Phil. I'm done."

I stayed silent, a sinking feeling growing in my gut as I watched him run a hand through his hair. What I had hoped would be a breakthrough, a resolution to my painful soul-searching, was now slipping through my fingers.

It was hard to remain focused on anything for the rest of the day, but I muddled through. By late afternoon, as the sun filtered into the dining hall, casting long shadows on the tiled floor, Harris and I quietly picked at our dinner plates, both numbed into a sense of disbelief and saying little to each other. Then, the Major walked in.

"Can I see *yous* two now? I just got back from my meeting with Joe."

I stared at her, trying to gauge her mood, but she quickly turned and strode towards her office. Harris and I followed her closely from behind, like two students who were about to be reprimanded.

We sat in the same configuration as the morning's meeting, although this time I was clenching the armrest of my chair, sitting upright.

"Joe says I should go with the venture capitalist," she said, her voice flat as she crossed her arms.

Harris started to rise from his seat.

"But … I don't want to partner with some person I don't know," she added, shaking her head as if wrestling with the decision.

As I pulled Harris back down, the Major proceeded to pull out a bottle of *Johnnie Walker*. Unlike at our first meeting, when she handed us chipped coffee mugs, this time she laid

365

out three crystal Scotch glasses in front of us. Pouring the Scotch, she then reached for her own glass and signaled for us to follow.

"To our partnership!" she declared, raising her glass in the air.

"To our partnership," we chimed in unison, raising our glasses.

As the agreement was signed, the weight of it hit me: I had gone from being an underappreciated administrator to the full-blown owner of a school. While the path ahead was clear, its burden now felt far heavier than I had imagined.

Chapter 37

Both Harris and I were humbled by the Major's willingness to partner with us, even if Harris didn't admit it publicly. With the Major ecstatic about the prospect of becoming an accredited school, Harris initiated the paperwork with the Ministry of Education. However, despite Harris' promise that the application process for private school accreditation was relatively straightforward, the reality of the paperwork required and the extent of the checklist we needed to follow was becoming overwhelming. To make matters worse, the Major, eager to get accredited, kept asking, 'Philly, how far along are you . . . we need to get this done!'

So, when Koji buzzed through on my office intercom to inform me that someone from the government was on the line, I couldn't have been less enthused.

Now what?

"Hello, Phil Gower speaking," I exhaled after picking up the receiver.

"Mr. Gower, thank you for taking my call. Mayor Archibald Figbot here. I don't think we've had the pleasure of meeting yet, but I've heard some damn good things about your school."

"Well, thank you. I appreciate hearing that," momentarily

taken aback. "You said you're the mayor?"

"I am. I'm the mayor of the Timberline District, a ten-mile radius that includes your town of Timberline Lake as well as the villages of Rutherford and Browettsville."

The mayor had a strange drawl to his voice that caused him to accentuate certain words in each of his sentences.

"Listen, I'll get right to the point," he continued. "Every April, over in Browettsville, we host the Timberline District Annual Fair. It's your basic company picnic. Our office provides free food and entertainment, and we also sponsor a parade."

"A parade?"

"That's right. It's fun for the kids, and our businesses get to blow their horns a bit. That's why I'm calling. Are you interested in blowing your horn, Mr. Gower?"

"You mean, by joining your parade?"

"Yeah. We'd love it if you guys could enter a float."

"A float? Really?"

"Sure. Why not? Decorate a trailer with a banner showing your school's name, have a few of your kids waving on it, and arrange for someone to pull it. It'll give you some great advertising in the community—to showcase what makes your school special. And your students can join in our family picnic in Browettsville once it's all over."

"Well, it certainly sounds like a wonderful idea, Mayor. I just need a day or two to discuss it with the rest of my colleagues. Would it be okay if I got back to you by … let's say … the end of the week at the latest?"

"Sure. You won't regret it," he replied, then paused. "Hey, I have to ask, though," he said, lowering his voice, "What's it like working for the Major?"

"Oh … you know … it's fine," I wavered.

"Better you than me. Anyway, looking forward to hearing back from you. Ciao for now," he said, and the line went dead.

After hanging up, I stared at the accreditation documents piling up on my desk and thought about Mayor Figbot's pitch to showcase what makes our school special. It struck me that this wasn't just a pile of mindless paperwork staring me down—it was an opportunity to demonstrate that Cothbert belonged. We weren't just another school; we were something distinct, something necessary. I needed to prove that what we were building here truly mattered. As the mayor put it, I needed to blow our horn.

I grabbed my *Moleskine* notebook and jotted down a few words: "*A place to belong. A place to be me.*" They were simple sentiments, but I felt they captured something essential— what Cothbert meant to us and what it could mean to others.

Glancing down at my watch, I realized it was already 6:30. *Hopefully, Janice and Peg have some dinner leftovers.*

As I walked towards the Dining Hall, I almost bumped into Harris. He was dressed in a heavy woolen jacket, sporting a deerstalker hat and being trailed by a group of students. Then I remembered — he was scheduled to chaperon a group into town to buy junk food from *Kipling's.*

"Why don't you join us?" he asked, as I got closer. "The walk will do you some good. You know, get away from all that accreditation stuff."

I gave him a dirty look but could tell he desperately wanted some adult company. While a quiet night in front of a roaring fire with a glass of Bordeaux, a good book and some left-over meat loaf from the Dining Hall sounded a heck of a lot better,

I reluctantly agreed to tag along.

"I'll catch up with you in a few minutes," I called out, dashing inside the Dining Hall, reaching for a muffin and banana from the buffet table. I whipped into my office, grabbed my coat, and caught up with Harris and his troupe a few moments later. They were leisurely wandering up the driveway, their shoes crunching on the remaining remnants of fallen twigs and dead leaves that had survived the last few gusty months of the winter term. The trees lining the entrance to the campus were already sprouting tiny chartreuse-colored leaves, while young squirrels darted up and down on the overhanging branches, scaring away the crows squawking from above. The air felt cool, and I tightened the top collar of my fleece-lined jacket. By the time we got to the main road that led into town, I had already briefed Harris on my call from Mayor Figbot.

"Well, I think it's a super idea," Harris said, filtering the students into a single-file formation. "Let's flesh it out at the staff meeting."

"You know, the mayor asked what it's like working for the Major," I said, peeling back my banana. "I didn't have the heart to give him the answer he wanted."

"Ha! He'd love to gloat about our challenges. There's no love lost between those two."

"Why?"

"Four years ago, after Mayor Parsons passed away and his position opened up, Figbot and the Major ran against each other. Figbot had a solid platform, the Major... just threw herself in."

"Figbot won?"

"By a landslide. He made a campaign out of mocking her

name: *Avoid a Major Disaster, Don't Major in Mediocrity*—it was genius!"

"How did she take it?"

"Not well. They haven't spoken since. Whatever you do, don't mention the election around her. She's liable to pull out her shotgun."

"Got it."

We finally arrived at *Kipling's* twenty minutes later and after Harris had given a quick pep talk to the group on shopping etiquette, the students entered the store, where they quickly emptied shelves of instant noodles, chips, chocolates and soda pop. While we waited for them to finish, Santiago and Matilde perked up when they saw us. Santiago stepped down from a rickety ladder where he and Matilde were stocking shelves.

"Hey there, you two! Join us for coffee!"

He pulled up a couple of chairs, grabbed two coffees from a nearby carafe while Matilde went to the back, returning with a plate of homemade Portuguese buns, which she proudly placed on a table that usually served as a communal chess board. Harris and I sat with our backs to the window. Since I was famished, I eagerly devoured a bun while Santiago and Matilde pulled up their chairs opposite us.

"So, how's business?" Harris asked, following my lead, reaching for a bun.

"Ah, you know," sighed Santiago. "Same old thing. We get by. This old building needs so much work." He pointed his hands at the ceiling, almost like he was praying in desperation. I also noticed him giving Matilde a somber look which she acknowledged with a shaking of her head.

371

"I'll probably have to take out a second mortgage, you know," Santiago admitted as an afterthought. "But, hey, that's life. We're happy in Timberline. And we've got good friends here — like you two and your lovely students," he smiled. "Thanks for bringing them over, by the way. We always appreciate it. Every penny counts, you know."

"Speaking of which," I smiled, pointing at the growing line forming in front of the cash register, "I'm not sure they totally get the meaning of 'every penny counts.'" I stared in disbelief at the students' overflowing baskets of junk food.

"One day they will," said Matilde soberly.

She and Santiago got up and stood behind the front counter, making an effort to joke with the group. The two of them seemed to have a natural way with young people, and the students respected them almost like loving parents. Matilde, in particular, was getting a reputation for being the go-to person for haircuts at the school. When Frank recently discovered an old barber-chair stashed away in the watchtower, Matilde began making weekly visits to the campus to cut hair. She had been a hairdresser back in Portugal, and the students soon recognized she knew what she was doing. And for only five dollars a cut, they also knew a good deal when they saw one.

A few days later at our weekly staff meeting, where everyone was already ecstatic about the prospect of Cothbert becoming an accredited high school, the idea of creating a float was met with unanimous enthusiasm.

"Oh, I love that parade," gushed Myrtle, bouncing up and down. "I can't believe they've invited us to join it."

"Like …. I can't wait to work with the students on it too,"

372

Chill piped in, pushing on her hair bun. "This is going to be so damn cool!"

"You know what?" Pancho exclaimed, "I think we should build a mini model of the School House?"

"Oh … hey, ya… like, that's such a neat idea, Pancho," agreed Chill. "My art classes can look after the painting of it if you want."

"I can help you too, Pancho," Koji offered eagerly. "I like building things."

"And, once the float is ready, what about if our jazz band performed in front of your model?" said Ida with an uncharacteristic amount of exuberance. "It's about time they had an audience."

"And let's not forget that Francis Ford Byung-ju will be getting everything on film for us," Harris touted.

"Sounds like a plan," I smiled. "I'll let Mayor Figboot know right away."

The next day, following lunch, I asked Frank to ensure the gym was set up for an assembly. We were going to announce our participation in the parade and what needed to be done in order to create the float. I also wanted to ensure everyone contributed in some way or another, whether it was building or painting the mini School House, decorating the trailer with flowers, performing in the band, or volunteering to be one of the school models who would be waving to the crowd. I felt it really important this was a team effort.

Once we were all seated in the gym, the project was announced, and each staff member outlined the various jobs in more detail. I noticed how the students leaned in, engaged. It was a small thing, but it struck me—an indication of how far we'd come and how much the school meant to them.

My thoughts were interrupted by the chatter coming from the other side of the gym. A group of girls was huddled together. I quietly slid along the wall toward them, where I could see Pansy, Hibiscus, Aki, and Minji Lee, our recent addition, looking down at an object Aki had in her hand.

"Girls!" I whispered, firmly but quietly. "Watch the assembly, please! And stop talking!"

They looked up at me defiantly, crossing their arms, before slowly turning toward the front of the room.

What's gotten into them? I wondered.

When the assembly was finally over, I looked back to where the girls had been seated but they were gone.

"Harris," I called out, stopping him as he was stepping down off the stage. "Some of the girls seem upset about something. Do you know what's up?"

"No. Maybe Myrtle does," he replied, distracted by a couple of students who were pushing and shoving from behind.

Even though it was Myrtle's day off, I decided I had better phone her. But as I turned down the hall, there, standing outside my office were the same girls I had reprimanded in the gym.

"Please come in, girls," I signaled. I can see you're upset about something."

I moved behind my desk and sat down, looking awkwardly up at them. They moved in together, remaining stoic.

"So, what's up?" I asked, forcing a smile, trying to break the tension in the room.

"Your *lice* has big problem," announced Aki, sternly.

"Excuse me? My what?"

"This," exclaimed Minji, laying a bowl of emerald-colored

rice on the table. "Your food is getting worse and worse. You served this rice for lunch today."

"I did? I mean … we did?" I replied, trying to hold back my surprise at the disgusting-looking green concoction staring back at me.

"I agree, girls …" I responded, hesitantly. "This doesn't look good. I'm sorry … I missed lunch today because I was busy preparing for the assembly and so I didn't have a chance to see this…

A knock on the door made me jump and Harris peaked his head inside.

"Ah, Mr. Tweedsmuir," I responded, relieved that I had some additional back-up. "I think you need to see this." I raised my eyes to alert him there was a problem. "We have a bit of an issue with our food. Luckily, these girls have brought it to my attention," I said, in an exaggerated tone to show I was taking their complaint seriously."

Harris listened while I explained their concern. He looked down at the green bowl of rice.

"Ah," he smiled, slapping his head with a look of recognition. "I think I know what happened. All of you, follow me, please!"

The girls looked at each other, shrugging their shoulders, while Harris led us back down the hallway to the Dining Hall. When we arrived, I noticed the entrance to the hall had been wreathed with green streamers.

"Please," ushered Harris, holding open the door. We walked inside the room, where we were met with bright green helium balloons used as center-pieces on each of the tables. A large cake, shaped like a four-leafed clover sat atop a steel trolley. On its emerald icing, bold white letters read: *Happy*

St. Patrick's Day, Cothbert!

Janice and Peg stepped out from behind the kitchen when they saw us.

"By any chance did you two dye the rice green today?" asked Harris, grinning.

"We did," chuckled Janice and Peg. But no one wanted to eat it. Did we go too far with our St. Patrick's Day concept?"

"Maybe. There are some things best left untouched when it comes to green food coloring. Girls, come and have a seat," ushered Harris, reaching for Pansy's translator.

I stayed back and let Harris work his magic. Before long, the girls were in hysterics. They looked back towards me giggling.

"Sorry, Mr. Gower. We get joke now," cried out Aki. "Very funny joke. No problem with your *lice*."

"Good to know!" I called back.

We take our lice very seriously.

Chapter 38

With the building of a float well underway, it wasn't long before the Major got wind of the plan and came barreling into my office. I had become so used to her abrupt entrances I didn't even flinch when she flung open my door without knocking.

"Good evening, Major. Everything okay?" I asked rhetorically.

"What's this I hear about us helping that lard-ass, good-for-nothing Figbot?" she thundered.

"Well… that lard-ass, as you call him, asked if we would like to enter a float in this year's Timberline District Parade. I thought it sounded like a good opportunity. But, of course, if you don't think we should do it, that's fine with me. Still, we were hoping you'd sit beside Frank in the cab of the truck pulling the float."

The Major went silent, and I could see she was giving the idea a second thought.

"Figbot didn't want anything else?"

"Like what, Major?"

"That useless excuse for a mayor has no idea what he's doing. He's always harassing the community for more money, and he continues to jack up our taxes every year.

I think he's on the take, if you ask me. Don't know how he got the job. He should be audited—probably fired."

"Hmm," I responded, not taking much stock in her inventive storytelling. "Like I said, I'm not married to the idea, but we all thought it would be a good focus for the students. Who knows, some local media from Vancouver might even be there."

The Major sniffed, rocking from one leg to the next, as she thought more about it. "No, no, that's fine. If that's all lard-ass wants, I'll look after the truck and the flatbed trailer. What are you going to stick on this float of yours, anyway?"

I outlined the various ideas proposed by the staff, and I could see her really beginning to warm to the concept.

"Well, *yous* let me know if you need anything from me. I can get you used boards and nails if you want."

"Used boards and nails are good, Major," I smiled, detecting a note of triumph. She then walked out of my office with far less intensity than when she arrived.

I leisurely followed her from behind, deciding to check in with Koji at Reception, who was signing for three large packages when I arrived.

"Anything for me there?" I asked, hopefully, as soon as the *FedEx* man bolted out the door.

"Let's see," said Koji, scanning the label on each box. "Byung-ju ... Byung-ju ... and, Byung-ju. No. Sorry."

"Spoiled little brat," I pouted.

It was a few evenings later, just after Prep, when I made my way down the hill to the parking lot to check on the progress of the float. A spotlight on the watchtower cast dramatic shadows over the uncanny reproduction of the School House towering on a flatbed trailer. The sounds of hammering and chatter filled the air, and I spotted Minji in blue coveralls, a plank of wood balanced effortlessly on her shoulder.

"Looking good, Minji," I called out.

"Thanks, Mr. Gower," she shouted back. "You should come up and see this—it's so cool."

"Alright, just a sec." I climbed up onto the float, landing beside Saburo, who was fastening bright plastic flowers to the trailer's edge.

"Those look fantastic, Saburo."

He flashed me a smile—happier than I'd seen him in ages, probably because he'd recently passed his driver's test.

"Thanks. It's fun," he replied.

Minji appeared beside us. "Do you want me to show you around, Mr. Gower?"

"Sure. That'd be great."

"Up here!" Kyong-Park's voice rang out from above. He was perched on a ladder, slapping dark brown paint onto one of the walls of the mock School House.

"Be careful!" I called up.

"I will!"

Minji tugged at my arm. "Come on—you've got to see this!" She led me to the far end of the trailer, where Thomas was sprawled on the floor beside the Huang twins. He was sketching the school's crest onto a massive canvas, every line sharp, every detail painstakingly perfect.

"Superb job there, Thomas."

Thomas nodded, then, surprising me, added, "Thank you, Mr. Gower. I'm glad you like it."

I hesitated, then asked, "Thomas, can I make a request?"

He glanced up briefly.

"Under the crest, can you add the words: *A Place to Be Me?*"

Thomas nodded, and I grabbed a scrap of cardboard to scribble the phrase for him.

By the time Minji finished the tour, the trailer felt alive with energy—Manfred hammering with reckless enthusiasm, Aki and the others rolling out Astroturf, Pancho and Koji assembling wooden stands for decorative trees. It wasn't perfect, but it was ours.

As Minji darted off, Pancho gestured to the bustling scene. "It's something, isn't it? Everyone's found their place in all this."

I looked around—Thomas absorbed in his painting, voices weaving together, hands moving with purpose. The energy wasn't chaotic; it was alive, whole. *A place to be me.*

"Yeah," I said, the words sinking in like they belonged. They were taking on a life of their own—just like the school.

The following morning, I stood beside the finished float for one final look, feeling like a proud father. The sound of a car broke my reverie, and I turned to see Harris's yellow Volvo approaching.

"Are you ready?" Harris yelled, leaning out of the driver's side window. "We need to get into town if we're going to find a spot big enough for everyone to see the parade."

"Okay, I'm coming ... I'm coming!" I said, jumping into the car and eyeing Byung-ju, who was sitting in the back seat listening to his headphones. I gave a quick thumbs-up to the students standing in front of the float before our car tore up the driveway.

By the time we arrived in town, I noticed several locals had already staked out some of the prime viewing spots. Below a colorful rainbow of fluttering pennants, balloons, and a swaying banner that read *Welcome to Timberline,* refreshment stands were being wheeled into position while a couple of local officials threaded yellow security tape through metal pegs they had installed along the main strip.

Harris parked his car just outside *Kipling's,* where Santiago and Matilde were standing under a red awning, preparing for the sale of ice cream.

"Hey, you two," I called out, removing Byung-ju's camera equipment from the trunk of the car. "Having fun yet?"

"Always," Santiago joked back. "It's a great day for Timberline ... but not so much for *Kipling's,*" he added. "Because of crowd control, we've been asked to close down until the parade is over. You can use our parking lot for your students if you want. They'll have a great view from there."

"Oh, perfect!" thundered Harris, rubbing his hands together. "Well, come on, you two," he ordered excitedly, looking over at Byung-ju and me. "What are you waiting for? Help me get this area cordoned off."

Using a stack of orange pylons he'd brought with him, we proceeded to completely block off the parking lot from the general public. Then, locating a slightly elevated piece of land nearby, we helped Byung-ju set up his tripod and camera equipment. Santiago walked over, carrying cups of coffee and juice for Byung-ju.

An hour later, Myrtle and the others appeared on the horizon, walking in a single-file formation over the hill leading into town. Byung-ju, who was still listening to his headphones, immediately started adjusting his camera lens. But no sooner was the camera rolling than his behavior became quite erratic. For no apparent reason, he started giggling to himself incessantly, panning the camera in 360 degrees. At one point, he swiveled it up and down and then from side to side, singing loudly.

"Is something up with Byung-ju?" I asked, drawing Harris' attention to his bizarre show.

Harris narrowed his eyes, watching in disbelief, while Byung-ju held his tripod in his arms like a dance partner, waltzing it from side to side.

"You okay up there, Byung-ju?" Harris called out.

No response.

"Byung-ju!" yelled Harris.

Byung-ju removed his headphones. "Yes?" he replied innocently.

"Are you alright?"

"Of course," he called down, just as Myrtle and the rest of the school descended on *Kipling's* parking lot. Santiago and Matilde walked over to join us and, as was their custom, started bantering with the students, eventually handing each one a chocolate bar and a small hand-flag on which was written *Shop Kipling's.*

It wasn't long before we felt hemmed in by the ballooning crowds around us, and when it looked like the endless hordes of people would never stop coming, the distant sounds of drumming signaled the parade's arrival as imminent. Everyone stopped moving about and turned eagerly towards the main road. A military band came trooping over the hill, marching under a tall sign that read *Greetings from Mayor Figbot.*

A larger version of Colonel Sanders walked behind the performers, grinning and waving to the crowds as the cheering and clapping grew in intensity.

382

If only the Major were here right now, I thought, imagining the colorful language that would be coming out of her mouth.

Behind the band were various local merchants and professionals unabashedly flogging their company logos. There were also Boy Scout and Girl Guide troupes, a high school football team, dancers from a ballet academy, and floats representing grocery stores, telephone providers, the Parks Board, and the *As You Like It Pub,* which had a humorous montage of an Oompah band performing to patrons singing and swaying beer mugs.

Finally, the parade's newest entry, *Cothbert House School,* emerged at the top of the hill. The parking lot erupted in loud applause, and the students started jumping up and down. As our float moved closer, I could see the Major sitting in the front of Frank's truck, lifting her hand up, swaying it back and forth to the crowds like she were the Queen of England. Behind her, Aki, Manfred, and Stanley were poking their heads out from inside the mock School House, bouncing with an unusual degree of excitement, while the Jazz Band performed the theme song to *Mission Impossible.*

The loud cheering continued unabated, but then I thought I heard new sounds—a rat-tat-tat and then a series of loud pops. For a moment, I froze, imagining a gun had gone off somewhere. Then, looking more closely at the float, I noticed Stanley lighting a bundle of firecrackers before pitching them out the window in front of him.

I turned to get a glimpse of Frank and the Major sitting in the front seat of the truck pulling the float. They were nervously flicking their heads from side to side, clearly in a state of panic, not knowing what was going on behind them. When the rapid blast of the firecrackers finally subsided, the crowd showed their appreciation with even louder cheering. Before I could even think about what to do next, bright spirals of light started whizzing and twirling out the windows of the mock School House.

"Are those fireworks?" I cried out in dismay.

Harris came storming up beside me. "What the hell is going on up there?" he yelled angrily. "Where did they get those bloody things from?"

"Probably leftovers from the Olympics," I said, looking on in dismay.

The zooming pyrotechnic display generated more gunshot noises followed by huge echoing bangs. Without warning, the truck carrying Frank and the Major slammed on its brakes. The trailer behind it shuddered before lunging forward, causing the Jazz Band players to fall on top of each other. This was followed by a terrible grating noise.

I then watched in horror as the trailer released its hitch from the truck and began drifting slowly towards us.

"Get out of the way!" I screamed, signaling frantically for the other staff members to move the students back.

The trailer continued to pick up momentum and, if not for Harris' Volvo sitting directly in its path, it would have come crashing into us. Instead, like a can opener, the hitch cut through one of the car's doors, cleanly stripping away a large yellow sheet of metal as the trailer came to a grinding halt.

I looked up to see Aki, Manfred, and Stanley laughing hysterically as they were thrown against one of the walls of the mock School House. Slowly, the building's facade began to buckle and creak and then, like an accordion, collapsed in a cloud of dust.

384

What happened next is still a blur. But once we were able to convince some of the worried onlookers we were all okay and had retrieved everyone safely from the trailer, I gave a quick call to Koji, who arrived in the school bus a few minutes later. In the meantime, Myrtle had pulled Aki, Manfred, and Stanley aside and was tearing into them.

I then realized the Major was marching determinedly in my direction.

"Who's responsible for this? Who?" she screeched, stepping in front of me.

"I don't know yet, Major. We're trying to get to the bottom of it all."

"This is a total embarrassment," she added, storming off.

A few minutes later, Myrtle walked back over, her face looking pale and tense.

"I think they're all drunk!" she said in a hushed voice.

Chapter 39

While Myrtle watched over the students, keeping a particularly close eye on Aki, Manfred, and Stanley — not to mention Byung-ju, who I now suspected was also complicit in the drunk-fest — I pulled the staff together for a quick huddle to consider what to do next. While my inclination was to return to the school and never show our faces again in Timberlane, I realized I was probably being overly sensitive.

"I really don't think we should punish everyone just because a handful of students showed poor judgment," said Pancho. "I say we still go to Browettsville for the picnic."

"I agree," added Ida. "You know, a lot of the other students are really angry about what happened, particularly given all the work they put into that float. If they sense we changed the plan because of the troublemakers, I think things will only get worse."

"Ya ... I think so too," Chill nodded.

"Harris, what about you?" I asked. "What do you think we should do?"

Harris thought for a minute and then turned to us, his eyes filled with resolve. "One of the goals of today was to allow the community to get to know our school. If we run away now, their only impression of Cothbert will be of a bunch of out-of-control pyrotechnicians who caused mayhem. If we go to the picnic, maybe we'll be able to convince people we've actually got some pretty responsible kids at our school. Anyway, I have to go and schmooze with Mayor Figbot and apologize for this colossal mess.

"Alright, then. But I still have to take our troublemakers back to school and get to the bottom of all this," I said. "And I'll need someone to help me." Turning to Koji, "Do you think you could assist me?"

"No problem," he replied. "But who drive bus to picnic?"

"I'll ask Frank to do it. That way, we can borrow his truck to shuttle the hooligans back to campus. It's got a back seat so we should be able to squeeze everyone in. Frank can arrange to pick up the trailer later this evening. I'm sure Santiago won't mind if we leave it here for a bit longer."

"You're assuming Frank's going to be able to pry the trailer away from my car door," blasted Harris, red-faced. "Honestly, I can't wait to explain this one to my insurance company."

Frank walked up beside us a few moments later and I quickly explained our plan.

"Yup, I can do that," he said willingly.

"Hey, what happened to the Major?" I asked him.

"Oh, she walked home. Never seen her this angry before."

With the rest of the school en route to the picnic, Koji and I began our return journey to campus. While I fully expected our Gang of Four to be contrite and quiet in the back, nothing could have been further from the truth. If anything, they seemed intent on laughing, joking, and completely ignoring the seriousness of what they had done.

The moment we drove under the portico to the School

House and got out of the truck, I asked Koji to stay at Reception in case Harris called. I then marched the troublemakers straight to my office and told them to line up in front of my desk. Keeping a poker face, I asked, "Who bought the alcohol?"

They exchanged grins and shrugged at one another.

"No alcohol," said Byung-ju at last.

"Then why are you all drunk? Is it drugs, then?"

"No... no. We would never use those," Stanley replied adamantly.

The frustrating part was they actually sounded like they were telling the truth. I glanced down at their knapsacks on the floor.

"Okay then. Open your bags and empty everything on my desk. Pockets too."

Without hesitation, they began unloading. Pens, papers, CD players, headphones, notebooks, candy, and wallets spilled across my desk. I waited, expecting a beer bottle or flask to appear, but there was nothing. Then, as I scanned the pile, something caught my eye—a handful of small vials containing an orange liquid.

"What's this?" I asked brusquely, holding up one of the glass containers.

"Gift from my mom," replied Byung-ju. "Ginseng energy shots."

"Energy shots?" I repeated, frowning as I turned the vial over in my hand. There were no identifying markings on the glass.

"Do you have the original packaging for these?" I asked.

"Maybe," Byung-ju replied, rifling through the heap now covering my desk.

"Here!" he said, producing a small, torn cardboard box.

I examined it closely. All the lettering on the box was in Korean, except for one detail—the number 56.

"Byung-ju, what does this number mean?" I asked, pointing to the box.

Byung-ju read it slowly. "Fifty-six percent alcohol," he said, his voice cracking as his eyes cautiously met mine.

Before I could respond, the intercom on my desk started buzzing. I put the phone on speakerphone. "Yes," I clipped back.

"Mr. Phil. Please come quick. Miss Wade is here to see Mr. Harris."

"Who the heck is Miss Wade?" I asked in a frustrated voice.

"The Ministry Inspector. You know, the lady who going to make us a regular school."

"What? Oh, right. Her. Why's she here on a Sunday?"

"She said she is in town and wants to drop off papers for Mr. Harris?"

"Oh, for goodness sake!" the annoyance in my voice unrestrained. "Okay. Koji, I need you to look after these students while I deal with this. Tell Miss Wade to wait. I'll be there in a minute."

"Got it!" Koji replied.

A few moments later Koji came charging into my office, sliding to a stop.

"Koji, you must not let these students out of your sight. Do you understand me?" I demanded.

"Yes. Got it."

Gathering my thoughts, I took a deep breath and walked as fast as I could to the front lobby. Standing by the door was a young woman who caused me stop for a moment and stare. She was tall, with short black hair and an endearing look.

"Miss Wade?" I said, with a strained smile.

Extending her hand, "Tina, please. I realize it's Sunday, but I was just on my way back from Whistler and wanted to drop something off for Harris Tweedsmuir. Would you know where I can find him?"

"Harris is not around at the moment. I'm Phil Gower, the Principal. Can I help you?"

"Oh, right. I'll give this to you then," she said, handing me a folder.

I peered inside at a fat wad of checklists and forms.

"More certification paperwork?"

"There will always be more paperwork, Phil," she said, her smile becoming broader. "Listen, before I go, may I use your restroom?"

"Of course, it's just down this hall," I said, walking with her.

"I hear you've done an amazing job with this school," she remarked, a twinkle in her eyes.

"It hasn't been without its hurdles," I grinned, once again noticing her pleasant facial features.

My reverie was broken when suddenly I eyed Manfred and Albert wobbling out of my office, checking each other into the walls. I realized they were moving in the same direction we were.

"Um ... you know what, Tina ... I just remembered, that bathroom is being serviced right now. Why don't I take you to another one ... upstairs ... if you don't mind?"

"Sure. No problem."

We returned to the front lobby, and I casually looked back

over my shoulder, relieved to see the hallway was now clear, when a "hello" from behind us startled me. I whirled around to see Aki. She was swaying from side to side, her eyes unable to focus.

"The grils washroom is fooded," she said.

"Fooded? Oh … you mean flooded," I said with a forced laugh, grabbing her hand. "Let's go to the one upstairs, shall we?"

"Tank you Mr. Grower."

"Is she alright?" asked Tina, looking at her curiously.

"Medication," I blurted, pulling her towards the stairs. "Allergic reaction, I think."

"Oh, I see. Well, if you think you need my help, I have some first aid experience. She really does seem a bit odd."

"Oh, no. She's perfectly fine. I know what the problem is. She'll be okay," I replied. "She just needs water … and rest. Seen it before. You go ahead … the washroom is at the top of the stairs … to your left," I said, rapidly flicking my hand.

"Are you sure?

"Yes!" I said firmly. "Very sure."

"Okay, then. I'll say goodbye now," she said, extending her hand again. "Your Interim Certificate should be here in the next couple of days. It was really nice to meet you, Phil. I'm sure we'll be seeing each other again soon," she beamed.

"Oh, right … good … thank you, Tina," I said, praying inwardly she would just vanish.

I then heard loud heaving sounds and before I realized what was happening, Aki had thrown up all over the floor.

My eyes angled back towards Tina.

"Bad reaction this time," I smiled awkwardly.

"It certainly appears that way," Tina said, looking concerned. For a moment I could see her hesitating and then, "Well, good luck with her," she said, climbing up the stairs.

I waited until she had disappeared and then moved Aki slowly up to the top of the staircase. Checking first to make sure Tina was nowhere in sight, I hurriedly pushed Aki inside the boys washroom.

"Aki. Listen to me," I said. "I want you to stay in here until I come to get you. Do you understand me?"

"I get it, Mr. Grower," she said, falling into a washroom stall. When I finally heard Tina's shoes tapping down the stairs and the sound of the front door closing behind her, I quickly returned to the boys' washroom. Aki looked even worse than when I left her. I didn't hesitate. With a firm grip, I guided her back to my office, my mind racing through the mess we had to clean up.

"Koji, what happened?" I said, as soon as we returned to my office, closing the door behind me. "I thought I asked you to watch over them."

"They said they were going to be sick and had to pee," Koji replied earnestly. "I was scared they would do it in your office unless I let them go to the washroom."

"I see," I sighed loudly.

"Now listen," I said firmly, turning to the group, who were all starting to look quite ill, "those Ginseng energy shots are dangerous; they are not for teenagers. They're not even for responsible adults. Do you understand me?" I suddenly felt the total weight of the situation.

They nodded their heads shamefully, and stared at the floor.

"Byung-ju, how many more of those boxes did your mom send you?"

"Ten," he replied.

"Okay. All of you are coming with me to the Boarding House. Byung-ju, as soon as we arrive, I want you to deliver those ten boxes to me personally. I'll be waiting for you in the Duty Office. Got it?"

"Yes, Mr. Gower."

"Then let's go!" I ordered.

In unison, everyone tottered out of my office, no longer laughing and joking.

It was well past 6:00 pm when I finally heard the school bus pulling into the parking lot outside the Boarding House. With the Gang-of-Four sound asleep and the boxes of toxic Ginseng confiscated, I dashed outside to greet everyone with a sense of relief. But as soon as the first group of students stepped off the bus, I could tell from their faces something was terribly wrong. When Harris finally appeared behind them, he acknowledged me with a pained nod and then made his way over.

"Harris, what..."

Before I could say anything more, he grabbed my arm. "It's *Kipling's*. They've had a fire. The whole store's been destroyed."

"What?" I gasped. "Was it ... us .... I mean, the fireworks?" panic rising inside me.

"No, no ... Santiago returned to the store after the parade and saw black smoke coming from behind one of his coolers. He could tell from the smell it was something electrical. But by the time he got hold of a fire extinguisher, the old wooden building never had a chance."

"Oh, God," I said, moving my hand over my face.

"The students got to see it all on our ride back. We had to stop to make sure Santiago and Matilde were okay; that they weren't badly injured. We saw them standing outside crying, surrounded by fire crews and TV cameras. About five or six of the kids raced out of the bus to hug them both, trying to console them. By the time they got back on the bus, they too were totally distraught. The whole thing's awful, just awful."

"Oh, God," I repeated. "Poor Santiago and Matilde."

"Phil, they didn't have insurance!"

Harris turned away, his face pale. His shoulders shook, and for a moment, I saw something in him I wasn't used to—raw emotion.

Chapter 40

What does it take to be a strong leader? This was a question I was often asked during my failed job interviews back East. It was a question I found myself asking now, as I tried to figure out how best to manage what Harris and I referred to as *The Day After* — the day after everything that could have gone wrong, did.

On that *Day After*, I knew I needed to address the community's pain and frustration in the morning assembly. While I wasn't sure how to provide all the answers they needed, I understood that as the leader of this school, it was my responsibility to guide them through this challenging time. Some students were devastated by the destruction of the float, while others were heartbroken over what had happened to Santiago and Matilde. Equally difficult were the phone calls I needed to make to the parents of the students involved, explaining how their teenagers had gained access to alcohol despite the school's strict no-alcohol policy. One mother, in particular, would learn that her decision to provide her son with illicit Ginseng contraband had sparked the chaos. Then there were Santiago and Matilde—two beloved members of our community whose livelihoods and dreams were now in tatters. What could I possibly say to them that would make a difference?

Of all the duties that day, none was more difficult than addressing the students. With the help of a professional student counselor Ida had found, my goal was to answer their questions while navigating their complex emotions. As I stood before them, the weight of their expectant gazes felt unbearable. My throat tightened as I composed myself.

"Good morning, everyone," I began, trying to keep my voice steady. "Yesterday was a difficult day for our school, and I know many of you have different thoughts about what happened. It's important that you are comfortable sharing whatever is on your mind. Today, we are joined by Ms. Jennifer Staunton, a counselor who will lead our assembly."

There was a scattered applause as Jennifer, a casually dressed woman with a red ponytail, stepped forward. Smiling, she began "People make mistakes," pausing deliberately to let the words sink in. "And bad things happen to good people. I can only imagine how difficult this has been for all of you. So, as Mr. Gower said, let's talk about yesterday. Let's begin by discussing the float."

The room went quiet as a few students cautiously exchanged glances, unsure of who would speak first. I noticed Minji slowly raising her hand. I quietly whispered her name to Jennifer.

"Thank you, Minji, for starting us off today," Jennifer said warmly. "Do you have something to share?"

Standing, Minji's voice began to tremble with anger. "A lot of us worked so hard on that float. For many nights!" She paused, her anger building. "We weren't shown the respect we deserved. And," she added pointedly, "I think our school looked terrible because of what happened." She crossed her arms and sat back down, clearly fuming.

"Yeah!" a few other students shouted in support. I glanced toward the back of the gym, where the Gang-of-Four sat huddled together.

"Ms. Staunton, may I respond to that?" I asked.

"Please," she replied, stepping back to give me space.

"Minji, I understand your anger. I'd feel the same way. But you should know that we've learned some additional details about what happened yesterday. One of the students received some energy drinks from home, and they were shared with others. Unfortunately, the parent who sent those drinks didn't realize they contained alcohol. A lot of alcohol, in fact. It seriously affected the students' ability to think clearly."

Some students snickered, and I overheard someone mutter the word "drunk." Minji, unimpressed, let out a loud, sarcastic laugh.

A hand shot up from the crowd.

"That's Kyong-Park," I said, turning back to Jennifer.

"Hello, Kyong-Park," Ms. Staunton greeted him with a nod. "What would you like to say?"

"How do you think the people in Timberline feel about our school now?" he asked angrily. "We looked stupid with those fireworks and our broken trailer crashing into that car."

I glanced toward the back of the room again, where the Gang-of-Four were now sinking lower into their seats.

"Just so you know," Harris called out from the back of the stage, "that car was mine."

There were gasps followed by restrained laughter from the students.

"Okay, Kyong-Park," Ms. Staunton continued. "Do you have any suggestions for what we should do about it?"

"Me?" Kyong-Park asked, sounding surprised. "I didn't make the trouble."

"No, but you are part of the school that you think had its reputation damaged," she said.

Kyong-Park thought for a moment. "Well… I think the people who did this should apologize to the Timberline community," he said, leaning back into his seat.

"That's a good suggestion. Anyone else have ideas on how they could do that?"

The room went quiet again, and just as I was about to speak, I saw Thomas rising to his feet, his hand waving in the air.

"Thomas," I said, turning to Jennifer.

"Yes, Thomas?" she asked.

"I think they should do something nice for the community," he blurted out and then immediately sank back down in his seat, drained from speaking in front of so many people.

"That's a *very* good suggestion, Thomas. I think the students involved in this need to think carefully about what he just said."

A few heads turned toward the Gang-of-Four before facing the stage again. Jennifer took a deep breath. "Let's talk about *Kipling's*," she said softly.

At the mention of the store, sobs began to echo through the gym. Jennifer stepped back, waiting for the room to settle.

"I'd like you all to bow your heads," she said.

The students leaned forward in unison, and Jennifer continued, "Now, I want you to think about a happy moment you shared with Santiago and Matilde, and offer a prayer for them. Maybe wish them better days, ask for strength, or simply tell them you love them. This is your private gift to them."

The room was quiet, save for the soft murmurs of students praying aloud.

Jennifer paused for a moment before saying, "I'll conclude this morning by giving a challenge. Think of ways your school can support Santiago and Matilde. You are their friends, and as friends, you need to be there for them right now."

By the time the last student had made their way out of the gym, I knew we had a long road ahead to help heal the wounds that had been opened. Standing alone on the now-empty stage, I allowed myself a brief moment to collect my thoughts. The students had shown strength in their vulnerability, but it was clear there was still much work to be done to rebuild trust and unity within the community. As Chill would say, the school's *qi* was out of whack.

As I stepped down off the stage, the Major appeared from a dark corner. She hesitated for a moment, her hands fidgeting at her sides, before walking toward me.

"That was good," she said softly, eyes fixed on the floor. "I know... this wasn't your fault," she stammered. "And this Kipling thing—it's just awful, isn't it?"

"It is," I agreed. "And thanks, Major," I added, giving her shoulder a reassuring squeeze. "We'll get through it. But it's just a lot for someone so young to handle all at once."

"Yeah," she replied, her voice trembling.

As she walked away, I could see it was a lot for her to handle too.

Given the time difference in Asia, my parent phone calls would have to wait until the evening. Instead, Harris and I chose to visit Santiago and Matilde, who we eventually found wandering aimlessly around a cordoned-off area of yellow tape that encircled a pile of embers that used to be their beloved *Kipling's*. A light shower was falling, and you could hear the odd hissing sound coming from droplets of rain landing on the lingering hot spots the firemen were still working on.

Harris and I stood beside Santiago and Matilde, remaining quiet in the smoky mist that hovered; Harris placed his hand on Santiago's shoulder while I held Matilde.

"Thank you for coming," Matilde whispered at last.

"How can we help?" I asked, though I realized it was probably a futile question.

"There's nothing to do but sell the property," Santiago said sadly.

"And we still have a $40,000 mortgage that's outstanding," Matilde added, her voice heavy with emotion. The sadness in her tone was hard not to feel deeply, and I tightened my hold on her. After a painful silence, she added, "We need to sell soon. Very soon."

"Do you have enough to tide you over in the meantime?" Harris asked.

"We've got a bit of savings," Santiago replied. "We can probably manage for about six, maybe eight months. But after that, it'll start to get hard." He glanced nervously at Matilde.

"It's not just the store," Matilde whispered, her voice breaking. "It's… everything. The memories, the dreams we poured into this place."

"I can only imagine," I said softly.

Before returning to campus, I agreed to join them the next day for a meeting they'd arranged with their real estate agent.

I wanted to ensure they were not taken to the cleaners for a second time.

Sitting down to dinner later that night, there was friendly chatter in the Dining Hall, albeit restrained. I sat beside Chill, who was about to go on duty in the Boarding House. I asked her to monitor the students' morale; if she sensed anyone was struggling emotionally, she should let me know right away.

"I think we need to do more than just monitor," Chill replied unexpectedly. "I'm going to organize a yoga class every night I'm on duty. Yoga really helped me through a tough time," she said, her voice steady but sincere. "I've been through a lot, and today it's the one thing that helps me clear my mind and get my emotions in check. I want to offer that same experience. I think the students need something to help them reflect on what we discussed in Assembly this morning, and yoga can help."

"Thank you, Chill. That's a wonderful initiative."

I couldn't help but smile, appreciating just how far she had come over the past few months. She was stepping up in a way I hadn't seen before. She was taking ownership. She was beginning to understand what it meant to lead.

My first evening phone call to Asia was to Aki's parents. I'd asked Koji to help translate and had given him some talking points before we began. As the two of us muddled through my apology, Koji informed me the parents were understanding and sorry Aki had embarrassed the school. I tried to explain to Koji they had nothing to apologize for but eventually realized my words were being lost in translation, and he'd taken it upon himself to give his own account of what happened, no doubt feeling Aki had shamed the school.

The next call was to Mrs. Lam in Hong Kong, who listened quietly to what I had to say, eventually translating for Grandmother Lam, whose familiar screeching I could hear in the background.

"My mother says Stanley's behavior is not becoming of someone who will be attending Harvard, and you must punish him," said Mrs. Lam.

There was more screeching.

"Oh, and she also says, if you want to, you can hit him … you have our permission." I could hear further deliberation, followed by, "A bamboo rod works best."

I thanked Mrs. Lam, agreeing to take what she said on advisement. As soon as I hung up, I sank into my office chair, shaking my head in disbelief. Now onto Korea.

"Let me guess, you're phoning about our friend Byung-ju?" joked Hee-young, picking up my call to Hyung-Bo Consulting.

"I'm afraid it's a bit more complicated this time," I said, delicately explaining what happened.

"Jesus!" exclaimed Hee-young, after I'd finished talking. "Did I not tell you his mother spoiled him rotten? And now this. She really should be ashamed of herself. Okay, I'll speak with her and let you know what she says."

"Sorry, Hee-young."

"Nothing to be sorry about, Phil. This is entirely Mrs. Lim's fault. I'll get back to you in a bit."

My call to Digby Ma worried me the most. He had become my trusted friend, and I could never repay him for all he had done to save me during the Kang situation. And yet here I was about to inform him I had failed in my responsibility to be his son's *loco parentis.* My stomach was churning as Lafayette picked up my call, quickly putting it through to Digby.

"Phil Gower! How are you, my friend?" Digby chimed back, with his trademark enthusiasm.

"I'm fine! Thank you, Digby. But I'll be honest, I have had better days," I replied, trying to posture my call.

"So I've heard. Sounds like my son and his friends caused you some headaches."

"You heard?" I asked, surprised to realize he already knew.

"As much as Manfred can be a challenge at times, he'll always be honest with me. He told me everything."

"Yes, well, I'm really sorry about that. I have to accept the blame for allowing him access to those Ginseng energy shots."

"You had no way of knowing. It's just one of those things. I'm just sorry he and his friends embarrassed you and the local community the way they did. If anything, that Korean mother needs a good head-shaking."

"True. Anyway, as for the community, it'll eventually blow over."

There was a short hesitation followed by, "Tell me about the fire."

"You heard about that too?"

"I hear about everything," he laughed.

I wondered if there was more to that comment but ignored it.

"The fire was at a local convenience store called *Kipling's,*" I said. "Electrical, they think. I'm not sure how the owners are going to survive it all."

403

"You mean Santiago and Matilde?"

"Yes. Santiago and Matilde Amelda."

"Manfred talks about them often. He was quite upset when he told me what happened to them."

"They're very popular with our students. Salt of the Earth people."

"Can you tell me a little bit more about them?"

I wasn't sure what he wanted to know, but I explained about them being immigrants; how they were taken advantage of and paid too much for *Kipling's*; about their great work ethic and respect in the community; that Matilde routinely gave our students haircuts; and that they had no insurance and were left holding a $40,000 mortgage.

"Hmm," said Digby, his tone becoming more serious. "Listen, Phil, I want to see if I can help in some way. No promises, but I'm about to go into our foundation's board meeting. There might be something we can do. Are you around for the next few hours?"

"Yes. You can phone me at home if I'm not in my office," I said, giving him my cell number.

"Good. I'll get back to you," he said as the line went dead.

It was almost 11:00 pm when Digby's call finally came in.

"Phil, I may have some good news for you," he said, getting to the point right away. "But before I can confirm anything, our foundation will have to do its due diligence. It'll need Santiago's and Matilde's tax records, accounting files, deeds, and a criminal check. But we can talk about those later."

"Sure, I can discuss all that with the Ameldas," I said, not entirely sure where the call was leading. I heard the sounds of papers being shuffled, and then he continued.

404

"So, here's what we can do. Our foundation is prepared to build a new store and stock it with all the necessary inventory in exchange for a nominal monthly rental fee to cover some of the upfront costs."

"What do you define as nominal?" I asked, starting to take notes of the conversation.

"I can't confirm an actual number right now, but we were looking at around $3000 a month."

"That's very reasonable."

"Like I said, we just need to recoup some of the costs. We're not interested in skimming off any profit from any of this. In exchange, our foundation will also take over the property as collateral but register it jointly in their name and ours."

"I see."

"Lastly, in the future, when Santiago and Matilde are ready to sell the store, any profit from the sale of the land and building will be entirely theirs."

"That is very generous."

"But Phil, the one thing our foundation can't pay for is their existing mortgage."

"That's understandable."

"That's where I want Manfred and the others involved to step in," he continued. "I told you that down the road, I want Manfred to take over the foundation. I'm going to explain to him our plan—in confidence, of course—so he understands how the foundation operates. Then I want him and his friends to look at ways to help Santiago and Matilde raise money to pay off their mortgage. Maybe not all of it, but at least some of it."

"We can help with that too," I added. "I'd like it to be a school-wide effort."

"Fair enough, but please give Manfred the opportunity to organize it. I want him to step up and show some leadership in all this. So he can redeem himself."

"Understood," I laughed.

"So, there we are," said Digby. "I hope that helps."

"Wow!" I blurted. "They're going to be over the moon."

"Let's give them a bit of time to think about it, and if they decide to proceed, I'll have Lafayette fax through a list of files they'll need to provide in order to finalize everything. He'll also include a sample contractual agreement explaining what we just talked about. And by all means, get a lawyer to look it all over to give them peace of mind."

"I can't thank you enough, Digby."

"This is what I now do for a living," he said. "Make people happy. We'll be in touch."

That night, I couldn't sleep. I just wanted to drive to the Ameldas and start shouting from the rooftops that they were getting a new store. I knew I had to move cautiously, though, and that they might not even like the proposal.

When I arrived at my office the next morning, a note from Koji sat on my desk: *Urgent: Phone Hee-young at Hung-Bo Consulting.*

More drama. I sighed, glancing at the time and realizing it was already 10:00 p.m. in Seoul. Still, I decided to dial the number. Hee-young picked up immediately.

"You're working late," I said.

"Yeah, for Mrs. Lim," she guffawed.

"Oh? What's happened?"

"As always, her way through any crisis is to use gifts. Phil, she's just couriered the school a money order in the amount of $100,000."

"You're kidding me!"

"Nope. For real."

"And what does she want us to do with this money?"

"Whatever you'd like."

"Really? What does Violeta think about this *gift*?"

"She was furious when she heard what happened at the parade. She said, 'Take the money and run'; that it's a drop in the bucket for Mrs. Lim."

"I see," I said, not knowing quite how to respond.

"Phil, this is her way of saying sorry, and I realize it's not subtle, but just put the money to good use for the school."

As I sat there, realizing the extent of the money order from Mrs. Lim, a strange unease settled over me. On the surface, it was a generous gesture, no doubt. But something about it felt off.

Putting down the phone, I walked down the hall and peeked into Harris' office. "Tomorrow, I think you and I need to have one of our soul-searching chats on the Adirondack chairs. There have been a few developments."

"Oh, goodie!" Harris boomed sarcastically.

Chapter 41

Settling into our blue thrones, I watched in amusement as Harris attempted to light a new cigar, while a strong breeze made every attempt to thwart him.

"I've missed this," he said, his cigar finally cooperating as he closed his eyes and sank deeper into his chair.

I allowed him a moment of peace while I stared out at the mountains on the horizon. They were getting their annual spring coating of deep hues of green. A few minutes later, I remembered I had wanted to ask about Browettsville.

"With all that's happened, you never told me how things went at the picnic," I said.

Harris' eyes slowly drifted back open as he reached for his cigar, taking a puff and then forming a slow, deliberate ring of smoke.

"They actually went better than expected. People came up to thank us for the fireworks, including Mayor Figbot, who only had one comment: next time, we should get a permit. There were others who asked about the well-being of the students who were on the float, but they also seemed satisfied the unhitching of the trailer was nothing more than a freak accident."

"So, no tarnished reputation?"

"No, if anything, they appreciated we livened up their parade."

"Well, I'm not going to share that information with the Gang-of-Four, although I wish I could tell Minji and Kyong Park. They're still convinced our school was humiliated by it all."

"That's for sure! They stood to one side during the whole picnic, refusing to participate, clearly embarrassed and angry by what happened." Harris folded his arms behind his neck. "Anyway, what are these new developments you wanted to talk to me about?"

I began by describing Digby's offer to rebuild *Kipling's*.

Harris sat upright. "What a bizarre turn of events. That's remarkable! You mean, all the hair I've been losing over these past few months trying to rein in Manfred's behavior was not in vain?"

"I guess not."

"When are you going to tell them?"

"The Almedas? I was supposed to be at a meeting with their real estate agent later this morning. I phoned Santiago and told him to put it off; that I needed to meet with them alone first to discuss a possible game-changer. Of course, he wanted to know more, but I insisted we had to talk in person."

"They'd be crazy not to jump at it."

"Except, I'm not sure they can afford $2,000 a month on top of their existing mortgage payments. That's why we have to spearhead some sort of fundraising strategy to help them out."

"Hmm. Forty thousand dollars. That's a lot of money to raise."

"Which brings me to the next bit of interesting news," I said, detailing my call with Hee-young.

Harris snapped his head towards me, his face furrowed in shock. "A hundred thousand dollars?"

"The cheque's in the mail, apparently. But, to be honest, I'm really struggling with whether we should even accept it."

Harris leaned back, drumming his fingers on the arm of his chair. So, here's my take," he said after a moment. "If the Gang-of-Four had walked into a store, bought a bottle of *Captain Morgan's*, and gotten drunk on their own, and now Mrs. Lim was trying to bribe us to look the other way, we'd have to reject the cheque. No question."

"Agreed," I said.

"But that's not what happened here," Harris continued, his tone more emphatic. "She didn't plan this. She didn't hand the kids the rum. This was a careless mistake on her part."

"Very careless," I added. "Regardless of intent, accepting the cheque still feels… questionable. Dodgy, as you might say. Like we're letting her buy her way out of this."

"Or," Harris countered, "you could see it as her taking responsibility. She knows she messed up. This is her way of making amends."

"But if we take the cheque, what does that say about us? What about the school? Doesn't it look like we're willing to put a price on accountability?

Harris leaned forward, his tone softening. "I think you're being too hard on yourself—and on her. She's embarrassed, sure, but she's also trying to make things right. Isn't that the kind of accountability we want to encourage?"

I sighed heavily, running a hand through my hair. "I hate the optics. If word gets out, people might think we took a bribe."

"Phil, optics are one thing. Impact is another. If we use this money for something that directly benefits the school, doesn't that show integrity—on both sides?"

There was a long silence as I mulled it over. Finally, I nodded. "Alright. If we do this, it has to be crystal clear how the money's used. No room for misinterpretation."

Harris nodded. "So, what are you thinking?"

"Well, first, we're *not* using it to pay off the Almedas' mortgage. That doesn't sit right. Hee-young asked us to put this to good use for the school, and paying off a private debt doesn't align with that."

"So what does?"

"We're about to open our doors to local day students, many of whom will come from families that may struggle to afford our fees."

"Ah, Financial aid," Harris said, nodding thoughtfully.

"Exactly," I replied. "An endowment that generates revenue every year."

Harris's face brightened. *"The Lim Bursary Fund?"*

"Perfect. It helps the school, it helps the students, and by naming it, we're being transparent about where the money came from."

Harris smiled. "Great call. So, now that you're on a roll, what can we do about the Almedas' mortgage?"

"I'm not sure yet. Digby wants me to empower Manfred to take on that challenge. So, let's see if he and the others can come up with anything worthwhile."

"That may have already happened," said Harris.

"Oh?"

"The Gang-of-Four has asked to meet us both after Prep

411

A PLACE TO BE ME

tonight to discuss a plan they're working on."

"Good for them. Let's see what they've got."

Feeling content with our decision, we simultaneously got to our feet to begin the trek back to the School House while I mentally prepared myself for my meeting with the Almedas.

The Almedas greeted me with nervous anticipation when I arrived at their home a couple of hours later. After handing me a mug of coffee, they sat opposite me on the couch, uncertain of what I was about to say.

"Manfred Ma's father wants to rebuild your store," I announced, smiling happily.

"What!" Santiago shouted. "No! You're kidding!"

Matilde put her hand over her mouth.

As I eagerly outlined all the details of the offer, the two of them looked back and forth at each other, their eyes wide as saucers. When I'd finally concluded, the room went quiet, and I watched while they tried to digest it all.

"It's a lot to take in," Santiago said, his tone uncertain. "Are we sure this is the right move?"

Matilde gave his hand a reassuring squeeze, her eyes full of hope.

Santiago exhaled, the skepticism fading as a small smile crept across his face. "Alright, we'll seriously consider it."

Matilde beamed, her relief clear. "Phil, why is Mr. Ma doing this for us?" she asked, as the two of them seemed to come alive with joyful energy.

"It's what his foundation does—helps people who are struggling to start a business. I know you're not exactly starting a new business, but I think he sees your situation in the same vein: that you're being forced to start all over again.

To be frank, he was also quite moved by the way Manfred described your plight."

"It's very generous of him," said Matilde, her eyes brimming with tears. "And Manfred is too kind."

"It will be a stretch for us financially in the beginning," added Santiago, "but I think we can make it work."

"Okay then, I'll let you mull over the offer. Make sure you have enough fax paper in your machine to receive the contract. And for your peace of mind, get a lawyer to look over the agreement before signing."

I didn't let on that we were also working behind the scenes to find even further financial assistance.

"Are you ready to go?" said Harris, looking through my office doorway. "The Gang-of-Four wants to meet us in the watchtower. It looks like they have a video presentation for us."

"Sure," I said, grabbing my coat and following him down the hall.

"How'd it go with the Almedas?" he asked as we made our way out the front door of School House.

"It went well. They couldn't believe it."

"I need to meet this Digby guy. Does his foundation invest in battered Volvos?"

"I don't think so," I laughed. "Have you spoken to your insurance company yet?"

"Yes. They're giving my car a new door and a fresh coat of yellow paint, so I guess it wasn't a total disaster—my hot rod will look good as new."

By the time we climbed the stairs to the top of the watchtower, the Gang-of-Four were already standing, waiting for us. I could tell they were on edge and feeling a lot more contrite about everything since the last time we'd seen each other.

"Hi, Mr. Gower. Hi, Mr. Tweedsmuir," said Manfred, guardedly, sliding quickly behind two swivel office chairs facing the large Apple computer Mrs. Lim had donated.

"Please have a seat here," he directed, patting the chairs.

The room had been transformed into a mini NASA mission-control center. In addition to the giant-sized Apple computer on the long counter the Major had asked Frank to build, there were two laptops displaying frozen video images in the process of being edited. Beside a huge multicolored mixing board with wires coiled like snakes were stacks of computer disks, assorted headphones, and a large microphone on a stand. Adjacent to the counter was a freestanding board on wheels displaying a complex flow chart with a series of notations and different-colored sticky notes.

"Impressive," I said.

"It's a good start," said Byung-ju, realizing my interest in the equipment. "Still need other stuff, but this is okay for now."

I looked over at Harris, who sneered back.

"I am going to introduce our idea now," announced Manfred, stepping in front of us. "Then Aki will explain it more, and then Byung-ju and Stanley will show you our video."

"Sounds great," I remarked. "Thank you for inviting us."

"Yes," said Harris. "We're looking forward to it."

Pulling a piece of paper out of his pocket and unfolding it, Manfred began to read from a prepared speech.

"Good evening. We've come up with a way to help Mr. and

Mrs. Almeda raise the money they need. Our idea comes from Aki, who got it from Japan when her village temple collapsed in an earthquake." He then flipped over the large board, which revealed the letters *CCB*.

"We call our proposal the *CCB*, which means *Cothbert Coupon Book*. I will now ask Aki to tell you more."

As Manfred moved to one side, Aki stepped out in front of us.

"Thank you for coming, Mr. Gower and Mr. Tweedsmuir," she said, with a half-bow.

I noticed she was not relying on any prepared notes.

"Our plan is to get the students to go to Timberlane and the villages of Rutherford and Browettsville and ask every business owner in those places to give us discount coupons. It could be for anything they sell and for any amount. For example, 10% off, 20% off, 50% off, or 100% off—well, maybe not 100% off," she giggled nervously. "But anyway, I hope you understand what I mean," she added.

I gave her an affirming nod.

"We will put all the coupons in a book we call the *CCB*. Each book will sell for $25. The money from what we sell will go to help the Almedas and *Kipling's*, and the coupons will help businesses in our community and make Cothbert House School look good because our name will be on every book. Thank you!" she concluded abruptly, bowing.

Without even a moment to reflect on the pitch, Manfred slid back in front of us.

"So, what do you think?" he said eagerly, looking back and forth between Harris and me.

"Well...it certainly sounds like a neat idea," I replied, tentatively. "But I think there may be a few things you need to figure out before you present it to the whole school. For example, who is going to print these books, and how much is it going to cost?"

I could see Manfred's face losing a bit of its animation as he realized what I was saying.

"Also," added Harris gently, "this is a type of fundraiser. We may need to get a permit in order to run it. But don't worry. Mr. Gower and I will look into all these things for you."

We will? Since when? Thank you, Harris!

Manfred regained his upbeat composure, turning to the others with a look as if he'd won a prize.

"All of you are to be congratulated for coming up with this wonderful idea," I said, realizing I needed to be more supportive. "Give Mr. Tweedsmuir and me a few days to sort out these issues we talked about."

"Now I show you video," said Byung-ju, as Stanley put on his headphones, seating himself in front of the mixing board.

Manfred lowered the lights.

With an opening score of inspirational music that pulled on your heartstrings, the computer monitor started displaying a slow-motion video montage of Santiago and Matilde at *Kipling's*. These were followed by photos of Matilde cutting Stanley's hair in front of a laughing group of students. From there, it transitioned to exterior shots of *Kipling's* and the Timberlane community and finally, a dramatic depiction of the fire's aftermath. Text scrolled across this last segment, which read: Cothbert wants to help *Kipling's*. You can help too. Support the *Cothbert Coupon Book*.

The footage concluded with an image of the school's crest filling the screen.

The ceiling lights were slowly raised, but this time Manfred sensed the need for a bit of space before returning to his sales pitch.

"Bravo! Bravo!" called out Harris, standing and clapping.

I quickly followed his lead. "That was so well done. You should be proud of yourselves."

"Thanks. We like it too," said Byung-ju. "Mr. De Metz helped us with editing. We are now going to copy it onto CDs and give it to all the businesses."

"Perfect," I acknowledged.

"We also have one more idea."

Harris and I slid back into our chairs.

"Byung-ju shrugged nonchalantly, "Manfred and I think we could raise some money by going bald."

Aki and Stanley exchanged unsure glances, clearly waiting for our response.

"Excuse me?" I said, struggling to keep a straight face

"Ya. If each student gives us about $30, Manfred and me will phone Mrs. Almeda and ask her to shave our heads so we will be bald. We could then have about $1,000."

I looked over at Harris, who gave me one of his shrugs.

"I see," I said. "Let me think about this one, too. Before you can even consider the idea, I will need permission from your parents."

"Ok. No problem," said Byung-ju. "My mother listens to me."

That is the problem, I thought.

"My father will agree too," said Manfred.

"Mine won't," blurted Aki.

"Ya, and my grandmother definitely won't...she'd kill me," admitted Stanley.

That's for sure. The bamboo rod would definitely rear its

ugly head again.

"That was interesting," I said, while Harris and I descended the stairs. "Oh, and by the way, thanks for volunteering us to look into those issues surrounding the coupon book. Like I don't have enough on my plate with all the accreditation stuff."

"Not us, my friend. The Major."

"Oh?"

"I actually believe this is one of those rare occasions where she might actually be able to help us."

"Okay, but before we ask her for any help or anything, we need to soft-pedal my plan to use Mrs. Lim's $100,000 donation for financial aid."

"True. Can you set up the meeting?"

"Oh, joy," I responded.

As always, I relied on the Major's executive assistant to arrange our meeting, and Koji followed through by convincing the Major to join us early the next morning.

"Thank you for coming, Major," I said, ushering her to a seat. The Major dropped into a chair, throwing her tattered briefcase onto the coffee table. Harris and I pulled up our chairs, and I noticed her eyes already beginning to narrow with suspicion as they shifted between the two of us.

"How did those parents take it when they found out we got their kids wasted?" she quizzed, like a lawyer in a cross-examination.

"Wasted is a pretty strong word, Major, but they were very understanding. That's actually why I wanted to talk to you. There have been two very interesting developments since I spoke to those parents," I said, carefully easing into Digby's offer to build a new store for the Almedas.

"Wow! That Digby is one interesting guy. So is his wife. Very special woman," she added, suggesting there was more to the story. "Do the Almedas know yet?"

"They do. They're very happy, although they still have a $40,000 mortgage to pay off on the previous store. Digby has asked Manfred and the others involved in the incident to come up with a plan to help them raise some money. I'll get to that in a moment, but first, I want to tell you about a second offer—this one from Mrs. Lim, and it's for the school."

"More computer crap?"

"It's a monetary donation, Major," I said cautiously.

The Major's eyes started twitching.

"And while we originally thought of using it to help the Almedas, we think it would be better suited for financial assistance; you know, to help some of the local students from the community who will be applying to Cothbert next year."

"How much is the donation for?" she asked, avoiding eye contact.

"A hundred thousand."

There were a couple of coughs and a few hand movements as the Major continued to stare at the floor. Harris and I waited for the impending explosion.

"That's not a bad idea," she said at last. I exchanged a surprised glance with Harris. Neither of us had expected her to agree so easily.

"I know the other schools do that," added the Major. "We need to offer that aid stuff here too."

"Just so you know, Major, normally the way these things work is that you will need to invest the money first. Once it starts to generate revenue in a few years' time, we can use that money for financial aid. But we'll never touch the capital. The $100,000 will always belong to the school."

"You mean to us," said the Major.

"Yes. To us, Major."

"I thought you said you wanted to use it for some of those local students for next year," she said, finally looking up.

"I think it's important that the community knows we have financial aid now. So, for the first few years, we'll probably need to be a bit creative by discounting our fees if someone asks for help. Like I said, in the future we'll be able to use the revenue from the donation. And who knows, maybe we'll have more donations by then."

"Hmm. Okay. I'll set up a meeting with Joe for you."

"Thank you, Major."

We then moved on to the Gang-of-Four's plans for selling *Cothbert Coupon Books*, a.k.a. *CCBs*. The Major immediately warmed to the proposal because of the exposure she realized the school would get in the local community. She agreed to look after all the printing costs through some local printer who owed her a favor but conceded she didn't know how to go about getting a permit.

"Major, I'll speak to someone at City Hall," I said. What I really meant was that I'd give Mayor Figbot a call, but I didn't want to upset what had been an uncharacteristically cordial meeting.

"Oh, yeah, one other thing," blurted the Major, opening her briefcase. "This arrived today," she said, pulling out an official document on which were written the words,

Interim School Certificate, Cothbert House School and dropping it unceremoniously on the coffee table.

"We got it," cheered Harris, picking it up to take a closer look.

"So now *yous* two need to get on the phones and speak to them agents and make sure we get all our students to come back next year. And you need to start enrolling local day students."

"Understood, Major," I replied, going out of my way to be conciliatory.

When she finally left my office, I turned back to Harris, giving him a high-five.

"Why do you think the Major was so accommodating with the 100 grand?" I asked.

"You heard what she said. The other schools have aid. So, we have to have aid. It has nothing to do with attracting students in need or leveling the playing field. She just wants to go head-to-head with the other schools. Anyway, that's okay. We got what we came for. And we're on our way to being certified."

"Which, I guess, means more calls to Asia to let our agents know," I said.

"Yes. And some local marketing too."

"Hey, why don't we highlight the financial aid in an ad on the back of those coupon books?" I suggested.

Harris gave a thoughtful nod. "That's a great idea. I'm starting to like these coupon books more and more."

Chapter 42

It was the Friday before the Victoria Day long weekend, and with only five weeks left of school, things at Cothbert were in overdrive. We were juggling the final Ministry evaluation and pushing for last-minute coupon sales for the *CCB* project. Thanks to local media coverage and Mayor Figbot's legal oversight, things were finally moving—almost two hundred coupon books secured, and preorders topping eight hundred.

In preparation for Tina Wade's visit next Friday, we had locked ourselves in my office and were scouring every last page of our report to make sure we hadn't forgotten anything.

"So, I want to revisit our pedagogy one last time," said Harris, sliding his glasses up his nose and leaning into the arm of his chair. "Our focus will be a holistic one," he said, picking up the report and reading from it. "Committed to the whole child, Cothbert's approach will emphasize critical thinking skills while teaching second-language students the specific language of high school learning, enabling them to transition to a mainstream secondary-school program quickly and seamlessly."

"Got it," I replied, having heard him repeat his spiel several times over the past few days. While I didn't want to dampen his enthusiasm, I had spent considerable time bringing my tagline—*A place to be me*—to life, ensuring it reflected the school's deep commitment to the individual and was entrenched in Cothbert's overall approach.

As we continued to cross our t's and dot our i's, my office door suddenly flew open, with a loud, hesitant knock following as an afterthought.

"Hello, Major," I said without even looking up.

"*Yous* two finished with that report yet? That Tina Spade woman's coming on Friday, you know. We need that certification to increase our revenue stream."

The Major had obviously been speaking with Joe; there was no way she knew what a revenue stream was. Moving directly in front of Harris and me, Harris made a point of releasing a particularly accentuated guffaw.

"So? Where are we with this fricken report?"

"We were just preparing for Ms. Wade's arrival before you walked in, Major. The report is finished, but we're double-checking everything," I said, glancing at Harris, who returned a cold eye.

"Well, you're certainly taking your time about it," she whined.

I could hear the faint sound of the word "Christ" just as Harris whipped off his reading glasses, pounding his fist on my desk. "Major, do you have any bloody idea how much paperwork is involved in this certification process?"

"Ah, Big Guy. Don't get your knickers in a twist. You just need to fill in a few forms and type a little crap about the school. No one's gonna read any of that stuff anyway. The inspection is what counts."

"Really? Fine then," blurted Harris, slamming the report shut and forcefully handing it to the Major. "You know best.

Oh, and because you are co-owner of this joint, you have to sign the fricken report yourself before submitting it. It also needs to be couriered to Tina by this afternoon—whose last name is Wade, not Spade, by the way. So, you better alert your executive assistant to double-check your mailing information. We don't want the report arriving at a local garden center now, do we?"

Looking extremely annoyed, Harris announced, "I've had enough, Phil. See you tomorrow!" He then marched out.

Without a word, the Major slunk out of my office, our precious report scrunched carelessly under her arm like the morning newspaper.

Talk about déjà vu, I thought.

When I arrived at the Boarding House later that evening for my duty, I had already been forewarned by Myrtle that this was the night Byung-ju and Manfred would be getting their heads shaved. In honor of the occasion, they had arranged for an extravaganza. As soon as I stepped into the house, I was reminded that Byung-ju never did anything in half measures. Taped around helium balloons, swaying above the banisters leading up to the second floor, were headshots of both him and Manfred meticulously Photoshopped to make them appear hairless. Above the archway to the stairs, a banner was taped to the wall that read: *Hair Today, Gone Tomorrow Event, starring Byung-ju and Manfred. Free Refreshments. 8:00 pm in the Common Room.*

I shook my head and smiled, just as something rubbed up against my leg. I looked down to see Tofu peering up at me happily. As I crouched down to stroke his head, Myrtle walked up beside me.

"Quite the characters, eh?" she giggled.

"Do you think any of this will help to redeem them?" I asked, standing back up.

"You know, at first, some of the students thought the whole *CCB* thing was just a publicity stunt for the Gang-of-Four to regain face. But after the coupons began pouring in and all of those preorders started arriving, I saw more respect being shown toward them. I think tonight's event will confirm their good intentions."

"Sort of like their penitence," I smiled.

Just before eight, Myrtle and I made our way into the common room, where the Jazz Band players were setting up in front of the fireplace. The room's pool table had been covered with a tablecloth and was overflowing with assorted junk food, while sitting in the center of the room was a solitary barber's chair awaiting its victims. The students slowly wandered in. Taking notice of the chair, their faces lit up with excitement. I could tell they were secretly anticipating the event. As much as this was an atonement for members of the Gang-of-Four, it was also a type of catharsis for the rest of the community, who needed to let go of the sordid events of parade day.

The sharp sound of clanging behind me caught my attention, and I turned to see Byung-ju setting up his camera equipment. I should have known.

"It's going to be hard to film yourself while you're getting your head shaved," I joked.

In his typical humorless fashion, he responded, "Set to automatic. Doesn't need me to film."

Suddenly, the chattering in the room erupted into loud

cheers. I looked over to see Matilde arriving, carrying her familiar silver metallic case of hair-cutting implements.

"So, who is going to be my first casualty," she asked with a playful smile.

"I will," cried Manfred, stepping forward eagerly and climbing onto the chair.

"I'm assuming you got their parents' permission for this, Mr. Gower," said Matilde, pulling a white plastic sheet around Manfred's shoulders.

"Oh, yes. They were more than happy to oblige," I replied.

Matilde removed her razor from the case and flicked the switch. The buzzing noise reignited the cheering, now punctuated by chants of "Manfred! Manfred! Manfred!" As Matilde guided the buzzing machine up and over Manfred's head, large tufts of hair drifted slowly to the floor, revealing a bright, elongated patch of skin.

The students responded with high-pitched, giddy laughter, as if they were part of something subversive. Caught up in the excitement, Manfred squirmed in the chair until Matilde gently scolded him to stay still. In minutes, he was gleaming under the bright overhead lights, nearly unrecognizable.

When Matilde finished, Manfred leapt from the chair, grabbed a mirror, and burst into manic laughter at the sight of his bald reflection. Matilde gestured for Byung-ju to take his place, and the room's energy subtly shifted. Where Manfred had been impulsive, full of nervous energy, Byung-ju remained poised, almost detached. But as the razor buzzed over his scalp, something in him shifted. His face softened, and a faint, almost self-aware smirk tugged at his lips as he caught his reflection.

The cheers grew louder, but they were different now—less

mocking, more supportive, more genuine.

As the Jazz Band kicked into full swing and students crowded around the food table, I stood off to the side, appreciating just how much Manfred and Byung-ju had embraced their roles here. They had risen above their past mistakes, not for themselves, but for the school.

Chapter 43

The day of Tina's inspection had been meticulously planned, with meetings scheduled for each staff member and classroom visits throughout the day.

"She should be here any moment," Harris declared, glancing at his watch for the tenth time as we paced the reception area, waiting for Tina to arrive.

"Remember... holistic school... focused on critical thinking and the language of high school learning," he reminded me.

"Right," I said, nodding. "I remember." Just then, the front door swung open, and Koji came running in.

"The inspector is here—outside, talking with Miss Major."

"Of course she is!" Harris blurted, and we both rushed outside.

We found the Major standing on the steps with Tina, who was asking, "So, Ms. Hunter, how would you describe your approach here at Cothbert?"

The Major hesitated before responding. "We offer a holy education... you know, with... critic skills?" she said, glancing nervously at Harris.

Harris slapped his forehead.

"You're a parochial school?" Tina asked, looking puzzled.

"What?" said the Major, clearly confused.

"Hey, Tina," Harris cut in, stepping between them with a nervous laugh. "I think what Ms. Hunter meant to say is that we offer a *holistic* program focused on critical thinking skills."

"Oh, I see. Yes, that's what I remember from reading the report. I thought I'd missed something. I always read those reports very carefully, you know."

Harris shot the Major a sharp, pointed glance.

"Yes, well, Tina," he said, eager to move things along, "shall we get started with your agenda? I know you have a busy day ahead."

"Absolutely. Ms. Hunter, I believe we'll meet again later. We can continue our conversation then."

Oh, God, no, I thought, but I forced a smile and nodded.

The day seemed to go smoothly as I accompanied Tina from one meeting to the next, though I could tell she found it a bit unsettling that the Major kept showing up in the hallways after each appointment, standing with a goofy smile and a little wave. By 4:00 p.m., Tina joined Harris and me in my office for our debrief. Janice had thoughtfully prepared refreshments ahead of time.

"I hope you enjoyed your visit," I said, pouring tea with a bit too much nervous energy.

"Oh, yes. It was very nice," Tina replied, reaching for her cup. "Impressive and unique school. Solid curriculum, a caring environment, and an energetic staff. I especially liked your report, particularly the rationale behind your motto: *A Place to Be Me*—a theme that seems to guide everything you do here."

Tina's smile lingered a bit too long as she nodded toward

me. "You've built something impressive here, Phil," she said, sipping her tea. There was a softness in her voice that made me wonder if there was something more behind her words. "Oh, and you, too, Harris," she added, almost apologetically

I stared back at Tina for a moment before responding, "We really appreciate your vote of confidence."

Harris shot me a quick look, then, eager to keep the conversation moving, asked, "Did you have your meeting with Ms. Hunter?"

Tina gave a dismissive wave. "Oh, yeah. Look, I know what you're thinking. I saw your reaction on the steps when she tried to profile the school. Don't worry, I'm used to dealing with business owners like her who think there's a fortune to be made in education. It's always a challenge for me, as I'm sure it is for you. But just so you know, I took most of what she said with a grain of salt. My focus is always on the qualified educators running a school. And like I said, you two have done a fantastic job here. I'll have no hesitation accrediting Cothbert."

"That's a relief," said Harris, clearly relieved.

"Yes, that is great news," I added with a smile.

Tina reached for a cookie. "How are your enrollment numbers looking for next year?"

Before I could respond, we were interrupted by a soft knock on the door.

"Come in," I said.

The door creaked open, and the Major stepped in, standing awkwardly as her eyes flicked nervously around the room. "I thought I'd join you... if that's okay?"

"Come in, Major," I said, gesturing to a chair.

"Ms. Hunter, you have some excellent educators running

430

your school," Tina said, addressing the Major, clearly for our benefit. "I just informed them I'll be approving Cothbert's accreditation."

"Oh, great news," the Major said, sitting up straighter. "Great news!"

"I was just asking about your enrollment numbers for next year," Tina added, turning her attention back to me.

"They're looking good," I replied quickly before the Major could interject. "In fact, I just heard back from the two large agencies we work with. All but three of our existing students are returning."

"And what about your domestic recruitment?" Tina asked.

"We've recently launched a small financial aid program, and the response from local communities has been very encouraging."

"Good. Well, hopefully, your permanent accreditation will help with that. I'll make sure the official paperwork is sent over in the next few days. Anyway, I'm afraid I've got to run," Tina said, rising from her seat.

"I'll walk you to the front entrance," I said, glancing awkwardly at Harris before ushering Tina into the hallway.

As we exited through the front door, I turned to Tina and extended my hand. "Thank you for all your help today."

"I have to say, Phil, I really admire what you've done here," Tina said, her voice warm. "This was no small task, and clearly, it's not for the faint of heart. You're obviously a strategic leader."

I felt a swell of pride at her words. It was the kind of validation I had been craving. I couldn't stop smiling as I watched her make her way down the front steps when suddenly, she turned back toward me.

"I was wondering," she said, a playful smile on her lips, "if you ever had reason to visit Vancouver?"

"Yes," I said, flustered. "Mostly for school business, like accreditation," I joked.

"Good to know. Maybe we'll see each other again?" she asked, her tone coy.

"Yes," I beamed back. "Maybe."

Returning to my office, still basking in the glow of the debrief, the Major turned to me with a serious expression.

"How'd you lose three students?"

"Excuse me?" I blinked in surprise.

"You said three students weren't coming back."

"Oh, right. Yes, Jonas Chen, Marcie Tu, and Minji Lee. Jonas and Marcie got accepted to one of the big-name schools in the U.S., and Minji... well, she hasn't been happy ever since the parade incident. We might be able to convince her to come back, but I'm not sure."

"You know," Harris said, "for a school of our size and status, those are excellent attrition numbers."

"What are you talking about?" The Major's eyes narrowed. "That's ninety grand out the window."

"There will always be students who go to greener pastures," I said, trying to calm her. "The other private schools in B.C. lose students every year."

"Humph," she said, standing up and strolling out of the office without so much as a congratulations for getting certified.

"She really has no idea, does she?" Harris said with an exasperated breath.

"No," I exhaled. "But we do. Anyway, I think the *As You Like It* beckons. Don't you?"

"At last, someone who makes sense," Harris beamed. "But before we go, what's up with Tina Wade?"

"What do you mean?"

"Oh, I don't know… let's just say she gave you a bit more attention than what I got."

"Don't be ridiculous!"

Chapter 44

For the majority of the students, they had shared close to three hundred days living, learning, and growing together in a tightly-knit community. With less than twenty-four hours before they left Cothbert House School, it was understandable their emotions were running high.

At a farewell luncheon in the Dining Hall, there were tearful speeches by students and staff alike. Chill, Pancho, and Ida recognized both effort and achievement with awards. But it was Aki's presentation of a cheque for just over $40,000 to Santiago and Matilde that caused the biggest stir. This act of kindness—the result of 1,700 Cothbert Coupon books already sold—was a testament to how our school community had come together as one. By the time a very bald Byung-ju had finished showing his retrospective video of the year, members of the community were leaning on each other for support as they looked back on their time together.

When the formal part of the luncheon was over, most of the students elected to remain behind, sharing stories, swapping contact numbers, and snapping photos of each other. I was beginning to feel a bit like a celebrity as I offered up my best smile to every cry of, "Mr. Gower! Mr. Gower! Photo, please."

The Major, neatly dressed for once in a clean, pressed gray-and-white checkered pantsuit, radiated pride in the school she had helped create.

As I stood and watched with my own immense pride, I heard a faint call of my name behind me. I turned to find Mrs. Kang with Thomas by her side.

Wiping her eyes, Mrs. Kang reached forward to give me a hug. "I should never have mistrusted you. Never! Thank you. Thank you. I have already enrolled Thomas for next year."

"Yeah!" yelled Thomas, as he and his mother left. It was the first time I'd ever seen such emotion from him.

"We did it, my friend," said Harris, swooping in beside me. "We actually made it to the end of the year in one piece. And if anyone needs proof, I think you and I have just been immortalized in close to four hundred photos. I don't know about you, but I'm totally knackered."

"I know, but, hey, take a look around the room."

Harris filled his cup with coffee, stirring in three spoons of sugar. "It's too bad boarding schools get such a bad rap. A regular school wouldn't generate anywhere near this type of sentiment."

"Did you happen to see our infamous shareholder at play?" I asked.

"Yes. You've got to give her credit. In the end, she always seems to get what she wants."

"Speaking of which, what's the story on Millicent these days?"

"My understanding is some of her friends rallied around her and got her into therapy, and the Major is covering the cost."

"Good for her. I hope it all works out."

Koji came rushing up beside us. "Major wanted me to give you these," he said, panting as he handed us each an envelope.

"What is this?" I asked.

"Gift certificates for Afternoon Tea at the *Bacchus Lounge* in Vancouver. Major's friend gave them to her."

"I guess this is her way of saying thank you," I said, waving my envelope in the air, grinning.

"Yes, well, if she truly wanted to thank us, she would have arranged for unlimited alcohol at the *As You Like It.* But a nice gesture anyway, I guess."

"Funny, though, how she struggles so much to say thank you to our faces."

"She obviously sees it as a sign of weakness. Anyway, an afternoon at the *Bacchus Lounge* sounds very civilized."

"Oh, and Mr. Phil," Koji called out, just as he turned to dash off, "Ms. Wade phoned again and wants you to phone her. ASAP."

Harris turned with a devilish grin. "ASAP, eh," but restrained himself from saying anything further.

"Well," I said, feeling totally embarrassed, "I promised to help Myrtle with student packing."

"How's that shaping up?" asked Harris, still with a lingering smirk.

"It should all go smoothly. The majority of students are being shuttled to the airport on the *Hyung-bo* and *Yingyucom* coach, and the rest are being looked after by Frank and Koji."

"I see. Well, I'll meet you in the parking lot by the coach tomorrow then."

"8:00 a.m., Mr. Morning Person."

"Christ!"

When the last of the students sauntered out of the Dining Hall, I returned to my office to lock up and check for any final messages. An oversized envelope was sitting on my desk, but it could wait. I needed to phone Tina Wade.

"Phil, I'm so glad you called," came Tina's bubbly response when she realized it was me on the line. "Listen… I was just given two tickets to the the *Vancouver Symphony Orchestra*. They're actually doing a Beatles retrospective."

"Sounds like fun."

"I thought so. Would you be free to join me?"

"Well… yes… sure, I'd love to," I replied. "That's very kind of you."

After confirming the day and time and ending our call with some additional pleasantries, I put down the phone with a smile that went from ear to ear. I then noticed the large envelope again. Opening it, I pulled out a tall card, the center of which was a painting of our float in the parade with Thomas' signature under it. My eyes slowly misted as I read the message:

We are very, very sorry for all the trouble we made, Mr. Gower. We will miss you. Have a good summer. See you in September.

Sincerely, Byung-ju, Manfred, Aki, and Stanley

The next morning, with the coach loaded, Harris and I climbed aboard. The mood on the bus was subdued, but as we explained, summer would fly by, and before they knew it, September would be here again. For the three students who would not be returning, we reminded them they were always welcome at Cothbert. As we exited, we noticed the Major standing to one side, waving and looking forlorn.

By the time the door behind us hissed to a close, the engines of the coach had already fired up, and moments later, we were watching as the large black bus lumbered up the hill. We followed it with our eyes just as a car horn sounded, causing us to step back. Frank and Koji waved to us as they drove by in the school bus, taking the remainder of the students. A few moments later, the Major joined us.

Sitting on a stone wall outside the front entrance to the boarding house, none of us knew what to do or say next. Within minutes, a strange silence descended on the campus. Even with Harris and the Major beside me, the emptiness of the place felt heavy.

I glanced at the Major. Her usual confidence seemed muted, replaced by something softer—vulnerable, even.

Harris nudged me. "Mission accomplished?"

I nodded but kept my eyes on the Major. "You think she's okay?"

Harris followed my gaze. "Maybe she finally gets it."

I chuckled, but it didn't quite reach my eyes. "Yeah, she doesn't exactly wear her emotions on her sleeve."

"No," Harris agreed. "But she doesn't give up. Ever."

I thought about that. The Major had pushed me harder than anyone ever had—through challenges, frustrations, and a million compromises. At times, it felt like she was more of a distant mentor than a partner, and yet, here we were, side by side, still standing.

"It's been a good year," the Major said suddenly, her voice cutting through the quiet.

I turned to her, meeting her gaze.

"You know, Major," I said, "I couldn't have done this without you."

She paused, her eyes softening for the briefest of moments

before she nodded, her usual walls sliding back into place.

Harris broke the silence with a smirk. "Well, I guess we all made it to the end."

Myrtle walked up carrying a picnic basket and leading Tofu, who instinctively jumped up beside me for support.

"This is your first time, isn't it?" she said.

"What is?" I asked.

"You know, saying goodbye at the end of a boarding school year. It's much harder than at a regular school, isn't it?"

"That's for sure," I said, wiping my eyes.

Harris nodded, trying in vain to remain in control.

"It was a special group of kids," added the Major, continuing to look a bit lost.

"Come on, you three! I know where we need to go," Myrtle said, waving as she bounded toward the steps leading to the beach, with Tofu trotting alongside her.

We followed her, eventually making our way to the bench I had installed in Duncan's memory. Each of us read the brass plaque that was now affixed to its back:

In Memory of my Dear Husband, Duncan Green (1943–1965).

I also noticed a newly planted spruce tree to one side.

"Phil installed this bench for me," she said, her voice breaking. "This is where I go when I'm feeling down. I wanted to keep this space private, but you're all family—so, what the heck, have a seat," she continued.

Sitting down, we watched as she opened her basket, pulling out a thermos and some homemade muffins. Pouring us each a cup of coffee, she perched herself on the end of the bench. I took a sip, realizing it was Myrtle's familiar alcohol-infused java, just as Tofu jumped on my lap.

Harris turned to Myrtle. "Remember back in the summer,

before school started, how unsure you were about all this?" he said, giving her a gentle nudge with his elbow.

"I do," Myrtle admitted with a giggle. "I do. And now look at me—consoling you three louts!"

The Major cackled, joining in our laughter, and the tension began to ease.

"Anyway, thank you for believing in me," Myrtle said after a moment, turning her cup slowly in her hands. "This year has been... something else."

"It really has," I agreed.

"Hear, hear," echoed Harris, raising his cup. "And here's to you, Myrtle. You're one of a kind."

"You're special, all right," added the Major with a smirk.

"I'll take that as a compliment," Myrtle replied, mock-serious. Then, meeting my eyes, she said softly, "And to you, Phil—thank you for showing me how it's done. I mean it," she added, placing her hand lightly on my knee. "You've made all the difference."

I noticed the Major watching Myrtle closely and thought I saw the faintest nod of agreement.

Myrtle's words landed differently than anything I'd heard about myself before. For once, I didn't feel like I had to prove anything—it just felt right. I smiled, letting the moment settle.

The following day, Harris and I agreed to go in separate cars to the *Bacchus Lounge* for their Afternoon Tea. Harris had a medical appointment later in the afternoon, and I wanted some private time. Winding down the Sea-to-Sky, I couldn't help reminiscing about my first drive to school and how quickly I had accepted a job offer from the Major.

It reminded me of Matilde's comment on Christmas Eve about fate. Here I was, coming full circle, heading back down the same stretch of picturesque landscape to where it had all begun, but this time as a co-owner of Cothbert House School.

When I entered the Bacchus Lounge, my eyes scanned the room for Harris. Instead, I was pleasantly surprised to spot Koji tucked into a corner table with a young woman. I absolutely couldn't resist.

"Koji!" I exclaimed. "Fancy meeting you here!"

Koji jerked his head up, almost choking on the sandwich he'd just bitten into. "Mr. Gower? Oh, yes, hi. Miss Major gave me a gift certificate too."

"How nice. Did you know Mr. Tweedsmuir is here somewhere? I just haven't found him yet."

Koji's face was turning red by now.

I turned to the young woman beside him. "Hello, I'm Phil Gower. Koji and I work together—although he'll probably tell you I'm his boss."

"Oh, yes! Of course, Mr. Gower. I am Midori. Nice to meet you. Koji talks about you all the time."

"All good things, I hope?"

Midori laughed. "Oh, yes. All good. No bad."

Koji nodded emphatically. "See? Only good talking!"

I leaned slightly toward Midori. "You've got a very nice boyfriend—though for some reason, he's never mentioned you. Hopefully, we'll see more of you in the future."

"I'd like that," she said warmly.

Koji shot me a pleading look, his eyes darting between us. It was time to put him out of his misery. "Enjoy your tea," I said with a smile, leaving them to their afternoon.

I found Harris by the window, already looking the part of a country squire in his plaid waistcoat and slightly-too-tight tie. He had that Sherlock Holmes air again—if Sherlock had been on a steady diet of scones and ale.

"Feeling more relaxed?" I asked, settling into the chair opposite him.

"I do," he replied, studying me. "You're looking very smart this afternoon."

"I dress to impress."

The waiter arrived, and I ordered Earl Grey. While Harris remained lost in thought, I gestured to the waiter. "He'll have the same."

"Penny for your thoughts?" I asked.

Harris turned to me, his face unreadable. "You know, there were days I wondered what the hell I was doing at Cothbert. And other days, I felt completely energized by it all. But now? Strange as it sounds, I'm already missing the bloody place."

"Funny. Me too. And you know why?"

Harris shook his head.

"I realized it while driving here. It's because the Major had the good sense to hire us. And Myrtle. Sure, the Major drove us mad half the time, but she made this all happen."

Harris nodded. "You're right." He shifted in his chair, then smirked. "You know what, Phil? You're always right."

"Can I get that in writing?"

When the tea was poured and the scones buttered, Harris raised an eyebrow at me. "So, do you want to talk about your new girlfriend?"

"No. I don't. Change the subject, please."

"Flaky Easterner."

I smirked, taking a sip of tea.

442

There was no way I was going to tell him about my date that evening. Family or not.

Manufactured by Amazon.ca
Acheson, AB

30310682R00247